MY SOLEMN VOW

A HIDDEN SHIFTER ROMANCE

THE MAFIA ARRANGEMENTS
BOOK ONE

JAEGER ROSE

BEARLY CONTAINED ROMANCE

© Bearly Contained Romance

E-Book ISBN: 979-8-9900360-5-5

Model Paperback ISBN: 979-8-9900360-6-2

Discreet Paperback ISBN: 979-8-9900360-8-6

Editing - Jeanine of Indie Edits with Jeanine

Proofreading - Cayla Cavalletto of Hey Bookworms Editing

Book Cover - Katelyn of Designs by Kage

Chaos Coordinator - Kelsey Schneider

❀ Created with Vellum

MY
solemn
VOW

JAEGER ROSE

THE MAFIA
ARRANGEMENT
book one

A NOTE FROM THE AUTHOR

Dearly Beloved,

We are gathered here today in the name of dark romance. Namely, within these pages, we will celebrate the union between Mafia and shifter romance. This union, forged by the circumstances, brings together a pair of feuding families. One of which is a family of wolf shifters. As with many wolf-shifter romances, there will be gruesome events such as on-page physical violence, murder, and biting. In addition to wolf-shifter romance violence, this does stay well within the realm of Mafia romance. There will be more realistic acts of violence, such as guns, knives, and fists used against individuals.

My Solemn Vow is the first book in the Mafia Arrangement series. As in many dark romance relationships, there will be events which, outside of the pages of this novel, would be abhorrent and grounds for divorce and a protective order. But here in the darkness, we say 'yes, sir' and 'please, give me more.'

In the event you find yourself uneasy with things that happen in the dark and you're looking for confirmation that this darkness is, in fact, safe for you, please read the below list of generalized events.

If upon reading the list, you find yourself further questioning this book and its handling for you . . . I might suggest you reach out to the author so she can disclose additional information that others may find to be spoilers. You may find a more in-depth list or contact information at:

www.authorsarahjaeger.com

Your mental well-being is important and should not be compromised for the sake of fiction.

If you are certain beyond a reasonable doubt that you are at home in all levels of darkness, please feel free to skip the below.

For those of us who . . .
can do all things through spite,
which strengthens us.

Holly

PROLOGUE

THE TRUCE

He's such a good dad. But I knew Valor would be.

It's not uncommon for wolves to be good fathers, but we are young and dumb. Most of his friends are still out partying — that reckless, rowdy, and damn near feral era that I watched my older brothers go through. May they rest in peace.

Instead, Valor is asleep, mostly sitting up in his recliner with our daughter lying on his chest.

He was so worried she wouldn't bond with him since he's been taking on more responsibilities with his father. But all it takes is one look at the two of them to know she's a daddy's girl. I've no doubt in my mind she'll be chasing frogs, digging in the dirt, and roughhousing long before she ever wants to wear a princess dress or have a tea party.

It's why I have to do this. But I can't pull my eyes off them. I can't look away for fear this life with them passes too quickly before my eyes. Kerrianne is already three months, and it's as if I brought her home from the hospital yesterday.

Our world isn't safe for her. The feud with the D'Medici family, the head family of the Italian Mafia, grows stronger each day. I don't want to live in a world where I worry if my little girl is safe. Not if I can help it.

Valor thinks I'm going to the Christmas market. It's the only reason he's letting me leave the house. Nestled deep in Cavanagh territory, it's safe, and he understands how important it is for me to get him a present. It's been our tradition since we met, and he wouldn't deprive me of that.

I watch them a little while longer. I promised to wake him up before I left, but they're so peaceful. I should let him sleep. He didn't come home until I was doing Kerrianne's three a.m. feeding. The late nights are hard for him. Especially since he insists on taking care of Kerrianne when he's home to give me a break. I couldn't have asked for a better mate.

Keys in hand, I walk toward our apartment door. In the new year, we get to move into our house, and I can't wait to decorate the nursery. *Don't leave without saying goodbye.* I turn back to him, admiring how he looks holding her. I do as he asked and a little extra.

Valor put his phone on the coffee table before sitting down, and I can't help myself. I grab his phone and open the camera app. Somehow a dozen photos are clicked before I look through them. I can't bear to delete any of them, but I find the perfect one and send it to myself. On the way home, I'll get one printed and put it in the stack to frame when we get to the new house.

"Valor," I whisper as I set his phone on the table.

His eyes open a crack, and that crooked grin greets me. "Leavin' already?"

"Well, she'll wake up in two hours and want to be fed. I figured I'd go and get back."

Leaning forward, I run my fingers through his chestnut hair. It's getting long. I'll have to remind him to get it cut before he leaves again. Otherwise, he'll be too freshly cut for the family photos.

"You know we have people who can go to the shops for us."
He moves ever so slightly to press his head into my touch.

"Yes, Valor," I groan, selling the lie maybe a bit too hard. "It is healthy for me to leave the house every once in a while. It's been three months. I'm going stir crazy."

"Fine, just take—"

"Four extra security guards and a bazooka." I get smart with him, knowing it'll only make him that much more . . . fiery for later. "I'm barely going two miles from home. Pretty much the entire pack will be there. I'll be safe."

"You're the mother of my child," he says in a low rumble. "If you thought I was overbearing and protective before, then you should have thought it through before having my heir."

The way Valor protects me — he'd move heaven and earth if it'd keep me safe. And he'll raise hell if he figures out I'm not spending all the time at the market. Some women might find him overbearing, but I know how to handle him. A little sass, and well, there's a reason I got knocked up on our wedding night.

I roll my eyes and ruffle his hair one last time before forcing myself to walk away. Being late to this meeting is unacceptable. If I don't show up on time, Berto D'Medici will think I'm trying to set them up. It was difficult enough to get Berto to take my call. I can't waste this opportunity to call the truce.

"I love you, Holly," Valor calls after me. It's a little louder and firm, but he stays quiet to keep Kerrianne asleep.

"I love you too, Valor," I answer with one last backward glance.

The ache of being separated from them hollows out my heart. *I'm doing the right thing. I'm sparking a change. Something for the betterment of all of us.*

3

Valor

CHAPTER ONE

LIFE AT HOME

Parenting advice is bullshit ninety percent of the time. The other ten percent, the self-help books are great for target practice.

No matter how prepared you are or how much reading you do, nothing can accurately depict the complexities of raising a daughter as a single dad.

Or maybe I just got lucky. It's the only explanation for the seven-year-old, who is probably the more stable one of the two of us.

Kerrianne dances around the big-box store's school supply aisle, and I have the heart-aching realization that my little girl is growing up faster than I'm ready to admit.

We've barely started our shopping trip, and I can tell Kerrianne is more excited about the second grade than I am. In a little over two weeks, I lose the joy of spending almost every day with her, and it's as if a sharp knife is jammed into my chest.

Practically at the end of the aisle away from me, Kerrianne spins her skirt in a big swoop.

"What do we need first, Dad?" She stops spinning to look at me.

"Alright." I start at the top and skim the list. "We need four different folders."

While Kerrianne peruses, I step a bit toward the far side of the aisle. Sean, her personal bodyguard and one of my best men, is standing partially out of sight at the other end. As I knew he would be, but I couldn't help double-checking.

I do what I can to give Kerrianne the freedom of a day out with her dad. But even in a big-box store full of other people, there are no safety guarantees.

My bodyguard and private driver, Jack, is a few aisles over, pretending to browse greeting cards or some shit like that.

"Why don't they have any tortoise folders?" Kerrianne sighs and her shoulders slump. "They've got dolphins, dogs, and cats but no tortoises or turtles."

"Well, it's probably because a tortoise isn't a very common house pet and not a common pet at all for school children?" I don't bother lying.

Kerrianne has been obsessed with tortoises since I brought her to the fancy fish store. We went looking for a betta as a family pet but walked out with a tortoise. The four-pound, seven-inch Russian tortoise, who is roughly the same age as me, named Captain, is most certainly not traditional. Not my first choice of pets by a long shot. Instead of a manageable twenty-gallon fish tank, I got a construction project to build the perfect indoor enclosure, a gardening project for summer roaming space, a tortoise that eats a wider variety of vegetables than my daughter, and a very happy pup. What can I say? I'm that dad.

"Let's get dinosaurs too." Kerrianne comes back with three folders — two different colors of T. rex and one with a variety of them mixed in with volcanoes and palm trees.

"One more, little raptor." I correct her, showing her that she only picked out three.

She wrinkles her nose but goes back to the folder selections.

Kerrianne surprises me when she chooses a brightly colored folder with pink fluffy kittens.

"You want the kitten one?" I question before I think better of it. I try not to judge her choices and encourage my daughter's uniqueness, but this is out of character.

She makes a face. "Yeah, maybe another girl will have the same one and we can be friends."

Her nerves about the first day are expected. I didn't want to change schools, but when the one she went to for kindergarten and first grade wouldn't undergo necessary security upgrades, I made the hard choice to switch. The new school is equally far from home but more willing to accept change. Her nerves don't stop her excitement though. When I offered a trip to get school supplies or to the water park, this is what she wanted to do.

"Ten glue sticks." I squint at the paper; *how much gluing is there really?*

I judge but comply with the list. Clearly the teacher knows what the students need.

Kerrianne counts them out and brings them to where I stand with the cart. We go through the list, and she picks a variety of pink, blue, and black items.

My phone rings while we're on our way to check out. I groan when I recognize the quiet ringtone.

"Uh-oh." Kerrianne looks at me with a pout, having learned that ringtone too by now. "Can't you tell work you're busy?"

"I'll see what they want. Maybe it isn't very important and I can play hooky with you." I run my hand over the top of her head, taming a flyaway, before pulling the phone out of my pocket.

My father's 'business line' is on the screen. He and I decided that if it's work related, he'll always call me from this number, and I'll lie and say it's not his fault that I'm leaving her. Someday, she'll figure out that, as I'm the next alpha of our pack, Grandpa's been giving me orders all along. Much like Santa

Claus, the Easter Bunny, and the tooth fairy, it's a little white lie to keep some of the magic in her world . . . And to stop Grandpa from looking like an asshole for taking her dad away from her sometimes.

"Yes?" I answer, trying to exaggerate my steadily growing annoyance. It's not difficult. He knows what I'm doing today and interrupted anyway.

"I need your skills. I can put him in your basement if you'd like to finish the day with your daughter. But we need information. Italy and Russia are making plans, and this guy apparently knows what both of them are up to, but he's less than enthusiastic about sharing," Dad informs me.

Information extraction. It's what I do, and I'm good at it, but in order to spend as much time as possible with Kerrianne, I built a secured section of the house, not on the official blueprints, so I can work while Kerrianne is at school or sleeping at night.

"Yes, I understand. I can accept the delivery, but it won't be processed until later. Be sure to secure it properly before you depart." I smile at Kerrianne and give her a thumbs-up.

She pumps her fist excitedly and tippy-taps on her feet.

"I'll see to it." Dad hangs up.

"Yay!" Kerrianne runs straight into me, wrapping her arms around my waist. "Can we get ice cream before lunch?"

"What's the rule for ice cream?" I tap my finger against my lips, pretending I've forgotten.

The groan she pushes out is accompanied by a pouty lip. "Green things before ice cream."

"So, what does that say about ice cream before lunch?" I move the cart forward as the person in front of us finishes paying their bill.

"Fiiiine," she huffs and stays close to my side while I unload the items from the cart.

My house is built like a fortress, equipped with state-of-the-art security. It's a sanctuary away from the world and a place to raise my daughter.

The unfortunate people who are dragged here, against their will, don't get to see all the amenities it has to offer. Instead, they only see what's sealed up behind the walls of my home gym, none the wiser that it's underneath my family home. They come, they talk, and then, when they're no longer useful, they leave dead as a doornail through a very long, secret tunnel.

This man is no exception. He's stuck in a custom chair I had crafted for maximum discomfort. Long nail-like spikes protrude into his body uncomfortably, between ribs and against shoulder blades.

Because my father called me before lunch, this human has been sitting in my basement for eight hours while I had a father-daughter date with my pup.

We ate lunch at an expensive restaurant, went to a hand-crafted ice cream store, played with Captain, watched a movie, ate steak macaroni and cheese laced with hidden vegetables for dinner, and read no less than three bedtime stories before she finally went to sleep.

That's a long time to sit in an uncomfortable chair screaming for your life. The acrid smells of fear and piss have me flicking on the ventilation hood before I ensure the last of the room's soundproofing.

I compartmentalize my life much like I compartmentalize my house. An electronic tablet rests on the table closest to the door, and I use it while ignoring my unfortunate visitor.

In a few quick clicks, I open the security feed to Kerrianne's room.

"Who the fuck are you?!" The asshole strapped to the chair coughs while I click away on the tablet. He screams for help as if someone will hear him.

I set the alerts to go off if there's sizable movement in Kerrianne's bedroom, if something crosses the threshold to her room, or if someone approaches the front door. The last one is in the unlikely event that someone gets past the property's roaming security guards, gatehouse, and massive fence.

The feed flicks back to her bedroom, and I steal one last look. She's curled up, fast asleep in her jungle-themed room. *Too precious.*

The asshole screams again, pulling my attention off my little raptor, and I finally deal with the problem delivery my father left for me.

As I walk around the worktable and lean against it, I answer his question from three or four screams ago. "I'm the last person who will see you alive."

It's a bit dramatic, but it keeps the fear response high. Self-preservation can be a good tool to wield against someone.

"No." He shakes, and the color drains from his face while I smile and cross my arms over my chest.

I cock my head and examine him. I've never known how to respond when they argue with me about their inevitable death. Just because they don't want it to be true doesn't mean it isn't.

Though I've found that offering them one last choice is amusing. "We can make this quick. You tell me everything you know, and the worst of your suffering will be the hours of sitting in that chair in your own piss."

"Let me go!" He struggles, even though it's no use.

No one escapes the chair. Far tougher humans and other shifters have tried.

"Or we can do this the hard way. I extract a variety of—"

Three beeps from the tablet behind me demand my attention.

Quickly, I move back to the tablet and find the alert for the motion detector in Kerrianne's room. She's tossing and turning in bed. *Go to sleep, little raptor. Deep breaths, count the spikes on a stegosaurus.* Because why would my child count sheep when she could be the little badass she is and want a stegosaurus instead?

"What's going on?" The man tries to get my attention, which seems counterintuitive.

If someone tells you he'll kill you, maybe try to get out of his way and be less seen or less heard.

Kerrianne rolls over one last time and stops moving. I give her another couple of seconds before turning back to the dead man.

"Listen, as much as I wouldn't mind staying up all night torturing you, I'm running out of patience. I would like to go sit down, pop open a beer, and enjoy my evening. How about you tell me what I know you know, I kill you quickly, and then I get on with my life?" I stalk back toward him, grabbing a tool off the table, not even looking at what it is until I'm closer.

"I don't know anything. I don't know who you are. I don't—"

He screams as I hit him in the chest with the tool. I apparently grabbed a handheld gardening rake, and the three tines dig in under his collarbone. It should miss the lungs.

"I don't have all night." I warn him, but if he wants to play stupid, then I'll let him know what I know. Maybe he'll fill in the gaps.

I leave the gardening rake in his chest—you're not supposed to pull out embedded objects, after all—and grab the paperwork my father left me. There's something nice about the analog nature of this act. Technology, no matter how good you are, is easier to hack into than a manila folder with contents printed on flash paper and locked in a drawer, rigged to start on fire at the flip of a switch.

"You're Mick 'The Brick' Sharpman," I tell him, looking him over. There's nothing very big or blocky about him to warrant that nickname but whatever. "You're a low-level money launderer. Apparently, you don't care too much about paying out your dues to the right family. Seems you've been paying us ten percent but taking fifteen percent to Don D'Medici and . . . delivering information along with that money to him."

"No. I never even. I don't know who Don is." Mick 'The Brick' stumbles over his words.

"No, Don isn't his name, it's his title." I pinch the bridge of my nose. "What about Gregorio, or are you working with his consigliere, Eduardo? They're slimy. Italian businessman types."

The realization has Mick sputtering. No words escape his lips, only broken syllables.

"Tell me." I step toward him, this time with a hammer in my hand. "Everything I need to know about what you and the D'Medici family were up to."

"I didn't know he was the Mafia guy. I didn't. This guy Greg and his brother, Ed, approached me. The guy . . . He said that if I gave him fifteen percent of my earnings, he'd invest it. If I could get him information on where the next big fights were at and if there were any shipments moving, he'd . . . he'd . . ." Mick eyes my hammer, and I heft it up, letting it flop heavily into my palm.

"He'd what exactly?" I lean forward, getting eye to eye with Mick.

"He'd make sure that my investment did well. That he'd personally back it with interest on the payout at the end of the year." Mick keeps his eyes on the hammer.

"Don't worry, Mick." I step back from him and put the blunt instrument on the countertop. "A hammer doesn't work when you're looking for more detailed information. It's more of a 'yes or no answer' kind of implement."

I exchange it for a pair of shears, and Mick bellows, imagining, I'm sure, what I'll do to him with these. The sound is so loud that I miss the first buzzer. But his wail dies in his throat, and the proximity sensor of Kerrianne's bedroom door going off.

I dart back around to the screen, abandoning the shears on the table. Kerrianne is in her wolf form. The little dark gray ball of fluff is destroying her already shredded pajamas and trying to tear through the bedding and the mattress.

Again? It's the third time this month. I let out an exhausted sigh and look back at Mick.

He's not in a good way, but he most likely won't die in the time it takes me to get my pup back to bed.

"Sit here and think about what you've done, Mick. When I get back, I want a full report of all the things you've told Greg and Ed." I wag my finger at him and walk toward the exit.

After closing all the layers of soundproofing, I head back through the secret passage to the main part of the house.

Up another flight of stairs and down the hallway, I hear her little growls and snarls. The ferocity of a forty-pound puppy brings out my wolf instincts. But I don't shift. Instead, I open the door, and the movement startles her.

When she sees me, she whines and cries. Kerrianne nearly trips over her big puppy feet as she hops off the bed and makes her way over with her head lowered, knowing what she's done wrong. I kneel on the floor before her, and Kerrianne crawls into my lap, nibbling and biting up my neck. Her puppy breath reminds me again and again that she's just a baby.

She won't be this little forever. I sigh and drop myself down to my butt and settle in on the floor. Her puppy form is so much closer in color to Holly's than mine. Dark brown markings are becoming clearer in her coat, and the lighter spots seem to grow smaller with each growth spurt.

My little pup is struggling, and I love her more than all the pajamas and bedding in the entire world.

I embrace the squirming puppy, cozying her tight against me

while I glide my fingers through her soft, plush undercoat until she lets out a massive sigh and sneezes.

She wobbles as she pushes herself out of my arms and then hops off my lap. When I'm sure this isn't a puppy ploy to get me to play and she's ready to shift back, I stand and grab her little bathrobe off the hook next to the door.

It's slow, and she seems to struggle, but with one last stretch, Kerrianne shifts back, and I help wrap her up into her robe.

"Hey, little raptor, what's wrong?" I ask.

She practically throws herself against my body once more, this time wrapping her arms around my legs.

"I had a dream, and there were big, bad men, and they wanted to take you away, and I couldn't ever see you again," she wails, and I bend down, scooping her up into my arms.

"Oh, hey, little raptor. That'll never happen, I promise." I pet her hair while holding her to me, swaying back and forth like when she was a baby.

At seven, she's probably too big to want to be held, but I don't care. I'll do it until she tells me no.

"How can you be so sure?" She wraps her little arms tighter around my neck and pushes words out between gasps. "They knew our secret and —"

"There isn't a force on this earth that will keep me from you." I rest my head against hers for maximum reassurance. "Besides, what did I tell you about big, bad men?"

"You and Grandpa are in charge of all the pack." She holds back a wail.

"And?" I prompt.

"And the big, bad men." She sniffles.

"Exactly." I squeeze her tight.

It might not be true yet, but it will be. I'll get rid of the scum the man in my basement was making deals with and slowly take over a territory so large, have a network so big, that my pup will never be afraid of the world around her. Shifter, human, or criminal.

Antonella

CHAPTER TWO

HOMECOMING

It's the funniest thing to experience homesickness when you've spent so long running from your family. But one little thing is all it takes to have you considering going back home. Then it snowballs.

"Toni. You must take this job. Please. Please. Please. Please. At least apply?" Leticia, my younger cousin, is begging me over the phone like she's dying, and I'm loving every minute of it.

"I don't know." I sigh, playing into the uncertainty of the prospect. "You know if I move home, I'll be forced back into the life. Berto and your dad will be terrible about it. Plus, I just started feeling like I can breathe without worrying about every person as a threat."

That last part is true, but my resistance is fake. After seven years, homesickness has won and I'm headed back to Chicago, at least for one school year.

The job Leticia is begging me to take, a full-time teaching position at one of the most elite elementary schools in the country, is already mine. I applied, interviewed, and accepted the teaching job at Rothschild-McClintock Magnet School, starting for the new school year.

"But, Toni," Leticia whines, "you don't have to be back into the lifestyle. I know my dad would much rather keep paying you to stay as a silent heir."

"And I'll resent him for it. It was my dad's wish that I take over his responsibilities." I groan as I think about living in Chicago again. The conflict between me and my uncle Gregorio, Leticia's father and head of the infamous Italian Mob, is bound to only get worse.

It's easier to accept that I'm not who my father wanted me to be when I'm not seeing the turnoff every week to the cemetery where my parents are buried. The Catholic guilt can't burrow in too deep if I'm not face-to-face with it every day.

The guilt and conflict don't stop me from packing. I put the sweater I folded into the suitcase.

"At least think about it? I'm graduating this year, and you know Dad won't waste any time trying to marry me off to some pompous douche canoe who thinks he's hot shit and gives me an allowance." Leticia gives a wistful sigh, a stark contradiction to the insults she spewed.

She would never say such things if she weren't in her room, tucked away from the rest of the family. Leticia is almost perfect for becoming a Mafia wife. Meek, docile, easy to control . . . everything I'm not.

"I don't know, Leticia." I hold out telling her a little bit longer.

It's nice to have someone on this planet who wants me in their life. She'll be excited when I tell her the news, but hearing her say how much she wants me back home is nice.

"Well, if you're not coming home, then maybe I should do what you did? Apply to grad school in some faraway land. Get a master's and then, one step further, a PhD to avoid everyone." Leticia tries to sound strong in that decision.

"I'd help you pack." I encourage her while knowing full well that she got homesick during the one spring break she spent with me out here in New York.

With one more look at my bedroom, I breathe a relaxing sigh of relief. I'm grateful I don't need to sell the big pieces of furniture since I rented this apartment fully furnished. It'll be a relatively easy move back to my uncle's penthouse in the Gold Coast of Chicago.

"You'd need to be here first." Leticia pauses. "Wait. Does that mean you're coming home?"

"Yes, I already got the job you're telling me about. Well, no, not that exact job. I'm teaching second grade, accelerated learners, not kindergarten." I quickly remove the phone from where I had it pressed it to my ear with my shoulder.

Leticia's scream is so loud I'm sure everyone in the massive seven-thousand-square-foot Casa D'Medici heard.

"Shhhh." I bring the phone back to my ear when her excited squeals subside. "I'm not sure where I'm living yet."

"Don't be ridiculous." Leticia scoffs. "Where else would you live if not at home?"

"I don't know, get an apartment in River North? Any place not in Gold Coast? It would be a closer commute to school," I answer, pulling out the next drawer to put more clothes into the suitcase. "The only issue is the bodyguard." I giggle, thinking about the conversation I already had in my head about this, and then choose to relay it to her. "'Oh, yes, hello, Mrs. Neighbor. Oh, for work? I'm a second-grade teacher, and this is my bodyguard Enzo' or maybe something like, 'Oh, yeah, my uncle, Gregorio D'Medici, crime boss, wants me to keep him as a pet. Feel free to give Enzo coffee or pastries when you see him in the hallway.' Those aren't normal things you say to people."

"Oh my God, could you even imagine if that was?" Leticia giggles before musing, "Poor Enzo. Not that he would be assigned back to you, it'd probably be one of the newer men. Enzo is getting close with Berto. I heard them talking about a supplier and Russians. Of course, when I asked, all I got was 'It's men's work. You need to go back to the kitchen with Mom.'"

"Ugh," I huff and try closing the lid on my suitcase. Even thinking about what kind of business they could be getting into has me on edge. "Gregorio is going with the Russians?"

"Hell if I know," Leticia murmurs. "It's not like they tell me anything. I'm a woman. Did I tell you I cut my hair?"

"You did it?" I gasp, letting go of the suitcase lid since it's not zipping easily.

Leticia was blessed with beautiful golden hair, an oddball among the family of various shades of brown. She's been through countless battles with her mother, Francesca, about how she's not allowed to cut it beyond a trim and light layering. Despite being twenty-three, Leticia has never gone against her mother's wishes.

I sit on the bed next to my suitcase to focus.

"I didn't do all of it." Leticia huffs in stiff disappointment with herself. "I was too afraid to do the splash of color we talked about, but I went from waist length to chest length."

"Okay. Wow." I've never had a problem telling Francesca and Gregorio that they don't run my life. But for their daughter? This is a huge step in breaking the cycle away from the overbearing parents. "How did that go over?"

"There was some crying," Leticia admits, and I can practically hear her wincing.

"You or Francesca?" I clarify.

The sweat from packing is making my skin sticky, so I shake my T-shirt to try and cool myself down.

"Both," Leticia mumbles. "I held strong until she started crying. I told her I'm an adult and she had to accept that I needed some change." She sighs, and I think I hear her flop down on the bed. "But then she said she didn't want me to turn out like you. That God wouldn't forgive her if she had a disobedient daughter, and how could I do this to her? She literally left to go to church and pray for me. And that's when I went to my room and cried."

"It's a haircut. You didn't deserve for her to treat you like that." My heart hurts for Leticia.

I'm the rebel of the family, but I come by it honestly. My father, the second-born son, was raised to be my uncle Gregorio's consigliere when Gregorio took over as head of the family. Dad tried to bring the 'family' business into a more modern era and away from the classic men's club sexist shit. As a result, unlike Leticia, I was always encouraged to be unique and do all the things my cousin, Berto, Leticia's brother, did.

"It's not like I took you to get a tattoo or another piercing."

"I know." Leticia's voice is small, and it pisses me off.

I stand up off the bed and then start pacing, angry on her behalf. I pull my other suitcase out of the closet and put her on speaker, setting the phone on the overfull suitcase I'm done with. "It'll be okay. I'll come home, show them my newest tattoo, and they'll be so focused on me that they'll forget all about your haircut."

"When are you coming home?" Leticia whispers like she's hiding some big secret.

"I'm finishing packing as we speak. My lease is up at the end of the month. And I figured I'd talk to Berto about where to live." I groan thinking about how that conversation will go. Berto and I don't see eye to eye.

He's a traditionalist and would gladly cut me out in a heartbeat if it weren't for my father's wishes. But once upon a time, when we were children in the same classes, we used to be friends. Sometimes, I catch glimpses of that boy, but they're getting fewer and further between.

"I would recommend telling him sooner rather than later and letting him book the flight," Leticia suggests. "He's been obnoxious about making decisions lately. Dad's been trying to give him more responsibility so 'every decision matters.'" Leticia uses a fake deep voice, imitating her older brother.

"Will do," I say while standing by my dresser and tossing my socks across the room into the suitcase.

"So, you'll be home when?" Leticia sounds all too pleased with the feeling that she 'won' my return home.

I finish tossing that drawer and move on to my underwear and bras. "Well, the school year starts in a little over two weeks. I need to pick up my class list and a ton of stuff, so the sooner, the better. I was looking at a flight out tomorrow afternoon. But if Berto is—"

"Berto!" Leticia yells, and I'm so glad my phone isn't up to my ear.

Her footfalls sound much quieter for a few seconds.

"What?" Berto sounds grated by his sister's presence.

I think back to all the times when he told his father how he asked for a younger brother.

"Toni wants to come home. She got a job here. Can you get her a plane ticket?" Leticia uses her sweetest voice.

"She's coming home?" Berto sounds just as surprised as I assumed they would all be.

"That's mine!" Leticia objects. "Call her on your own phone. Later—"

"You're coming home?" Berto's deeper voice is closer now.

I stare down at the phone, and the dread I had for this conversation smacks me in the face. I was enjoying being excited with Leticia, but now this. Begrudgingly, when I can't not answer any longer, I explain. "I accepted a position at Rothschild-McClintock Magnet School. I'll get an apartment in the city, maybe River North, so I'll be closer to work."

"No." Berto is firm. "You'll stay here at the house. It's too dangerous for you to live and work in neutral territory. You should have spoken to me before accepting a job. The

Cavanaghs are up to their bullshit again. It's not safe to talk on open lines like this. I'll send you details for your flight secured."

Interesting. I don't bother arguing with him, but I do catalog what he is saying. "Thank you, cousin."

Berto says nothing more, and Leticia is back on the line. "Ugh, I have to go too, or I'll be late for dinner."

"Go. Go." I encourage her while I finish packing the necessities and can manage without needing her to body double.

"I'll see you so soon!" Leticia smacks her lips in a kiss. "Love you! Bye!"

"Love you too," I call out, but she's gone, and I'm left back alone with the silence of my apartment.

Am I really moving back into La Casa D'Medici with all of them?

But the longer the silence drags on, the longer I ache to be with people. The ties of community found in a large family aren't easily replaced.

CHAPTER THREE

A VILLAGE

"I don't understand why we can't hit them where it hurts. The D'Medici family has been coming after everything we do. They were at the human underground fighting arena. What happens if they find the wolf fights next? If humans find out about us ..." One of the older men of the pack growls his opinion. The threat is left off because no one likes to theorize what would happen if wolves were made known to the public.

Rumbles from the twenty men in the room fill the air as they voice their agreement, and someday it'll be my job to answer these questions. But not today.

My father and his pack second, my uncle, Neil, are in charge. Both are in their fifties, but there's another decade or more before they step down as heads of our business. Until then, I get to sit on my father's left, a symbol of my status, at the table set up in the front of the room before rows of chairs where pack members sit.

They won't find us. We protect the human fights less than the wolf fights for a reason. My wolf echoes my thoughts on the subject. Usually, my opinion isn't being asked for. I'm here to be involved and show my support without directly having a say.

But I would be lying if I said I wasn't itching to do exactly what the man is suggesting. I want Gregorio D'Medici dead and buried long enough for his son to take over the family business and get his feet underneath him. I clench my fist, trying to dispel some of my own feelings about our situation. I don't go off half-cocked though. Mine is a personal vendetta. I have a mate to avenge, and I'm playing the long game. I'll be a patient hunter.

"We all know the risks," another man, probably irritated with the length of this meeting, snaps.

I shuffle in my seat, not liking his tone. But my father stays relaxed, unbothered. Neil, however, is clenching his fist like he's holding something back.

Movement in the front row draws my eye. My younger brother, Royal, had shuffled in his seat and is now leaning back in his chair. With his phone in his hand, his thumb flies across the bottom. I know before I feel the vibration in my pocket that he's sending me texts.

There's no point in hiding it. Everyone in the room heard it go off. Wolf hearing.

I open the message quickly and look at it.

ROYAL:

Fix your face you look like an axe murderer.

Unless that's the vibe you want to go for, make everyone think you're unhinged.

I really don't want to be Alpha though, and as younger sibling . . . it was never my job. That's why I learned IT like we discussed. Look less unhinged or unhinged enough that someone challenges you. K thanks.

And I told Mom and Dad I wanted a little brother why? Regardless, I relax my jaw, unclench my fist, and try not to 'look like an axe murderer.' I try for my usually cool and unaffected inter-rogator facade and put my phone away.

Because he's a good uncle to our pup. My wolf tries to offer support for Royal.

But it's not needed. As much as he gets on my nerves, we're brothers. We always have each other's backs.

"Let's go over what we know." My father tries to be diplomatic, and I'm ready for him to disclose the edited version of what Mick told me about 'Greg and Ed' D'Medici after I put Kerrianne back to bed in the wee hours of the morning. "I don't want to put too much information out there and be wrong about it."

"Ian. I want to hear it from Valor direct." The older man from the pack, Thomas O'Halloran, coughs. The years of cigars are catching up to him.

Neil scoffs from the other side of my father.

My wolf growls, but I suppress it. Civility is best suited right now. For the longest time I only handled the non-pack part of our business, but recently, my dad has requested my involve-ment more and more with the pack operations. I understand his reasoning, but it can be disruptive to the established hierarchy. Three dominant wolves at one table trying to lead isn't easy.

"Fair enough." My father looks over at me with a silent warning to keep it to the basics.

Heat warms my collar with that glare. Dad's usually more forgiving when the pack wants to hear something from me.

Did I fail to silence that growl? I check with my wolf, but he plays dumb to the question. *Fuckin' hell.*

I straighten in my chair, raising my gaze to look more point-edly across the room, and start with the important pieces. "We know the D'Medicis are looking to branch out. Drugs and information aren't enough for them to sell. They're trying to fill the gaps with the special kinds of shipments we refuse to touch."

"Fuckers," a man toward the back of the room barks, a thick

Irish accent giving away that it's one of our more recent transplants. "Traffickin'. Disgusting."

"What are we doing about it?" Thomas raises his voice with a growl, clearly ready to issue a challenge.

"The obvious." Neil cuts in.

"From Valor," someone toward the back shouts.

Neil grumbles, but over the murmurs of the pack, I can't hear what he said. Dad huffs the way he does when he disagrees with something. Like when I used to tell him I was going to a friend's house, but I was really hooking up with Holly. It wasn't a lie; she was a friend. He didn't believe me, but he didn't stop me either. Disagreement but not an objection.

I clench my fist again but don't take Thomas's bait for a challenge. Ready to defer to my father, I give him a sideways glance, but instead of stepping in, Dad remains silent. He gives me a nod of approval.

The huff wasn't directed toward me. I don't look down the table because the tension in the air is enough to know a discussion is coming after this meeting.

Taking a second before speaking, I uncurl my fingers and drum them on the table. "The rat I worked last night didn't have enough answers for me to confidently say we should make a move. If we were to err on the side of caution, we should suspend the fights until we have a better handle on what is or isn't going on — D'Medicis or otherwise."

Groans of disappointment fill the air, but no one contradicts me. While we, the 'Irish Mob' as the government agencies have dubbed us, make many decisions through votes and open forum discussions, at the end of the day, the pack alpha makes the final call. The pack not disagreeing with me is a good sign that Dad's silent support of my decision to wait will go uncontested.

"We need to end the war once and for all. The D'Medicis' numbers keep growing while our pack keeps shrinking," another man pipes up from the back of the room.

Yes, they have more children than we have pups every year, but I've been slowly and diligently wiping out illegal business after business of the D'Medici empire. The end game is to remove them as a threat entirely. But in the process, I also want vengeance for Holly's death. It's been seven frustratingly long years of searching for evidence of who killed her, and when I have it, that person will pay for the pain he has put me through and the impact of Kerrianne never getting to know her mother.

Berto and Gregorio D'Medici are on the top of my suspect list, and when I have proof and the opportunity, I'll drag them to my basement, kicking and screaming. I'll take pleasure in dismantling them piece by piece as I force them to tell me why and apologize for what they've done. I'll make them beg, with false hope, for their lives.

Royal clears his throat, and I know it's his way of telling me to fix my face. I spare a glance at him, and he's pointing to his lips. I'm so tired that I'm smiling at the thoughts of murder. *Maybe the pack should be concerned about me.*

We're wolves. Death is normal. My wolf defends me all while thinking of the taste of blood.

Yeah, the pack should be concerned about me.

"I understand the frustration postponing the fights will cause. It's valid for us to worry about the next moves." Dad puts a voice to the decision he, Neil, and I made in his office earlier this afternoon. "Let's reconvene at the next full moon. We'll talk about resuming the fights. I'll have better answers for you then. Valor is working a lead on how to hit the D'Medicis back. We all know when my son goes on a hunting expedition, he comes back victorious."

"Objections?" Neil shuffles in his seat, and when I stretch back in my chair, I catch a glimpse of his features pinched together.

No one raises any additional concerns.

"Adjourned." Dad pats his palm on the table.

I try to contain my sigh of relief at this day being that much closer to over. But Royal snorts, and I know I failed. *Fuck it, I'm done for the night.*

Murmurs around the room meld together as pack members stand, some heading outside to run under the light of the full moon while others, including myself, head to the main meeting space of the home, where refreshments have been set out as prepared by my mother and some women of the pack.

A few women make eyes at me as I navigate the space full of shifters. Some of them, the more stubborn or more delusional ones, are still vying for an opportunity to be the next alpha's mate, and they try to put themselves closer to the path I'm walking with hope I'll give them a chance. It'll never happen.

One or two hopefuls used to wander up at every function and offer a drink, a meal, or more. But now they know my lack of interest isn't a side effect of grief. I've made it clear I'm not to be approached. It's not that they aren't great options. Most will make good mates for someone else someday. For me though? There are no sparks.

When I became a single dad, I decided I would only bring a woman into Kerrianne's life when I could be sure she would be a good influence, would understand the life and expectations on her, and wouldn't try to step in and replace her mother's memory.

There's only one woman I'm looking for. I find her in the crowd, in black slacks and a bright red sweater, and navigate toward where she's chatting with a couple of her friends, a Bloody Mary in her hand.

One of her friends clears her throat when I approach.

My mother glances at me, her short gray and brown hair springing around her face. The silver necklace Dad gifted her for their anniversary glints in the light. Her face bright, she beams at me. "There he is. I was wondering if your father would ever adjourn the meeting. It's like he forgets full moons are for celebrating and not just another business meeting."

"We had some concerns regarding the plan. You know how business is. I take it your meeting went well?" I ask, only half caring and mostly for appearance's sake.

I force out a smile to make it look right and like I care. Royal's reminders to hide some of how I'm feeling are still fresh, but exhaustion is setting in.

"Well, I won't bore you with planning parties and festivities." She turns to look at me head-on, and her face falls. "Oh dear." She waves to her friends and then wraps her non-drink-filled hand around my bicep. Mom's intuition picks up my bullshit. She knows now I'm not here to say hello and that I love her. "Ladies, please excuse me."

Quickly, she ushers me like a small boy away from the party. We head down the hallway toward my father's office. Before we get to the door, I hear him and Neil inside, chatting about a trade route we established.

"Neil, could you give us a minute?" Mom isn't really asking. Her tone is short and impatient.

"Can't this wait?" Neil asks, eyes narrowed at her. "We're talking —"

"Neil, out!" Mom snaps while pushing me into the room and waving toward the door.

Neil scowls. Then he draws a slow breath, becoming more neutral before he stands slowly, not ready to piss my mother off. Ducking his head out of respect, Neil obediently moves past us out to the rest of the festivities, scotch glass in hand.

I wouldn't want to risk my mother's wrath, but getting a front-row seat to him debating it was amusing. Mom is not a violent wolf unless she needs to be. But she's the alpha's mate for a reason, and there's no point in pushing her buttons after she delivers an angry bark like that.

And Dad would never stand for someone disrespecting her. No matter how close he and his brother are.

"What's wrong?" My father looks me over, brow furrowing. He unbuttoned the top buttons of his dress shirt and rolled up the sleeves. "Is this about the text message?"

"No, that was Royal being . . . Royal. Mom is making a bigger deal out of it than it is." I scrub my hand down my face.

"You look like you're about to fall down with exhaustion." Ma gives me a pointed look, and then, with a hand on my chest, she pushes me, gently-ish, to the chair in front of Dad's desk. "Sit."

Once I'm seated, the exhaustion I apparently wasn't masking well settles in further. My eyelids grow heavy. The comfort of the chair and privacy of Dad's office give me the feeling of safety, and I yawn.

"Now." She sits in the other chair, looking me over. "What's going on?"

"Kerrianne is shifting in her sleep, again. I thought we'd gotten past this back in kindergarten." I shrug and let my shoulders slump in defeat. "She's having nightmares and saying that big, bad men were trying to take her from me. She's afraid and terrified that they know our secret."

"Well, she is that age." Dad runs his hand over his five-o'clock shadow and then across his mouth before letting it fall with a thud to his desk. "I don't envy you. It was bad when you went through it, and hell when Royal went through it. I thought we'd have to buy mattresses in bulk the way he shredded them."

"True." Mom laughs and takes a sip of her drink. "It's normal. She is starting to really understand how different we are. It's also clear that she's understanding more about people leaving. Of course she's afraid to be separated from you. You're all she has."

"I am not." I look at the two of them, bewildered at the

suggestion that my daughter is alone. "We have the three of you."

"It's not the same as having two parents." Mom taps her finger against her chin and pointedly lets that statement go, shifting the conversation. "I think what helped Royal most was shifting before bed. Wore him out until he could hardly keep his eyes open, then he'd sleep through the night."

"Yeah. Then he hit that growth spurt." Dad laughs, clearly taking a trip down memory lane. "Practically wore the same size clothes as you overnight. That's why we stopped after him. We couldn't hardly afford the two of you growing like weeds."

I can't exactly focus on what they're saying though. *Could this be better if I had a mate?* I hate that thought. *No, Royal and I grew up in a home with both parents, and they're saying it happened to us. If it happens to everyone, then it's something I can get her through. We've made it this far, just the two of us.*

"It's normal?" I confirm against the warring tension in my gut.

Mom nods and rubs my shoulder, comforting me. "It'll pass. Leave Kerrianne with me for the night. Go home and get some rest. She's downstairs playing with some of the other pups from the pack. It'll be fine."

"What about school in two weeks?" I run my hands back through my hair. The more I think about this, the more worries for Kerrianne's safety come to light. "We opted to send her to the school with the advancements but —"

"But nothing." My mother raises a stern brow. "Is she shifting uncontrollably during the daytime that I'm not aware of?"

"No."

"Then she should go to that school. The school the pack goes to is very nice, but you'll have the same issues you had before. She's smart, Valor. She needs to be in a place that challenges her with kids her own age. Putting her in the advanced grades won't make her well rounded." Mom reasons with me.

I groan before pushing myself up out of the chair because the world is getting blurry, and I refuse to sleep in my father's office. "I wish the first one had agreed to the security updates. I hate moving her again."

"It'll be okay. Kerrianne makes friends anywhere. She's bright and kind. She's a good pup, Valor." Dad reassures me. He walks around the desk and gives me a hug.

I don't know what I'd do without the two of them in our lives. Beyond that, as I walk back through the house, past the gathering of pack members who give waves and smiles, I can't imagine trying to raise her without the support network I do have. Every failure I have, someone can help fix it. My family may be small, but my pack is large and full of love. *What more could I ask for?*

CHAPTER FOUR

THE GREAT DISAPPOINTMENT

After a long week of paperwork, fingerprinting, drug testing, and new-hire orientation, I'm finally provided with what I've wanted most: my class list. The rest of the teachers at the school all 'pitched in' to help fill my class after a long debate about which students would go well together. I got a small rundown of the 'who's who,' and my excitement is next level.

Some new schools can be less than considerate and give the new teacher all difficult students, but I feel like I've got a good mix.

My first month's lesson plans had to match exactly with the other second-grade classroom, so I'm off the hook for planning while I learn a little bit more about my students and their abilities. That's a weight off my shoulders because one week does not make for adequate time to lesson plan for a whole month, get them approved, decorate my classroom, and take the time to move back into my uncle's home.

However, it is long enough to make cute 'fall in love with learning' themed meet-your-new-teacher crafts to send home, and do all the other things.

I don't announce my presence when I come home, opting to open and close the door to the penthouse as quietly as possible. My assigned bodyguard chose to stay at the front desk and security office rather than come up the elevator. I made him ride in the passenger seat so I could drive all the way home. . . and make passenger princess jokes.

Berto, Gregorio, and Eduardo told me I couldn't have Enzo back on my detail despite the fact that he offered and stated it as his preference. If I must make the concession to live at 'home' with my family, then I would at least like a bodyguard I know and trust. So, I'll make this one's life hell until he complains enough.

It's childish. I know it is. But in the last week it's been made abundantly clear that the 'heads' of the family are once again trying to appease me by keeping me paid out as my father wished. The issue is they're ignoring the rest of his desire that I be made a partner, that I become Berto's consigliere and not be restricted to only financially benefiting from the business.

I don't even necessarily want that responsibility or involvement, but I want respect as a person and not to be treated like Gregorio and Eduardo treat their wives and daughters.

I refuse to be less.

Settled in at the dining room table, I'm thirty minutes into working on my art project when Leticia comes waltzing into the dining room.

"Oh my goodness!" Leticia clasps her hands in front of her chest, looking over my shoulder.

I'm mounting the images of the little hands to glue the leaves to while Leticia fawns over the pile of the finished pieces.

"Ooooh, look at this one. I could take her home." Leticia holds up a picture of an adorable blonde-haired little girl, pulling off the sticky note on the front with her name to give me an unobstructed view.

"They're not for adoption, Leticia. It's not a pound. You can't bring a child home." I laugh, teasing my younger cousin while searching my brain, trying to practice my students' names. "That's Emma?"

"Yes." Leticia sets down Emma's photo and picks up another, repeating the process. "Oh my goodness. He looks like a little Berto."

The little boy in question has dark hair and olive skin, like a more modern version of Leticia's brother, my cousin, Berto. *Huh, he really does look strikingly like him when he was that age.* But I have no idea what the boy's name is, and I make a wild guess, remembering some names on the list. "Liam?"

Leticia shakes her head. "Noah."

"What are you two squealing about now?" Berto, the man whose ears must be burning, struts into the dining room. Laid-back swagger, hands tucked into his pockets, he looks across the table with more of a grimace than a smile. "Aaah, that time of the year already? You've started making your little art projects."

Get fucked, Berto. You're not ruining this for me. I narrow my gaze at him. "Yes, you knew I'd have art projects. You act like it's been so long since I was making projects over Christmas break."

"Look at how cute they are, Berto." Leticia, ever the peace-maker, draws his attention back to the photo of Noah, stopping any argument we might get into. "This one looks just like you did."

"I never had a haircut that bad." Berto has a single defense, mock outrage, and he loosens up a little bit. "Now, if his parents got him a real haircut, then yes. He could possibly be cool enough to be a mini me." Apparently remembering that he's decided to constantly be a frigid bastard, Berto straightens his stance and squares up to where I sit at the table. "Well, you better clean up. We're having family dinner tonight, and we're expecting guests."

Oh joy. I fake smile at him. "Yes, cousin dearest."

He walks away without further comment.

Once he's gone, Leticia mutters, "Our guests aren't even arriving for three more hours. It's not like I'm in the middle of setting the table."

"He likes to think he's the boss." I scoff and keep working on my project. "He'll remember soon enough that he'll never truly be the boss of me, and he'll chill the fuck out."

"God, I hope so. But he's been this way for a while. Something must be going on." Leticia sighs.

"When I figure it out, you'll be the first to know." I reassure her.

After school starts and I adjust to the new schedule, I'll start worming my way back into the business. *I'm not nosy. I'm concerned.* I smile at that distinction my roommate in college taught me. I'm totally being nosy, but 'concerned' sounds so much nicer when someone asks why you want to know.

There's more than enough time to spare to finish my art project, for Leticia to set the table, and for us to both get freshened up before our dinner guests arrive. I come down the stairs in a little black dress. Some battles aren't worth fighting, and a dress to family dinner is one of them.

Aunt Francesca is waiting at the bottom of the staircase. Her long raven-black hair is in a bun, her designer dress is tailored to fit her like a glove, and as always, her diamonds showcase the money and status Gregorio has accumulated, or not squandered . . . whichever. She's ready to entertain whoever is coming to dinner.

Her presence is purposeful. It's to scrutinize me and stop me from coming down wearing something not to her liking. Which is most of my current wardrobe.

She eyes me from top to bottom, then top to bottom again. "Toni, would it have killed you to wear something other than black?"

"Probably." I give her a saccharine smile. "It has long sleeves and hides my tattoos."

"At least there is that. Though, that skirt is a little short."

She approves enough to walk away, and I look down, checking the hem length.

It's above my knees but barely. I pull my long brown hair over my shoulder. The curls I purposefully styled a little tightly, naturally relax a bit. My straight hair doesn't always hold them well, but I do my best. She'd rather it be up, but I try to do at least two things that annoy her at every family dinner. I have several options since most things I wear, do, or say frustrate her.

With no demands from Francesca to go and change, I continue down the stairs until my heels are clicking on the terrazzo floors.

Following the sounds of voices, I start analyzing and trying to determine our guests. Uncle Eduardo, the loudest of our already loud family, is telling a story and garnering laughs from the group. Nothing gives away who we may be entertaining.

Leticia, however, hears me coming and meets me at the door to the sitting space with a glass of wine. *Oh, it'll be one of those nights.*

Stepping into the room, I see why Leticia brought me wine right away. Our guests are four gentlemen, two seated, two standing, and a single woman, seated between the two men on the sofa. Of the entire party, the only one I recognize is Igor Popov, head of the Bratva. He's . . . well, unique looking to say the least. Where la famiglia hands down their reign from oldest son to oldest son, the Bratva fight for it, and in his fight to be

Pakhan, he took a gruesome attack to the head, leaving him scarred across one eye.

Igor stands, as does the younger man sitting on the sofa, which, by my logic, tells me it's his son. Their strong jaws, dirty blond hair, and semitruck-like builds give away the genetics they share.

Even if he does have to fight to be Pakhan, I have no doubt this man could fend off anyone coming for his position.

Igor speaks, a smile pulling at his lips. "You must be the lovely Toni I have heard so much about."

Oh, oh no, he did not. I cast a sidelong glance at Gregorio, but he's keeping a tight lid on things.

I don't bother to smile. "I am."

Igor reaches out for a handshake, and I reciprocate the gesture, but he wraps his fingers around my hand and doesn't let go. *I am going to slit Gregorio's and Berto's throats in their sleep.*

"Come, I'd like you to meet my son." My hand still clasped in his, Igor practically pulls me toward him. His accent isn't as thick as I'm guessing it was when he first immigrated. "Toni this is my son, Nikolai."

Nikolai isn't unattractive with his blond hair, striking blue eyes, and prominent jawline, which I'm sure women dream about. If I wasn't currently revenge-plotting to take over the family business, I'd maybe even flirt. Except when my hand is placed in his, Nikolai kisses it.

I cough to cover my gasp.

"Little flower, are you okay?" Nikolai reaches out to steady my other arm but takes my wine glass instead.

"I'm fine, thank you." I pull myself out of his reach and try to take the wine glass back.

The oaf holds it up to his eye level. Which is quite tall, given I'm wearing two-inch heels and he still towers above me. "Is it customary for women to drink wine before dinner?"

I abandon him and the glass and head to the bar cart, letting

Gregorio and Francesca smooth over with our guests that yes, it's quite common for Italians to have one . . . or four . . . glasses of wine with dinner.

Wine won't dull this experience enough anyway. I grab a rocks glass and pour myself an old-fashioned using the ingredients already laid out.

Berto hisses as he approaches me, "Do not make a fool of this family. You knew this would happen."

"Mmm, did I?" I pitch that as a question despite knowing this was a risk of coming home. This must be record timing though.

Gregorio will always try to marry me off for a business deal. I'm honored he got me the head of the Bratva's son rather than some lowly enforcer or captain this time. Like any of Gregorio's previous attempts, Nikolai and I won't be paired.

I return to the sitting area, purposefully avoiding the side of the room where Nikolai has my wine glass. I draw a long, slow sip of my drink.

"So, Toni, your aunt tells me you're a teacher?" the beautiful blonde woman in the center of the sofa asks me.

I have no idea who she is. But if this is an engagement dinner, she must be Mrs. Popova.

"I am." I smile, stiffening slightly and crossing my legs demurely. Then I lay it on thick. "I graduated from Columbia, summa cum laude and valedictorian, the highest honor they offer in education. Then I went on to teach for two years at private elementary schools in DC. I felt it would benefit me to pursue my master's, so I returned to Columbia University in New York and graduated summa cum laude, again."

"Oh." She raises her eyebrows. "Impressive."

"A bit overeducated for a woman in your line of work, isn't she, Gregorio?" Igor laughs like he's told a funny joke.

Leticia slides her hand next to mine on the sofa and gives it a squeeze.

Don't worry, cousin. I won't hurt their feelings . . . much.

"Well, you know her father, Antonio, may he rest in peace, always wanted a child who could fill his place someday. God gifted him with a bright girl like Toni. It seemed only fair to honor his memory by letting her go to school," Gregorio answers before sipping his drink.

"Yes, and she's made the family quite proud. If anything, Toni is a perfect example of how we are continually striving for greatness," Eduardo answers as he walks behind me.

It's a threat to behave.

Not happening, Eduardo. I draw another long sip of my drink and ignore him.

Aunt Francesca saves us from the horrors of small talk with the announcement of dinner being ready. I make sure to move from the living room in the middle of the pack, staying close to Eduardo's middle child, Sarena, who came from the kitchen with Francesca. My seat, customarily at Berto's left-hand side, has a place card on it.

"I thought we'd do something fun for dinner." Francesca smiles. "Everyone has a place setting just for them."

It doesn't surprise me that 'somehow' I'm 'magically' seated next to Nikolai, and the place setting contains a little extra, nonstandard piece of decor.

Our large family has filed in with our guests, and I pull my chair out.

Nikolai places his hand over the top of mine, stopping me with it halfway out. "I am sorry for my interference. I tend to be a bit overzealous."

He reaches over to the table for the piece of decor, a red chrysanthemum.

I force myself to remain still as he tucks the stem behind my ear. *Is this guy for real?*

"I do hope that we can make this arrangement work. I think you'll be very happy with me as your husband."

I bite my lips together, and Nikolai pulls out an engagement ring from his pocket. He tries to raise my left hand to slide it onto my finger, but I tuck that hand behind my back.

After the first surprise proposal, the novelty wears off. Though, as far as rings go, this is one of the nicest I've been offered. If I was accepting based on rings alone, Igor and Nikolai would win the alliance with the D'Medicis through marriage. But I'm not chattel and I'm not being married off.

"How much?" I ask him quietly.

"I don't understand." He furrows his brows.

"No, of course you wouldn't." I turn to look at Igor and Gregorio. "How much? Two million?" Neither of them flinch. "No, more than that. What, five million and opening a shipment for direct imports on guns?" Gregorio cocks his head, and I know I'm closer. "Opening the direct import and my share in the family business."

"Toni." Berto warns in a low voice from across the table.

"I'm getting closer, then." I look back to Nikolai. "I'm sure you're very nice, and of the men Gregorio has tried to marry me off to, you're the most attractive, and your ring is lovely, but my answer is no."

"You can't say no," Gregorio says from behind me.

But I remove the chrysanthemum and hand it back to Nikolai. "I wish you well."

"Antonella!" Gregorio shouts as I leave the dining room.

I don't bother trying to leave the house, but I do ascend the staircase, heading directly to my bedroom.

If I leave, they'll chase me and drag me back. It'll appear childish and like I'm a prisoner here.

If I stand my ground, they'll have no choice but to remember who I am. My pull is limited. I'm still a woman, just another possession in the D'Medici home. But I am my father's daughter, and guilt of his death hangs heavy on my uncle's conscience, but he's never spoken of why. It's been enough, but I don't feel like it will be enough for long.

I'm not dumb enough to think this is the end. The first possible opportunity Gregorio can find to make a proposal stick . . . he will.

Berto must have taken the other stairwell. He meets me at my bedroom door and starts scolding me. "Quite a temper tantrum you threw."

"I didn't even throw a wine glass. Hardly a temper tantrum." I unlock my door and step inside.

"You're coming back downstairs." Forcing his foot over the threshold, he stops the door from closing.

Ice runs through my veins. Back when we were classmates, dare I say friends even, there was always something in Berto that made me afraid. It's there now, rearing its ugly head. *Stay strong. He won't hurt you.*

"Change, put your hair up, come back downstairs, and sit to eat with the family." His order is clear.

"I'm not marrying him."

I think about the hurt on Nikolai's face. Poor, naive man seemed so sure we could be a good match.

"Did I tell you that you had to?" Berto gives a fake lackadaisical shrug.

He's trying to disarm me. I wait him out, knowing that Berto likes the sound of his own voice enough to tell me if I don't ask.

"Eduardo really wants to marry Sarena to Nikolai instead. But Igor had it in his head that his son could handle you."

Berto's explanation makes my stomach roil.

"She's eighteen!" I huff.

I don't know what has me angrier, that they're marrying off a practical child, forgoing the usual 'college first' requirement, or that I'm a pawn in Gregorio's game of chess. I mean, yes, it's obvious I'm turning down the marriage proposal, but this is a new mind game that I didn't expect from Gregorio. He's not that smart.

"They are a good match on paper. She and Nikolai both enjoy . . ." Berto shakes his head.

That's when it hits me. *This was Berto's plan.* Leticia said every decision mattered and mocked Berto. This is much more his speed.

"Come downstairs. Switch seats with me and see for your fuckin' self. I know you think I'm some sort of monster, but I care for Sarena." He mumbles, "Probably more than I care for you."

He clears his throat. "It's not like we're marrying her off to one of those Irish pigs, the Cavanaghs, and calling the fucking truce. Could you imagine? No. It's the Russians, they've been good friends for a long time. Even if you weren't here to witness it for yourself."

"You're sure Sarena will like him?" *How the fuck will I get her out of this?*

Berto crosses his arms. "I swear on Grandmother Sofia, may she rest in peace, and her Bolognese recipe. Sarena and Nikolai will love each other before the meal is even over."

"Fine." I raise my chin and look away from him. "But I'm wearing something slutty."

"Wouldn't expect anything less, cousin." Berto backs out of my doorway. "Mom hates that red dress you wore for Labor Day."

"I own it in green too," I tell him before closing the door.

His appearance upstairs and the offer of information were unexpected, to say the least, but I agreed to rejoin the 'dinner party,' if only to see for myself what he's so certain about. So, I change into the floor-length green jersey-knit version of the dress I wore on Labor Day. With a massive slit up my thigh, it's even more daring than I'd usually wear, but most importantly, it has a single shoulder strap and shows off all the tattoos on my arms.

I strap a holster to my inner thigh down by my knee, on the opposite side away from the slit, and slide in the smallest gun I own. I'm not sure I trust what Berto said, and if it's a lie and they try to send me with them tonight, then there will be bloodshed at Casa D'Medici.

Fuck Gregorio, fuck this power play, and fuck the deal with the Russians.

Valor

CHAPTER FIVE

THE FIRST DAY OF SCHOOL

"Dad!" Kerrianne giggles as she jumps up and down on my bed, pulling me out of the half-hazy sleep state I was trying to cling to. "We'll be late. Get up, sleepyhead!"

Making a big show of it, I moan and groan, then stretch and immediately regret it when I feel the tug of the freshly healing skin on my side. I hide the pain with a big yawn that I talk through. "What time is it?"

"Time to get up!" Kerrianne repeats. She drops to her knees next to me, bouncing.

I push myself up onto my elbows before reaching over and tapping my phone screen. It lights up and shows five thirty in the morning. Kerrianne's school starts at nine. Sure, we may live under an hour away from it, but it only takes her an hour to get ready and eat. *Bloody hell, child. You got being an early bird from your mother.*

I flop back down and look at her. "No chance you're gonna let me go back to bed for at least another hour, huh?"

She shakes her head. "Nope."

"Alright."

I push my blankets down and make like I'm getting out of

bed, but then I dart up and wrap her in my arms. Holding her against my chest, I pull her with me back down to the bed.

She fights back, little arms pushing and knees curling up to press against me. One of her bony knees hits last night's bullet wound on my side, and I let out an 'oof' before rolling to protect it from her.

"Daaad," she groans. "If we're late, I'm not gonna be a happy camper."

"I thought you were going to school not camp." I tease her, tickling her sides.

She giggles and shrieks. It's loud and fills the room despite all the noise-dampening measures I've installed. I'd hoped if I got her to lie back down, she'd be tired enough to fall back asleep. But I was still at work at bedtime, and at my mother's insistence, Kerrianne went to bed early.

Last night was a fucking mess. My hunt to determine how the Italians are getting information came back with a good quarry. That prey, before it died, led us to hit an Italian store-house. We came out victorious, but that doesn't mean it wasn't without problems.

The Italians had significantly more firepower than they've ever had before. Russian firepower. It's a new development, and one we're not pleased with. Beyond that, had I not been shot during the raid, I would have been home and could have dictated her bedtime myself. *Well, isn't this the consequences of my own actions.*

I let my little girl free, and she scrambles out of bed. Waiting by my door, she's hoping for a chase. She's fast and, for seven, keeps me on my game at all hours of the day.

I remember a time, nine years ago, when I could come home, flop down into bed, and sleep for twelve uninterrupted hours. But I wouldn't go back to those days, not if it meant losing her.

"Alright, go downstairs, feed Captain, and you can have thirty minutes of tablet time. I'll be down soon."

"Okaaay. But if I come back up and you're sleeping." She eyes me and must be practicing her stink eye with Grandma again because she almost looks intimidating for her forty pounds.

"I'm up. I'm up." I nod, waving her away because I'm starting to feel wetness spread on my side.

Kerrianne closes the door behind her, and I wait a minute to make sure she doesn't storm back in before rolling out of bed.

There's a small red mark on my white sheets, and the tank I wore to bed has a larger red spot. I pull it off over my head and look at the sutures, finding one popped open.

The bullet would have killed a human. It was a clean shot, straight through and punctured a lung.

Our healing is faster, but that doesn't make us invincible. From this morning's light exertion, I'm out of breath, and when I try to inhale deeply, the pain is sharp. I cough, and blood comes up, but that's not unusual for it only being four hours since it happened.

I need two large raw steaks, a painkiller, and the grace of God to heal my body and get through this morning. Little mercies for being wolves. The fuel for our body is simple. Raw proteins, mostly red meat for the blood loss, fish for omega-3s for inflammation, and lamb for help with muscle healing.

Of course, as a father, I firmly encourage eating other things besides proteins, which is a struggle, but for myself, I cut a few corners.

Gunshot butterflied closed, cleaned up, and dressed for the day, I carry my suit jacket downstairs to where Kerrianne is messing around on her tablet. I try to keep her screen time to a minimum, but if it's a little bit of extra screen time or explaining why Dad's bleeding, well, I'll take her up north to our property in the woods on an extra-long hike this weekend and pray I'm doing a good enough job.

I toss my suit coat over the back of a chair, and Kerrianne is quick to close out of her game and close the case without argument. *I don't deserve such a well-behaved child.*

"Let me guess. You want a big plate of soda bread French toast, two pounds of bacon, and a bowl of fruit for breakfast?"

"It's tradition, Dad." She gives me snark.

I raise an eyebrow at her. The sass can only go so far because, Lord help me, I'm not having that as a teenager.

"Yes, please." She smiles, and it's too cute to even scold her any further.

This is the part I hate. Kerrianne is fed and dressed, hair braided and backpack put together. I have to say goodbye. I hate goodbye. We always do it at the house because it's safer. I can get all the hugs before she goes.

Kerrianne reassures me she'll be fine.

I threaten Sean within an inch of his life to keep her safe, at all costs. He nods, knowing how serious I am. It's a risk bodyguards like him take when agreeing to work this closely with the pack alpha's family. The risk is magnified when the pack alpha is so predominantly involved in the darker parts of society and his granddaughter's life.

Kerrianne spends the drive hypothesizing what school and her class will be like, based on the info packet from Mrs. Neidermeister detailing what second grade will bring.

I half listen while reminding myself that I'm not the only parent who sends his kid to school with a bodyguard. Half of the students at Rothschild-McClintock Magnet School have one. If I could get away with it, I'd hire private tutors and lock her away from the world to keep her safe. But she thrives in a classroom with peers, and I won't take that from her.

How do other parents live with this?

We pull up in front of the school, and Kerrianne ambles out the back of the vehicle. Sean is right by her side with his head on a swivel, cataloging the world around them.

On the first day, bodyguards are allowed to stay the full day and report back with any potential security issues. They'll be able to report any deficiencies in the school's security — not that they'll find any — directly to one of the few legitimate businesses I run. It made the parents happy, given the new security system, to have an input in its execution.

But it's flawless. Between my eye for weak points and Royal's expertise in state-of-the-art technology, there's very little anyone could do to compromise the school and the safety of the students.

"You okay, boss?" Jack, my driver, asks.

I'm sitting in the front seat, dressed in a suit and sunglasses, matching Jack. I don't look any different from any other security professional escorting a child to school.

Kerrianne has always gone to school under a pseudonym. To the outside world, she's Kelsey Clark, the daughter of a faceless tech mogul and nothing more. If my enemies were to find out she's Kerrianne Cavanagh, daughter of Valor Cavanagh, next head of the Irish Mob, she'd be dead.

Keeping my pup safe while letting her be a pup is a constant balancing act. She doesn't completely understand the importance of the fake name while she's at school. But we've done it for so long now that it's normal, and we made a small concession by keeping her initials the same to help ease some of the transition for her in the beginning. And I prayed it wasn't too obvious, but it's served us well for this long.

"I'm okay." I watch as she and Sean stand in line to enter the school.

Full-body scanners and infrared technology are hidden in the entryway. Nothing is visible, to make the kids feel like they're entering a normal school all while providing state-of-the-art security.

It was an important upgrade to me. The school board loved the donation and that they could now market the school as 'a normal, everyday experience for children of the elite.' I don't care how they market it so long as she's safe every time she walks through those doors.

It's not a perfect system, but it's better than ninety-eight percent of the schools in this country. Her bodyguard should make up for the other two percent.

"Ready, then?" Jack asks after they've disappeared through the doors.

It's a formality because he's already got the gear shifter moving to drive.

"Yeah. It's a whole new day of bullshit to deal with." I tuck my heart away.

There's no room for me to be soft. I have an empire to run, a legacy to build, and a rival family to destroy. Not exclusively in that order.

CHAPTER SIX

THE MELTDOWN

The heart attack I get when Sean's phone number pops up on my screen will kill me someday. Before I hit answer, I'm already closing my laptop and on the move.

I don't bother with hello, fearing for the goddamned worst. "Go."

"Valor." Sean is calm, and the gentle sound of the SUV on the road is in the background.

I take half a second to relax. *She's safe.*

My wolf goes from violent and snarling to on edge and growling.

"Yeah, Sean?" I grab my keys out of my top desk drawer and start gathering my stuff to leave.

"Kerrianne and I are detouring for a sundae at the ice cream parlor." Sean isn't asking, which is fine.

He and Kerrianne have privileges to make a stop up to twice a week at preapproved, very particular places if she doesn't have other commitments after school.

But he usually sends a quick message letting me know. Communication is paramount when it comes to Kerrianne's whereabouts, but a phone call means there's more than just a slight change in plans. Given his casual tone, though, it isn't life threatening. It means my little raptor is within hours of a meltdown. Hopefully, we're pre-meltdown, but it could likely be post.

"Well, the two of you have a good time." I cautiously proceed with my offer, knowing the call is on Bluetooth in the SUV and Kerrianne will be listening. "Maybe, if I can get away early, I'll meet you, and then raptor and I can get dinner."

I close and lock my office door at our legal business front and head out to the parking lot.

"Can we get pasta?" Kerrianne's words tremble.

So, it's post meltdown. Which is why Sean called. School has only been in session for three and a half months, and this is the third time she's had an issue.

I scrub my hand down my face, not from frustration with her falling apart but that I wasn't there.

Pup needs to learn. This is learning. My wolf groans and hangs his head with the defeat I feel. We want to protect her from all the heartache of the world, even if we realistically can't.

"Sure thing," I answer, but I fake needing to cut the call short. "Okay, I'm going into my next meeting. You two have fun, and we'll get pasta for dinner."

"Okay." Kerrianne's little agreement wrenches my heart from my chest. The single word is laced with frustrated sadness.

I hang up before starting my car. The ice cream parlor is a ten-minute drive from the office, and I get there in time to watch them walk inside.

I force myself to stay in the SUV rather than rush in and save the day. But she's expecting to get ice cream with Sean before I show up, so I let them enjoy. She trusts him. Hell, they've been paired together since prekindergarten.

The lighting at this time of day is perfect, allowing me to watch from my parking space through the ice cream shop's big plate-glass window.

Her cheeks and nose are red. Her hair is a little more ruffled than it was this morning, and she wipes her nose with her sleeve while she waits for Sean to pay. They sit toward the front, for my benefit. Sean skims the parking lot and gives a small nod when he sees me.

After about five minutes, he's got her at least chatting and not shut down.

Normally, no ice cream before green things is the rule, but everyone needs a mental health day now and again. The school lunches are balanced meals anyway.

I take my time getting out of my SUV and walking to the front door. Kerrianne sees me coming and gives me a big, excited wave.

Sean stands up, giving me his seat at the little café table. It's the changing of the guard — smiles, handshakes, and nods. After he gets out to his SUV, he'll text me anything he knows about what triggered the meltdown so I can assess if there needs to be a change. There's no need for me to get hung up on that right now, though. Instead, I focus on what Kerrianne might need from me in the moment.

"Hey, little raptor." I smile and sniff her ice cream, acting like I might take some.

She snatches the bowl off the table and gives me a pointed glare. I laugh and settle in. Sean takes off through the front door. He isn't going far but gives us the feeling of privacy. He'll be our armed escort.

"Dad, can I go back to the other school?" Kerrianne hangs her head and stirs the ice cream in her cup that's slowly turning to soup.

"Why do you want to go back to the other school?" I cock my head.

Parenting books are bullshit. Parenting books are bullshit, I chant in my head against the barrage of intrusive thoughts thanks to the books I tried to read for 'reasoning.'

Obviously. My wolf huffs, angry that I distressed her by changing her world.

"I don't think my teacher likes me." Kerrianne furrows her little brow, and I reach over, smoothing it out and then tipping her chin up to me.

"Let's go walk, and we can talk about it before dinner." I smile at her. I want to know her side before I make any assumptions about what happened today.

There are three sides to every story — hers, the teacher's, and the truth. Determining whose story is closest to the truth isn't the easiest thing, but it's literally my job in all aspects of my life.

Antonella

CHAPTER SEVEN

THE TROUBLE

The way I was called 'new teacher' in the school's canned emails has created a conflict that is now grating my nerves. The first day was filled with parents, bodyguards, mannies, and guardians questioning my ability and credentials to teach.

But as I've done my job over the past couple months, the questions about me being a fit for Rothschild-McClintock Magnet School have almost completely died down. I plan to put the rest to bed today at the mid-semester parent-teacher conferences.

If I'm lucky, I'll even get some insight into why one of my students isn't demonstrating the same readiness for the accelerated materials as his peers.

I have a high tolerance for kids behaving like kids — you don't grow up in a large Italian Catholic family without it. So I didn't take it personally last month when he shouted out into the hallway, 'Mom said you're not even a real teacher' every day for a week.

Today he crossed a line. I will not tolerate violent behavior in my classroom.

Throwing a basket of markers across the room and narrowly

missing two students in the process was the catalyst for escalating parental involvement. And on conference day, of all days.

During lunch, I sent an email reminder to his parent about tonight's conference being mandatory and urgent. Truthfully, I expected a curt email requesting I move the meeting forward or to be blown off completely. But surprisingly . . . she waited her turn.

"Ms. Mancini." Peyton Hopkins, mother of my student, David, butchers my relatively easy pseudonym as she rounds the corner of my door.

Peyton Hopkins is as fake looking in real life as she is on her billboards, which are plastered all around the Chicago area. Her brassy-blonde hair is so stiff with product that it sits on her head like a helmet as she wobbles into my classroom in her six-inch platform wedges, and her navy blue 'power suit' is so starched that it barely moves.

"Yes, I'm so glad you came in so we can discuss David's behavior. Please, have a seat." I offer her a chair at the work-table, which has adult-sized chairs for this purpose.

"I'd rather stand." She glares at me.

"Very well." I take a seat at the table.

She can't rattle me by attempting to come off 'imposing' while I sit as she stands.

"I'm concerned about David and his developmental differences compared to the other students in the accelerated class. We're three and a half months into the school year, and I'm not noticing an improvement from when we talked during the first couple of weeks. I've noticed his homework is coming back only partially completed. Now his behavior —"

"His behavior is fine," she snaps.

I blink dumbly at her, waiting for her to change her mind about the words she's chosen. She amps up the entitled bullshit instead.

"Do you know who I am?" She scoffs.

"Yes, Mrs. Hopkins." I can't help it. Really, I don't want to, but I couldn't even if I did. "You're the self-proclaimed realtor tycoon who, by my calculation, spends far too much money on billboard advertising. You're the donor who plastered her name all over the field house and athletic compound for the entire academy. And last but not least, the mother delusional enough to think that her son will be some great American all-star sports player but is doing nothing to further his education to ensure he can compete academically."

Her face turns fifteen shades of red.

"Well, I never." She shakes her head. Her hair still doesn't move. "Just you wait until the principal hears about this."

"Yes, well, tell Doctor Thatcher I say hello," I barely get out before Peyton Hopkins storms out of my classroom. I mutter under my breath, "And don't let the door hit you on the way out."

Valor

CHAPTER EIGHT

THE AUDACITY

I've been called to the principal's office before, but with Kerrianne shifting in her sleep, I don't know what to expect with this latest summons. Conferences are today, and rather than meet with Kerrianne's teacher, I've been sent here.

"So, if you're okay with it, I'd really like to see what options we can offer Kelsey as far as ac . . . celllll . . . errrr . . . ated . . ." Doctor Thatcher trails off with a disturbance coming from outside her office, which is fine because I'm listening to the same thing she is.

"No, I demand to speak with Doctor Thatcher right now. There is no one more important at this school than me."

I snort because the self-importance of some parents is ridiculous. I'm no more important than any other parent here.

The door opens three seconds later.

"Doctor Thatcher, we need to talk about that new teacher. What's her name? Ms. Mancini? She is out of control," Peyton Hopkins, realtor and insufferable woman, fumes as she storms into the office.

The door slams closed behind her, and I'm not one to run

JAEGER ROSE

from a conflict, but this conversation regarding Kerrianne feels like it isn't so urgent that it can't wait for another day.

Peyton drops into the chair in the same manner Kerrianne does when she pouts, practically slamming her ass into it. Her perfume assaults my nose, and I hold back the urge to cough. I debate getting up and leaving.

No, let's stay. This will be amusing. My wolf and I have a similar thought, seeing as how Peyton is breathing heavily, and her face is almost purple with rage.

"Peyton, Mrs. Hopkins." Doctor Thatcher corrects herself. "I am with another parent. He had an appointment."

Peyton seemingly notices my presence for the first time, and she sits up in her chair a bit taller. Which is weird since I settled in, assuming this would be a long conversation with Doctor Thatcher. It's not like I've adopted an intimidating stance.

"Victor." Peyton coos at me, using the fake name everyone from outside the pack is given. "It's lovely to see you. I'm so sorry to barge in, but you don't mind, do you?"

I don't get a chance to answer for myself because Doctor Thatcher tries to intervene. "Mrs. Hopkins, could you please step outside? Mr. Clark and I are in a meeting."

"No, he should hear this too. It concerns all the school's donors," Peyton snaps, cutting off Doctor Thatcher.

It's no secret that my security company has fortified the entire place, including the ridiculous sporting complex she donated, so I'm not surprised she knows who I am.

This'll be good. I steeple my fingers, ready to listen.

Doctor Thatcher sighs and gives me a preemptive apologetic look.

"Well, as you know, my son is in Ms. Mancini's class." Peyton starts telling this story like I would tell Kerrianne a bedtime story. "It started off as a few emails about his behavior in class. Apparently, he had a tiny outburst."

"Outburst?" Doctor Thatcher pulls out a notepad from her

62

desk drawer. She tilts it up and poises the pen over the paper, except the cap is still on the pen.

Outburst as in, he's thrown something. I translate from my and Royal's time in school.

"Yes." Peyton Hopkins nods but doesn't even notice the cap is on the pen.

This is peak comedy.

"Well, according to Ms. Mancini, my David has been having behavior issues, and she's not teaching him the same thing as other students. Ms. Mancini told me my son is stupid." Peyton starts to fake shake.

It's too rigid and uniform to be real shaking with rage or any other emotion.

She's terrible at lying. My wolf sighs and lies down. *Could she at least pretend to care about her kid?*

I clench my core to stop myself from laughing at his inner monologue and the fact that Peyton's son is stupid.

"Ahhh." Doctor Thatcher nods, pretending to write on the pad. "I do remember seeing that David's scores were quite low compared to the rest of his class. And he may be missing assignments?"

"Yes, but I told her it's because the school year is new, and he needs time to warm up. It's like warming up for a ball game, it's getting back into the swing of things," Peyton huffs, the fuming anger still there. "But what's worse is that she insulted my intelligence and business sense."

"Your business sense?" I can't help but cut in, leaning forward, trying to see if she's joking. I'm confused about how this is 'worse,' and it feels like some sort of practical joke. "Her insulting your business sense . . . is worse than thinking your child needs help with school?"

"Exactly. You get it." Peyton thinks I'm agreeing with her.

I look at Doctor Thatcher, who meets my eyes and shakes her head.

At least I'm not alone in experiencing this.

"She seems to think I don't know what I'm doing with my business and that my child's clearly not smart enough to attend this school despite the fact that I donated, very generously, mind you, to the new field house." She sniffles despite not having any actual tears to generate mucus. It's disgusting.

Oh, here we fuckin' go. I pinch the bridge of my nose, trying not to get myself involved in what clearly does not belong anywhere near my business. But a field house for an elementary school seemed a little excessive, because it is.

"And we are very thankful for the field house and your donations for it." Doctor Thatcher appeases Peyton's need for praise. She goes on to add, "And it would be impossible to take care of the lawns, landscaping, and snow removal without your generous contributions."

The pack has a lawn care company, my wolf thinks. *This woman is not necessary.*

I almost pull out my phone to file a note on the subject when Peyton turns the conversation again.

Her fake tears precede her words. "I just don't know how an educator of such a high-caliber school could ever talk to someone who gives them so much. I mean, surely Mr. Clark's child isn't being treated with this much disrespect."

"I —" Peyton doesn't give me a chance to confirm or deny that assertion.

"I think, maybe. if my money and my son aren't respected enough, I'll pull David out and go back to Dalton-Davis Prep." Peyton lets out a few fake tears that she wipes away with the knuckle of one of her talon-length fingernails.

"Well, surely we can give her a chance to apologize." Doctor Thatcher looks like she might pass out with how ashen her face gets. "The school would like to make it right."

"No. I don't want my David in a place where he's clearly not being taught." Peyton shakes her head adamantly.

She means catered to. The smart-ass in my brain cracks another joke.

"Well, Ms. Mancini is in charge of the accelerated program that you wanted David to be a part of, despite my warning otherwise." Doctor Thatcher looks to me.

Ahhhh, the accelerated program for Kerrianne. The dots start connecting. *But also, who insists their kid goes into a special class-room if they're . . . no, that's a dumb question. Peyton fuckin' Hopkins, obviously.*

"I mean, for class numbers, I would be glad to consider switching Kelsey into Ms. Mancini's classroom." I step in, trying to help, not knowing if it's the right move, but at the bare minimum, Peyton Hopkins will get out of this room.

"And who is Kelsey with?" Peyton looks at me, almost hopefully.

"Mrs. —"

"Well, she's married. I think that's for the best. I don't know that David respects a woman of Ms. Mancini's age who isn't married."

Bewilderment, between me and Doctor Thatcher, leads to us both shaking our heads and giving wide-eyed looks.

"Victor." Peyton puts a hand on my thigh, and I move enough to dislodge it discreetly. "Surely, you know what it's like being important and trying to run a business and raise a child. You only want what's best for them."

Ew. She touched us. My wolf shudders, and I manage to suppress it.

"I know what it's like to consider professional opinions to make an educated decision for my child." I don't agree with her on purpose.

"Thank you so much. You know, I'd love to meet up, we can catch up. I have some great . . . properties we can see together." The proposition in Peyton's tone is poorly masked.

"Unfortunately for you, all my property needs are being met.

Though, I wish you the best." I try a soft smile and fake my phone vibrating in my pocket. "Oh, I've got to take this. Doctor Thatcher, would you send me an email with perhaps the details on Ms. Mancini for a deeper background check and what the accelerated program entails? But I think if this needs to be an expedited switch, it could be made as early as next week before the optional courses over winter break begin? And if there's an issue, we can reevaluate."

I had Royal run background checks on everyone in the school, literally everyone, when we looked at transferring Kerri-anne here. But a more thorough one for the person she spends every day with would be an extra precaution I won't pass on . . . but for a few days, it can't possibly hurt for her to be in Ms. Mancini's class.

"Of course. I appreciate your flexibility." Doctor Thatcher stands to walk me out.

I beat her to the door and head out into the main office, letting out a sigh.

The women working the front desk snicker. The closest one to me, a little louder than perhaps she should be, says, "She has that effect on people."

Well, I knew it would be a difficult conversation about Kerrianne's behavior as she was being overly helpful, independent, and talkative, but that wasn't what I expected. The first choice to fix it, popping her into another classroom, seems straightforward.

I text Royal.

VALOR:

> Little raptor is moving to a new classroom. I'll have details. Need a background check on the new teacher.

Per usual, Royal is glued to his phone:

ROYAL:

Sounds like a plan. You're ready to go hunting
or am I going?

A picture comes through of Kerrianne wearing one of Royal's headsets, intensely focused on something off camera. The headset is ill fitting, but the one in her size 'didn't feel right,' and really, she likes using Royal's and feeling big, so I didn't argue.

VALOR:

Promise me I'll be back for Thanksgiving?

ROYAL:

You'll be back by Thanksgiving and you're the
best older brother ever.

Remember this when you have a pup, and I
kidnap it rather than letting you stay home
with it.

Antonella

CHAPTER NINE

TINY SCOLDING

I finish tidying up my classroom from conferences and reset it for tomorrow's first activity when Doctor Thatcher knocks on my door.

"Ms. Mancini?" The principal pops into my classroom.

Shit. Shit. Shit.

"Hello, Doctor Thatcher."

I know I'm in trouble because the woman who walks around with a broad smile has let it fall, not entirely but enough.

"I'm assuming what Peyton Hopkins said was a gross exaggeration, but I promised I'd have a word with you." Doctor Thatcher clutches her pearls. "Mrs. Hopkins is a massive donor for the school. We're counting on her . . . and her husband's landscaping company . . . to keep the playground and school grounds in pristine condition. They're also our snow removal company. I managed to talk her down from pulling her son out of the school entirely, but I will transfer her son Mrs. Neidermeister's room. I'm sure you understand."

Thank fucking God. I could almost squeal with delight. *Play it cool. Play it cool.*

"I'm supposed to remind you to temper your language and

try to be a bit more diplomatic with the parents, especially during first-time conversations." Doctor Thatcher drops her hand to her side and stifles a laugh. "In some of these homes, the children are more well behaved than their parents. Proceed with caution. Even if we all want to tell Mrs. Hopkins where to shove it, we can't. We're professionals."

"Yes, Doctor." I answer quickly so I also don't have to pretend like I'm not laughing.

"We'll rotate another student into your class to keep the numbers equal. I think your class will be better for her anyway. You seem to have a way with the more advanced students."

The way Doctor Thatcher lays on the compliment seems genuine rather than a patronizing attempt to make me feel like a valued employee after a major fuckup. It's only been a couple months of classes, but I've been shadowed by more senior faculty, including Doctor Thatcher, several times already.

"Completely understand." I agree and take the barely there reprimand with a single nod.

"Good." Doctor Thatcher sighs. "I'll email you her information. She'll be transferred in next week before the optional winter break classes begin. Could you have a packet ready to go home to her father? Mr. Clark is the donor for the security system. It'll be his utmost priority to be informed."

"Absolutely." I think back to the extra packets I made 'just in case' while setting stuff up at the beginning of the year.

Doctor Thatcher doesn't linger and leaves me to my business. It's a relief to have the confrontation over and done, but boy, do I wish it was Friday instead of Friday eve.

CHAPTER TEN

THE NEW STUDENT

Uncle Gregorio has forgiven me for the botched engagement attempt. Berto's idea to let me turn the proposal down publicly at family dinner was remarkably the right move. But I don't love that he didn't tell me. While his reasoning of wanting a 'real reaction' is valid because I'm a terrible actress, it doesn't justify his actions.

However, watching the relationship between Sarena and Nikolai bloom has been unique. It's a little weird to me that he's thirty and she's eighteen, but when I came home one day to a plastic sword fight, I was a little more forgiving of that. Their level of obsession with the same science fiction fandoms likely made this love at first fight.

Today I came home to an 'argument' of sorts. Nikolai was on one side of the table and Sarena the other. Nikolai was arguing for the number four, while Sarena insisted on the number six. I finally figured out they were arguing about the number of children they wanted. I laughed it off and grabbed a glass of wine before heading up to work on my lesson planning and the packet for the new student.

After changing into something more comfortable, I venture

up to the rooftop patio of the penthouse, where the gorgeous view of Lake Michigan awaits. The chilly but still fresh air is a nice reprieve from being holed up in my room and indulging in old seasons of reality competition shows, and it's probably one of the last nice days of the year. There are perks to living in Gold Coast over River North.

Leticia joins me, reading from her tablet, and we're at peace when Berto finds us.

"Ladies." He greets us, walking over to me and reading over my shoulder.

He gets bored and walks past me to sit in the other chair.

In a split second, Berto freezes. His spine goes rigid, and it's like everything in nature pauses with the shift in his demeanor.

Dark eyes narrowed, Berto snatches a picture up off the table and shows it to me. "Who is this?"

"Kelsey?" I hesitate to answer, looking at the new student packet I added her information to when I got home.

"What's her last name?" Berto snaps, shaking the photo at me.

"Clark. I think. Why?" I shake my head, raising a hand in a 'what the fuck' motion. In true Italian fashion, half of our conversation and tone is in the way we talk with our hands, so he should know I'm equally frustrated with him. "You're being weird about a seven-year-old. Not a good look."

"She looks exactly like Valor Cavanagh's kid, Kerrianne," he informs me, holding the photo out.

With a huff, I snatch it out of his hand. The little girl has bright green eyes and a slight red tinge to her brown hair. Even if it wasn't completely stereotypical, it is believable that she'd be the daughter of the heir to the Irish Mob.

But I refuse to let him bring my work into the ridiculous family feud. "Well, she's Kelsey Clark, so you're wrong. I don't know what you think the Cavanaghs are planning, but it's not like we've had bodies dropping all around us again. Right? The feud has been mostly quiet?"

Berto stays rigid. He doesn't answer me.

Fuckin' hell, we're going back to war with the Cavanaghs. I set the photo back down on the table. Sure, I work under an iron-clad pseudonym with a pristine set of false documents, but it's because the Cavanaghs aren't our only enemies. Discovering my true identity and planting a child in my classroom is elaborate and far fetched. *Right?*

He takes one long last look at it. "Kids all look the same at that age anyway. But I know those Irish bastards are up to something, more than usual."

I don't believe, not for a single minute, that Berto will let the idea that Kelsey is a Cavanagh go. But there's nothing I can do, even though I want to, because if Berto wants to investigate it, he will. And I don't doubt he's about to incite another skirmish that'll end in bloodshed. *Moving home was a bad idea.*

Apparently forgetting why he came to bug us, Berto heads back into the house. The foul mood mostly follows him.

Leticia jumps up from the couch and follows him to the door, looking down the hall — probably to make sure he's not returning — before she runs back. This time she sits right next to me and picks up the picture of Kelsey. Extending her arm, she holds it out before us.

She whispers, "How weird would it be if you had a Cavanagh in your class? That would be dangerous, right?"

I roll my eyes. *I'm so not entertaining this line of thinking.* "There's a reason I work under a pseudonym. It's fine, how would anyone know? Besides, Berto has a hard time telling the little second and third cousins apart when they all get together. I hardly believe that he could possibly remember what Valor Cavanagh's child looks like."

"True." Leticia lets out a huge sigh. "No, you're right. I'm sure it's fine. Besides, it's not like you're a real soldier or anything.

Berto and Gregorio make sure everyone knows that's how they see it. Feud or not . . . no one is wasting their time on a school-teacher. Even if you're supposed to become his consigliere, we're not likely targets."

"Exactly." I shake my head and keep working on the lessons but look back at the picture of Kelsey.

It's not her. The school is elite but not that elite. We don't even send the little cousins there. Berto is wrong. She can't possibly be a Cavanagh.

Antonella

CHAPTER ELEVEN

THE TRUCE

Kelsey Clark and I are standing in the 'safe zone' after school, where kids wait for their pickups. It's a viewing area with a big picture window that allows them to watch for their ride. And from a lifetime of being surrounded by bulletproof glass, I know it's not a single bulletproof pane but two.

Bodyguards — in many cases, expensive 'mannies,' who do a lot of caring for the children of the elite — are the primary pickup and emergency contacts for the students here. I remember seeing the bodyguard type picking her up yesterday.

I take in the nervous child, who has only been in my classroom for two days. She seems to be taking her time to break out of her shell with her new classmates. Despite what Mrs. Neidermeister said, Kelsey has been nothing but respectful, most of all when talking to me.

Kelsey turns toward me, prying her eyes away from where she's had them glued to the window. "I don't know. Sean always picks me up, but he's not here, and he didn't text me that he'd be late. Do you think he's okay?"

No. No, I don't. The 'danger' warning in my brain is firing on all cylinders. I have only ever worked at elite schools like Rothschild-McClintock Magnet School, and never, not once, has a bodyguard or parent ever been late for pick up.

The rich, famous, and notorious are, in general, much more protective of their children than your regular parents. They pay through the teeth for that protection, and the paychecks for those bodyguards do not lend to one willingly being late or putting their ward's safety on the line.

Kelsey holds her little black device out to me. The screen lights up, and I confirm there aren't any messages or anything of that nature.

This isn't good at all. The hair on the back of my neck, and all the way down my arms, stands on end.

"Let's go call your family." I give her a smile and offer her the device back. "I'm sure it's nothing more than some traffic."

A pit in my stomach has me wishing I had a sidearm with me. My nervousness is probably unwarranted because I'm in an elementary school. The most worrisome thing should be a pack of gum, but the call of danger singing to me says otherwise.

"Okay." She bites her lips together.

I stand and, walking slowly, lead Kelsey to the office down the hallway from my classroom.

It'd be easier to contact someone programmed into Kelsey's device, but protocol dictates we're not allowed to use students' devices. Only the admin can call the designated phone numbers in the office system.

Please let her have more than her bodyguard as a contact.

I pop the office door open, and it swings inward, nearly hitting another teacher with their student. The office is *packed.*

Slowly my shoulders drop, my body attempting to relax. *See, traffic. There are others here with students. It's traffic.* I try to talk my inner self down from the nervousness.

Based on the number of people in here, there's no way I'll be able to squeeze through and get to the desk with Kelsey and her backpack. But the office's large windows offer an unobstructed view of benches across the hallway.

Stepping back out of the office, I motion toward the bench across the way. "Have a seat, I'll be right back."

Kelsey sits on the bench, her little green backpack leaning against the wall. I take one last look down the hall toward my classroom, but it's empty.

I open the door, more carefully this time, and weave around the masses to get to the second office admin who is typing on her computer. She looks busy, but no one's standing in front of her. I turn myself to face her as best I can while keeping Kelsey in my peripheral vision.

"Ms. Mancini, what's going on?" the school admin asks after a few moments, looking up from her desk.

"I need to call the guardians on file for Kelsey Clark. Her bodyguard hasn't shown up yet." I give her a soft smile.

"Oh." The admin furrows her brow with the same uneasy suspicion bulging her eyes. "That's odd."

"I agree." I look over my shoulder one more time. *Should I take her back to my classroom and have admin call me with answers?*

The admin dials and then begins speaking with whoever the emergency contact is, explaining the situation. She puts her finger in her opposite ear to hear over the ruckus two of the teachers are causing, laughing on the other side.

I flit my gaze to them, trying to figure out what's so funny, and then the world fades to a dull buzz as a hand, presumably attached to a person who is standing outside the view of the window, extends toward Kelsey.

She looks hesitant to take it.

"Okay, Ms. Mancini, Grandma and Grandpa are on their way—" The admin continues beyond that statement, but my feet are already moving.

That they're on their way is enough to know that my gut

feeling is right. Whoever that is isn't who Kelsey should be going with.

I dart out into the hall, and my heart practically comes to a stop as I see Kelsey being all but dragged down the hallway away from the office. She's leaning back, heavily resisting.

Despite the two-inch heels I chose to wear this morning, I sprint to get in front of the man.

The man I know.

My cousin Berto.

He's coaxing Kelsey to go with him.

My fingers clench into a fist. He didn't let it go. He investigated her over the weekend. *That bastard.*

Luckily, we're only a few feet from my classroom door, and with a quick extension of my arm, I push it open.

With a smile, masking my grimace, I instruct Kelsey, "Go ahead and play for a little bit. Your grandmother is sending someone to get you."

Kelsey looks between us, no doubt confused because Berto told her some sort of lie. She shuffles into the classroom, and I lock the door behind her.

"Antonella." Berto warns me, using my real first name. "Do you know who that is?"

I shake my head, not even wanting to hear what he's planning. I lower my voice to an angry whisper despite a scared bird fluttering behind my ribs. "She's seven. You're not taking her."

"That is Valor Cavanagh's daughter." He grits his teeth and matches my low tone. "We don't have a lot of time. We are taking her. Gregorio is waiting. If you know what is good for you, then you won't be here when the Cavanaghs show up."

"This is too far, Berto," I hiss, raising a finger sternly toward him.

I can't let him take a child. But what do I do?

"She's a child. A girl. Hardly matters." He scoffs, brushing me off.

Berto moves one way, and I mirror him, keeping myself between him and the door.

"Exactly. She's a *child*." I can't believe what I'm hearing. I could smack him for being so obtuse. "She matters more than anything."

Berto isn't married, but he's talked about having children a dozen times before. His 'dream' is to find the perfect wife and have a family. It must be easier to care about the fantasy in his head than living and breathing people.

"Think this through, Berto." I look at the door and then meet his glare before attempting logic to override this ridiculous kidnapping. Once upon a time, before Berto spent more time with the made men than people our own age, he used to listen to me. "If you take her, what's to stop them from doing the same to any of our younger cousins or to your children someday?"

"It wouldn't happen," Berto snorts and waves me off with a flick of his wrist. "It's not even a Catholic school."

Not even a Catholic school? God fucking help him, for he does not know he's stupid. I fervently shake my head. "Berto. No, this is enough. Go home."

"I'll call my father." He threatens me like I'll back down if he calls the head of the family. "You're disobeying a direct order."

"Do it, then. It's not even the first time in a week I've disobeyed him." I call his bluff and stand my ground. "There's no way I can let you take a seven-year-old for this war. There is a line somewhere, and this crosses it."

Berto pulls his phone out and threatens me at normal speaking volume. "Just let me take her. This doesn't need to be a big deal. I take her out of here like her bodyguard, and no one will know anything beyond that."

"No." I'm firm, raising my voice for emphasis but then trying to bring it back down, remembering where we are and who's on the other side of the door. "You're not taking her. Call your father if you think it will make a difference, but she will not be leaving with you."

"And what will you do about it, Antonella?" he huffs, dismissing me as always.

Our eyes lock, and I know what I must do.

It's dangerous.

It's shameful.

For all I know . . . it will be the end of my life.

But if I let Berto take her, it will be the end of Kelsey's, or I guess, Kerrianne's, life.

The truce between the D'Medicis and Cavanaghs may be called when a member of one family raises a weapon against their own to defend a member of the feuding family.

The story, the warning, or maybe the call to a greater good, that's been told to us from the time we're small, echoes in my head. It's more like a legend rather than a real thing, but I'm running out of ideas.

As firmly as I can, I threaten him. "I'll call for the truce if you don't leave, Berto."

Berto shakes his head in disbelief. "You're calling for the truce?"

He doesn't believe I'll do it. Do I believe I'll do it?

"And what happens when Valor decides that his daughter, a worthless eldest child from a dead woman, is expendable?" Berto gives me a pitying frown before the more serious, threatening Berto comes back. "If they don't accept the truce, you're a dead woman and the kid dies anyway. Get out of my way. This is why women aren't involved in business. Your father was a fool to let you think you could handle the work that must be done. Mind your place, Antonella."

His words sting, and tears threaten my eyes, but I refuse to feel the sorrow they deliver.

Berto grabs my shoulders and tries to get me to move, but my feet are anchored to the ground, shoulder width apart.

He trusts me, or more likely underestimates me, too much as he puts himself within arm's reach.

My breathing is erratic and not as steady as I want it to be, but there's only one way forward. I put it all on the line.

It's all too easy to reach into his suit jacket.

With shaky hands, I draw his gun from the holster under his arm.

My entire body screams at me. *I shouldn't do this. This is wrong.*

Before he can stop me, I have the muzzle pressed into his chest.

The violence has to stop somewhere.

"I'm calling the truce."

"Antonella." He draws my name out in warning but takes a step back from me and the gun rather than trying to snatch it out of my hands.

Berto has seen me shoot. He knows I'm not afraid to pull the trigger when I need to.

He lifts his hands, not in surrender, but on instinct, as one should when faced with a gun.

"Let me take the girl. No one will know you tried to stop this. It's not too late to be less of a disgrace."

"Call Gregorio." I keep my voice level. "I'm calling the truce."

"You're making a mistake." He shakes his head. "They killed three of our men this week alone. It's a child. It's nothing," he says, trying to peddle his rhetoric like some sort of shady market merchant, downplaying the negatives.

"Call Gregorio D'Medici." I snap each word, further cementing my decision and the separation between us.

How can he be this way? I grew up with Berto. This isn't him. It can't be. My heart is beating faster than the ticking seconds of the clock. *No, this might not be the Berto I thought I knew, but he's still my family.*

I talk as fast as I can without stumbling over my words. "If you want to shoot me to get to her, then you better have an explanation for why you killed me in cold blood. Her grandparents are on their way to collect her. They'll find me dead and her gone. When they figure out you took her, you'd have killed a D'Medici and taken a Cavanagh. It will be obvious what happened here."

"You're a coward," Berto spits. "Too soft for this life. You're lucky Sarena was a good fit for Nikolai. My father is ready to marry you off against your will. Maybe he'll get his wish with your antics."

I've never known Berto to be so cruel, not to me. Mean, sure, but today is a whole new low, even for him.

"Maybe so, but I'm the one with the gun. Make the call."

Please, God, don't let me be wrong. Let them love this child enough to spare her life and mine.

I draw deep breaths, locked in a staring contest with Berto.

He hangs his head and dials before holding the phone up to his ear.

My classroom door opens behind me, and Berto leers at her.

I reiterate my stance and move my finger to the gun's safety, a threat Berto notices but Kerrianne can't see.

Trying to be comforting even though my voice wavers, I softly say, "Go back inside, Kerrianne."

She gasps. "You're not supposed to know that name."

"I know, but you're gonna have to trust me that it's okay." I don't dare turn to face her because it would give Berto my back. "Go back inside and close the door. Your grandparents are coming."

The door closes behind me with a soft thud, and at the same time, Berto says, "We've a problem. Antonella is . . ." He runs his tongue across his teeth, pausing to give me one last chance before finally saying, "Antonella has called for the truce."

I can't hear my uncle on the phone, but I know whatever he's saying isn't good. Especially when Berto says, "Yeah, she's squeamish over the Cavanagh heir."

I bite my tongue before I argue with him. Kerrianne is hardly someone he considers to be a legitimate heir. I want to yell, to smack him and remind him of that. He should be ashamed of himself for coming for a child like this.

Which is it, Berto? Are women heirs, or are we chattel to be married off? Am I a disgrace or a brave soldier?

But I don't say it because I know the answer. Besides me with this gun right now, no woman in our life will ever be taken seriously.

My actions scream 'women are weak' and 'women are too emotional; they form bonds to children they don't even know' and back their argument. It will further their belief women have no place in this business. *I* have no place in this business.

Not even my father's final wishes could gain me entry into the boys' club entirely.

"You better prepare yourself." Berto shakes his head, hanging up the phone. He warns me while looking at the screen as it goes dark. "Don D'Medici is pissed. Your head will roll if this doesn't work out. Pray the Irish give you an easy husband."

Berto walks away down the hall, leaving me with his weapon. In smooth, practiced movements, I flick the safety on and lower the weapon to my side.

I called for the truce.

The warning stories and consequences of my actions slowly sink in. What I've done, beyond turning on my family, is incite a massive negotiation. It could be days or weeks in the making. I've put my and Kerrianne's lives on the line. If they don't come to an agreement, the families have the right to kill us both.

Uncle Gregorio will kill me without issue, and if the Cavanaghs don't kill Kerrianne, it'll become a blood bath.

Finally, Berto walks out the door at the end of the hall, and I can draw steady breaths. My shoulders relax slightly, but I'm still tense. My heart returns to a steady thrum. It doesn't matter what I'm feeling though. There's a little girl in my classroom. One who is probably terrified from being dragged down a hallway after her regular bodyguard didn't show up. She needs her teacher, a constant in her life, to be strong for her.

She doesn't know what I've done. I saved her from one danger but put her in another. My heart aches for a little girl I've barely met and the unfairness of the world she lives in.

Maybe, by the grace of God, we'll be saved. In the unlikely event an agreement is reached, then the final acts to bind the families are a wedding to join the families as one and two funerals, where we'll place our dead in each other's cemeteries.

D'Medici or Cavanagh, both families believe in one covenant: you don't kill your family if they haven't betrayed you first.

Calling the truce is not a betrayal, no matter how Gregorio chooses to see it. We are safe from death until the negotiations are rejected. But after that . . .

"God, forgive me for what I've done," I whisper. It's been a while since I've prayed, but now is as good a time as any. "Shield her from harm."

I've basically walked myself right into the arranged marriage I've fought so hard against. It'll be no surprise when my family offers me at the negotiation table. They don't want someone 'weak' or, as I'm sure it'll be spun, 'uncontrollable' in their ranks. And no matter how much we'll have become 'one family' because of the truce, their opinion of me will be set in stone.

Taking a deep breath, I turn toward the cubbies stacked two high along the wall beside my classroom. The one closest to my room has a bright red scarf hanging out of the basket. I pull it out and wrap it around the gun.

Kerrianne may be a Cavanagh, but that doesn't mean she's used to seeing guns every day. Not out of a holster and certainly not in the hand of her teacher, no matter how natural it is for me.

I leave the door ajar so I can better hear if someone approaches. Their footsteps should echo in the hallway before they ever get to my room.

The scarf-clad gun comes with me, and I set it on the closest chair, hidden from the play area by my desk. Then, cross-legged on the ground with Kerrianne, I engage in play the best I can. Thank God she doesn't ask questions. She's more excited to get to play with the newest classroom toy.

Not even ten minutes later, a mix of footsteps echoes down the hallway. A pair of heels, a pair of loafers, and at least two pairs of combat boots. I reach for the scarf-covered gun, resting my hand on it, ready to pull it out if it's more of the D'Medici family rather than the Cavanaghs. I wouldn't put it past my uncle to bring one of my aunts to talk sense into me.

But in walks a guard I don't recognize, gun drawn but held low at his side. He must not see the bundle concealing my weapon because he holsters his before waving in the rest of the people.

Ian Cavanagh walks through the door first, followed by his wife, Elizabeth. I've only ever seen them in pictures as targets and adversaries.

They're so lifelike and human. Especially when Elizabeth's hand goes to her chest. Her words are pinched and breathy. "Kelsey, there you are."

Kerrianne screams in excitement while running toward her. "Grandma!"

But her relief is in contrast to Ian Cavanagh's speculative gaze toward me and the heavy hesitation in his voice. "Ms. Mancini, is it?"

I nod, moving to stand now that Kerrianne has rushed to her grandparents' side. "Yes, that's me."

"Grandma, is Daddy home yet?" Kerrianne stage-whispers while trying not to speak when the grownups are.

The guards with them eye me suspiciously, and Ian Cavanagh rakes his eyes down my body.

Elizabeth steals careful glances at me while assuring Kerrianne that her father will be home soon.

A powder keg of uncertainty, hesitation, and disbelief is primed and ready to blow. I'm outnumbered, and maybe Berto was right.

Maybe they won't respect the truce. Maybe I'm not safe after all and this is how I die. There is a chance, though, that they don't know it's a pseudonym. It's possible Gregorio hasn't called them yet. Maybe he never plans to.

Part of me wishes I'd pulled the gun to show that I won't go down without a fight.

"Interesting." It's all he says, and it isn't the usual midwestern 'interesting' to show disgust or distaste, more of the acceptance of a calculation.

"And you're the one who called the truce and saved Kerrianne?" Elizabeth asks, holding her granddaughter against her.

Yeah, I should have grabbed the gun.

I hang my head for a moment but then look at them. "I couldn't, in good faith, risk the life of one of my students. No matter who they are."

Ian Cavanagh's single nod lifts a weight from my shoulders, but his words remain solemn. "I've already accepted the first call with the arbiter."

"I appreciate your cooperation. Gregorio will likely ask for something large."

"We will do everything we can to assure that a deal will be cut." Ian offers me a somber smile.

It's a reassurance and the best I can expect given the circumstances.

I don't have regret or remorse for what I've done, but the

reality is that my uncle may remain obstinate. No matter what Ian Cavanagh brings to the table, it's possible no deal will be reached.

Once the Cavanaghs leave, I wait until their steps are out of earshot before, with trembling fingers, I reach for the scarf-clad gun.

In the silence of my classroom, I give myself time to decompress. But I fight back every tear that threatens to escape. *I've survived more. I'll survive this. Probably.*

Straightening chairs, I focus on deep breaths and slow steps before finally making it to my desk at the back of the room. I grab my purse from the cupboard to the left of it and tuck the gun inside, concealing it before I pull the scarf out, sans gun. Folding it, I prepare it to go back in the messy student's cubby.

With nothing more to do, no way to keep myself here in the sanctuary of my classroom, I leave, closing the door and locking it behind me for what could very well be the last time.

Valor

CHAPTER TWELVE

THE PHONE CALL

The wheels of the jet touch down in the middle of nowhere, Brazil, and I'm ready to get off the plane. It's been four days and six cities of stalking this asshole who claims he can sell off information about our organization for the right price.

We're inching closer, and now we know for certain they're trying to sell information on our gun-running operation directly to the D'Medicis, with the intent to strengthen the Bratva and Russian arms dealers.

It will ruin my carefully laid plans. Revenge is on the line. It feels like every year, I get closer and closer to figuring out why Holly had to die.

But the problem is, I can't focus on it.

It's midafternoon, and my burner satellite phone hasn't pinged through with the updates I'm expecting.

I double-check the time.

Sean hasn't messaged me that my little raptor has been returned to the nest. *Okay, if there was traffic . . .* No, they should have been home at least thirty minutes ago, even if traffic was an extra half hour.

Fuck the mission, fuck this asshole, I need to make sure Kerrianne is home safe. I'm headed back to the plane when the burner phone rings in my hand.

The ringing, followed by my mother's name on the screen, puts my hair on end. My whole body locks into place, but I force myself to bring the phone to my ear. The worst-case scenarios run through my head. "What's wrong?"

"Calm down." Mom is calm, her voice steady.

"What's wrong?" I repeat, feeling no less tense.

"So much like your father," Mom muses, but with a deep breath, she levels with me as only my mother can. "I wanted you to hear it from me that there was an incident at Kerrianne's school today."

My blood runs cold, and I clench my fist. *Don't crush your only communication device.* "What happened?"

"We're not entirely sure. Not yet. Ambushed by the looks of it. Kerrianne is fine. Sean is dead."

Sean is dead. He was trained by the best of the best. How the hell did this happen?

Mom's reassurance soothes the worry but sparks my anger. She's not giving me details, and I don't know if it's because she really doesn't have them yet or she's keeping them from me. Dad tells her everything, but I get left in the dark when I'm out of range to help. Frustrating. I hate not being there when my girl needs me.

"I didn't want you to panic and do something ridiculous like fly back home. We're keeping Kerrianne home for the rest of the week as a precaution. So, there won't be any more updates on the school trips. She's a little flustered, and she complained that Captain must be lonely and that Jack doesn't feed him enough. So now the three of us are at your house. Royal came with. There's no harm in being at your place, but I wanted you to know. You can check in on the security cameras at any time."

"I'm coming home." I bang on the door for the pilot.

"Valor. Go about your work. Kerrianne is currently learning

to count cards with Royal," Mom tells me, knowing that mentioning my brother will calm me some. "Go get your job done and come home."

The pilot opens the door and looks at me with a raised brow.

"Yes, Ma," I answer, gritting my teeth while thinking about whatever happened at my daughter's school.

It was bad enough that her bodyguard is dead but not bad enough that I need to come home. It's a massive gray area.

Kerrianne is my world, and I'm on the cusp of throwing off the whole mission to run home and be with her. To protect her.

Kerrianne's safety overrides any logic, but because there isn't any arguing with my mother, I shake my head at the pilot and deplane again.

Dad may be head of the crime family and the pack, but Mom is head of our house. While we may not live under her roof, my mother's reach extends to me and Kerrianne anyway. I trust her judgment, and since she does the caring for my little velociraptor while I'm away, I let her make this call.

Royal isn't the best in close-quarter combat if the house were invaded, but no one, absolutely no one, can outshoot him.

"I agree, keep her home." Anger fuels me. I was exhausted and sick of being on the road before, but now it's a rage-fueled rush to the finish line. "I've got to get going. The car's waiting."

"Go with God," Mom says and hangs up before I can even tell her I love her too.

Getting the last word in and refusing to say goodbye is how she deals with us doing such dangerous work. Her faith that God wouldn't let us die if she didn't get to say goodbye hasn't done her wrong yet.

I trust that whoever tried to get to Kerrianne will pay with their life. My father won't make it a swift death.

Antonella

CHAPTER THIRTEEN

THE AFTERMATH

"Antonella!" my uncle yells the minute I walk across the threshold into his home.

He storms toward me, his shoes clicking across the terrazzo floor. His face is red and his eyes are narrowed. I know that look. It's the one he gets seconds before a rash decision.

Uncle Gregorio grips me by the shoulders and shakes me. "What did you do?"

"You know what I did." I force myself out of his grasp, knocking his hands away. What I did might have been wrong . . . in his eyes. But it was right in my soul. "And you know it's not up to you alone if I live or die. Killing me means they will have the right to destroy you."

He puts up a hand and works his jaw back and forth. "I always knew you were weak. I thought letting you go to school and then teach would keep you in your place. I gave you what you wanted until I could find someone willing to lower themselves by marrying you. Instead? You pull this bullshit. My brother is rolling in his grave with how ungrateful you are."

I ignore his jabs and barbs. Before I went to college, Uncle

Gregorio's tantrums would sting. Anytime he brought up my parents, it would bring me to tears.

Anything Gregorio said, I believed. I was a child and didn't know better.

While part of me is still a scared little girl, hiding away in the darkest parts of my mind, the rest of me has grown, healed, and accepted that Gregorio is a bully used to getting his way.

Keeping Gregorio honest about my father's wishes already infuriates him. The audacity of a woman as consigliere and being entitled to my father's share of the family business stings his sexist ego.

Now, I don't waste the time or energy answering his brutal attacks, no matter how awful his words are. I never let him see me crack. He doesn't know what to do with that, and he grapples with my refusal to engage in the volley of violence.

"Well, at least I've gotten you married off. You'll no longer be my problem. This weekend, you'll marry whomever Ian Cavanagh offers for the truce. I've proposed that he offer his own son. It would work out perfectly, seeing as how you're already willing to throw your life away for Valor's spawn. Once you're part of their family, they can do whatever they want with you. Maybe their inquisitor won't kill you like he did your cousins." Gregorio steps closer to me. Getting in my face, he lowers his voice and threatens me. "He's killed six of them personally. This year alone. Maybe he'll make you lucky number seven."

"Then that will be God's will and not yours," I reply.

That earns me a head shake, a withering glare, and an expression so pinched that you'd think he smelled rotten cheese. Finally, Uncle Gregorio storms past me, heading in the opposite direction of my normal course through the house.

Gregorio thinks he can control everything and everyone, but he can't claim to be a man of God and be omniscient. It's a fact he doesn't like to be reminded of.

I'm not even halfway to my room when Berto finds me. Walking down the hallway with me, he asks, "You didn't happen to bring that gun back, did you?"

With a massive eye roll, I reach into my purse and retrieve the handgun. I spin it in my hand and offer him the grip while holding it by the barrel. "Yes, I brought your precious gun home. I knew it was one of your favorites, so I narrowly stopped myself from tossing it into the river on my way home."

Taking the gun with a soft smile, Berto sighs. "You know, Antonella, it didn't have to go this way."

"Save the lecture. We've had our piece of the argument." I give him a soft smile.

I'm nicer to him than Gregorio because Berto doesn't know how to handle it when people are nice to him.

"Well." He shrugs, backing down. "We'll see how that ends for you."

The reminder of the uncertainty of my future sets my heart hammering in my chest for the second time today when he walks away from me.

My fingers shake as I unlock my bedroom door and step inside. Under normal circumstances, in a normal family, I'd be a hero. I'd have saved a child's life.

But the drug-smuggling, gun-running, money-laundering, information-brokering D'Medicis are the original Italian Mafia dating back to the fifteenth century. The name may have suffered a variation, the business undergone a dozen or more transformations, but the blood is the same. So are the traditions.

Until me.

I toss my purse down on my bed and strip out of my work clothes. Normally, I'd hang them up to wear another day, maybe next week even, but they feel dirty, the corruption of today staining the fabric. I toss them in the wash.

I have two hours before dinner, and I want a long, hot shower and a half hour to stare at the ceiling, disassociating, but

I know that'll be too much to ask. I put on my robe and head into the bathroom.

After showering quickly and drying my hair, I pull on a wrap dress for dinner. While I'm tying the fabric, the door to my room opens. I go straight to my nightstand drawer and draw my gun. As I point it toward the door, my thumb naturally rolls over the safety.

Leticia, who was sneaking into my room, screeches and quickly covers her mouth to muffle the sound.

She steps inside and, after closing the door, hisses, "Antonella. What on earth? Why did you pull a gun?"

"Because my door opened unannounced," I answer logically. I put the gun back in the drawer and groan. "Please, by all means, let yourself in."

"What happened today? All Berto would tell me is that you're getting married." Leticia climbs onto the bed and flops down on her side, looking at me. "I don't see a ring."

"They really don't tell you anything." I sigh and wave for her to move over.

Leticia rolls onto her back, leaving me room on the queen-size bed to climb on beside her. We lie there, looking up at the ceiling, in silence for a bit.

When I can stomach the answer, it comes out. "I called the truce today."

"Oh. My. God." She raises her head and looks over at me. "The truce, as in, if they can't come to an agreement, you'll end up dead. There needs to be two funerals and a wedding?" Eyes wide, she draws a deep breath. "The truce where you had to pull a weapon on one of our people and make a solemn vow to protect a member of the other family with your life. That truce?"

I nod. "That truce."

She pales and falls back down to the bed, her body stiff as a board next to me. "I'll pray so hard for you."

"Thanks." I look at the stucco on the blank ceiling.

"My dad will kill you," she groans.

She's being metaphorical because despite Leticia being the daughter of the head of the family, she has zero exposure beyond what I tell her of the family business.

"Well, not if the Cavanaghs kill me first." I hold my hands up in a demonstration of weighing the options.

God, I hope Valor Cavanagh loves his daughter. At least enough to spare the person who saved her.

"Okay, so tell me everything." Leticia slaps my side with the back of her hand.

It takes me a whole ten minutes to relay the two-minute interaction with Berto and the three-minute communication with the Cavanaghs back to her because Leticia asks a million questions.

"Well . . . I guess we should get dinner out of the way. Mamma already has a dress on order for you. It's waiting on tailoring." Leticia sighs.

"Good, I won't have to shop then." I let out a massive sigh to match.

If Francesca is ordering a dress, it would be because Gregorio told her to.

It won't be much longer, and Leticia will have a marriage arranged for her. There will be a long engagement and a big fanfare leading up to a full weekend of events beyond a traditional wedding. Leticia is every bit ready to be the good Mafia wife. She's been poised to please. Whereas, deep down, I've always known that however I ended up married, I wouldn't be fawned over like some Italian Mafia princess. Leticia has hundreds of inspirations tagged away in her internet pin board, and her sliding off the bed and straightening her dress nervously is more than a tick. She's itching to do something for this wedding now that she knows what's happening.

"I'm getting you the something old, something new, something borrowed, and something blue. So that'll be covered. It's amazing how fast this all moves."

I get up off my side and shake out my dress but keep my eyes on her. I don't know how to tell her that it doesn't matter. None of this really makes any difference to me.

Her eyes well with tears, and her bottom lip wobbles. "I wonder where you'll live. Whoever it is probably won't let you work. Oh . . . no. What will we do? I won't get to see you every day. I just got you back."

I want to comfort her and tell her that it'll be okay. That I'll be fine. But I won't lie to her, and it's too easy to get lost spiraling into the unknown. If I get soft and give into fear, then Berto and Gregorio win.

Neither Leticia's tears, quivering lips, fallen shoulders, nor her arms wrapping around her middle break my resolve. She so easily shows all the feelings I wear guarded close to my heart.

Briskly, I round the bed and pull her into a hug, trying to protect her. I give up being honest. I can't let her be this afraid. *Ignorance is bliss. Spare her feelings.* "It'll be okay. They won't keep us apart. I'll call you all the time."

"Promise?" she whines into my shoulder.

I squeeze, wobbling us back and forth. "Besides, it's me they're marrying off, not you. I'll get married to an underling who's happy to be considered important enough to be married off. No one will want the woman who called the truce. He'll be easy to manage. Nothing will change between us at all."

Valor

CHAPTER FOURTEEN

THE WEDDING

"You expect me to what? Fuckin' bring an enemy whore into my bed, into my home, and let her play mother to my daughter?" I snap at my father, my teeth clicking with the force.

Rage stews, swirling up my spine. My muscles coil and strain, pushing to shift to the form better suited for this much conflict. Here and now, I'd rather start a war than live in love.

I pace inside the small space by the church confessionals, fists clenching and unclenching, as I think about the ridiculous differences between me and a D'Medici. The most notable being how breakable she'll be. "She's a goddamn human."

"Ahem." Father Michael clears his throat.

"Sorry, Father," I growl, trying to remember my language. At least to keep the higher power out of it, for his sake.

The collar of my white dress shirt is too tight. I want to unbutton it. I adjust the dark green tie, but it's not enough. *No, I want to be in my other shape.* The messier and more destructive one.

When I married Holly, I promised her the usual 'until death do us part,' but it wasn't supposed to be such a short time frame. It wasn't supposed to be months after our little girl was born.

In the seven years I've grieved, I accepted that a new wife was eventually in the cards for me. But clenched fist, fangs fully bared, and squaring up with my father, I'm ready to fight for my new wife to be anyone but a fuckin' D'Medici.

I shrug out of my suit jacket. My mother having picked out the most luxurious one I have, should have been an early indicator of the trouble to come. Silver cufflinks, dark green tie rather than black, and she bought me new shoes. *I should have fucking known. How did I accept that this was only Sean's funeral?* I'll blame the jet lag and being too trusting of my parents. Jack didn't even lie to me because all I asked him as I changed in the back of the SUV was where we were headed. We are, in fact, at the church. *Is it a lie through omission?* I snarl.

We'll put him in his place. My wolf decides.

The responsibility of being alpha wasn't something I was ready to ascend to, but I can best my father and stop this. I can control my own fate. The memory of the taste of blood floods my mouth.

We can take his place. My wolf thinks too closely about killing my father, and I pause.

"Yes," Neil answers shortly, and I had forgotten my initial question. Lucky for me, I guess, Uncle Neil doesn't miss an opportunity to talk down to me. "Yes, we do expect you to do as we say and marry the D'Medici woman because once our families are joined and the bodies are buried, the bad blood can be put to rest. The truce was called. We all have a duty to do."

"Fuck. The. Truce," I snap.

I tried to keep my voice down before, the echoing in the main part of the church always feels so loud, but now I'm at full volume. My fingers inch closer to my gun. *I could kill Neil . . .*

"We have what we need. The information I got should stop the bleeding out and their attacks on us. This would be the leverage needed to take the D'Medicis down." I try to bargain with them and remind them where I was.

My wolf snarls, *End them both, and we can stop all of this. All. Of. This. We can protect our pup.*

No. I stop myself, leaving my gun in the holster, pacing back and forth before him. Neil isn't the man I'm taking an issue with. Beyond that, Uncle Neil isn't worth the bullet, the penance, or the cleanup. He has never made a move to become alpha or take over the business. Probably because he knows he can't.

I let out the snarl from my wolf. "Bring the person who called the truce here, and I'll kill them. It's not too late to fix this mess."

Neil takes a step back.

If I were having this conversation with my father in front of anyone more than Neil and Father Michael, one of my father's chief advisors, I'd be out of line. It would be grounds for a gun to my head or teeth around my throat for openly questioning, challenging, showing distrust of the head of the family.

"I don't think you'd like the outcome of that." My father is barely even showing emotions. But his hands are in his pockets, and his eyes are bright gold. I'm pissing him off even if he refuses to say it. "Before you try to void the truce, perhaps a little information about it would be prudent." This time, he releases a small growl, warning me. I stop pacing again. "It was called to protect Kerrianne."

It's as though he threw a bucket of ice water on my soul. *Fuck.*

"And the woman you're supposed to marry is the one who turned a gun on her own people for Kerrianne. So, if you'd like to kill your new wife and violate the well-calculated truce, you'd better have a foolproof plan to keep your daughter safe from the retaliation they'd be well within their right to take . . ."

I didn't put it together. An incident at the school, Sean being dead, and the truce. Nausea rolls through me. I rest my hand against the pew beside me, bracing my weight. *If the D'Medici called a truce to save Kerrianne and I were to kill the truce caller, then they would come for Kerrianne.*

"You don't have to like the situation. You don't have to like your bride." My uncle tries to justify this as he hems and haws. "It's peace. We could only wish to be so lucky to see true peace in our lifetimes."

"But you will." My father cuts him off, reassuring me with a hand on my shoulder. "You will see peace. She'll be a good wife for you. Antonella D'Medici was raised in this life. She knows her place. It doesn't hurt that she's beautiful, and don't think I'd let just anyone be in my granddaughter's life."

Antonella D'Medici, a niece of Gregorio D'Medici, then. Fuckin' Mafia princess.

I drop my head and scoff as sounds of vehicles pulling up in front of the church filter through the thinner panes of stained glass above our heads—easily heard with wolf ears.

"You were mated to Holly before. Wolves surviving their mate's death isn't usual, Valor. She might not have been your fated mate, but living a life alone isn't good for you." Dad throws his and Mom's concern, one they don't bring up, at me.

I desperately wanted Holly to be my fated mate, but it wasn't in the cards. We claimed each other and had Kerrianne, but losing her didn't make me feral. Sad, but not feral.

Car doors slam just outside.

"That'll be them, then." Father Michael nods toward the back of the church, where I'd been brought into this mess thirty minutes ago.

I assumed today was Sean's funeral. Instead, it's a nightmare that happens to lay a loyal soldier to rest.

"It would be better if the truce was never called. We were so close to decimating them all." I scoff, snatching my jacket off the pew before following Father Michael and the pack's leaders back to the church's entryway.

No one contradicts me, and with each step, acceptance seeps

in. I shrug on my jacket, relaxing my shoulders, and focus on the light of my life. Surviving the loss of Holly was easier because my little raptor needed me. Kerrianne couldn't lose both her parents.

We descend the stairs in the vestibule and approach the main doors.

Once the final car of the caravan parks, the driver gets out and rounds the hood while two guards from the lead cars walk along the wall of vehicles. The driver opens the front passenger door, and Don D'Medici steps out. But the rear passenger door is opened from the interior. A guard blocks her from the rear of the car, but no one helps her as she maneuvers her dress and gets out of the car.

I catch sight of the four-inch heels she's wearing and keep that in mind for judging her height against me.

She's not struggling, but it's clear she'd move more easily with assistance.

Her dress is fitted from her collarbones to her thighs, just above her knees, where it flares out around her. It isn't a traditional white wedding gown. Instead, the black fabric catches the early morning light. Sequined or some sort of sparkly lace fabric covers a simple, but not plain, black gown of some nature. It's long sleeved, and the garment's modesty is unexpected, but I can't put my finger on why.

Because she's not flashy like the usual Mafia wives we've stalked, my wolf supplies. *She's beautiful.*

I can't take my eyes off her. Somehow, I've become transfixed on the human I'm being forced to accept.

I step slightly to the side to keep my eyes on her as Gregorio D'Medici and his consigliere leave her to navigate on her own.

Her head is bowed, watching where she walks rather than owning the space around her.

Antonella is accompanied, not escorted, up the three small

steps of the church, raising the hem of her dress in one hand to allow herself to step up each of the stairs.

Neither man holds the door open for her.

Maybe it's that I'm already angry, but that lack of action heats like coals stoked to a roaring fire of hatred.

Antonella D'Medici may be the niece of my sworn enemy . . . but she's also my daughter's savior. That counts for some loyalty. *Enough for her to be treated better than that.*

She takes us in with her brown eyes, flecked with the gold of autumn leaves, clear and bright but wary. I hadn't put much thought into what she'd look like, but my father wasn't lying. She is beautiful. Heart-stoppingly so. A calm washes over me when we lock eyes.

I shake my head and shoulders, trying to brush the feeling off. She could be a wolf in sheep's clothing for all I know.

"Are you ready to take custody of the disgrace?" Gregorio D'Medici asks me. His disgusted half snarl reflects his perpetually ill state. "I'm sure you're not very happy that Toni has ruined your personal vendetta. It's not too late to kill her and call off the truce."

Toni? I hate this asshole. I hate him more than I hate having to adjust how I'll kill him and his filthy son. This truce won't change the fact that, if they're guilty, I'll find a way to kill the two of them. It just means I'll no longer be putting their heads on a spike in their own front lawns after I do it.

Ignoring his taunts, I extend my hand to Antonella, not as if to shake, but flat for her to rest her hand within mine.

Gregorio wants to make a show of being a dick to her, then I'll make a show of possessing her like she's a prize. This may be a truce, but nothing says she can't be the spoils of war. I'll just have to tread carefully to ensure she's not a Trojan horse.

My heart flutters, and we lock eyes again. She doesn't wear a long veil. Rather it's one of those small hats with tulle or something that's customary for mourners. A suit is a suit, but some women dream of the day they get married. The dress and dancing, food, cake. But there'll be none of that because our wedding will be celebrated graveside. There's a curiosity to it.

Did Antonella mourn having to wear black on her wedding day? Better yet, why do I care?

Antonella puts her hand in mine. It's cold, and I resist the urge to shrug out of my jacket to offer her warmth.

What the fuck is wrong with me?

With her proximity, I inhale a bright citrus scent layered with something lightly sweet and floral.

I clear my throat and lead her two steps closer to Father Michael.

He nods and leads us up the stairs into the main portion of the church, down the central aisle, and to the altar, where he stops before God.

"Formalities' sake." Father Michael looks between me and my new bride but focuses on her. "You are here of your own free will?"

"Yes." She gives one single nod.

Her voice is strong in volume but hollow in quality, like a well-loved tavern after the bar closes.

Antonella's eyes are constantly moving, assessing her uncles and the Cavanaghs around her. If I couldn't hear her deliberately slow, steady breaths, I'd think she was poised, but they're there, their shallowness helping her steel herself.

My wolf catches the scent of fear and looks for the cause. But I'm not concerned. I'd worry if she was oblivious to the threats in the room.

Father Michael sweeps his gaze to me, and I debate the truth, but there's no way I'm letting the D'Medicis see that I wasn't involved in this.

"Yes."

Back on Antonella, Father Michael asks, "Do you, Antonella D'Medici, take Valor Cavanagh to be your husband?"

I don't take my eyes off her, holding eye contact. Neither of us wants to be here, but it's born of necessity. Our fates are intertwined now. Would either of us be willing to risk the truce for the sake of bloodshed?

Antonella doesn't answer right away. It's as if she's giving me a calculated once-over. There isn't fear or sadness in her eyes. She's almost too calm to be marrying the heir to a bloody empire. Whatever she sees in me, it's enough.

She turns to Father Michael with a determinate nod. "I do."

The movement exposes the column of her neck, and it drags my wolf forward. *Just one bite.*

No. I push him down.

It's my turn, and Father Michael formally asks me, "Do you, Valor Cavanagh, take Antonella D'Medici to be your wife?"

I clench and unclench my fist before I answer. "I do take Antonella D'Medici to be my wife."

"You may exchange rings." The priest smiles, gesturing between us.

Apparently, every detail has been thought through because my father offers an open box to me, and Gregorio D'Medici offers one out to Antonella. I take a beat to look at the ring. It has a classic look with a single stone set in a flat gold band. The diamond is nice, but it's not nearly nice enough for what I would have picked, even for an arranged bride. It screams Dad's taste.

Not bright enough. My wolf laments.

Slipping a ring on Antonella's finger tarnishes the memory of the same experience with Holly, the mother of my child and the woman my heart holds steadfastly to. This ring, a symbol of an unbreakable truce, marks the second time in my life I'll make a promise until death. With Holly, I believed it would be when we were old and gray. Now I know better. *How long will it be before death catches one of us this time?*

Untraditionally, we step closer to the altar and a pen is

passed between us. Five people sign legal documents binding us as one before God and for the government.

No one suggests I kiss my new bride. Which is for the best because tonight, after the bodies are buried and the families are consoled, I'll have to fuck her and provide the sheets as proof of our union. Consummation, the final 'step' in a marriage.

Tender kisses aren't what our world is built on. Our marriage won't be built on them either.

Unfortunately for Antonella, the truce and its less-than-savory stipulations won't be the only change in her life. She unknowingly just married a wolf shifter. If death, by some miracle, evades us, our laws demand that I turn Antonella within the next year.

The requirements of the truce are nothing compared to the bloody ordeal of being gifted a wolf and surviving. It's not for the faint of heart.

After signing the documents, Antonella links her fingers with mine to walk back down the aisle.

Maybe she'll have what it takes to be the alpha's wife. But then again, what choice does she have?

Valor

CHAPTER FIFTEEN

THE FIRST FUNERAL

After our short wedding 'ceremony,' we walk back to the church's entrance, where Sean's casket is arriving. We escort it, as pallbearers, to the front of the church, and I can't believe he's gone. I rest my hand on the center of the casket. Closed because it was too brutal. He fought until his lifeblood ran dry. But that doesn't answer any of the questions that haunt me. *How did this happen? How do I console my daughter through this? How do I find someone else she'll feel safe with? How do I trust anyone else to take care of her?*

I turn back to the vestibule to greet my pack, and Antonella is waiting for me. With her hands clasped in front of her waist, she radiates patience and understanding.

She doesn't need direction. When I step toward her, she offers me her hand. I help her down the stairs, and as the first few cars arrive, she takes her place by my side. She casts her eyes down, trying, and succeeding, to look as respectful and subservient as possible. Gregorio's and Eduardo's wives adopt similar positions, practically shrinking into invisibility beside them.

It irks me that this is the norm for her. It's evident there's a stark contrast between our families. The way they treat their woman like filth. We should have kept eradicating them. *Stupid fucking truce.*

I place my hand on her mid-back, and Antonella tilts her head and eyes up to look at me. "We're a proud people. My wife needs to be strong and show a united front."

She gives me a single nod and straightens her spine.

I know I should take my hand away, but I like the way it feels to touch her. The possessive bit of my soul clings to her. *Antonella is mine, after all.*

Ours, the animal inside me corrects. *Could be more than just our wife.* He practically bites his tongue, but I feel it anyway and stiffen with the thought.

Cars and SUVs full of people unload, and pack members climb the stairs, greeting me and nodding to Antonella until the church is nearly full.

Then my SUV pulls up with Kerrianne and my mother. *How the fuck do I explain this to Kerrianne?*

I finally drop my hand from Antonella's back.

It's not that I keep Kerrianne completely closed off from what I do, but there's an appropriate time to explain what's going on. The day Kerrianne buries her bodyguard is not the day to tell her I'm married and another woman will be living with us.

Antonella slips her fingers into my hand and squeezes, and I look to her.

She whispers, "I'm going up to the visitation and will take a seat in the second row. You can take Kerrianne up to visit and get through the services. If she asks why I'm here, explain that funerals are when people come together to show that they care for those who have lost a loved one. I'm here to be supportive."

I'm barely done processing those words before she steps away from me, her hand slipping from my grasp. Everything she said makes logical sense. It's exactly the right sort of thing to do in this situation.

How does she know how to do all this when I don't? What information does she have that I'm lacking? How is she more of an expert at this than I am?

I can't come up with a reason to distrust what she says or does in this moment.

Antonella continues up the stairs as Kerrianne comes through the door. She runs over and wraps herself around me.

Her little tears and sniffles tug on my heartstrings. Kerrianne hugs my legs until I pull her off me, but only so I can get down to her level for a full hug.

"I've missed you so much. I don't want you to go ever again." Her crying panic gets her nose running, and my heart breaks into a bunch of little pieces.

This isn't the first funeral she's attended, even recently, but it's the first time it's been someone she had contact with daily. Well, that she'd remember anyway.

I pull tissues out of my pocket and hand one to her. She blows her nose and hands it back to me, and I shove it in my opposite pocket.

"I love you, little raptor. I won't go away unless it's absolutely necessary."

"Sean died." Her words have tears threatening my eyes. Her voice is so small. "He was supposed to protect me. Then Grandma came and got me."

"It'll be okay. You'll always be protected," I promise, already running through the names of people in our organization who I trust, but more than that, who I trust with Kerrianne's life. It's an exceedingly short list. "Until then, you'll be with Grandma, Grandpa, Royal, or me full-time."

Kerrianne nods in understanding and hiccups. I offer her another tissue. She cleans her nose and then, lip still quivering, gives me another hug. I give her one more tight squeeze before standing and setting her on her feet.

I turn back to the church and lead her up the stairs and down the aisle, to the final visitation of the wolf who gave his life for her.

My parents lead the way, Kerrianne and I following them closely.

Our people are silent as we walk by. Their heads bowed in respect. *How different are our traditions from hers?*

After the funeral services, I sent Kerrianne home with my mother, and Antonella returned to my side. The December air is cold against our skin, and while Kerrianne's a wolf, there was no need for her to stay out in this weather.

The part I hate the most in all this is that we drove across the cities, deep into what was — arguably, still is — enemy territory, to lay him to rest among the D'Medici people. Graveside service, the final prayers as he's lowered into the ground, and the toast to his afterlife are done in less than thirty minutes.

Antonella sat by my side through the burial, and it was an easy, comforting silence.

Normally, we'd head back to the pack house and tell stories, share memories, eat and drink in Sean's name. But with a second funeral to attend today, we hold a small reception here, among the D'Medici headstones.

When Antonella asked to stretch her legs, I didn't have an objection. The opportunity to gather my thoughts was welcomed, but now I'm watching her from a distance as she seamlessly integrates herself with my people.

Our people, my wolf corrects.

We've been at this cemetery for about an hour, and one thing

I hadn't thought about was how similar or different our families would be when it came to mourning. Gregorio D'Medici is here with his wife out of respect for the truce. They're respectful but not overly chatty among the pack, and they completely ignore Antonella's presence. The jury is still out on the 'good' or 'bad' in that dynamic.

The cemetery isn't exclusive to the D'Medici empire, but it's clear that Italians take their dead as seriously as we do.

The plots, headstones, and monuments are similar. There are fewer crosses and trinity knots but more angels and longer epitaphs. Flowers sit at almost every family monument and individual headstone, solar lights dot the grassy areas, and little flags mark the graves of those who served our country's military.

Sean's body may be separated from the pack and laid to rest here, but at least we know it will be respected and not forgotten.

My eyes leave the slabs of granite to find Antonella again. It doesn't take long. She makes her own introductions and offers condolences. I note the way she positions herself, never tucking behind trees or monuments. It strikes me as purposeful that she never leaves my sight. Even when someone stands before me to speak, she finds a way into my peripheral.

One of the quartermaster's sons, who's younger than Kerrianne, approaches Antonella as she speaks with Sean's mother, who flew in from Ireland.

The boy gently pats Antonella's thigh, and without breaking the conversation, Antonella wraps her hand around the boy's and gives it a squeeze. He stands, patiently waiting. In less than a minute, when her conversation with Sean's mother is done, Antonella turns to the little boy.

Her long dress restricts her movements, but Antonella shuffles the skirt and gets to a low crouch, despite wearing four-inch heels. In a lull of my conversation, I catch her talking the boy through the steps to tie his shoe. It looks like the bunny and tree method I used with Kerrianne. She then double knots it and gives him a low five.

You'd have to be blind in one eye and not able to see out of the other to miss the fact that she's good with children. It's appealing, and I don't like how this observation makes my slacks tighter. *Kerrianne doesn't need a sibling.*

Doesn't she? My wolf thinks about how much fun it's been to play and see the little raptor grow.

"Valor." My name is said with a thick Irish accent.

I force myself to look away from Antonella. It's harder than it should be. When I do, my uncle and the alpha of the Northern Ireland pack, Patrick Doyle, comes to stand beside me. Patrick, who is mated to my dad's sister, Deidra, made a special trip for the occasion. A truce between families is monumental, and the effects are so widespread that it made waves all around the world.

"Patrick." I shake his hand. "Good to see you."

"It's good to see you. Especially on such a happy day. Congratulations." Perhaps scarier than my father, who can be straight faced through anything, Patrick smiles.

"Thank you, Patrick."

Losing Sean and signing a meaningless truce don't seem to lend to a happy day, but according to him, my father, and my uncle, we're to be celebrating peace. So I let it go.

"It's a shame about Sean." He nods to the grave. "Of all people, I never thought a D'Medici would get the drop on him. Humans like that taking down a wolf with his skill set. I trained him myself since he was a teen. What we don't know about this is aggravating, yet a moot point, I suppose."

"Kerrianne was quite attached to him. I don't know what to do." I admit.

"I've got a few good wolves looking for a change of scenery. I'll have them shipped over for you. Take your pick." Patrick purses his lips. "I know it was your preference to have someone less familiar with the current pack. Makes 'em more objective."

"Much appreciated. Now more than ever, I would like someone who sees everyone as a threat. The not knowing what happened and all." I've always seen Patrick as an adviser of sorts, and I've never taken his generosity toward me, and Kerrianne, for granted.

"Whoever you don't need here in the cities, we can move about the country to deal with the issue with the Bratva. D'Medicis really fucked the duck with that before the truce," Patrick adds.

I wasn't here and don't know the extent of the information we have on the D'Medicis now, but what I learned while in South America is confirmed with his words. The D'Medicis married one of their women off to a Bratva heir.

Patrick rotates, turning to look in the same direction as me. It's obvious he's watching Antonella talk to Aunt Deidra, just like I am. "She seems to fit in. Deidra has taken to her. You could have gotten a much worse shake in this deal."

He's not wrong. Everyone seems so happy for us and genuinely accepting of her, but I don't care for the observation. I haven't come to a decision about her yet, and everyone's assurances are falling into the unasked-for-opinions pile until then.

"Why are you so excited about this deal?" I examine him, trying to figure out the big secret I've been left out of.

"We need this truce to stick . . ." Patrick answers, adjusting his cap. "You and the D'Medici girl have given us a much-needed break. Your father negotiated a strong deal in our favor. The Italians think we took the short end of the stick by giving us this woman." Patrick shakes his head and laughs. "The D'Medicis are backward on the deal with the Bratva. The craic is that the Russians wanted your bride over the one they received in negotiations. Though Nikolai is quite chuffed, Igor is bent over it."

I raise a brow at that. *Interesting.*

Patrick draws a breath and keeps explaining what I missed while I was away. "Now the D'Medicis are buyin' the shipment we couldn't sell to the Syrians because they ended up with the Gardaí. The Bratva don't have a place to send the shipment they stole from us."

"And based on information I found while hunting . . . we know where they're keeping it." I see why Patrick is getting excited over the dealings.

"We can get those back, and my son can find a buyer so we turn a tidy profit." He smiles.

"And now, two massive arms dealers are linked to the D'Medicis. If we play our cards right, it'll no longer be a competition. We can control which wars we back." Patrick pushes his shoulder against mine, trying to make light of everything and reassure me. "And you get a woman who will make a good mate. If for no other reason to like her, she was strong enough to tell Igor Popov no. Could be worse."

"It seems a little too good to be true." I try to express my concerns diplomatically and concisely. "She's so willing to come and be part of our family. I'm supposed to believe this isn't all a ruse?"

"Well, not everyone grows up with a silver spoon in their mouth that isn't laced with poison." Patrick raises an eyebrow. "You're turning down a mother for your child?"

I can't withhold my glare. I shouldn't have shown my hand like that. But no one knows my daughter better than me. No one should have more of a say over her life than me. 'She doesn't need a mother' is on the tip of my tongue.

"Don't think ya can do both jobs. In our world, youngins need a woman who has been raised in this life. Your daughter could do far worse than to have a schoolmarm for a surrogate." Patrick warns me. "You may not have picked Antonella, but would you have ever picked someone? A head of the pack must have a family. Men like us aren't meant to be alone."

Schoolmarm? Makes sense if she was at the school when she called the truce.

My silence clearly not appeasing Patrick, he leaves me with one last thought. "Take a look at how they treat her when you're at their funeral later today. Maybe it'll clear up the differences."

I let Patrick's words stew as he walks away. All the while, I look at Antonella as she listens to some of the younger women in the pack.

Antonella looks over, as if to check in on me. Her brow knits together as she observes me, but one of the younger women places a hand on her forearm and draws her attention back.

There are many people here that I should speak with and family members I could catch up with, but I can't take my eyes off her.

What do I do with you, darling? What is this pull?

My wolf cocks his head, and I mimic his movement, looking at her intensely.

She says something to the small group and then dismisses herself. Gracefully stepping around the fresh grave and past headstones, she makes her way to me.

Her sultry voice is low in volume, keeping the conversation between us. "Are you okay?"

I nod. "Why do you ask?"

"Well, the older man came to talk to you. It looked like you were debating hurting him. I thought maybe you needed a buffer." Antonella's offer is unexpected and oddly settles some of the rage burning in my gut. But the calm I feel doesn't cross my face, and Antonella interprets my lack of response as a dismissal. "Alright, well, let me know."

She takes a step to walk away, and I wrap my hand around her wrist, spinning her back to face me.

"Thank you for coming to check in with me. I appreciate your awareness of the world around you."

"You're welcome." Antonella doesn't try to pull away from me, though her eyes lock on where we're joined. My fingers are nearly white where they're pressing into her wrist.

Why is she so calm? Did they drug her?

Patrick's words come back to me. She was raised to be a wife in this life.

Why are you the way you are? Let me figure out what makes you tick, darling.

"What's going on?" Antonella stands a little taller and meets my gaze. "You're upset by something, and I think it's more than being married to me."

"I don't understand why you're so calm." I'm honest, but I can't pinpoint why I trust her with any information. She's too disarming.

Antonella grimaces, her little nose wrinkling, and I'm drawn to kiss her.

Kiss her . . . of all fuckin' things.

I stand my ground in the short distance between us, trying to ignore my inner desires. Holding her here, the warmth of her wrist in my grasp, I wait for her answer. Despite being human, there's something unbreakable about her.

"At the end of the day, there isn't a choice in the matter. The best thing I can do is make the most of my situation and hope you do the same." Antonella chooses her words carefully and, with a soft, sad smile, lowers her volume even further. "I'm committed to making this partnership work."

"I'll do what I can." I slowly remove my fingers from her wrist, and my skin mourns the absence of her warmth, cold again in the early afternoon sun. "We should get moving. I don't want to be late."

Antonella nods and waits for me to take the lead. With her

head held high, she has no problem holding my hand and following my lead.

Everything she does, I want to question. I want to know everything.

Antonella

CHAPTER SIXTEEN

A DIFFERENT WORLD

I don't know how they decided on the order in which the funerals would take place. But in the familiar St. Catherine's cemetery this morning, surrounded by people I had never met before, the people I've called enemies my entire life, I felt the most at home I have in a long time.

Hugged tightly and welcomed to mourn with them, I was not Antonella D'Medici but instead Antonella Cavanagh. No one even suggested I wasn't. There wasn't a question if I belonged there.

Valor Cavanagh, *the* Valor Cavanagh, makes me feel *something*. He's not outwardly warm, and the pictures I've seen over the years confirm it's him, but they don't do his devilish good looks justice. They don't capture the bright fire in his eyes nor the way he keeps his hair well kept. And pictures can't convey the thick smell of warmth that comes from him. It's heady like bourbon but sweet like chocolate.

I feel a connection to him. Maybe it's blatant attraction and the relief of being safe clouding my mind, but I don't know that Valor Cavanagh really is the worst man to be married to.

Graveside, the mother of the decedent, Sean, told me how grateful she is to have me in her family and that someone was able to pick up the duty when her son couldn't. I wanted to weep with her.

I'd never met him, never known him, only saw him in passing, but anyone who comes from a woman with such grace in adversity must have a heart of gold as well.

During Sean's graveside service, I meandered and mingled with his family and their close friends. The Irish aren't as many cousins and uncles and nephews deep as we are, but it's built more on chosen family. Maybe that's what makes them more accepting of someone new from the outside world and why they extend kindness instead of judgment.

The divine providence that put me in this position had me dreading 'going home' all over again.

My 'family' is cold.

Valor and I sat together in the third row during the service.

My cousin, a fourth cousin from Aunt Francesca's side, was killed on an undisclosed, to me, job. We weren't close. Having only seen him a few times a year, I was apathetic to his passing.

By now, everyone knows I was the one who stood in the way of family business. They all knew the day it happened because gossip travels fast in an Italian family. The silent treatment, the scornful sideways glances, and flat-out snubs were to be expected.

They're pissed at me for ending this war. I'm not sure they even know the reason I interfered was because of an innocent child, but a family quick to anger and staunch in tradition won't see the turning tides of life as anything but a tsunami.

But their disappointment is nothing new. It fills me with useless indifference.

Valor held my hand through every second of the service he could. We're practically attached at the hip, and the lack of emotions I feel toward my family is drowned out by the stiffness and simmering anger toward the circumstances that have led us here.

The ride back across the cities into the suburbs of Chicago wasn't long. We're in Barrington at St. Patrick's Catholic Cemetery. It's the heart of Irish territory.

Blessedly, the burial wasn't all that long, and they lowered my cousin into the ground twenty minutes after our arrival at the most. But the fifteen minutes we've been standing graveside, being offered condolences, has felt like a lifetime.

Leticia is the only friendly face in the crowd. However, the minute I got too close to her, she held her fingers low by her waist, crossing them, as if to say wish for something good, and then separated them. Our secret gesture we use to tell each other when it's not a good time to talk.

I know she's not upset with me because when I walked past her, she brushed her pinkie against mine, a solidarity of our pinkie promise to always be friends. But it's pointless to be here.

Valor tried to branch off on his own, but every time he does, it's clear those loyal to Gregorio D'Medici are not receptive. They step away from him, denying all attempts at conversation.

Now, he wraps his arm around me, drawing me close as if to console me for a hug. He bows his head, bringing it to my ear, and whispers, "I'm getting the distinct feeling we've overstayed our welcome."

"It's not just me, then." I let out a slow breath, whispering back to him.

He releases me from the partial hug and grabs my wrist. It's less gruff than when he did it at Sean's grave site. This time it's almost caring. When I pull back, he lets me slide through his fingers until my hand is intertwined with his.

Valor looks down at our joined hands with the tiniest change in his demeanor — raised eyebrow, parted lips that threaten a smile, and a slight head nod. It sends butterflies throughout my body from where our hands are linked straight to my stomach, where the fluttering is concentrated. Our eyes meet, and his look is dark and full of desire.

I don't know that Valor will ever fully approve of me, but he sure as hell can't be worse to live with than the D'Medici family. Especially when he looks at me like that.

"There you two are." Berto's voice breaks us out of our little bubble.

Berto uses his 'I'm about to take a beautiful day and ruin it with a fist fight' tone.

I immediately shift, giving Valor my back to face Berto. *Maybe if I'm between the two of them, this won't escalate.*

"Valor, it's good to have bested you." Berto offers his hand out to shake, which wouldn't be problematic, but Valor's right hand is wrapped up in my left and tucked between us.

Valor doesn't make it an issue. He runs his free hand around my waist, pulling me closer and pressing my back against his chest, then releases my hand.

"I would like to say good job, Berto, but it looks like I'm the one with a wife." Valor doesn't let Berto win, but he does shake his hand.

I bring my left hand up and touch the one he has wrapped around my stomach. At my touch, though, Valor's grasp relaxes slightly. The constant touch, a sign of ownership, will further his appearance of claiming me.

Appearances are everything, and Valor wants Berto to know I'm his.

"The problem is, Valor." Berto's voice drips with condescension, slick like the grease in his hair. "I mean, it was so easy to just stroll right up once I had —"

"Berto," I snap.

"Now, now, Toni. The men are talking, maybe be a good wife and go see what the other hags are up to." Berto is cold to me.

I open my mouth to snap back at him, but Valor's arm hugs

me tighter to him. "My wife stays with me. But do tell, Berto, how do you think you're better than me?"

"Well, it was almost too easy. That fancy, high-tech security system of yours really shouldn't allow an override with the key of someone so easily killed. That was a nice touch. I was able to waltz right up to her. It's a shame the truce was called before I could finish the job." Berto doesn't stop poking.

He's trying to start an incident, isn't he? I grip Valor's arm, silently begging him not to let this keep escalating.

"It takes bravery to put someone's life above your own. Though, I'm sure you aren't familiar with that concept." Valor gently trails his hand up and down my stomach. "Bravery, that is." Valor's deadly sharp tone softens a hair, and he must look down at me. "It seems fitting that the woman willing to put her life on the line becomes my wife."

Berto huffs and rolls his eyes.

"If you'll excuse us. We have a marriage to consummate and celebrate." Valor's voice is low and gravelly.

I've never heard someone make that noise, but the intensity lights my whole body on fire.

How the fuck did I forget about that?

I don't know if he means his words to be so alluring, but their heaviness and the straightforward declaration of our required physicality have my lower abdomen clenching with a need I haven't experienced. Not like this.

Well, as far as first male partners go . . . At least I'm attracted to him? Fuck.

Berto steps backward to walk away rather than turn his back on us. "Enjoy your new life, Mrs. Cavanagh."

My new moniker is foreign, especially coming from Berto, but I can't get lost in the thoughts about it because Valor clenches his fist against my stomach and grows rigid behind me.

I spin in the tight space between us and look up at him, his jaw clenched and eyes narrowed.

My stomach tightens, and I try to smooth over the mess Berto made. "I'm so sorry."

Looking down at me, he shakes his head. Valor's shoulders drop, his jaw unclenches, and he kisses my forehead. "Don't be." He pulls away a little, and a sultry smirk crosses his face. "He's helped me make an important decision, and he doesn't even know it."

My stomach swoops. That little single kiss makes me light-headed, and his smile does nothing to slow my rapidly beating heart.

"You should find the cousin you like and say goodbye." Valor's tone is unexpectedly sweet. "I'll have Jack bring the SUV around."

I search for her but find Leticia standing with her parents and Uncle Eduardo as they chat with one of Berto's friends. She's locked in place, the same old routine of being seen and not heard. The disassociation and her roaming gaze are evident from here.

We lock eyes and exchange small smiles. Going over there will be pointless.

Instead, I look back to Valor. "The potential conflict isn't worth trying to say goodbye."

"I'm sorry," Valor says, offering his hand out for me to hold rather than taking my wrist. "It isn't fair that shit men like Berto get to dictate how women live. I'll make sure the two of you get to connect. When we set you up with a cell phone, the two of you can talk. Maybe we can all do dinner."

My brain short-circuits as he leads me away.

My questions about their family, their life, and the differences between us are growing two- and threefold. But I, not so patiently, wait to address him again until we're tucked into the black SUV and the doors close behind us.

"You'd really let me talk to her?" I practically whisper.

"Of course." Valor's eyes are wide, but he quirks an eyebrow. "Antonella, this isn't a kidnapping, it's a truce."

I nod because, with the pause, it seems like I should answer him. *Is Valor trying to make me want him? Does he know it's working?*

Valor

CHAPTER SEVENTEEN

THE HOTEL

I knew there would be a guard in the hotel suite because we'd gotten here early and were told they'd be doing a security sweep, but when I open the door, he's just standing in the living space, fucking around on his phone.

My wife, behind me, is tired. She was practically falling asleep in the SUV on the hour-long drive over here, but she kept jolting herself awake. Probably because she doesn't trust us enough to rest in our presence. Not that I blame her.

The way her people treated her was unacceptable. The frustration I feel on her behalf will exhaust me if I linger on it too much. I will, however, hold it against them and add it to the grievances I intend to make them pay for.

I hold the door open, and Antonella shuffles in behind me. I'm not sure she notices, but she releases a soft groan that lasts less than a fraction of a second, presumably when she sees the guard and yet another obstacle. I walk away from the door, clearing a path for him to make his exit, and Antonella follows me closely.

Is it instinct or conditioning that she knows to stand behind me like this?

The guard stands at attention, and I can't believe I have to command him.

So I do, the full weight of the alpha command behind my words. "Leave. Us."

The growl I hold back as I try to remember to be human is practically choking me from the inside out.

He gives my wife a look. A look like he thinks she's his to even lay eyes on, drinking her in. I move to keep myself between them until he's finally looking over his shoulder for one last glimpse of her before going out the door.

That fucker is getting his ass kicked later, my wolf grumbles, like it wasn't already happening.

I wait, watching the door, until it clicks shut and the lock whirs. My fist finally unclenches, and I turn to look at her.

Antonella is completely calm, almost bored by the situation. Either because she knows better than to get involved since she was raised in this life or because she's not smart enough to know the dangers.

It's not that she's not smart. It's that she doesn't know wolves exist. It's that she doesn't know she married one. I sigh because I'm being too hard on her. *It's that she has always been able to defend herself against the dangers she knew about, and clearly, a single man ogling her is nothing new.*

"You're an interesting woman, Antonella." I try to open the conversation between us but immediately realize the error of my statement.

"I am?" She cants her head, looking at me as if to see me in a new light.

We've been watching each other all day. We've played the respectful newlyweds that our families were expecting. She integrated with my family, and I claimed her, keeping her at my side as best I could and making sure her family knew they lost.

Now, though, in this hotel room, I don't want to be respectful anymore. I want to know who this woman is and if she was given to me simply because she called the truce or if there was more to it.

And in a sick way, I want to take what's been given to me.

Antonella begins to unpin her hat. She makes it look so easy, removing whatever held it in place and then pulling down the intricate updo. I didn't expect such long hair. It runs down her back, stopping above where her hips dip one last time before the curve of her ass takes over.

Maybe the truce won't be so bad after all.

My cock twitches. It's not like I've lived a celibate life since Holly . . . but there's something about Antonella. It started with being unable to take my eyes off her, and it hasn't stopped.

The rich brown locks hold the waves from having been pinned up for so long. When she shakes it out, it sways around her waist, sexy in a way I wouldn't have expected. I've always loved long hair on women, and I want to wrap my fingers in hers, first to explore the array of deep browns and second for something much more primal.

In public, I didn't feel like this. Maybe it was the buffer of an audience or expectations to be civil and in control. But that reservation is gone.

I get to look, to touch, and to use as much as I want. If she needs an adjustment period before submitting to the demands of being mated to a wolf, then that's all on her.

She'll want us. My wolf assures me, but I don't need his approval. Not for this.

"Like what you see?" She flirts with me while running her fingers through her hair and tousling it from the roots.

I'm no stranger to someone flirting, but the way she does it affects me in a way I've only experienced once before. I clear my throat. "Enough."

She scoffs a laugh and looks around the room. "I know it's customary to consummate and for you to deliver the evidence, but I was hoping I could wash this day off me first. Do you mind?"

No, I don't mind. It's on the tip of my tongue. It's what I should say.

Be a good husband and not the alpha asshole. Instead, I slide off my suit jacket, unbuckle my cuff links, roll up my sleeves, and pull the knife out of my pocket.

Antonella watches me, eyeing the knife, but there isn't fear in her eyes or in the air. Not like there should be. Then her lips barely twitch, almost like she's fighting a smile.

So trusting of me, princess. A man you've never met, but surely, you've heard the stories.

The woman doesn't even question it when I bring the knife up toward her face. She tilts her head and moves her hair out of the way. The second time she's bared that graceful neck to me.

My cock is rock hard at the view and the thought of putting my mark right there at the base. *Submit to me more, darling. Give it all to me.*

Antonella doesn't flinch when I slide the blade under the high collar of her dress. The knife has no problem cutting through the thick hem and then slicing the lace and backing fabric like butter.

Inch by inch, I slice down the front, between her perfect tits, showing off a black lace bra. As the dress parts, her skin becomes more visible. I stop at her waist and slide the pommel of my knife down her shoulder. The fabric slides away, revealing black ink tattooed into her skin.

The warm, rich scent of her arousal mixes with the bright citrus and lightly sweet floral fragrance I caught earlier. I wet my lips, anticipating what she'll taste like.

Don't get attached. I don't know her yet. We're married, not mates. I warn myself, trying to think with the head on my shoulders, not my raging hard-on.

Could be? My wolf debates.

I shove him away.

I go back to the front of her dress, and this time, I position the blade tip closer to her body. The razor-sharp edge connects with the smooth skin of her belly, and while I notice a small twitch, a minuscule flinch, and a hitch in her breath, Antonella doesn't object.

As I unravel the material with my knife, black lace panties are exposed, and I work lower yet, finding a matching garter and stockings.

God damn . . . I have to stop myself from palming my dick.

Right before the seam where the fabric furls out around her hips, I stop the knife's descent. I've sunk to my knees, but it doesn't feel shameful to lower myself before her.

She's too perfect. She's too fucking perfect. I can't let myself fall for her. It's lust. It's lust. It's lust.

Rising back to my full height, I offer my non-knife hand out to her. Antonella takes it and lets me assist her as she steps out over the now ruined not-wedding gown.

"Thank you." She gives me a soft smile. "I'm sure the zipper would have worked, but your way seems like it was faster."

The sass. The perfect, flirty little sass. "Did Gregorio D'Medici put up with your attitude?"

Antonella shakes her head and gives a single-shoulder shrug. "I think you know the answer to that question. Perfect nieces don't get married off to the enemy's inquisitor."

"It's for the best." I flick the blade of my knife away and tuck it back into my pants pocket. "Go get cleaned up. I'll meet you in bed. Don't take too long."

My fingers itch to take her out of her undergarments, but some part of me wants to let her have a reason to like me. Though, I don't even know why.

She walks away in four-inch heels and a set of lingerie that could have been custom designed for her form. I squeeze my dick to stop myself from following her. If I follow her, then I'll fuck her in the shower and then need to manufacture consummation proof. Dirty sheets are easier. Showing someone else a video of us fucking is out of the question.

The growing possessiveness over her isn't healthy.

A chill runs down my spine. I know this feeling, this attachment, and when I lost it before, it almost ruined me. Holly wasn't my fated mate, but losing someone I was that close to, that I'd let myself bond with . . . If God takes that from me again, I don't know that I'll survive.

Don't betray me, darling, and I won't fall in love with you.

CHAPTER EIGHTEEN

THE ANTICIPATION

Valor cut my dress off.

Cut, with a knife.

And I feel . . . different about it. Especially since I know the tip of his knife running along my skin wasn't an accident. It could be seen as a threat, but it didn't feel like one.

My heart keeps banging against my ribs, and I'm a little lightheaded.

He knelt before me. Actually knelt before me on his knees to remove my dress. And Valor looking up at me with those deep, soulful hazelly-green eyes? *Kill me now because surely, I won't survive a lifetime of him looking at me with that kind of heat.*

I could have caught on fire from how hot it was to be the object of his desire. The attention warmed my body all over, and I've turned the shower cooler than I normally would to try to subdue the flames.

Physical attraction aside, we were sworn enemies before today. An arranged marriage and desire don't mean he trusts me. I can't let him disarm me. There's still a chance I die before we consummate the marriage. *Maybe I shouldn't shower first.* When we consummate, the truce is fulfilled. Until then, killing me and calling it off is still an option. It's a thought I struggled to avoid all day.

But why would the Cavanaghs have paired me with Valor if they wanted me dead? Why the fuck did they offer out the next leader of the Irish Mafia at all? *Because he's the best for killing me?* I fully expected what I told Leticia to happen. Married off to some underling who wouldn't have a care in the world for me. I could be a wife, teach school, and exist. This is not what I bargained for. Not at all.

The bathroom door opens, and I look for a weapon but know there isn't one to wield. A hotel shower isn't the most common place to find a weapon stash. But it's just Valor. As he leans against the counter, his demeanor is more approachable, with his red-brown hair mussed like he's clearly been running his fingers through it and an unbuttoned dress shirt.

"You can join if you want," I offer. The hotel shower is large enough for two.

Besides, if everything goes 'well,' he'll be inside me soon. *Fuck.* It feels so new. Not feels. Is. It is so new.

I thought I saw a bulge in his pants, but black slacks aren't ideal for dick ogling. The longer he doesn't say anything, the more tense my body becomes. I'm not a virgin, but none of my past relationships prepared me for Valor. He's intense and intimidating. There's a significant difference that makes me feel out of my depth.

I finish rinsing the suds from my body and the conditioner from my long locks.

When I step out, Valor is holding a towel toward me like a wall between us. *Unexpected.*

I take the offering and wrap it around myself, and then he offers me another one for my hair, taking me by surprise at first, and then the reasoning clicks into place. *Kerrianne.*

Valor is an enigma. He cut my dress off and looks at me like

I'm a sexual object in one minute, and in the next, he's offering out towels. A gentleman. If only he'd talk to me.

"I'm guessing I'll need to cut you for the tradition. I can't expect you to be a virgin." Valor's voice . . .

I spoke too soon. Maybe I don't need him to talk to me. But, sweet baby Jesus, his voice when it's gravelly like this. I guess if he wants to talk and say semi-crude things, then it's mostly acceptable if the words sound fucking hot.

But the response he's looking for isn't one I know how to give him. My sexual history isn't long, but for people with our upbringing, staunch within the Catholic church, I've done a lot of things that are off putting.

Years of aunts' talks in the kitchen come flooding back. *Be desirable. Downplay it. Men like conquests and being first.* The words from my first partner that convinced me to take the plunge hit next. *Some of them don't even think being with another woman counts.* Justifications and instructions swirl in my brain, and I try to get it together enough to form a coherent sentence.

I choose an educated and science-based response. "A stretched or broken hymen isn't something that can det—"

Valor shakes his head. "I'm not judging you, Antonella." His voice and tone say otherwise, but he draws a breath and lets it out slowly, speaking again with a more level tone. "I won't judge you."

"Are you serious? I can't expect you to be a virgin is an incredibly judgmental statement." I fight to not roll my eyes.

"You're radiant." Valor sweeps his gaze over my towel-clad body. Arguably, I look like a drowned rat with my hair stick-straight after a shower. "I can't be the only person who has seen you naked. It's not possible for you to be this beautiful and untouched."

I'm not sure if he's trying to make it better or worse. Valor is great at saying the wrong thing.

He scrubs his hand down his face, and I keep my mouth closed.

Be a good wife. Don't give him a reason to want to be rid of you. Consummate the fucking marriage and solidify the truce. Stay alive. Just. Fucking. Lie. Apparently, I have no desire to do any of those things. I open my mouth to say more, but words don't come out because Valor's hand wraps around behind my neck.

In the span of a heartbeat, his lips press against mine.

I didn't have any expectations of what kissing him would be like. He didn't kiss me at the wedding ceremony. This makes up for it. His lips against mine are soft, but the kiss is firm. When his tongue prods my lips, I open and let him take my mouth.

I've been kissed but not like this. Valor isn't demanding, but he's not complacent as he explores the depth of the kiss. Heat builds between us, and he nips my bottom lip. His fingers clench into my wet hair, but it's not to control me further. Neither hurried nor slow, this kiss reignites the warmth I subdued with my shower.

The cold tile beneath my feet doesn't stop the desire radiating through my body. And when I don't think I can take it anymore, Valor groans against my mouth. "Fuck, darling. Making this easy for me, aren't you?"

"Making what easy?" I whisper against his lips, panting.

I don't remember the last minute, but I'm pretty sure I wasn't breathing.

He laughs and releases my hair but doesn't let me go. "Falling in lust with you."

Valor tugs at the towel I'd wrapped around myself, and I don't resist because what's the difference anyway?

But he doesn't rip it off me and haul me to the bedroom. Instead, he runs the soft cloth over my skin, drying me off. On his way down my stomach, he trails his tongue along the same path his knife took, the space where I'd noticed a tiny red line when washing.

And when he's done, he pulls at the towel I'd wrapped my hair in. "Do you need to do something with this?"

I shake it out and gather it, twisting the strands around each other and in opposite directions until it's in a wrapped rope. I twist it up to the nape of my neck and secure it with a binder I'd pulled out of my hair from the updo. The joys of straight hair and heatless curls . . . Product would have been nice, but one day of mistreating my hair isn't the end of the world.

"Come to bed, darling." Leading me by the hand, he walks backward out of the bathroom.

Valor

CHAPTER NINETEEN

THE TALK

Kissing Antonella was unlike anything I've ever experienced before. I'm thirsty for more, but Antonella is timid. She hesitates to follow with small, unhurried steps as I lead her to the bed.

I stripped off the covers earlier, leaving the sheet to make this easier, but does it look like I'm too eager?

When the backs of my knees bump against the mattress, I sit and spread my legs. Antonella obediently stands between them. Her height has her head slightly above me, the bed here lower than mine at home. I'm practically eye to eye with her beautiful tits, her soft pink nipples demanding my attention. I restrain myself from touching, pinching, exploring and instead take the opportunity to admire her body, bared before me.

There's something enchanting about her. Her soft, smooth skin, slightly pinkened by the warmth of the shower. Freckles dot her body in various places, and the tattoos on her arms are the only ones I can see.

I want this, us, to be about more than checking a box for the sake of the truce. I remember what it was like to be married, but nowhere in this relationship has there been room for it. It's unfair of me to ask for more from her. Especially now.

With each second that ticks by, she becomes less self-assured and confident. There's no getting out of this, but I'd rather it not be something that happens *to her* in this way. Not if it's something we can do together and enjoy. Maybe, if I'm lucky, the little glimpses I got of her submitting are more than a conditioned response. Maybe it's who she is.

"What's wrong?"

Antonella shakes her head and denies the tension in her shoulders, despite the way they're pushed up toward her ears. "It's nothing. Everything is fine. For the record, I'm not a virgin. It's just that it's been non-penetrative, fingers and tongue only."

Alarm bells sound in my mind. I study her face and features.

She diverts her gaze and turns her head away from me.

Submitting again. My wolf tunes in, watching now that I'm on edge once more.

Her refusal to admit sexual partners must be because Antonella is afraid of what I may do or say. My stomach settles, and the murderous thoughts quit fogging up my mind. Clarity takes over as I think about the way she danced around her virginity but isn't completely timid and shy.

Old-fashioned values are staunch in her family.

Men and women, in the biblical sense.

I feel ridiculous that it took me this long to come up with it.

I try to be gentle with my question. "Antonella, you're not a virgin, but you've never been with a man. You're bisexual or . . .?"

Her face pales. She swallows hard, jaw setting tight, and her breaths come ragged and fast.

Acrid fear wafts off her body. *God, a kiss that hot, and it'd be my luck that she's only interested in women.* My palms are sweaty, and my mouth is dry. *We'll find a way to make this work.*

She wants us. My wolf reassures me. *You know it. We've smelled her arousal.*

But that's not how any of this works. We only work if she can tell me more.

I use my thumb and forefinger to turn her face as gently as I can, despite her heavy resistance. "Darling, are you attracted to me?"

"Yes." Antonella rakes her rich brown eyes down my chest, not because she needs to see me to confirm her attraction but because she's unashamedly checking me out.

Apparently, I'm not the only one giving into the lust. The fragrant perfume of arousal that I thought I scented is real. And the smug wolf retreats from me.

Her single word is all the reassurance I need. It goes to my head. *My wife thinks I'm attractive.*

"Then it doesn't matter which box the world puts you in." I bring my hand to the back of her neck and pull her closer. "All that matters is the here and now. Let's stay in this moment."

She climbs onto my lap, and I close my legs, making it easier for her to straddle me. With her thighs spread apart, the warmth of her core presses against me and the scent of desire floats into the air. I relish the weight of her in my lap.

I turn my head and start kissing her from her collarbone to her ear. "I'm not gentle, but I'll try for you. They'll be expecting blood, so we'll see what we need to do when we're done fucking."

She relaxes into my touch as I run my hands up her body, coming to play with her nipples. At first, I manage to play gently, teasing her, but then Antonella moans. She shifts forward into my hands, and I squeeze the little buds. I twist, testing her tolerance.

Antonella gasps, "Valor."

My cock throbs. My name on her lips already a siren's call.

I kiss her neck again, this time up the center column,

143

pushing her head up away from me. Antonella's breaths come fast and irregular. She's stock still on my lap, breathing through whatever's going on in her brain.

I drop one hand to her pussy, finding her wet, and when I pinch her clit, she bucks forward. "Are you fighting it, Antonella? Are you denying yourself pleasure?"

She whimpers, and I'm trying to restrain myself, but my cock is pressing against my zipper. I don't want to wait her out. I want to be buried in her warmth. I'm not falling into lust with her. I'm deep within its grasp, and I haven't even been inside her yet.

I roll her clit between my fingers, pinching it firmly. Antonella's mewls are sexy, and her head tips down again as she squeezes her eyes shut.

A shiver courses through her, shifting her closer, and she sinks lower against me. Abandoning her clit, I slide my fingers to her opening. Her core is warm and her arousal coats my fingers as her breathing becomes shallow.

"Is this all for me?" I tease her, knowing it is.

Her body got wet for me with barely any prompting.

"Yes," she breathes out.

I take that as permission. It might not have been, but it doesn't matter. Not right now because this woman is mine. I want her, I'm married to her, and I'm about to fuck her exactly like I need, and if she's meant to be mine, then she'll love it too.

I roll her onto the bed, and she lies back onto her elbows as I strip the rest of the way out of my dress shirt before undoing my belt.

Antonella has her knees pressed together, and she's openly eye fucking me. Her thighs clench as if trying to relieve her needy little cunt. I may be her first in this area, but it's not intimidating her. No. Her heated gaze and verbal answers are confirmation that she's attracted to me. Antonella needs me.

I pull my belt from my pants and toss it on the bed beside

her. Her eyes follow the movement, but before long, they're back on me, watching as I undo the fly and slide my pants and boxers down my legs. I'm almost painfully hard for her. Upon approach, I grab one of her ankles and extend her leg, pushing it over and opening her before me. She's not completely bare, just shortly trimmed, and I love it.

Antonella is self-conscious and looks away.

"I—" Her tone wobbles.

I kneel between her legs and push her up the bed a bit farther, cutting off whatever she was going to say.

"Such a pretty pussy." I lower myself on the mattress between her thighs.

Antonella

CHAPTER TWENTY

THE CONSUMMATION

He darts his tongue out from between his lips and licks up my inner thigh. His fingers press into my skin as he drags himself up my body and hitches my leg up above his shoulder.

The light tickle of his short, few-days-old beard against my thigh exhilarates me.

I squeeze with my leg, trying to pull him closer.

"What's the hurry, darling?" he murmurs against my skin. "We have all night."

Then he kisses closer to my apex and follows it with a playful nip. I gasp and freeze, and that draws a dark laugh from him. The breath from his exhales taunts my clit.

I expect him to slide his hands up my legs, but he doesn't. Instead, he grazes his teeth against my bare skin. It's so fucking hot watching him as he moves, easily shifting my body to accommodate what I know will be the biggest object that'll have graced the walls of my pussy.

I've experimented with small-sized toys and have come on the fingers of my past partners, but Valor's cock is bigger than all of them. *Intimidated? Completely. And yet . . .*

Never in my wildest dreams did I anticipate someone

JAEGER ROSE

looking at me the way he is right now. Eyelids heavy with lust, chest heaving with ragged breaths, and a flush of warmth along his skin.

Maybe he's right, and what's between us is strictly sexual. If all we ever have is a spark of burning-hot desire, then I'll wring out every ounce of pleasure I can from this man so long as he looks at me like this, and I'll love every minute of it.

"Valor," I beg, wanting to feel his tongue.

Holy hot mother fucking damn. This man will eat me alive.

With the first lap of his tongue, my body relaxes, remembering the ecstasy of this act. He groans against me, and the vibration pulls a shudder from my body.

He slides the bottom of his tongue down my clit, and I buck into him. I don't even remember how long it's been since I've done this.

"So needy," he murmurs. "I love the way you smell, the way you taste, and how you feel in my hands. So sweet."

He drives home his point by thoroughly licking me and running his hands up my body. Wrapping his fingers around my nipple, he squeezes.

The urge to feel how soft his chestnut hair really is has me clutching the sheets to stop myself from lacing my fingers through it.

My need for more is ever growing as Valor relentlessly teases my clit. Pushing, rocking, grinding against his face isn't getting me what I need, only drawing huffy laughter and more teasing.

Flickers of his tongue on my clit have me losing all self-control. I abandon my grip on the sheets and fist my fingers into his hair, pulling him closer.

A groan or growl comes from him, and he nips my clit. Shocked, I let him go.

He lifts his gaze to mine. "Naughty girl." His words are punctuated by the heat in his verdant eyes.

148

My heart flutters. My breathing, already ragged with the thrill of arousal, nearly stutters to a stop.

"Do I need to bind your hands or spank you to get you to behave?"

I swallow hard, unable to answer. *Holy fuck. He's perfect.*

Valor

CHAPTER TWENTY-ONE

THE CONSUMMATION

Being between her legs is glorious. From the way she writhed, resisting her building desire to touch me, it was expected she would break. I want her to break.

If she had any idea of how I want to push her to every breaking point she has, maybe she would fight. Well, more than the adorable attempt to make me eat her further.

I grab my belt from the bed beside her. Antonella doesn't object as I grip her wrists and bind them tight. After restraining her arms, I drag them above her head as I close in on top of her, rendering her helpless against what I'll do to her.

"Leave those there, or I'll punish you with it."

Her eyes go wide, like she's truly afraid, but there's no fear in the air. No, only her natural, sweet smell and the sticky scent of arousal fill the room. She wets her lips and nods.

I lean down and kiss her, exploring her mouth with my tongue, letting her taste herself.

She kisses me back like her life depends on it, rocking her body up against mine.

The intensity between us is undeniable.

I stroke my cock. Not because I'm soft but because I'm already dripping pre-cum and this kiss is testing my patience. I lower myself until my chest presses against hers and line myself up with her entrance. A gentleman would have finger fucked her first. He'd have let her come, but I'm neither gentle nor man. And I need her to bleed for me.

It's painful to slowly inch into Antonella's tight pussy. Her cunt grips me so well that it's hard to take her sweetly. "Fuck, Antonella, do you have any idea how good your cunt is? So tight and wet."

Antonella's stopped breathing, her body rigid. Her eyes are closed, and she's holding perfectly still. The pain in her expression isn't the good kind. It isn't what will lead to her pleasure. I don't revel in making her hurt like this.

I kiss her again and draw myself out of her, already missing her warmth. "Talk to me, darling."

She scrunches her features. "I'm good."

I don't love the way she isn't looking at me, but even if she wants to revoke her consent, it can't happen. We both have reasons to finish this act. I can make this terrible experience up for her later.

"Then I'll take you."

Antonella nods.

Did I misread her?

When I don't move, she opens her eyes. Her pupils have practically taken over her irises.

She likes the bad pain?

I thrust into her fully, sheathing myself inside her. She screams out, her eyes clenched tightly, but it turns into a moan. After a few more deep thrusts, she raises her hips to meet mine.

"Valor." She gasps, and her eyes open. They're pleading and soft. "More."

"You like that?" I kiss her and then murmur against her lips,

"You like me owning your pussy? That's it, isn't it, Antonella? You're so much wetter because I fucked you hard."

"Please," Antonella groans. Her pussy flutters around my cock, the sensation sending a tingle down my spine. "Valor."

"Yes, darling." I kiss her lips again. "I'll use you like the good little wife you are."

I thrust into her and pull almost entirely out before slamming my hips back into her.

Tears well in her eyes, but she's still pushing her hips up to meet mine. Her hands stay mostly above her head, but she's gripping the sheets and yet trying to pull toward me.

"You look so pretty crying for me," I praise between thrusts.

Her eyelids are heavy with lust, so I shift my weight to one elbow and grind into her as I bring my fingers down her body.

With my middle and index fingers, I slide through her sensitive flesh. Tightening them against her clit, I rub in the same rhythm of my hips.

I squeeze a little harder, and her pussy tightens around my cock. She was already so tight, but this is practically strangling. I'm on the edge of my own orgasm trying to outlast her. And finally, with two strokes of my cock and working her clit faster, Antonella's body tightens.

She screams and goes rigid. The only muscles not locked up are the ones pulsing around my cock.

My orgasm hits me hard, and I let it take me from the state of vigilance to letting my guard down. I drive into her one last time and keep myself deep inside her, pushing cum into her cunt.

Antonella gasps and writhes, her body bucking up into me.

She's so fucking perfect.

"Fuck, that's it, darling. Take what you need from me." My balls throb as she milks every last drop from me.

I can't take watching her anymore. I need to taste more, to

feel more. I kiss her frantically until both of us finally slump, relaxing from our releases.

Pulling out of her and leaving the heaven that is her pussy is a disappointment. I'm drunk on the feeling of her, and I already want more.

She turns her head toward me, blinking, her widened pupils more sensitive to the low light coming in from the windows. The post-sex glow painting her skin further ingrains her in my brain.

My wife.

I lick her slick from my fingers, hoping she sees how much I love the way she tastes, and a slight copper taste hits me. *Thank God.*

"Holy shit," Antonella whispers, lifting her still-bound hands from above her head momentarily before putting them back where I left them.

I effortlessly release her from the belt, and when I do, she brings her arms down and rests her hands on her stomach.

"Yeah, okay, dick . . . better than expected," she murmurs. "So much better than expected."

The confession strokes my ego, the pride swelling in my chest. Who wouldn't like to hear their woman loves their dick? *My woman.* It's true, and I know it, but accepting it isn't as daunting as before.

"Should have done that before." She sighs, eyes falling closed.

No. I dislike that. It's better this way. The possessive nature of wolves would have me hunting down her past male partners. It's best that she never had another man before me. I want to tell her that but don't. *Now is not the time to explain being a shifter.*

But as my post-sex high fades, the disgusting reminder of reality sinks in. I scent the air, and the coppery note of blood confirms what I tasted on my fingers. Guilt runs in waves down my spine. *Did I go too hard, or is it the strain of the first fuck?*

Antonella's eyes are still closed.

"I'm sorry, darling. You have to get up." I kiss her nose and then her lips.

She groans, opening her eyes. "Okay. Just a minute, still lightheaded. Too good."

I don't know that I've ever gotten such sweet praise.

CHAPTER TWENTY-TWO

THE SHEETS

Antonella bled enough that I didn't feel like I needed to cut her for further proof. I made certain to use the same sheet to wipe my cum off her, carefully looking for blood.

Guilt that I hurt her comes between waves of exhilaration. The way she looked beneath me and how she liked me to take her have me stiff in my pants, but with every step away from her, those thoughts fade. The stiffness in my back grows as I carry our cum-stained sheets down the hallway, to the private elevator, and then down to the private meeting room.

I remind myself again and again that she's not a virgin. It's that she hadn't done *this* before. I haven't corrupted her. It's a bunch of fabric and bodily fluids.

It sickens me that this is part of the truce. The proof of *it*. Why isn't it enough that I bound her to me before God and in the court of men? I have to show proof that I physically attached myself to her. *Would Antonella and I have even had sex if it wasn't for this?*

That doesn't seem to matter though. No, we might not have, but I dislike sharing her vulnerability with the world. I don't want anyone to know about her body in its most exposed state.

No one should be thinking about her underneath me. The beautiful woman in my bed deserves respect and more than being reduced to cum and blood stains on sheets.

Fuck. I pause outside the conference room. A thick wooden door separates me from the group of men waiting for this delivery. *No, I'm only protective of her because she's mine. I'm only thinking of her this way because she's mine.*

My inner beast decides to chime in. *Wolves protect what's theirs.*

Exactly. It's nothing. I'm in lust with Antonella. It's a normal biological function.

My father and his second, Gregorio D'Medici and his consigliere, and the arbiter will be there to take custody of the sheet.

If the men who had set the terms of the truce weren't already dead, I'd dig them up and kill them again for making me do this. Truce be damned. She shouldn't have to suffer this for their disgusting traditionalistic ideals.

Thankfully, I didn't need to walk through the busy lobby. I'm certain I don't look entirely human, my eyes unmistakably the color of a wolf. It takes me a full minute of focusing on the door's wood-grain pattern to force myself back to the controlled state that is me pretending to be human.

The room is dead silent when I come in. Apparently they gave up pretending to be able to engage in conversation. Unceremoniously, I toss the white fabric down on the conference room table.

My father doesn't give any emotion away as he draws a single shallow breath. My uncle, however, wrinkles his nose at the smell before schooling his features back into a careful mask of indifference. The scents of sex and blood on the sheet are strong. The arbiter nods once. There isn't enough blood that he's triggered by the scent. But a vampire will always know.

The two humans in the room can't seem to smell it, and that

irks me. *How the fuck have we had to compete with them all these years? We should have been able to easily wipe them from the earth.*

Gregorio D'Medici doesn't take the wadded-up fabric as proof. He greedily grabs the mass and pulls it across the table with a scowl.

My father slides back from the table and the mess, shaking his head with the same disgust I'm hiding. It's not that we're prudish. Wolves, as a culture, are open about sex and relationships. And it's obvious, given Kerrianne's resemblance to me, that I've most certainly had sex before. But physically inspecting the sheets is vile. I don't blame Dad for moving away from it.

"Are you fuckin' serious?" I snap in Gregorio D'Medici's direction but then force myself back to being human again. *Get a fuckin' grip.* I look to the arbiter and try again. It still comes with a growl, but the words are more human. "Is this necessary?"

"Call it . . ." Gregorio D'Medici looks at me, and his eyes are wild, like an animal before it attacks. "Morbid curiosity. I wouldn't want you to have a less-than-perfect bride."

The sick fuck cares that his niece was or was not a virgin? I can't believe my ears. *Puritanical fuckin' bullshit. Sex isn't only for reproduction. And sex isn't only dick in . . .* Holly would be proud of me wanting to go Woman's Studies 101 on his ass, but I don't have the crayons or patience to explain this to him.

He straightens the fabric across the table and pulls out a magnifying glass to inspect the blood. There isn't a lot of it there. Antonella bled only slightly. *It should be enough. Blood is blood.*

"How do we know you didn't cut her for this?" Gregorio D'Medici looks to the arbiter.

The arbiter, clearly sick of his shit, glares at him before snidely remarking, "Yes, because obviously, Valor cut Antonella with a knife and then rubbed one out onto the sheets? It seems awfully extreme when the easiest answer is to fuck. They're adults and knew what a marriage would entail." At last, he decrees, "The truce is valid and binding. Violence between the families is strictly prohibited. Breaking the truce is grounds for annihilation at the hand of the arbiters."

I've never heard what would happen if the truce were called. I honestly have no idea what arbiters do beyond the legal definition and, well, be vampires. Their immortality makes them perfect candidates to keep the families' feud's negotiations true to the original intent. The feud began over a century ago, and while I'm not sure why the fighting started, I can name enough grievances in my lifetime to know that us coming together is a big deal. But more so now . . . My curiosity is piqued by them openly mentioning annihilation in front of the — human — D'Medicis, who, as far as I know, are ignorant about things that go bump in the night . . . But maybe the D'Medicis assume it's a figure of speech. Or, have I misjudged, and they've known we're wolves this whole time?

I don't ask, not here and now, because standing here in this room with the disgusting pig, Gregorio D'Medici, is a ninth circle of hell I had no intention of ever visiting.

Dad stands and walks toward me. Neil follows him, and when they pass me, I turn to follow Neil. We head straight out the hotel entrance and step to the side, waiting for the valet to bring his SUV around.

"Valor." My father gives in to the stifled grin.

It's the same attempt at a disciplining smile when Kerrianne misbehaves. He can't handle being the disciplinarian for his children or grandchild, especially when he's amused by what's happened.

The man is a seasoned alpha, all but convicted murderer, and made my childhood a living hell, but that grin makes me wonder how the pieces of him can seamlessly fit together.

God grant me the patience. We lock eyes.

He pulls me in for a hug and claps me on the back. "I told you so."

Our conversation from this morning, almost twelve hours ago, has been in the back of my brain, taunting me. *You will like her.*

I hug him back as his SUV pulls up and wait for him to get inside.

But Dad reaches in and turns back to me with shopping bags. "Your mother thought that perhaps wedding clothes wouldn't be fun to come home in tomorrow."

Keeping her naked in bed forever? Not a problem. My wolf supplies his ideal outcome.

With a single head bob, I accept because I sure as fuck hadn't thought of that when I cut her dress from her body. Though, the wolf has a point. "Thank you."

I stand at attention as they climb into the SUV and then until it leaves the parking lot.

Antonella is mine. She'll make a good wife. We're compatible. I can stomach those things about her. I turn back to the hotel and keep my thoughts on her, absently navigating back up to our room. *She may be mine and we may be good together, but that doesn't mean I can trust her.*

Antonella

CHAPTER TWENTY-THREE

FOUR CHEESEBURGERS

"Hey," Valor says from the bedroom doorway of our hotel suite.

The disheveled look suits him.

I toss the last pillow up toward the headboard and finish remaking the bed after having grabbed spare sheets from a closet in the suite.

The rigid Valor of this morning has faded to something softer. He's not without edges but more relaxed. I guess that's what an orgasm does to most people.

"I was thinking." He doesn't approach me. Instead, he leans against the doorframe, crossing his muscular arms over his chest.

That's a dangerous thing. I keep my comment to myself and wait patiently. It's not like I could go anywhere. He's blocking the only entrance to the room.

"Let's get out of here. This feels . . . shameful." He gestures to the bed, his top lip curling and eyes hard. "We shouldn't be forced into this. It's done. It's over. But I don't want to stay here, in this space, under the weight of the situation anymore."

Shameful? Situation? His words are pointed and sharp, and I can't tell if he's angry with the circumstances or something

JAEGER ROSE

else . . . like me. The sharp juxtaposition of Valor makes my chest throb.

When he left, he was visibly frustrated, but I attributed it to the garish act of having to provide proof. He was tender and kind toward me, like he had been since I got out of the shower. Albeit a little awkward, but he was still tender. There's nothing I can do but ride it out.

"Sure." I shrug, trying to be accommodating. But I gesture to the hotel robe I'm wearing. "You wouldn't happen to have clothes for me?"

Valor nods and disappears into the living area of the suite. He returns a few moments later with a shopping bag from a boutique store and hands it to me. "This should all be close to your size."

I'm quick to accept the bag and take it to the bathroom to change. The skirt, blouse, and sweater are my size. It's a put-together outfit, and while they're not things I would normally pick for myself, they are beautiful. *Is this what Valor wants his woman to wear?* I could absolutely work more of this into my wardrobe. *No. Nope. I don't dress for men. Especially if they want me to.* But I pet the sweater again, and my resolve crumbles a little bit . . . *Even if they do have good taste.*

With the fresh clothes on, I take a little bit of extra time to blow out some of my hair. I try to keep the heatless curls fluffy, but I know without any hair product, they'll fall flat and be gone before bed, but at least it's something for now.

When I exit the bathroom, Valor is in dark-wash jeans and a gray T-shirt. They're practically molded to his skin. *Is there anything he doesn't look sexy in?*

Shoes are set out for me next to the bed with a small handbag beside them. The small clutch I left in Valor's SUV will likely fit in it.

"Ready to go?" Valor checks his watch, the door, me, and his watch again.

164

"Jesus, rush much?" The utterance comes out unchecked and unfiltered, and regret sinks in almost immediately.

"Sorry." Valor's apology holds sincerity. "I fuckin' hate that we had to do this, like this, and I could really do with like four cheeseburgers and a stack of wings right about now. It's not my intention to be a complete asshole to my wife."

My wife. My whole body shudders, and I try to force it down. But no matter how hot he is, I can't keep doing this back-and-forth.

"I don't know where I stand with you." I put the words out while slipping on the new shoes. They pinch a bit, but I ignore it.

Valor tilts his head and seemingly looks me over like I've said something incredibly complex. "Oh?"

"I'm serious, Valor." I sigh and scrub my hand down my face, glad it's free of makeup so I can be as tactile as I like. "What is it? How will this work? I can't imagine this was how you saw your life going. It isn't how I envisioned my own."

But that last bit is a lie. I knew this would be my fate. I assumed it would be to someone less . . . *What exactly? Attractive? Complicated? Powerful?*

Valor stalks forward. The pumps I'm wearing give me a slight edge, but I miss the four-inch heels that brought me closer in height to his over-six-foot frame. I'm not short at five-and-a-half feet tall, but Valor doesn't hesitate to use that difference to his advantage. We're chest to chest when he slides his hand up my arm, across my shoulder, up my neck, and into my hair. The way he interlaces his fingers into my hair is soft and intimate, a contrast to the stern look in his eye.

"I like the fire, princess." His voice rumbles low. "I like that you feel comfortable enough to show me this spark. My people appreciate women who stand their ground. But I'm still your husband, and that spark is fine as a spark." He narrows his eyes as if to emphasize his point.

I'm blaming the wetness in my panties on the way he fucked me. It'd be a lie. But I'm crediting the sex we've already had for the pull he has on my body. I lower my eyelids, unable to look away but giving him the respect of not looking at him.

"Now." He dials back the intensity, and I can practically feel the change in the air as the dark, deadly side of Valor gives way. "I thought we'd go out, get some food —"

"Four cheeseburgers and a stack of wings." I parrot back what he said earlier despite having been scolded for being bold.

"That and whatever you want to eat." He pulls my hair gently, and I look up at him in response. There's that sultry smile. "We'll get to know each other and together come up with a plan of what the fuck we're doing while being married."

"Okay."

It goes against my norm to let a man take control. But different, letting the experience happen, isn't wrong. It's survival.

Valor unthreads his fingers from my hair and gently runs them through the long strands, never getting them caught up or tugging too hard on a tangle.

I expected a driver and car waiting for us out front, but Valor fished keys out of his pocket and unlocked a black SUV parked in the hotel's underground garage.

Like a gentleman, he opens my door for me and helps me up and inside before closing the door.

A glance over my shoulder tells me this must be his personal vehicle. A car kit featuring children's essentials sits on the back seat, and a little trash can on the floor has a cereal bar wrapper in it.

Valor climbs in and notices me eyeing the back seat. "She's a good kid but turns into a feral little beast if you don't feed her

166

regularly, and God help me, she went through that phase where they only eat like four things."

"Then a giant growth spurt?" I offer, trying to keep him in this good mood.

"Yes, thankfully she still likes dresses because finding pants and shorts to fit her long legs is a nightmare." Valor starts the SUV, and the radio lights up to a satellite kids' station. He's quick to turn the sound off and moves the vehicle into gear. "Do you eat cheeseburgers and wings? Or would something else be better?"

"Depends. Does your favorite cheeseburger and wings place serve beer and mixed drinks?" I don't care if that makes me sound like a bad influence on his child. This day has been stressful enough that I deserve a drink.

"It wouldn't be my favorite place if they didn't." Valor sighs and settles into his seat. "After dealing with your uncle, I believe we both deserve a couple of cold ones."

"A-fuckin'-men."

I feel safe with Valor behind the wheel. He's not aggressive or erratic like Berto nor does he sit hunched over the steering wheel, gripping it like his life depends on it, driving like he's afraid of the gas pedal, like Gregorio.

But perhaps most notable is that no one has tried to get ahold of him. I can tell his phone is in the vehicle because it automatically connected to the screen, but no message notifications or calls come through.

Is it because of the respect people have for him or something else that no one is contacting him? Maybe they expected us to still be fucking?

Valor

CHAPTER TWENTY-FOUR

AND A STACK OF WINGS

Antonella and I aren't completely uncomfortable and awkward together. But the drive from the hotel to the restaurant is more silent than I'd like.

We're back and forth with random, meaningless nonsense as Midwesterners do — the weather, the changing colors of the leaves, and how neither of us cares for sports. But we can't find a groove. Instead, we're stuck somewhere between overly familiar and perfect strangers, which is exactly what we are. We've fucked, but unlike a one-night stand that I can send on her way, Antonella is mine. *Mine.*

My wolf thumps his tail in agreement.

I refuse to be miserable for the rest of my life. I'm not living with awkward trips out into public. I've got to fix this. Figure out how to make this a working relationship. If I can negotiate with a massive language barrier in place, crack some of the top mercenaries in the business, I can certainly handle Antonella D'Medici.

When we reach the bar and grill, I back the SUV into a space so we're facing the door. I ask mostly politely, "Wait for me?"

Antonella nods, and I climb out and walk around to her door

while casually glancing at our surroundings. We're deep in the middle of Cavanagh pack territory, and the chances of anyone bringing any sort of trouble here are slim, but odds are never zero. Being aware of your surroundings is free.

I open her door and offer her my hand. Antonella takes it, and once she's clear of the closing car door, I drop her hand and walk backward away from her.

I try for playful rather than intimidating as I explain myself. "I was thinking we could make this like a date."

"Like a date?" she asks, raising an eyebrow.

The suspicious side-eyed look is cute as fuck.

"Why not?" I shrug, taking another step away from her. "We're already married, we can't date too?"

I want to hold out my hand, to walk hand and hand with her to the restaurant even though the parking lot is small. But I don't because I'm a coward, afraid to be rejected by the woman I've married, fucked, and met this morning. Not in that order, but why would I put myself up for rejection?

"So, you're taking me to a burger joint for our first date?" She looks up at the sign above the door with an overexaggerated squint.

"And wings," I add, pointing to that part of the sign before holding the door open for her.

I like this easy banter. The sassiness from her. I wasn't lying when I told her I like her spark.

"This place is a favorite," I say as she walks through the door.

Other women, especially those who come from a lifestyle with money, would, without a doubt, feel some sort of way about me taking them to a burger joint, but Antonella's disgust is fake and all in jest.

She's smiling and her shoulders are relaxed. Composed-and-calm Antonella seems to be fading away, and I'm seeing more of the woman underneath. The woman who isn't there for display purposes only.

Usual friendly service sees us seated in a booth in a quieter portion of the restaurant, and with drink orders taken and delivered, silence settles between us.

I try to come up with something that won't sound like an interrogation, but 'tell me about yourself' is such a basic conversation starter. *This isn't an interrogation. Get to know* her, *not what she knows.* But the longer I sit with that, the answer is obviously to do both.

"What's something that's always been on your bucket list that's easy to do, or visit or whichever, but you haven't done?" Antonella asks, breaking the awkwardness before I can.

It's unexpected, and I find myself stuck with the question. My mind goes a little blank at the thought, and despite knowing that not having an answer is generally not what people want to hear from a leader, I tell her the truth. "I'm not sure . . . I have anything."

"What?" Antonella scrunches her face, giving me a slightly disapproving look. "Everyone has a bucket list. Something you want to do or see before you die. It can be as silly as, like, wanting to swim with sharks."

I shake my head but wobble my hand. "No? I guess. I have goals but not set things I'd like to do."

"Such as?" Antonella presses.

"I'd like to go a full year without being shot at." I can't help but smile. "Though, maybe . . . my luck has changed, and the next year will be the one."

Antonella, who had been taking a sip, almost spits it out in a laugh. "Oh, good God. Can you imagine life without always looking over your shoulder? I was close in grad school, but . . . well . . . men."

I hum my agreement. While it's not the same, even if I'm not getting shot at, I know there are plenty of enemies looking to take the pack down. And it's possible, even within the pack, that someone is looking to unseat the Cavanaghs from the alpha position. My birthright is not a guarantee. A challenge could come.

"What got you into teaching?" I ease myself into the dozens of questions I want to ask her.

Be friendly, take an interest not an interrogation. When did my job become an interference in interacting with people like a regular person?

"I've always loved kids." Antonella's smile comes back. "I guess it comes from having a big family. Teaching was something I thought I'd be good at. College was the only way I was getting some separation from the life that was expected of me. I knew I'd never fully get away from it, but it was something I could do for me. It's why, uhm, I kept things so —"

She struggles for a word, and her cheeks flush. I can't smell her arousal over the other scents in the restaurant, but I assume it's there.

I offer her an out. "Platonic?"

"Divinely feminine." Antonella corrects me. "Bringing someone home would never have been acceptable. Gregorio kept bouncing around having a plan for me. It was easier not to argue with him. And it was easier to hide something going on between me and someone I could pretend was a gal pal, not a girlfriend."

I hold back my next question and try to come up with something relatable to what she shared, but we have nothing in common in that regard. Until today, there had been options, and had I found my mate, I could have been with her, no problems. Sure, I had an expectation that it may be arranged if the time came, but my parents wouldn't have denied me someone if I truly wanted them.

I've also never had to hide who I was from the people who care for me. It seems that maybe Antonella and I have very similar thoughts toward Gregorio D'Medici if I read between those lines.

"What about you? Did younger Valor ever think about leaving the chaos and never looking back?" She prompts, chaos clearly code for criminal lifestyle.

"I never wanted to escape my destiny. I knew from an early age I was the next head of the family. I've wanted it for a long time. Maybe it's too 1950s of me, but I always knew what my life would look like, and I liked what I saw. Maybe that's more an answer to your bucket question. Life with a ma — nsion, a kid . . . and a wife."

I nearly blow that sentence, and I can't believe it. Normally I'm better about keeping my guard up when talking to humans. Antonella will learn soon enough that we're not the same. But a restaurant is not the place to tell her that wolf shifters exist. It's hardly even a place to have the 'mate' sort of conversation.

"I suppose that's probably a good thing." Antonella gives a resounding sigh. "It'll be interesting to learn your expectations of me."

I take a sip of my beer before extending an olive branch. "If you want to teach, there's no reason you can't continue to."

Antonella quirks a brow, and her lips part a fraction. It's not intended to be sexual, but I'm stuck somewhere on the spectrum between interrogating and fucking. On one end, I want to know everything about her, from what makes her tick and what she knows about the D'Medici empire. I want to grill her for information and see how long before she cracks. On the other hand, I want to bend her over the nearest surface, make her scream my name, and then watch my cock disappear between those slightly parted lips.

"I would really like to keep teaching," Antonella softly says.

The restaurant isn't the place to have this sort of conversation, but it's also not the place to bend her over and fuck her. It's been a long time since I've been attracted to someone like this, and leaving the hotel room is quickly becoming the worst mistake I've made today. It's probably just the year-long, self-imposed dry spell making it all that much harder to keep my thoughts tame. The dry spell I implemented after some serious guilt over spending time with hookups instead of Kerrianne.

Yeah, we'll go with that, my wolf huffs.

I force myself out of the fantasy of fucking her mouth and let the burning questions bubble to the surface, disguising them as polite conversation rather than demands. "I'm interested to know how you were the one to come to Kerrianne's aid. I'm equal parts grateful and, as I'm sure you can understand, suspicious of the circumstances. Are you a teacher in a neighboring class?"

"Sooo . . ." Antonella runs her fingers through her hair and then sighs. "Funny story about that. I had no idea Kerrianne was a student at the school. I wouldn't have taken the job had I known she went there, Valor. But I had a . . . well . . ." Antonella backtracks. "How friendly are you with Peyton Hopkins?"

I shake my head, thinking about the exchange in the principal's office.

Antonella draws one long breath before a massive string of words. "Well, depending on who is telling the story, I told her that her son was stupid and she was ugly, and then she pulled her kid out of my classroom and almost pulled out her funding for the school. So, I was slapped on the wrist and they transferred Kerrianne into my classroom."

I'm dumbfounded. I'm stuck in neutral. I don't even know how to shift gears.

Ms. Mancini.

Antonella huffs, expelling the last bit of air from her lungs before sipping her beer.

She's telling the truth. I can hear the honesty, but I dislike the answer. I take a long pull of my beer, trying to stave off the irrational, angry, overprotective parent in favor of the logical, levelheaded nature expected of me.

"I know that has to be hard to believe." Antonella rises to her own defense as if she hears my innermost thoughts. "But I wouldn't have put us in this potential position. The school is in neutral territory, so I assumed it would be safe to accept the job. I teach under a pseudonym because well . . . everyone knows the D'Medici's and what they do. It's hard to get work that way."

She's telling the truth. My wolf has been as equally interested in her as I have.

Why didn't this come up in the background check Royal ran? Is her cover identity that good? I hate that I have more questions than answers.

What I do know though . . . "I believe you."

I'm thankful for her saving Kerrianne, even if it's put me in a shit position. I still want vengeance for Holly, but Antonella has put an end to my vendetta. "It's been a lot to process. I was out of the country, and to come home to this . . ."

"Mess." Tears well in the corner of her eyes. "Thank you for saving my life."

Saving her life. She's thanking me for saving her life? It was either save her life or risk Kerrianne's. She must know that, but it seems like the wrong thing to say right now. I only nod in response.

I finish my beer at the same time the waitress comes back with our main courses, and she offers to get me a new one. I look to Antonella, and she asks for a second.

With a nod of agreement, I tell the waitress, "Looks like we're having another round."

Antonella smiles and wags a finger at me. "Don't get any ideas that I'm some sort of big drinker. I've had probably the worst week of my life, and I want to enjoy the good things when they happen."

I lean forward. "Am I the good thing?"

Her tongue peeks out of her mouth, wetting her lip before she bites it. My cock stiffens in response, but before Antonella can give me an answer, the waitress returns with our second round.

Antonella takes the out of the waitress coming by and bites into her burger. She hums in approval. "Oh, this is really good."

"I'm telling you, they have the best burgers in the area." I pick up my burger and take a bite.

As expected, it's cooked to the bare minimum, meaning it touched the grill long enough to sear the outside and not let any humans think the restaurant is serving raw food. It's a perk of being a regular and recognized by the server. Do I need the burger raw? No. Do I like it raw? Yes.

"And wings." Antonella runs the joke another time, the basket of wings on the table untouched.

"I'm a burger first, then wings and fries intermixed kinda guy." I shrug. "Setting a good example for Kerrianne. She's a typical kid and wants the best part first and then fills up before she can eat the protein and veggies."

"Yeah, it's so hard because at that age, they're so particular about food, and it can be hard to help them establish good habits while not —" Antonella cuts herself off. "I'm rambling. You don't need me to tell you how to parent your daughter."

"You're right."

As soon as I say it, I know how it sounds. But it doesn't make it less true. I don't need someone else, especially a human, telling me how to parent my daughter. And yet, she knew exactly how to handle this morning with Kerrianne at Sean's funeral.

Antonella looks away from me, focusing on her dinner, and I do the same.

There's so much more I could learn about her. Namely how she could pull a weapon on her own family member . . . for Kerrianne. She's not loyal enough to her family that she'd let them take an 'easy' target from our side of the chessboard.

Because she's not a loyal person in general or because she's not loyal to them for some reason?

We're both narrowing down on our food, and the waitress stops by to ask how we're doing.

"Excellent, thank you," Antonella answers as if we haven't eaten in silence.

Antonella dips her fry in the blue cheese dressing that came with the wings and stalls before putting it in her mouth. She looks up at me, and our eyes lock.

She draws a deep breath and sighs, shaking her head. "For one night, let's pretend we're not Valor Cavanagh and Antonella D'Medici? We're Valor and Toni. Two people on their first date and hanging out? We've got a lifetime to unpack the feud between our families, but I don't think either of us wants to be in a long-term relationship with someone we don't even know."

"Committed," I add.

She furrows her brow but knowingly adds it in. "Long-term, committed relationship with someone we don't even know."

"One thing to know." I smile at her, attempting to do exactly as she asked by letting go of what stands between us in order to be two people — strangers — trying to find love. "I don't share. I'm the oldest sibling, and I'm not a fan of sharing."

"As an only child, I completely understand." Antonella smiles back.

I gesture to the wings, offering her first pick. We ordered a flight sampler of five flavors, four of each. She starts with a medium spicy one.

"What's your red flag?" Antonella asks. She quickly adds, "And no, it can't be that you're a single dad."

She puts the whole wing into her mouth and pulls the bones out clean.

Fuck me, that's . . .

I clear my throat, willing my dick to calm down. "Uh, can it be that I found that so hot I want to take you home right now, throw you down on my bed, and fuck you until I know what it's like for you to scream, whisper, and moan my name?"

Antonella drops the bones on the plate, and her whole body stiffens. She chews, swallows, and then, in a tone low enough that I think it was meant to be an inside thought, mutters, "Is he trying to kill me talking like that?"

I whisper back, "My real red flag is that I'm a control freak when it comes to my relationships. I will dominate you if given the chance. I don't want a meek woman. I need someone willing to put my ass in check and who isn't afraid to tell me when I'm being a dick."

The sly smile she passes me precedes her sultry words. "Well, aren't you lucky. Because my red flag is that I have both a problem with authority and like it when my partner puts me in my place. I don't need to be saved, Valor." Her pupils are wide, and that 'look' is in her eyes. "But that doesn't mean I'm disinterested in seeing how far we could take this."

My resolve is gone. The original intention was to leave this as a 'get to know you' and maybe 'figure out if we have any interests in common' dinner. But I can't. Not when she's saying things like that.

I reach into my pocket, pull out two one-hundred-dollar bills, and throw them on the table. Standing, I hold my hand out to Antonella.

She glares at me and then the wings. "Rude. These are delicious."

"This restaurant isn't going anywhere, and the wings never change." I narrow my gaze at her and curl my fingers in encouragement before relaxing my hand again, beckoning her to comply. "Come, Antonella."

Antonella takes one last sip of her beer and then places her hand in mine.

On the way out of the restaurant, I give the manager a two-finger wave and don't bother with anything else. I've got

Antonella tucked into the passenger seat and the SUV on the road in less than a minute.

I try and fail to keep my hands to myself on the drive. I let my hand leave the steering wheel and find its way to her leg. But the fabric of her skirt is in the way.

Antonella rests her hand on mine. "Just drive. It's not like we don't have all night."

All. Night. I relax at that. I want to enjoy every inch of her, but we do have all night. *What's a little more lost sleep when I can be taking her?*

She watches out her window, and I continue the usual route home. The thirty-minute drive passes slowly. And when we're ten minutes from the house, I hear the change in her breathing.

Her head is leaned against the headrest, tilted to support itself on the seat belt, and her eyes are closed. Antonella is out like a light.

Sleepy mate, my wolf observes. *Much like the pup, she drifted right out.* His tail thumps, and a warming feeling of affection prickles along my skin. *We'll sleep beside her at home.*

His assumptions don't normally bother me, but it's not like she's a wolf. It's not like we know she's ours. *What if I don't want her in my bed?*

Don't be stupid. Your bed is good enough to fuck her in but not good enough to let her sleep in? My wolf's words make me pause.

You're really claiming her as our mate? After we had Holly? I feel my pulse beating in my head. He's been possessive of her all day, but she's a woman we were gifted. I've always taken care of and protected my things. Antonella is another object to possess.

Holly was good, but she wasn't like Antonella. If you'd look, then you'd see that. My wolf is hyperfixated on her, and it has me sitting at a stop sign at an empty crossroad.

The turn signal clicks with the passing seconds, and I let them tick by, examining the raven-haired beauty beside me. There's no doubt about it — she's beautiful. Round, high cheekbones and the angular, yet feminine, shape of her face, with that adorable button nose, are all attractive and beautiful together. But beauty does not make for a mate.

She's the enemy. I try to argue, thinking of the people we've lost, the friends and family no longer at the dinner table, the dwindling numbers of our pack, and Holly.

I tear my eyes away from her and make the left-hand turn toward our home. *She's a D'Medici. She'll sleep in my bed because it's the easiest way for me to be sure she's not wandering into something that's not for her to know.*

My wolf doesn't argue with me. I sense his annoyance, but I conceded to his demand that she sleep in our bed.

But . . . It's not a difficult concession to make. Even if I don't want to want her . . . Antonella is appealing, and I've already admitted it. I've fallen into lust with her. There is no reason this can't be a physical relationship.

Valor

CHAPTER TWENTY-FIVE

THE MORNING AFTER

My phone buzzes on the nightstand, and I roll over to ignore it. Then I'm enveloped in Antonella's sweet, fruity scent. *Mmmm. I could do with more of that.*

I drag her to me, thoughts of sleepy sex rolling through my mind, and then my phone begins to ring again. *What could possibly be so urge —* Kerrianne. I bolt upright and turn toward the nightstand, pulling my phone off the charging cord.

Guilt turns in my stomach and floods throughout my body as I answer. "Hello?"

My heart hammers in my chest. *How the fuck did I forget she wasn't home with me?* Yesterday's memories are far more vivid now.

"Good morning, sweet boy." My mother is singsongy and cheery, and my tension eases.

My shoulders fall, and I pull the phone away from my ear to steal a glance at the time. *Nine? It's fucking nine?* I scrub my hand down my face but can't think of the last time I slept this late. "Good morning."

"Your father told me that you're home today. Odd, I thought the hotel for a few days would be a better adjustment period but . . . nonetheless. Kerrianne needs to come home for at least a little bit today because Dad and Royal are doing something loud. We don't want to hurt her sensitive ears. You know how it is at that age."

Meaning, Royal and Dad have work to do, and Kerrianne would want nothing more than to be helpful, but whatever they're working on isn't age appropriate. Mom would normally come here under the guise of playing with Captain, but I'm here with Antonella.

Fuck. Shit. Damn.

"I thought I'd give you a call and let you know we'll be there in about an hour or so." Mom keeps chatting as if my silent panic isn't a problem for her. "You know, Kerrianne is so excited to go back to school."

"I'm sure. We'll get it sorted. I'll be ready to take the package in an hour, but ninety minutes would be much better for me." I look over at Antonella.

She's awake, eyes still heavy with sleep and her gorgeous brown hair draped across the pillow.

"Sure, I think maybe we'll take a trip to the market on the way there. That'll give us some extra girl time. We'll pick up some treats for Captain." My mother hums. "Well, I'll let you go, then."

"I'll see you in ninety minutes." I fight the groan out of my voice and hang up before flopping back down next to Antonella. *That gives us plenty of time for one more round since she fell asleep on the way home last night.*

When I drag her into my arms, she releases a soft, breathy moan. I kiss her deeply.

But she pushes me away. "Ew, I have morning breath."

I kiss the tip of her nose instead. "It doesn't bother me. In lust, remember?"

"Yes, lust. Got it." Antonella puffs out her cheeks. "But I'm pretty sure that was your mother calling and the package is Kerrianne."

Perceptive. I nod, my forehead pressed against hers. "Yes. But that doesn't mean we don't have time for ourselves for a bit first."

"Mmmm." Antonella's coy smile is a knowing one. She's already lying as close to me as possible, so I know she can feel my length pressed up against her. "Is that so?"

"I know so."

I nudge her head and inch closer, bringing my lips to her skin and kissing down her neck. Kissing past the point where someday, soon, I'll bite her and mark her as mine. The possibility of it makes my cock throb.

I've known her barely twenty-four hours, but I'm already attached. I'm thinking about marking her, keeping her . . . Acknowledging that hurts because, at the end of the day, I know very little about her. And truce or not, the unknown can get you killed.

I push myself back from Antonella, my thoughts sobering me. "No, you're right. We should get up."

My cock is quick to take the hint with the change in my mood. I climb out of bed, headed toward the bathroom to shower and get dressed. Antonella may be my wife, but it doesn't make her good for Kerrianne. I shouldn't have brought her home so soon. I should have dated her. Given her an apartment in the city and around-the-clock guards. We could have taken it slow and introduced the idea to Kerrianne at a more reasonable pace. *What was I thinking?*

But I know what I was thinking. I was thinking of the drop-dead gorgeous woman thrust into my life, into my bed, and how good it would be to not be lonely. Not in that way.

The solid sleep from the time we got home until my phone rang . . . I don't remember the last time I slept without waking at least once during the night.

I've gone through all the motions — starting the shower to warm it up, brushing my teeth, taking a piss, and then stepping into the spray. The water wakes me up and drags me into the present.

There's a knock on my bathroom door before Antonella steps in, her figure obscured by the fogged-up glass.

"Valor, is there another bathroom you want me to use?" Antonella is quiet, soft spoken. She's the softer, reserved woman from during the funerals again.

Why would she ask that? I wipe the steam off the glass and look at her hovering near the open door. "Is there a problem with this one?"

She shakes her head. "I noticed that you seem tense with Kerrianne being on her way home. Maybe the distance between us isn't a bad thing."

"Come in here." I try not to demand, but I can't talk to her when she's so far away.

I can hear her just fine, but she might not be able to hear me between the running water and the wall of glass.

Antonella heads to the toilet first, gracefully covering herself while she does her business. I turn away from her, giving her a bit of privacy since humans expect it. I take the opportunity to quickly wash my hair, and about the time I'm ready to wash my body, the shower door opens, and she steps in. Expectantly, Antonella stands naked before me, and my dick twitches because how could it fucking not with a stunning woman bare before me.

She pulled her rumpled hair over one shoulder and crosses her arms in front of her gorgeous tits. I want to rip them down so I can savor the view.

"Valor." She scolds, a bit of the fire I like coming back.

"Yes, I'm hesitant about Kerrianne coming home," I admit and offer her my hand, inviting her closer. "I don't know you or how Kerrianne will handle this. You're not her mother."

Antonella declines my hand and remains where she is. "I'm not trying to be Kerrianne's mother. That's the furthest thing from my mind."

It's what I wanted to hear, the reassurance that Antonella knows her place, but the fact that I feel satisfied with her answer frustrates me. *Fuck, I'm an asshole.*

"Before you get to be this overprotective, domineering father, just hear me out." Antonella is firm. She tilts her head slightly before squaring back up. "I'm not trying to be anything more than your new wife. It's my duty to you. Last night was . . . I had a great time getting to know you, Valor. However, that doesn't change our reality. We're practically strangers."

"Arguably, strangers don't know how the other tastes when they're aroused."

I regret those words instantly despite how true they may be. Apparently I'm really leaning into being an asshole.

"Regardless." Antonella dismisses me without so much as a rueful glance. "This doesn't have to be a big change in your lives. If you don't want to tell Kerrianne we're married, you don't have to. I can simply be a —"

"Absolutely not," I snap and then shake my head. My shoulders tighten. "I don't lie to her any more than I have to. I'm not telling her the woman sleeping in my bed means nothing beyond a roommate. But you're not her mother."

"Fair enough. Then we tell Kerrianne exactly that." She solidifies her statement with a firm nod. "We tell Kerrianne the truth. I'm here as your new wife. It's new and unexpected. But that doesn't change the fact I'm her teacher, you're her father, and the same rules apply."

The backbone she shows me, not backing down with my aggression toward her, has me fully hard.

"No, there isn't another bathroom you should be using." I circle back to the question that started this all. "You're my wife. You sleep in my bed. You use the en suite bathroom. There's plenty of space for your stuff in the closet. I'll take care of you now that you're mine."

Antonella leans backward in shock.

I hadn't meant to say that out loud. She is mine, but saying it that way isn't 'normal,' and I'm sure there was a better phrase.

But she is mine. She is my wife. She's —

I cut that thought off and resolve to keep the facts in place. *She's my wife.*

Antonella

CHAPTER TWENTY-SIX

THAT AWKWARD MOMENT

Valor finishes rinsing off and steps out, leaving me alone in the warm, steam-filled, luxury shower to get clean. Yesterday, it was easy to overlook the lack of clothes, phone, and personal belongings in general. Gregorio refused to let me take my phone because, until the marriage was consummated, he didn't want them to possibly get information they shouldn't have. The clothing and toiletries were one of his bullshit excuses that I didn't want to waste energy arguing about.

But my selection of bath products is limited to his. *Shampoo is shampoo.*

I sigh and begin washing my hair. By the time I'm washing my body, my brain has taken over processing, trying to figure out the back-and-forth Valor brings and the way he takes command of my body.

Oh fuck.

Earth-shattering dread hits me, and I drop the washcloth. It splats as it hits the floor, and I crouch to pick it up.

I'm still stuck in my head as I finish showering, moving on autopilot despite the new surroundings. A warm towel is waiting for me when I step out of the shower.

Valor and I didn't use a condom.

I came off birth control three months ago because the ring was the only one that controlled my symptoms, but it needs to be stored in the refrigerator. I hid the small foil packages behind the condiments in the far back while I waited for the tiny fridge I ordered for my bedroom to be delivered. But foolishly I picked the slower shipping option.

It wasn't even four hours before Francesca started stress cleaning out the refrigerator and found the supposed evidence of my deviance. She showed Gregorio, and the meeting with the priest was scheduled for after dinner — about how I shouldn't be hindering the natural order of things or having premarital sex. I can still hear Berto snickering like he doesn't have condoms stashed in his room.

Fuck I'll never pick slow shipping on anything ever again. It's not like I couldn't afford it. I didn't want the delivery guys rushing.

Tears well up in my eyes, and I brush them away, but not before I see Valor standing against the bathroom counter.

"What's wrong?" He, of course, doesn't ignore it.

"Uhm." I chew on my bottom lip. I can feel tension between us, but it isn't expected. I wait for it to implode. "We didn't use a condom, and I'm not on birth control."

"Not an issue." Valor is quick to answer.

Got it. I nod, not voicing the screaming thoughts in my brain. *I'll be pregnant before the school year ends. It's okay. I've thought about kids. I'll be happy when it happens.* Gaslighting myself isn't exactly working, but I try to calm myself down with it.

"It's not an issue" — Valor cuts into my inner self-loathing — "because you can't get pregnant with my kid."

"What?" I narrow my eyes at him.

Please say this isn't some sort of education system flaw where I have to have 'the talk' with him. He had Kerrianne, for fuck's sake. He should know how pregnancy works.

He pauses as if trying to figure out how to say the words. "It's physically impossible for me to get you pregnant."

"Okay." The words 'I had a vasectomy' would be more reassuring. "And that's because . . .?"

Valor shrugs. "For all intents and purposes, at this time, I'm sterile."

I don't love the way he said that, but vasectomies are reversible, and maybe it hurts his manhood too much to say the words. I nod and let it go. The panic is still there, but I'm confident with reading between the lines.

"What else is on your mind?" Valor asks, stepping closer to me.

I dislike being naked, or only wearing a towel, when he's still clothed. It's becoming a trend, and I'm feeling more vulnerable.

"I would love if you could show me what is acceptable for me to use. I don't want to step on your toes or get in your way." I hate that I sound so weak and timid, but it would go a long way to have something that I can cling to for comfort.

He stops, our eyes locking, and he picks up one of my hands. "Don't say that."

I play my sentence back in my head but can't decode what he's trying to tell me. I look at our hands together, and he squeezes, drawing my attention back to his face.

"Whatever is in this house is for you to use." He levels me with a glare. "You can't get in my way or step on my toes. You're my wife. I take that and all the responsibilities that come with it very seriously."

Valor steps back and pulls me through to the closet. Much like the rest of the house, it's massive. Custom built-ins line the walk-in closet, and Valor leads me to an empty section. He presses a button, and a wooden panel slides back, revealing a custom safe.

"Jewelry and valuables can go in here. Fireproof, waterproof, and if you lock it, theft resistant. Obviously, I'm using this portion of the closet, but I'm not attached to it. As long as I have a place to hang stuff, I'm fine with it."

He steps away from me and pushes his palm to a portion of the wood nearest the door, and there's a beeping sound. "Hidden handprint scanner. You'll find several throughout the house." Valor opens what I assumed were drawers for storage to reveal another safe. This one, however, isn't for jewelry and valuables. It's a weapon cache with a few handguns. "It would be beneficial if my daughter has you as an added level of security. Even if you're not comfortable with carrying daily, being able to take a gun in a crisis would be ideal."

I don't argue that I know how to shoot. Now isn't the time to start being sassy. He's . . . being friendly and warm with me.

Valor closes the compartment and turns to face me before walking over to a set of drawers in the closet. "Do you have many things to move in?"

"I'm not big on material things. I do have a curated collection of clothes, a couple family photos, nothing big."

I wonder why my stuff hasn't already been dropped off. Maybe Gregorio D'Medici didn't want to spend the time in hopes that Valor would kill me before any movers would be necessary.

Valor pulls out a pair of loose-fitting boxers, sweatpants, and then a T-shirt off a hanger before offering them to me. "Is it possible for someone in your family to box up your belongings?"

"They already are? I was trying . . ." I furrow my brow, and despite the little voice in my head saying 'be complacent,' the question bubbles out. "Is there a problem?"

"No." He shakes his head.

Our hands brush as I take the clothing from him. Warmth floods through me again. Even my body seems to be doing a push and pull with him. I've never felt anything like this, and it's confusing, to say the least. "I have to assume there is if you're ask—"

"Antonella, I don't want my wife going back to Casa de D'Medici alone. The stupid fucking truce gives you access to their house — if I come with you — but if I walk in that house with a loaded gun and see Gregorio D'Medici, I might shoot him in the face."

"The feeling is incredibly mutual." I stifle a laugh before walking out of the closet toward the bathroom again.

Valor follows me, and I catch him looking at me in the mirror. His eyes are wide like I'm growing a second head.

"What?"

"Is it mutual that Gregorio wants to shoot me or that you want to shoot Gregorio?" Valor seems so serious.

"I mean both are true, but I was mostly talking about me wanting to shoot Gregorio." I sigh and pull at the end of the towel.

Valor stalks closer and carefully, with a hesitant touch to my shoulder, turns me. "What did he do to you?"

I tsk dismissively, waving him off, and shake my head while working the towel over my long strands. *Guessing he doesn't have a blow dryer. Maybe in Kerrianne's bathroom?* "He's a shitty person. My parents died, and Gregorio did the noble thing of raising me with my father's wishes in mind. It's the only reason I got to be a teacher and not a housewife."

"But also why you were his first choice to offer up as a tribute to the truce." Valor pieces that together however he sees it to be true, but he's also not wrong.

Even if I hadn't called the truce, Gregorio would have continued to try and use me as a pawn in this game.

"I never want you alone with someone from your old life. You'll always have me or one of our guards with you when you see them." Valor cups my chin and tilts my head up toward him before placing a soft kiss on my lips. "I don't trust them not to hurt you, and I don't trust you to not take revenge."

Never once had I considered the opportunity to be violent toward the D'Medici family. With the truce in place, it would be dumb to put my life on the line like that. It doesn't matter, though, because Valor kisses me again, and this time, he dips his tongue into my mouth. Butterflies take flight in my stomach, and I can't believe how loving he's being once again.

It doesn't last because he withdraws.

"Kerrianne will be here soon." He sighs like this pains him as well. "There's a blow dryer in her bathroom until we get your things here. You can buy whatever you need that you didn't have before. I know you're not big on material things, but anything you need is yours."

Valor doesn't wait for me to object or remind him that if my stuff gets here, I'll have everything I need. He turns at the door with one last look at me naked before walking off, I'm guessing downstairs, to wait for Kerrianne.

CHAPTER TWENTY-SEVEN

AND A STACK OF WINGS

"Dad!" Kerrianne squeals, running through the foyer.

When she's a few feet away, she launches herself at me.

I scoop her up into my arms, spinning her around before one last squeeze and nuzzling my nose in her hair for a comforting breath. "I missed you so much."

"I missed you more." Kerrianne tightens her grip around my neck.

After a few seconds, I rub her back and set her on her feet. Kerrianne wraps her arms as far around me as they'll go and squeezes like a little constrictor snake.

"I doubt it." I stroke her hair, comforting her.

Kerrianne steps back away from me, finally letting go, and her eyes go wide.

The footsteps on the stairs tell me Antonella is dressed and making her way down here.

I turn as she descends toward us. I love seeing her in my clothes. They're too big for her, but she's rolled and folded them until they fit her well enough. I want her in my clothes always, as unpractical as that is.

"Ms. Mancini?" Kerrianne tugs on my hand, suspicion pitching her voice higher.

The tension I'd forced myself to forget about is . . . slowly returning. I wait for chaos to set in. I'm unaware of what it'll look like, but I don't anticipate any of this going well.

Kerrianne narrows her eyes at me and then cups her hands up over her mouth, whispering, "Dad, you didn't kidnap my new teacher, did you?"

I'm immediately drawing a blank. *First of all, how does she know I kidnap people? Second of all, how did she jump to the conclusion that I kidnapped Antonella?*

Antonella gives a small wave. "Hello, Kerrianne. I'm not kidnapped. I promise."

Then they both look at me like I'm the problem and need to explain myself. "Well, there will be a few new things," I start, looking to my mother, who's coming into the house carrying grocery bags, for guidance. Mom pointedly ignores me and my problems. I redirect Kerrianne to give myself time to figure out what to say. "Let's go see if we have any food left in this house."

"We do!" Kerrianne shouts, running back to the kitchen. "I'm making sandwiches!"

"Take your shoes off," I call before turning my attention to Antonella.

Antonella offers her arms out to Mom. "Please, let me help you."

"Oh." My mother offers a bag out to her. "Thank you."

Antonella turns and heads through the house, following Kerrianne.

My mother looks at me, raised eyebrows and an approving smile on her way past me.

Does everyone know something I don't? I assumed it was only a business dealing, but . . . the way Mom looks . . . *It doesn't matter. Let it go.*

We follow Antonella to the back of the house and find Kerrianne making a peanut butter and jelly sandwich with the refrigerator door open and beeping. I push it closed and walk around the island to where she's working.

Kerrianne doesn't stop making sandwiches. "Ms. Mancini, do you want strawberry or grape? And do you like crunchy or creamy peanut butter?"

"Strawberry and creamy," Antonella answers as she takes in the big space in the light of day.

The kitchen and living room are open concept and span two stories. Doors off the kitchen lead to the slate patio and modest-sized yard with the fenced-in tortoise run off to the side.

"I'm heading out. Your father wants a pot roast for dinner, and if I don't put it on now, we won't eat until ten." Mom makes a big deal out of appeasing Dad, but I know for a fact she loves every minute of it.

I give her a hug. "Thank you for bringing her home. Jack should be at the bottom of the driveway with an escort."

"You and your father worry too much. Everything will be fine. We're with much closer friends now." Mom looks at Antonella with a smile. "It was good to see you, dear."

"You as well."

Antonella's shoulders are rigid, her spine straight and hands clasped before her, and when she moves, it's with small, steady steps. It seems like she's prepared to walk on eggshells, if needed, to navigate the situation.

After I hear Mom close the door behind her and Kerrianne makes three creamy peanut butter and strawberry jam sandwiches, we head out to eat on the patio. She picks her favorite chair, and I sit across from her, leaving Antonella to sit between us.

The elephant in the room is too big even for our patio, so I try to lessen the blow the best I can. "So, Kerrianne, you like having Ms. Mancini as your teacher?"

Kerrianne nods, her mouth full.

I don't know how to tell her we're married, so I start with what I know how to explain. *She's your daughter. Talk to her like you always do.* I scold myself. "Well, do you think you'd be okay if she lived with us?"

"Obviously." Kerrianne sasses.

Antonella snorts, choking on a giggle. I look to Antonella, hoping for some sort of help, and she takes mercy on me. "Kerrianne, do you remember when Sean didn't come to pick you up?"

"Yeah." Kerrianne drops her eyes to her plate and picks at her sandwich. "That's when he got hurt."

Her words break my heart.

Even though I protect her from most of the death in our world, it still seeps into her life. Not having been here for her afterward hurts. Mom and Dad broke it to her gently, but I'm her father. *Maybe the truce will be a good thing after all.*

"I'm finding a replacement for Sean." I reassure her and myself. "We'll make sure you two get along just as well."

"Captain too." Kerrianne's features slip into puppy dog eyes.

It's not even something she tries for. It's natural for a wolf her age to do.

"Captain too." I agree and then nod to Antonella. *Can't wait to show her the family pet and see how squeamish she is.*

"You know how I knew your real name is Kerrianne and not Kelsey?" Antonella continues, circling back to the difficult conversation.

Kerrianne nods but stays silent.

"My name isn't Ms. Mancini. I'm really Antonella D'Medici." Antonella's eyes flick to mine and then back to Kerrianne.

"We're not supposed to talk to D'Medicis." Kerrianne sits back in her chair and looks at me.

"Well, the day Sean went away, a big meeting was called between the D'Medici family and the Cavanagh family, and they decided to make an agreement so no one else would get hurt.

We promised to all get along together." Antonella draws a deep breath before continuing. "As part of that deal, it was decided that your dad and I had to get married."

"Like Grandma and Grandpa? They got married a long time ago. There are pictures." Kerrianne squints at Antonella, studying her.

"A little like that." Antonella agrees. "Your dad and I agreed that we would live together and be friends so the rest of the families could learn how to be friends."

"So, it's okay to talk to you?" Kerrianne looks at me and scoots forward in her seat.

"Yes, you can talk to Antonella," I answer. "Antonella and I have to spend time together, but you'll always be my number one."

"Well, obviously." Kerrianne giggles.

She's pushing the respectful line a little bit too far.

I raise an eyebrow, and she self-silences, pulling her lips between her teeth, acknowledging that she's getting a little too brazen.

She eats more of her sandwich, and I'm mid-bite on mine when Kerrianne asks, "Okay, so can Antonella sleep in my room?"

"No." I'm quick to answer, swallowing hard. "Antonella and I are sleeping in my room."

Antonella freezes like we hadn't talked about this already.

"Oh, okay." Kerrianne pouts and changes the subject. She gets the expert-level manipulation from me as a learned trait. As much as I try not to lie to her, my ability to redirect has somehow rubbed off on her. "When am I going back to school?"

I lock eyes with Antonella over the table. *When can I send them back to school?*

"Well, your dad and I talked about that a little." Antonella takes over from my silence. "Probably not Monday with me but maybe by Wednesday?"

It's news to me that Antonella is going back to school tomorrow. But I don't argue with her in front of Kerrianne.

"Really?!" Kerrianne gets excited and is back to all smiles.

She starts rambling a million miles a minute about a game they're playing at recess and how Antonella let her play with the new blocks after school until my parents got there to collect her.

I dislike the amount of information I'm missing from the week I was away. But soon, our sandwiches are gone and Kerrianne is bouncing, ready to show Captain off to Antonella.

Hanging back while Antonella helps hold things for Kerrianne to make her tortoise's breakfast, I fire off a text to Royal.

VALOR:

> Can you text me the dumbed-down version of what happened while I was gone?

> Why didn't you catch Antonella was a D'Medici?

> Need a phone for Antonella. Clothing too. Was that negotiated for at all? Can you investigate that or get Mom and the pack ladies to get her outfitted accordingly?

It doesn't take long, and I get the line-by-line answer that is probably as bare minimum as Royal can make it while still answering my questions.

ROYAL:

> Sean died. The arbiter was called in. D'Ms demanded you marry A. Funeral planning. Taught K how to play Texas Hold'em.

> Didn't catch because her documents were tight. Now that I found the flaw, double-checking everything else. Won't happen again.

> 10-4 phone, negotiations, and lady stuff.

The problem with opening and looking at my phone in this spare second of time is that I see how many people are no longer respecting that I was married yesterday. There is one, however, that can't wait.

PATRICK DOYLE:

I've sent six Stateside this morning. I've sent you and Royal their qualifications. I highlighted my two personal best guesses given Kerrianne's unique personality. Was good to see you. Best wishes and congratulations again on the wedding. Perhaps for Christmas we'll catch up again.

I flip open my email and lean against the kitchen island. Kerrianne doesn't need me there to introduce Antonella to Captain, and as much as I wanted to see her face when she sees the reptile, this is more pressing.

The files take a bit to download, but I start with the two Patrick flagged as his top choices, taking a cursory glance before opening the others. I close out of the others and return to Patrick's picks. The two are the most skilled, and he has always been fond of Kerrianne, never shying away from the endless conversation about whatever subject she's most interested in.

VALOR:

You're right on the selection. I'll set something up with them. I want Kerrianne to have a chance to meet them first. Thank you.

Patrick isn't big on responding to text messages, so I don't expect to get one back. Which is fine because Kerrianne's and Antonella's footsteps are drawing nearer.

Antonella

CHAPTER TWENTY-EIGHT

THE GUN RANGE

After a trip to visit Captain, Kerrianne leads me back through the house. She was so pleased I thought he was handsome and that I wasn't afraid of him.

We find Valor in the kitchen, furiously typing something on his phone. But he's quick to tuck it away, putting it out of sight and out of mind. His face lights up as he looks at Kerrianne.

"Antonella likes Captain and thinks he's handsome." Kerrianne yawns and looks up at Valor.

I've seen them together throughout the morning and early afternoon, but I can barely get over the family resemblance between them. It's much stronger than I had noticed originally. It's no wonder Berto was able to see it.

"Can I take a nap?" she asks in the cutest voice.

Kerrianne is beyond the normal age you'd anticipate a child wanting a nap, but Valor doesn't argue with her, and I don't question his parenting choices. He clearly knows his daughter, and I think I might have overstepped with talks of school.

Valor takes her upstairs for a nap. I love how glued together they are.

A sad longing for the absence of that feeling pains me.

I take my time to observe the living room as a distraction from the sharp sorrow at the loss of my own parents. The large fireplace has a few family pictures posted on each end, and I move closer to them.

The first must be last year's Christmas photo as they're all sporting festive clothing. Another of Kerrianne's kindergarten graduation. Another of her and her pet tortoise, Captain. I'm guessing the day they brought him home, and the last one catches my eye. Valor is sitting in a recliner. His feet up, he's leaning back, and a baby is curled up on his chest.

Tears prick at the corner of my eyes, and I blink them away. It's the kind of photo a mother takes of her family. One where she's seeing the beauty of their lives together, and knowing that Valor has raised her on his own for a long time . . . It's possible his mother took it, but I don't think she did.

"It's from the night Holly died." Valor's voice is low and quiet behind me. "She took the photo before she went out to the Christmas market. I got a call from the pharmacy that the photos were done a few days later. We still can't prove Berto and Gregorio killed her."

I turn to face him; he's standing almost directly behind me, but I didn't even hear him come down the stairs, let alone get that close to me. "I'm so sorry for your loss. If I knew the answer, I would tell you."

"Thank you." His response is automatic. "I'm a little frustrated that you'd tell my daughter she's going back to school on Wednesday. It's given me the difficult task of hiring her a bodyguard before then." He takes a step back from me and motions to the sofa.

I take a seat, and I assumed he'd take the recliner across from me, but instead, he sits down beside me.

His statement didn't give me a lot to work with beyond drumming up a bland apology, so I try to add value to the conversation. "Well, we live in a bit of a different world. The truce is in full force, and I'm qualified to protect Kerrianne. I've no doubt I could keep her safe. However, it was a discussion that could have been had, you're right."

Whatever I said was wrong. Valor sets his mouth in a hard line and raises an eyebrow. "I know you pulled the gun on Berto, but point-blank is much easier than anything long range or with multiple assailants."

I don't know if he's trying to be condescending, but it comes out that way.

I take the condescending tone and give it back to him. "Well, I know I'm just a little old Mafia wife now that I've been married off, but my skills lie far beyond making pasta. Which is it, Valor? Did you want the perfect and docile Mafia wife or not? Tell me which woman you want, and I'll force myself to fit that mold even if it hurts, but I can tell you right now that I'm stronger than I look. I can protect Kerrianne, and Berto was afraid that I would shoot him because despite the hallway being close range . . . He knows I'm a better marksman than he is."

Valor's jaw clenches, the muscles twitching under his short beard. He rakes his eyes down my body slowly, in a calculating way, not in the lustful way like yesterday.

"Alright." Valor pulls his phone out of his pocket and punches in his code before poking the screen a few more times. "Kerrianne's asleep. Let's get down to the range."

"The range?" I shake my head at the absurdity of it.

"Yes?" Valor doesn't seem as amused as I am, but he does nod. "I never gave you the tour. Let's do some of that on the way down, I guess."

I explored some of the upper level when I looked for Kerrianne's bathroom, so escorted to see the rest is more formal.

"Alright."

I'm positive Valor is underestimating me. It's not the first time someone has in my lifetime, but it's wholly unexpected.

I get a tour of the house — main floor with an open-concept

eat-in kitchen to the living room, which I'm already familiar with. There's a formal dining room and formal sitting room back toward the front door. Off the garage is the mud room with a washer-dryer stack and the tortoise room with the adorable Russian tortoise.

Back by the stairs, Valor opens the door to the basement. He leads the way down the staircase, turning lights on at the bottom. There's a game room with expected game tables, a decently equipped gym, and a movie-theater-style room, and then he opens a large, thick metal door at the end of the hallway. Valor doesn't hide the code as he punches it in, and then he places his hand on the scanner next to the door.

"I'll get you programmed in the system; you'll be able to open the hidden exit, the panic room, this vault, and the small one in my closet upstairs." He slides the door back and steps inside.

It's a marksman's wet dream. Racks of guns, ammunition, targets, and other explosives. I poke my head in behind Valor, taking it all in. "Holy smokes."

He laughs. "We have an arsenal, but what did you really expect?"

"Well." I hesitate. We don't talk with outsiders about the family business, but business and my family have changed drastically. Yet, Valor is actively sharing things with me, so I go for more honest than maybe I normally would have. "I don't think it's a surprise to anyone that the D'Medicis' weapon suppliers aren't as good as the Cavanaghs'. Mercenaries and marksmanship are kind of the Irish's calling cards."

"I suppose you're right." Valor selects a small handgun for me. It's one Berto gave me a while ago that I hated. Part of me doesn't want to say anything, but Valor pauses briefly, looking at my face while loading the magazine. "Do you . . . have a preference?"

"Well, when you say it like that, I sound like a snob." I cross my arms in front of my chest, tipping my nose up, pretending to be pretentious. "In the nine-millimeter, I prefer a compact over a subcompact. I'm not opposed, but the thirty-two and twenty-five are my preference over the thirty-three."

"Damn. Say that again slowly." Valor's eyes have that warmth to them again like at the restaurant last night, only different.

The lighting must be playing tricks on me because it's almost like they've changed color completely.

"May I have a thirty-two, please?" I give him a wry smile.

Valor unloads the thirty-three and then moves to the wall behind him. He selects a thirty-two and moves to a different rack. "Have you ever used one of these?" I shake my head, and Valor huffs. "No, of course, Berto prefers one, so that's all you'd be exposed to."

"Well, in his defense, he didn't want to do this at all, but it was my —" I hang my head and stop myself from defending him. What Berto did was inexcusable, and Valor has every right to be pissed off at him. "It doesn't matter. What's happened has happened. I'd be glad to try anything."

"I'm sorry." Valor loads two guns and sets them on the table in the center of the room before grabbing holsters for them. As he undoes his belt to fit a holster, he surprises me. "I know you called the truce. I know that of everyone, I benefited the most from you calling the truce. But I've wanted justice for Holly. For so long that part of me is mourning the ability to finally catch Berto and Gregorio vulnerable."

"I . . ." There aren't words for this conversation.

Valor walks around the central table and picks up the gun he hadn't holstered, bringing it over to where I am at the door. He offers it out to me, and I visually inspect for myself that it is, in fact, loaded and ready to be fired before flipping the safety back on.

"Start you with something you're comfortable with, but I

have a feeling you'll like this other one better." He gestures for me to turn back to the firing range.

I move to the preparation table closest to the shooting line. Valor approaches with earmuffs, plugs, and safety glasses.

"No lecture about how these aren't something I'll have the time to put on before I pull the trigger?" I set my gun down before slipping my safety glasses on.

Valor uses his middle finger to push his up the bridge of his nose, the cheeky fucker smiling. "Nah. But I've got excellent hearing, and I'd like to keep it that way."

"So, when you pretend to not hear when I ask you to take the trash out?" I narrow my gaze at him.

"Won't happen." He assures me. "I've been properly . . ." He laughs, a single chuckle to himself. "Domesticated once before. I don't play the game boys do, nor am I looking for someone to mother me. We're a partnership."

Valor hands me the earplugs first, and I take them. He might only be falling in lust with me, but if he means everything he says, I'll be in love with him before the end of the week. My heart warms at the prospect of having someone who respects me in my life.

After we take our time putting on safety gear, Valor offers to let me take the line first. He stands close to me as I line up to take my first shot. I look at him over my shoulder, but he doesn't step away. Not even when I raise my gun.

With calm and even breaths, I pull the trigger for three shots on an exhale before lowering the weapon. Valor reaches forward and pushes my arms up again. It's evident he wants me to keep shooting.

Did I miss? I don't think so.

I fire off another set of three, but Valor again stops me before I can lower my arms. I empty all thirteen out of the magazine before trying to lower the gun one last time. For obvious reasons, Valor lets me. He pats my shoulder and then must press a button because the target comes down the range toward us on the overhead track. It's fancy as fuck, but this man converted a whole room of his house for the sake of a tortoise.

Valor takes off his earmuffs and pulls out one of his earplugs, so I do the same. With the target hanging before us, we get a good look at my shots. Of the thirteen shots, all but one are in the nine and narrower portion of the targets. One is in the upper right quadrant in the eight section. It would still kill if it hit someone.

"Not bad at all." He approves, but his blank expression irks me. "But I want you to try something with a little more fire-power. It's better for more powerful assailants."

"Big dudes. Big bullets." I try cracking a joke, but it's apparently over Valor's head, or I'm back to square one in 'bonding' with him again.

"Something like that." Valor pulls the gun out of his holster. "This is the civilian version. There's a military grade one that's a little sleeker, but I want to see how you handle this."

The gun he offers me is much heavier, but I still feel like I can manage it.

While Valor clips the target, I look at the size of the ammu-nition and familiarize myself with the weapon. After sending the target back down the track, he stands behind me once more.

Having him so fucking close unnerves me, but I don't try to warn him away or make him back off. Whatever his reason — overprotectiveness, fear of my failure, or trying to make me squirm by increasing my awareness of him — it's working.

I recall the way it felt to have his hands on me, and I curl my toes at the memories. *Focus.*

I raise the gun and level the sights. I have to make more adjustments than I'd like in front of him, but it's a new gun and there's expected to be a learning curve.

I squeeze the trigger nice and slow and am hit with a massive kick. I falter back a step. Square into Valor's chest, but beyond that, his arms are right there in an instant, so fast I barely saw them move to steady mine. My face heats, and I'm glad he's behind me and can't see it. I should have braced more. I knew this would be more forceful.

After a second, he lowers his hands and places them on my hips, directing me back to the shooting line. It's evident, without him even needing to tell me, that he wants me to shoot again.

I push all the air out of my lungs, holding myself as steady as possible.

This time I'm ready for the kick and I handle it better. Three more, and Valor's hand finds my waist. I lower the gun, ready for him to pull in the target. I'm pretty sure some of the shots missed completely. *He'll think I'm a complete mess.*

Valor doesn't retract the target. Instead, with his long arms, he adjusts my grip on the gun ever so slightly. He presses down on my supporting elbow, giving me a less extended support. He guides me to rotate my other elbow up before squeezing my shoulders. When I roll them forward, he steps away.

I send two more bullets down the range, and Valor steps in again. This time, he adjusts my stance, staggering my feet a bit farther. It's like learning to shoot all over again. My face flames hot and tears well in my eyes. *I'm better than this. I know I am.*

We repeat the process three more times. Each time, I get closer and closer to letting more emotions show. My red cheeks can be explained away because of how warm it is in the range. But tears would be inexcusable. I'm not weak.

By the time Valor recalls the target, my arms are wobbly from supporting the weight of the gun and the recoil. Being away from home, I lost a lot of the muscle I had gained. It shouldn't have been this way. I shouldn't have let myself get lax.

Valor takes out both earplugs this time and pulls off his safety glasses, then unclips the target and lays it next to the one from earlier. This time, rather than a nice tight spread, the shots are in a variety of places.

"Not bad for the first time with that weapon. You got better the more I helped you find the sweet spot." Valor taps the shots in what must be the order they landed.

The end of the range isn't that far away, but I couldn't even pretend to know which shots landed where and when, and I don't remember seeing all of them even hit the target, but they did.

"How did it feel?"

"Heavy. Big." I go with simple answers. *Fucking scary, and I don't want to shoot this again.*

"We'll try something else another day. You're good enough with the thirty-two that I think you're right, and Kerrianne can go back to school this week. I don't love not having a dedicated staff with the two of you, but I'm not leaving anytime soon. I've got meetings with the pa—" Valor seems to correct himself. It's the third time I've noticed him do it. "People in our organization, but I can have them at the house. Jack, my driver, can act as escort for you both."

Gut instinct says argue. I can drive us, but it's his daughter. The same daughter who was almost kidnapped and killed this week. I can't fault him for not wanting her to be out of his sight and under the care of someone he's known for less than a week when returning to school.

Valor offers to take the firearm from me, and I hand it back. He holsters it and then hesitates as he watches me. His lips part as if to speak, but he closes them again around the tip of his tongue, which is then pulled back behind the seal, keeping him silent.

It's sexy and heartbreaking all at once.

"Did I do something wrong?" I know he commended my abilities, but it felt more like a clinical acknowledgment of the facts and not true approval, which is gutting me.

"No." He brings a hand up to my face and cups my cheek. "I'm impressed, princess. The D'Medici women have all been worthless as far as I've been concerned. You're changing my opinions and making me skeptical."

"I'm an anomaly." I move my head out of his hand as I let it drop to look away from him. "Leticia wouldn't even be able to line up the sights."

Valor grips my chin with his thumb and forefinger, returning my eyes to his. "Don't hide from me. I want to see your beautiful face as you talk to me."

Why? Why is this man so back and forth? Frigid and then warm.

I nod dumbly and try to come up with an answer.

"Dad?" Kerrianne calls from somewhere nearby.

"In the range," Valor calls, his fingers lingering against my skin before he slowly lets me go like he's physically suffering for it.

"I need another snack," Kerrianne says from the doorway as she looks at her toes, getting them as close as she can to the transition from the carpeted floor to the absorbent rubber under our feet.

"You gonna grow on me or what, little velociraptor?" Valor gives her the smile I wanted to see.

"I don't know. Grandma says I'm gonna be big like you." Kerrianne shrugs. "Royal says I eat more than he does, which isn't possible. He ate a whole pizza all by himself, and I only had two slices."

"He definitely eats a lot." Valor agrees with her. "I'll put these away, and then we can figure out an afternoon snack."

"Okay." Kerrianne nods and walks away from the door.

When she's gone, Valor begins cleaning up, and I help carry safety gear back to the vault he got it out of. After putting it all away in silence, he closes the door behind us. I lead the way back toward the rest of the house, but his fingers wrap around my wrist, and he spins me to the wall.

His lips crash into mine, and the kiss is full of heat. An inferno brews in my belly, and I want more of the offerings Valor has pressed against me. After a nearly breathless minute, Valor lowers the intensity of the kiss between us.

"Thank you," Valor says softly, his lips barely pulled away from mine.

"For what?" My voice is breathier than I'd like it to be.

Valor frees my wrist and then runs his hand up along my arm and around the back of my neck. I stiffen as he holds me on the rougher side of gentle. "For explaining us to Kerrianne. This wasn't something I was expecting to have to explain to my daughter, ever."

"Ever?" I bring my hand up to his chest, but I don't know if I want to push him away. "I find it difficult to believe that you thought you'd never find a woman to marry."

"I never wanted to bring a woman home to my daughter. She deserves all my attention, and no woman was worth ruining that connection I have with her." His words sting, but he brings his other hand to rest on my waist.

It's reassuring in contrast to the near accusation that I'm here to ruin things. In a few more breaths, Valor leans away. My eyes take a moment to focus, but I see him clearly.

Hard lines etch into his forehead as he's stern with me, narrowing his eyes. "I'll never choose you over her."

"I would never ask you to." I shake my head and then sigh, dropping my hand from his chest and casually letting it knock away the one he has resting on my waist. "Besides, I'm not sure I would pick you over her either."

A smile tugs at his lips.

Hot and cold . . . Hot and cold . . . If only I could figure out how to navigate him.

Valor

CHAPTER TWENTY-NINE

LATE NIGHT VIEWING PARTY

"So . . ." Antonella looks at the king-size bed in my suite as she comes out of the bathroom after her bed prep routine and changing into pajamas. "Which side is mine?"

"Take your pick. I get pushed around to whatever side has the most room when Kerrianne comes in if she has a nightmare, wants to snuggle, or wakes me up way too early trying to pull me out of bed." I strip out of my shirt and yawn, releasing tension from my body.

"Alright, well, I've been sleeping in the middle of a queen, so aren't we a pair." Antonella sighs but then picks the side of the bed closest to the window.

Tactically, it puts me closer to the door and to Kerrianne, and I realized that I did have a preference after all. *Works out, then.*

Despite feeling like I could sleep for a good sixteen hours, my brain doesn't turn off when I lie down. It's filled with the buzzing sound of too many thoughts and situations that haven't been sorted. Antonella's still form is beside me, and I can't keep tossing and turning. It's not fair to deprive her of sleep because it's eluding me.

I slip out of bed and go down to my office, where I open my laptop. Normally, I lean on my tech-genius brother, Royal, to handle a lot of things. But there is something I have unfiltered access to without needing his expertise.

The school's security system feed filters right into my security company's cloud. Only three people have access to view footage: me, Royal, and Doctor Thatcher. So, it doesn't take me long to log in through a few firewalls and select the date files.

After pulling 'Ms. Mancini's' room number off the roster, I have a camera to start with. On fast-forward, I start playing back the events of the day Antonella called the truce.

At the end of the day, Antonella escorts the kids down to the safe zone. Kerrianne has her little smartphone in hand, looking at the screen, brows furrowed. She'd be waiting for a text from Sean saying he's nearby. Minutes tick by and no Sean.

A pit forms in my stomach knowing he won't arrive.

Antonella and Kerrianne come out of the safe zone, and I slow the speed down to real time. Antonella leads her toward the office.

I flick to a closer camera, facing the opposite direction.

Antonella walks into the office but comes right back out and leads Kerrianne to the waiting bench. From this angle, I can see into the office, and Antonella continuously checks to maintain a line of sight through the office window to my daughter.

It's reassuring how much care she's taking with Kerrianne. And yet, my hackles rise, knowing something will happen. Something will shatter the little bit of sanctuary the school should be.

At the top of the screen, in the hallway that leads from the classrooms to the office, feet come into frame first, then legs, then a torso, and then Berto's smug face.

My wolf growls, ready to snap.

Berto holds his hand out to Kerrianne. Antonella sees from

the office and starts moving at the same time that Berto grabs hold of Kerrianne's hand and pulls her off the bench.

Little raptor fights back, pulling against his hold and leaning, trying not to follow him, but Berto's a man and she's a wolf pup. I'm transfixed and can't even breathe, waiting to see what happens next.

Antonella bolts out of the office, her eyes wide and fearful. It's the kind of panic that can't be faked. I can practically smell her fear through the video footage. She races down the hall, and I flip through cameras and fast-forward to the right time stamp until I get to the best view of the hallway in front of Antonella's classroom.

The protective way Antonella moves Kerrianne from Berto's side and proceeds to lock the classroom door eases my ache of dread. Finally, I draw a breath.

The fierce way Antonella shakes her head, points to the door, and then gestures for Berto to leave swells my heart with a little pride. Seeing her tell off the man I've wanted to do the same to a hundred times over soothes that bit of my ego.

The slimy fuck is a foot taller than her in her heels, and yet she stares him down. He moves in, threatening her maybe?

She pulls his gun on him.

That's our mate. My wolf wags his tail in pleasure.

It's not a practiced move by any means, but she does it well.

Berto's eyes are wide, the whites clear in the image as he backs away. He shakes his head and raises his arms in surrender before he slowly and unthreateningly pulls out his phone, then dials. When Antonella flicks off the safety, I'm wishing she would have shot him.

I could turn the audio on. I could listen to what they said, but as I move to plug in the headphones, Antonella's classroom door opens from the inside.

Kerrianne pokes her head out, and Antonella steps, blocking

her from Berto. Then Kerrianne disappears back through the door again.

More words are exchanged, and finally Berto leaves down the hallway toward the back doors.

Antonella lowers the gun to her side. She breathes for a moment before checking her surroundings, pulling a scarf out of a cubby, and hiding the gun.

She protected Kerrianne from seeing it. My wolf notes. *She tried to protect our pup from the darkness.*

I sit in silence, looking at the screen where I hit pause. Antonella looks down the hallway, watching to make sure the coast is clear. I don't know Antonella well, but that scene told me everything I needed to know about her.

She saved Kerrianne. It wasn't an act. My wolf presses the facts, the genuine fear in her eyes, the way Berto fumbled when she took his gun, and this image on the screen. Antonella's soft features are pulled together pensively, fighting for calm.

None of those motions were practiced or rehearsed. They were live, in the moment. It was real. Antonella put her life on the line to save Kerrianne. I close the lid to my computer, letting my eyes adjust to the darkness.

Our mate. My wolf settles inside me, content for the night. For a heartbeat I consider if he could be right.

When I get back up to the top of the stairs, I check on Kerrianne before heading back to bed. Little raptor is curled up, hugging her dino nugget plush toy, and it sinks in how close I was to losing her . . .

Movement in my bedroom draws my eye. Antonella steps toward the bedroom door. "Is everything okay?"

I draw myself away from Kerrianne's room. "Yeah, I'm coming back to bed."

Antonella doesn't move when I get to the doorway, and she repeats her question. "Is everything okay?"

I'm caught off guard by the repetition. "I needed to see she was okay. It's alright."

"I can go somewhere else." Antonella offers.

No. I keep myself from protesting as loudly as that word was in my head. "No, it's okay. Really. I'd tell you if it wasn't. It set in for a second how close I was to losing my entire world."

Antonella steps back and turns away from me, but I reach out, ensnaring her hand in mine. When she turns back to look at me, her eyebrows are raised. "Valor?"

My mouth is dry, and I don't know how to explain without sounding like the overprotective father I am. How do you tell your new wife that the reason you're not in bed is because you were downstairs watching the footage of her saving your daughter's life? So, I settle with the beginning of how that conversation would go. "Thank you, for keeping her safe for me."

"You're welcome," Antonella answers, squeezing my hand and pulling me with her back toward the bed.

Ours, my wolf reiterates, and it resonates in my soul.

CHAPTER THIRTY

BACK TO SCHOOL

I didn't know what to expect when I walked into school for the optional winter break classes. My entire life has changed but my badge worked fine. There was no substitute listed for my class, and by all accounts, it's a normal everyday bonus school day.

I don't know why I was ready for a call to the principal's office, but I get a visitor instead. Doctor Thatcher pokes her head into the classroom shortly after I send my students to gym class.

"Hello, Mrs. Clark!" She beams at me, nearly startling me as I write the math items we'll be working on up on the board.

Clark? I freeze, stunned by that statement. *As in Kelsey Clark. How the fuck would she know that?* I turn to look at her and plaster a smile on my face, hoping my 'teacher face' is as good as my 'Mafia wife face' and will keep me from broadcasting everything.

"Sorry, Victor, Mr. Clark, sent me an email yesterday explaining things about Kelsey and your very recent wedding. I had no idea you were engaged." She's still smiling as she walks into the classroom.

Victor? Oh, wow, he went all out with the pseudonyms. Okay . . . I don't know if I'm grateful or angry that Valor sent an email. *I guess that depends on how this turns out.* "Oh."

"You snagged a good one. Rich, tech mogul, and handsome. No wonder he's never paid anyone else the time of day. But why didn't he give you a recommendation for the available position? We could have put Kelsey in your class from day one," the principal asks, heavily implying the nepotism and buying spots that I already knew took place in institutions like this.

Lie your fucking ass off. I force myself to keep a nonchalant tone. "Well, I didn't want anyone to think I wasn't capable of the position. I wanted to earn it. Victor respected that choice. And we were even nervous to have Kelsey in my class."

"Nonsense. I'd much rather make sure she feels safe. Poor kid. I know the Appletons lost their manny last year, though that was a bad accident with a zip line. They pulled their kids for a week. I was shocked Victor will be sending Kelsey back by Wednesday, especially with this being a bonus class. I would assume he'd wait until the new year. You must have a new body-guard or someone in the works for her?" The principal keeps rambling, not even letting me breathe and answer the question. "Well, regardless. Congratulations. Victor is quite the catch. Please let us know if you're interested in moving up in classes with her or want to remain in the second grade. We don't mind either way, especially since Victor's contribution to enhance security at the school has really resonated with the school board and brought in some well-influenced families."

I'm still slack jawed and not even sure how to cut in to this.

Doctor Thatcher's watch beeps. "Meeting with the board." She heads out of my classroom in a whirlwind with a wave over her shoulder. "Gotta get going!"

I'm stunned and shocked until I see why.

Valor is standing in the hallway. She's barely out the door when he strides in like he owns the place, which . . . given he's literally a major donor to the school, I guess he does.

He approaches and places his hands on my hips, holding me to him. "I'm sorry."

"Oh?" I look at him, raising an eyebrow. "What for?"

"Well, I figured you'd be a little angry that I meddled in your school life but —"

I shake my head. "I'm appreciative that you have no problem with me working. It's fine. It also seems like you're taking care of literally everything in my life, so that's an added perk I hadn't anticipated. It's like when your friend says, 'I planned a whole trip,' and you get to go along and see the sights."

"Well, I would promise not to be so overbearing, but it's not going to happen." Valor smiles and gives me a quick peck on the lips. "I came to give you this. I don't like not being able to reach you."

Valor pulls a phone out of his suit pocket. It has a green case and a grippy on the back. Then out of the other pocket, a smartwatch.

"Oh." I don't object as he hands me the phone, but then he picks up my wrist and puts the watch on for me. I'm stuck somewhere between thinking this is kind and feeling like he's putting a tracking device on me like I'm some sort of dog. "I don't think the watch is necessary."

The sly grin tells me this isn't a negotiation, and I save the fight for something else that I'm sure he'll try to bring into my life.

With his grip on my wrist, Valor pulls me closer to him. He wraps his arm around my waist and drops his hand to the globe of my ass. The fact that I'm wearing the outfit I wore after our wedding doesn't help with the memories and warmth his actions elicit.

"You're taking care of Kerrianne. There is no such thing as not necessary in my eyes." He bites his bottom lip like he wants to kiss me but steps away instead, and I don't like the absence of his warmth against my body. Valor clears his throat. "I called Berto."

I raise my eyebrows. That's a sentence I never in a million years would have guessed, and I'm waiting for an the sky to fall, ready to take cover under my desk.

Valor nods, flaring his nostrils. "He's letting us send someone to collect your things on Saturday. So, my mom offered to buy you a bunch of work outfits. I told her you may wish to shop for yourself, and she told me to mind my business."

He laughs. "I tried to remind her you are exclusively my business, and then she scoffed and hung up."

I nod. "Your mom is buying me clothes for the week?"

"I've been instructed to gather your sizes because it was a lucky guess for her with the after-wedding outfit." Valor brushes a wayward lock of hair out of my face, and I swoon.

I fucking swoon like a teenager in love for the first time.

"I'm guessing your number is now programmed in my phone?" I wiggle the device at him. "Thank you, for this. I'm sure there was no way in hell Berto would hand mine over."

"I did try, but he was adamant. And yeah, I'm in your phone. As are my parents, Royal, and Jack, my driver. *Our* driver." He corrects himself, and it's causing more heart palpitations and butterflies. "Want to text her the sizes directly?"

"I can." I look at the classroom and then the clock.

I have ten minutes before the students are back. I've known Valor a few days, a few being a generous term, but I don't want him to leave.

"If it's too soon for you to be back in the classroom, you can come home." Valor offers, and I dislike how, again, it's as if he's reading my mind.

But I shake my head. "It's silly. I know there's no threat. I'm safe."

"That security patch has been fixed. I've hired an armed security agent for the staff and teacher entrance, and the others remote lock, so no other door is accessible without two different key cards." Valor shakes his head. "I underestimated Berto's resourcefulness, and it won't happen again. You're also linked into the school's silent alarm and will know immediately if there is a breach. This weekend your classroom door will be switched out and will be bulletproof against a higher caliber than the rest already are."

"The doors are bulletproof?" I look at what I assumed was a heavy oak door.

Valor huffs. "Of course they are. Windows too."

"Windows, I assumed, but the doors, I had no idea." I brush that same lock of hair out of my face again.

Valor watches my every movement, and I think his jaw twitches as he partially turns away from me. "Alright, I've gotta move on with the day. I'll see you tonight at home."

I don't even get a chance to say goodbye. His long legs carry him on silent footsteps as he strides out of the room as if he'd never been here at all.

CHAPTER THIRTY-ONE

THE CHANGING OF THE GUARD

It's been exactly a week since Sean died. Kerrianne reminded me this morning when she tried to go to school with Antonella that Antonella and I said she could go to school tomorrow.

I know she should go to school. The bonus classes over winter break are 'optional' and meant to allow families the flexibility to take their kids out during the regular session for vacations or whatnot that fall outside of the school's scheduled days off. It would be smart to utilize those extra days in the event she gets the summer sillies and needs to take summer break early. Wolf pups and season changes aren't always the most conducive to learning.

My little velociraptor is safe with Antonella, I have proof of that, but I'm being a nervous and overprotective father.

Not overprotective. My wolf disagrees, furthering my belief that I'm letting the situation control me and not the other way around.

If these candidates are up to my standard, then, and *only then*, will I let her go back to school.

Patrick's top two candidates match my choices. The oldest guard in the group at fifty years old, who tragically lost his mate and son in an 'accident' twenty years ago, and the youngest in the group, a twenty-eight-year-old who has formal military training as well as working in Gardaí. I'm not concerned about either candidate or their ability to take care of my daughter, only that they'll be able to connect with her.

The doorbell rings, and I leave the kitchen, where I've been cleaning things that aren't dirty, which Holly used to call my 'stress tell,' to go answer it.

Kerrianne and Antonella are in the living room and had been working on some of her makeup homework.

She whispers loudly to Antonella, "What do I do if I don't like him?"

It's refreshing to hear that my daughter has the same concerns I do, which is why it felt like the right time to involve her in the interview process. She'll spend a lot of time with her guard, between the commute to school and anytime she's not at one of the main properties. They have to get along.

Antonella certainly isn't the damsel she could have been, but she isn't a wolf. *She isn't a wolf yet.* I'd feel better knowing that they get along with and trust their primary security and that it's someone who respects them.

"We finish the interview. Then you tell your dad," Antonella answers her.

I pause to be sure I hear the rest of their conversation. The interviewee can wait.

"Remember that kindness is important. We can have opinions, but that doesn't mean they're good to share out loud."

"We can be nice without being friends." Kerrianne recites something they must have talked about.

It's a much nicer way than I would have phrased it. I open the door, and the first interviewee, the older of the two wolves, is waiting.

"Alpha." He greets, turning his head away from me, exposing his neck.

I'm not the pack alpha, not yet, so being treated with that same respect is overly formal. But it shows that he takes who I am seriously.

I step aside and let him in. "Thank you for coming."

"An honor." Declan looks around my home as we walk through.

It's not in the curious, snooping sense of what my home looks like, but his eyes look at the security of it. Window latches, entrances, potential hiding places, and potential weapons.

Kerrianne opts to sit in my chair with her little legs curled up cross-legged. I sit with Antonella on the sofa and offer the last wingback chair to Declan. He walks over to Antonella first and offers his hand out to shake.

"Afternoon, Mrs. Cavanagh." He nods.

Got the memo she doesn't know. His thoroughness is impressive.

I like him. You can feel how calm his wolf is. My wolf takes note, cocking his head and watching as Declan goes toward Kerrianne.

"Miss Cavanagh." He extends his hand. "My name is Declan O'Toole."

"Nice to meet you." Kerrianne smiles at him, shaking his hand.

Seems he's already winning points. I look over to Antonella, and she gives a tiny nod, disguising it as moving her long hair from one shoulder to the other.

He sits forward in the chair and looks at Kerrianne, pretty much ignoring me and Antonella. "So, tell me, Kerrianne. What is your favorite subject in school?"

It's a strange question, and I want to cut in, but Antonella places her hand on my knee. So I keep my mouth shut and let the two of them talk.

"I like science. I'm really good at math." Kerrianne beams.

"That's fantastic. I'm partial to it as well. Good at countin' things." Declan nods.

His file said he worked inventory for the Doyles when he started. My wolf reminds me.

He immediately asks her another question. "What changes in your schedule the most?"

Not the direction I anticipated.

"Uhm." Kerrianne's nose crinkles, her mouth moving back and forth as she thinks. "Sometimes Dad gives me an allowance to go do things, like if I have a bad day at school, we can go get a frozen hot chocolate or ice cream. And I really like it if we can stop and get treats for Captain too."

Declan passes a quick glance to me, and I nod. "And Captain is probably not a boat captain?"

"He's a tortoise," Kerrianne explains with an exaggerated eye roll. "Not a turtle. A tortoise."

"He wouldn't happen to be a Russian tortoise, would he?" Declan raises an eyebrow in suspicion.

"Yeah?" Kerrianne looks at him with the same suspicion, narrowing her eyes.

"I've one of my own. Her name is Magdalena." Declan makes slow moves to slide his phone out of his pocket and open a photo gallery, which he shows to Kerrianne.

At the excited little wiggle of her butt in the chair, I imagine the puppy in her wagging her tail. "That's so cool!"

I can pretty much text the other guy and tell him not to come to the interview. It'll be a waste of time.

They start bonding over tortoises, and before I know it, Kerrianne leads Declan through the house toward the tortoise room.

Antonella stops me from following too closely, her hand coming to rest on my chest. "You know he's the right choice."

Her opinion feels right. My wolf immediately agrees with her.

The three of us are clearly thinking the same thing, but

asking her opinion anyway feels right. *No, I'm just testing her. This isn't asking for an honest opinion. I made up my mind.* But I let the words leave my lips anyway. "Text the other not to come?"

Considering it for a moment, Antonella looks down the hallway. "No. This is a good experience for her, but she'll pick him. Start whatever extra background checks you're planning, and let her interview the other. But Declan is your man."

The contradiction to my line of thinking causes me to pause. I'm so used to efficiency and moving within a set system that I didn't consider my pup's development. *How will she learn to do this if I don't give her the opportunity?*

"You know, how much you know about this business doesn't speak well to Gregorio's ability to keep quiet." I tease her gently.

My arms ache to wrap her up into a hug, but we haven't made any sort of moves of affection toward each other in the last couple of days, and with Kerrianne so close . . . How do I explain this? It's safer to deny myself the touch.

Antonella smiles coyly. "Well, my father wanted me to be involved. It's the 'insignificant things'" — she uses air quotes — "that Gregorio was willing to let me know parts of. Security checks were one of those things."

For a moment, I wish I had been able to meet her father. The man who made his daughter capable may have been able to give me advice in raising my own. *She'll never be Kerrianne's mother, but she could be a mentor.*

She'll be her mother and mother our next pups. My wolf imagines her belly swollen with a sibling for Kerrianne.

I stuff it out of my mind. Starting to trust her sure as fuck doesn't make her a good mother. There is still a chance this is some grand plan at deception.

But you want her to be. My wolf scoffs. *Quit fuckin' kidding yourself.*

Kerrianne and Declan come out of the tortoise room and

then lead the way back to the kitchen and the living room where they sit down again.

We follow their lead and take our seats.

Again, Declan takes charge of the conversation. "What's your biggest worry about security?"

Kerrianne's eyes get glossy with tears. "That we don't all get to go home."

"You're upset about losing Sean?" Declan asks.

My hackles rise. *Why didn't she tell me?* I want to interject, but Declan seems to have it under control.

"I don't like that he died protecting me. And I know that it's supposed to be better now but . . ."

"But even though it isn't your fault, it feels like it." Declan gives her a reassuring smile.

Where is this conversation going?

"I promise you, Kerrianne. Guys like me and Sean, we know the risks of this life, and it's an honor to get to protect you. If dyin' is what it takes to get the job done, then God says it's our time to go. We don't argue with God about it." Declan mostly faces Kerrianne, and he levels with her.

Treats our pup with respect. My wolf approves with a firm nod. He settles inside me, retreating with the lack of threats.

"Okay." Kerrianne's voice is small, and after a few seconds, she asks, "Do you like going on field trips?"

"Field trips, approved, can be fun. Do you ride on the bus, or do we drive separately?" Declan cocks his head with the question that's security-minded but benign enough that she doesn't notice.

"I ride on the bus." Kerrianne eyes him suspiciously. "Do you listen to music or podcasts?"

"Music. Got too many voices in my own head to be hearing other people blabber," Declan answers, letting Kerrianne take charge of the interview now.

"Are you gonna yell at me?" Kerrianne glares.

"It's not my job to parent you. I won't yell. If I raise my voice, it's to shout, and it'll be because you're not being safe. But once you are safe, then it's up to your da how things get handled." Declan is firm about it. "I won't lie or keep anything from either of ya where your safety is concerned. It's not my job to do anything but make sure you're safe."

Antonella's movement of her hand, low on the couch, is out of sight for Declan and Kerrianne, but I take a quick glance, and she's holding her thumb up in approval. First with a firearm and now with a member of the security team, Antonella is quickly proving that she's capable and competent for this life.

I don't know if I should be excited or even more wary about her presence because of it. If Antonella really is only the truce caller or someone who is fed up with the violence, what does that mean for our life together?

A year where we don't get shot at. My wolf thinks about a life with her again. Taking a walk down the pier with Kerrianne between us.

CHAPTER THIRTY-TWO

ANYTHING BUT ROY!

Sleeping in Valor's bed, eating breakfast with him and Kerrianne, and leaving for school have almost become normal. It's so weird. Now that everything changed, I don't know what to do with myself. So much so that I took a deeper inventory of the pantry and lamented that I need more hobbies now that I don't have my master's program to throw myself into, friends to grab brunch with, or a cousin to annoy.

Kerrianne comes running down the stairs, and the whoosh of the front door opening has me on edge. I step around the wall in the kitchen to witness Kerrianne squeal in delight as she practically tackles an imposing dark-haired man.

I stop, stock still. I recognize him. I know who he is, and it makes sense for him to be here. But how many times will it take for me to come face-to-face with the Cavanaghs before I'm not afraid for my life?

"Dad!" Kerrianne shouts. "Dad!"

Valor comes in from outside where he was working and, I think, spying on me. He stands behind me, resting his hands on my shoulders with a soft squeeze. "Little raptor, how did you catch Royal?"

"I can explain," Royal starts, and he spins Kerrianne around as he walks toward us.

Valor steps back, retreating toward the kitchen, and I follow, going back to where I was making some quiche for breakfast.

"Hey, Antonella, nice to meet you. I'm Royal. You can call me anything but Roy." Royal, Valor's younger brother, doesn't offer his hand to shake, but he does give me a warm smile.

"Well, Anything But Roy, it's a pleasure to make your acquaintance." I wrinkle my nose at Kerrianne, and she starts laughing, clutching her stomach.

"Charmed, I'm sure." Royal shakes his head, and his cheeks turn pink.

He purses his lips, and it's clear that I've broken some of what could have been discomfort between us.

"Have you had breakfast?" I offer him a plate.

"He ate," Valor grumbles, and I put the plate back. "Royal, why are you here?"

"I told him about show-and-tell, and he said he'd come right over." Kerrianne looks up at Valor and shuffles herself between the two titans.

"Show-and-tell?" Valor looks to me.

"As in show-and-tell happening in January after the holiday break?" I try to decode where Kerrianne is coming up with these things.

I've been working on next semester's lesson plans each night, so that's the only thing that comes to mind.

"I don't know what to bring. And last time Dad said I can't keep bringing Captain." Kerrianne looks around the house like she's expecting a magical thing to appear that she can show.

"So." Royal beams at his brother before hoisting Kerrianne up and holding her to his side. "Maybe we can finish the robot for show-and-tell."

Kerrianne screeches in excitement, and it echoes around the open house.

Royal scrunches his shoulders up around his ears and puts a finger in front of her lips. "Yikes! Kerrianne. We talked about that."

"Sorry," she whispers and repeats what must be a rule. "No screaming like woo girls or howling in the house."

"Oh, good, we're teaching my daughter what woo girls are." Valor scrubs his hand down his face.

"I didn't tell her what they were, just that they scream." Royal defends himself, pointing between Valor and Kerrianne.

I try to do something intelligent, but I'm at a loss, watching the Cavanaghs and this whole new dynamic. Valor walks around the island and starts dishing out quiche.

"If we're doing a robot for show-and-tell, then I need robotics parts," Royal starts as he sets Kerrianne down and shudders a little bit, pulling on one of his ears. "And the convention is in town this weekend."

"Declan hasn't even started yet," Valor groans, scolding him. "I don't have a —"

"Really? I'll be with her," Royal snaps. "We get more free stuff if I bring her with. Tech dudes love to see little tech girls getting into this sort of thing. Please?"

"You make it sound creepy when you say it like that," I stage-whisper, at least finding something to add to the conversation.

"Fair enough," Royal stage-whispers back over his shoulder.

Valor sets a plate down in front of the stool where Kerrianne usually eats breakfast. She hops up and starts shoveling food into her mouth.

He scolds her softly. "Slow."

"What I mean to say is that there aren't enough young girls interested in STEM and STEAM, and they get the most free stuff because of it, and some of the free stuff is stuff you can't get until the new year. So, even though we're absolutely loaded and my tech budget is through the roof, I can't physically get these things." Royal beams at his older brother.

"You want my child so that she can con the tech guys into giving her stuff for you to use to build her robot?" Valor crosses his arms.

"Daaaaaaad." Kerrianne pouts, her whole bottom lip jutting out. "Please?"

Valor turns to look at me.

I freeze and weigh the options. *He doesn't want a mother for her.* I shrug and give him the educator's perspective and keep it as impersonal as I can. "Well, it is a good opportunity for Kerrianne to experience things her regular activities at school won't start supplementing until she's a bit older. The robotics lab starts next year."

"Seee!" Kerrianne shifts back and forth on her stool before having a few more bites of food.

"You're taking a team of six. If I hear one single incident of something not being right, you're coming home." Valor has to shout the last part of that sentence because Royal has already scooped Kerrianne off the stool and is charging back through the house.

"I already got a team together! I'll have her back by dinner!" Royal calls back, and in less than ten seconds, the front door closes.

"Was she already wearing shoes?" Valor groans.

"She had shoes. No jacket though." I nod while plating some of the fluffy quiche.

Valor accepts the plate from me and draws a long sniff before wetting his bottom lip. It looks as if he'll lick it straight off the plate. "She'll be fine. It's not that cold yet."

"Valor, it's December. It's one thing for you to sit out there . . ." I stop because he turns his back on me going outside to collect his laptop. *Clearly, we're not talking about that.*

On returning, he picks up the conversation. "I've gotta make some calls. Are you okay? Need anything? Jack can take you into town to . . ."

I shake my head. "It's okay. I'm working on some lesson plans."

There's a fleeting few seconds of awkward silence, but then Valor leaves me to my own devices.

Guess I am the Mafia wife, married off and left alone. Could be worse.

Drumming my fingers on the countertop, I pick up my phone, where I had been plugging ingredients into a search engine to look for a new recipe.

I hesitate over her name. *Leticia D'Medici.* It's so formal written out like that. But it's not my phone. Not really. I'm guessing Royal put it together and organized it, so it made sense to him. The apps are sorted alphabetically with a little folder separating the 'Tools' — the weird apps and things that are preloaded on the device that I don't know anyone ever uses — and tucked away out of sight.

ANTONELLA:

Hey, it's Toni. Are you still alive?

I send her a picture of my hand in a half-heart shape, so she knows it's me. Just another one of our childhood symbols.

A split second later, I get her hand in the other half of the heart followed by a flurry of messages.

LETICIA:

OH MY GAWD. YOU'RE STILL ALIVE?!

I miss you so much. Ugh. It's been so weird without hearing from you.

Tell me what you can without getting killed.

I love you so much.

Valor

CHAPTER THIRTY-THREE

LITTLE BOXES

"The boxes of your stuff are on their way up the driveway," I tell Antonella as I come into the kitchen.

The morning spent on the patio, doing paperwork for the pack's hunting registrations, calling Doyle in Ireland, and calling the vendor my mother has been struggling to track down for the winter festival is squandered time I could have spent with my girls . . . *My girls, that stupid fuckin' thought again . . .* But when Kerrianne pulled out the puppy dog eyes and imitation of a tail wag, asking to go to the robotics convention, how could I say no?

I confirmed that Royal did line up a full six-man team of guards. It might be overkill at a convention of a bunch of nerds, but after Sean, I'm not risking it.

"Oh, that's great." Antonella gives me a smile, looking up from the dough she's been kneading. I knew she wanted to cook dinner for us today, but fresh bread was unexpected. "This'll have time to rise then."

I'm mesmerized, stopped dead, as I watch her. Her movements are so graceful around the kitchen. She places the dough in a bowl with a dishcloth covering it before moving it to the stovetop. The apron tied around her is sexy, cinched in around her waist. I wonder if she'd wear just that apron and only that apron for me on days we're alone like this. I push that from my mind. She hasn't shown any signs that she's interested in a physical relationship.

Antonella washes her hands, pulls off the apron, and then walks toward me.

Ours. My wolf is locked onto her. *So fucking ours.*

The sway of her hips has me feeling like a teenager, wanting to enjoy her in any sort of way she'll allow. It's unusual. It's not who I am. Yet, I act cautiously, testing the waters by wrapping an arm behind her and resting it on her waist as I turn us toward the front door, where her boxes will arrive.

Antonella follows my lead, fitting in against my side as we head toward the front of the house. I open the door as the cargo van Neil took over to the D'Medicis' comes to a stop.

We opted to send Neil to pick up Antonella's stuff because he brings authority without directly risking the path to the head of the family or line of succession.

Dad and Gregorio will start taking meetings together and try to strengthen the bonds with the families, but there's still a freshness in the animosity. The discussion of me going was quickly thwarted when I mentioned, offhand, that it would give me an opportunity to poison Berto.

Neil tips his hat in a mockery of being formal. "Top of the morning to ya."

I laugh, keeping Antonella tucked into my side. "That'd probably be more realistic if you had an Irish accent and not a midwestern one."

Antonella bites her lips together, but her shoulders quiver as she holds back a laugh.

"I think this vehicle may have been overkill for the number of boxes." Neil opens the back of the van. "I thought surely it was a mistake, but they said you packed your luggage by yourself. I double-checked three times, but they were sure this was everything. If they went through it or took stuff out, I can't be sure, but it seemed pretty well sealed up."

I step around to the opening and find the cargo net holding down four medium-sized moving boxes, two large suitcases, a dress bag, and a carry-on. A hollow pit forms in my stomach, and I clench my fist. Neil is right.

This has to be a mistake. No woman has this few possessions. I don't care how sexist that sounds, it's true. She's twenty-seven. She should have accumulated more than this.

Why is our mate's life so small? My wolf questions it too.

"Antonella, could you come confirm this?"

Antonella peeks around the van door. "Yeah, that should be all the stuff. Assuming no one went through it, but the tape doesn't look cut."

"This is all of your stuff?" I reiterate, pushing out each word while gesturing to the van. "A handful of boxes and some suitcases?"

"Yes. Why are you being weird about it? It's not too much, is it?" She shakes her head. "I can help you carry?"

"That's . . ." I put my hand over my mouth. I let it go. I don't know what situation she came from. I'll ask when we don't have an audience. "Neil, let's get these in the door."

"Of course." He unclips the cargo net, and I grab hold of the suitcases.

They're at least heavy and clearly full. Neil carries one of the boxes, following me, and I hear Antonella pulling another box forward, so I rush back to take it from her.

"You don't have to help. We've got it." I try to keep the growl out of my voice, but I'm pissed.

Antonella raises her hands in surrender, turning to go back to the house, and I try not to focus on how the hollowness moves from my gut to my heart with that. I don't want to be a place of fear for her.

"You think maybe she didn't pack all her stuff because she's not planning on staying here long?" Neil murmurs.

"That'd be an odd assumption." I dismiss him, but silently I wonder the same thing.

I go back to inspecting the boxes by scent as I carry them. The one I grabbed from Antonella smells of books and paperwork. The box Neil picks up smells like leather — purses, maybe, and shoes for sure.

Neil's next box seems to contain more books and toiletries. And the last one is light. Probably mostly empty. I can't make out any particular scents. Must be miscellaneous items.

This is really it? Or is Neil right?

When I close the door behind us, Antonella is standing in the foyer on the defensive. "I didn't know where I was going so I packed everything I owned back into the boxes I moved from New York with. There's nothing I'm really attached to if we need to get rid of some things —"

"Antonella." I place a hand on each of her shoulders. "I'm concerned because I know if I packed up Mom's 'essentials' for a long-distance move, it would fill the back of that van."

She shrugs my hands off her shoulders, and I want to touch her again, to pull her into my arms, but I don't feel like I can. Something about whatever it is between us stops me. I don't know if it's the short time we've known each other or the situation. Or the fact that Neil made me question why she's here . . . But I didn't expect the desire to comfort her to hit me so hard.

It's because she's not just a wife, she's our mate. And you're being a dick about everything. My wolf scolds me. He pushes me to get closer to her again.

"I don't have a lot because I haven't really called any one place home for a while. College, then two years teaching, back to grad school. I rented apartments that came furnished so I wouldn't have to ask Berto for help moving." Antonella looks at the boxes, stepping toward them to maybe pick one up. She stops herself, her hand bent at the wrist as if to make a stop gesture toward the floor.

The truth in her words is undeniable, and I'm relieved that it's not what Neil thought. She doesn't have things for a valid reason, but I get an inkling there's more to what she's saying, the same inkling I get that tells me when to push someone in my basement a bit harder for information. "There's more to it than that."

She's ours, and we want everything about her to be safe and happy, my wolf adds.

"Gregorio is on all my bank accounts except for one, which I set up to filter some of my paycheck away to hide from him. It's spending money." She sighs and turns to look at me. "I'm entitled to a one-quarter pay out of the family business." Frustration looms, her eyes getting cloudy and her jaw tightening. "But God forbid I touch it. Any purchase or dollar amount beyond what Gregorio deems appropriate is labeled as a bad decision. Which he then uses as further proof to support his opinion that Eduardo's son, Romeo, would be better to take over as consigliere. Women are too frivolous for business."

I'm stiff, rigid, my body begging for violence. I want to shift, stalk, and to kill him.

Kill all of them. To hell with our laws. My wolf is ravenous. *I want to end each and every one of them.*

I hold him back, pulling calming breaths and forcing my shoulders down and back. "That ends now. I'll take you to our credit union on Monday after school, and we'll get you a new account and then request a wire transfer from your bank. I want you to have access to it anytime you want." I try not to smile, already glad that I've done this, but my lips are traitors, and I do smile at her as I pull out my wallet. "I'm sorry this took me a bit of time to get. I paid to have your license expedited, but it would have been faster for our forgers to make one for you."

The two cards flick out easily from where I tucked them, and

I hand over her new ID and the credit card connected directly to mine.

"Valor," she huffs, frustrated, looking at the two of them. Then Antonella offers the credit card back to me. "I explained."

"Wasn't offering, princess." I don't accept it back, picking up her suitcase instead. "Gregorio may feel obligated to take care of you per your father's wishes, but it's my honor and duty to make sure you're cared for. There's an expectation of our people that you're well taken care of."

At least I'm getting good at not calling it the pack in front of her. No more slipups.

She grabs her garment bag and follows me as I carry the suitcases upstairs. "Well, the good news is that I'm well stocked with clothes, and I believe I can meet those expectations of your people with my salary. Rothschild-McClintock Magnet School pays quite well."

"They better," I grumble. Kerrianne is worth every dollar I've put into the school and the tuition I pay, but I never considered looking into the teachers' salaries. But she's either misunderstanding that it's supposed to be my privilege to make sure she's well taken care of or she feels like she needs to prove something to the pack. That privilege is one I gladly embrace. "Let me take care of you."

My heart aches with that. Soul deep. I want to take care of her. *Maybe the damn wolf is right. She could be ours.*

Antonella

CHAPTER THIRTY-FOUR

SKIN DEEP

Valor carries the boxes to the second floor, where the bedroom is, and sets them down inside the massive walk-in closet.

"Books and other —" But his phone rings. Valor looks down at the screen and shakes his head. He raises a finger to indicate that I give him one minute before answering. "Valor."

His phone volume is low, and I can't hear the caller. "No, bring him through the back. Don't be stupid. I don't want blood all over my floor. Just because I have a wife doesn't mean she needs to do housework."

Valor rolls his eyes at me. "Yeah, we'll be down in twenty minutes. Don't bother securing the delivery. We can do it ourselves."

Valor hangs up and sighs. He starts taking off his dress shirt. "Change of plans. I've got to work, and I need your help."

"Okay." I draw that out, eyeing him. "What are we doing?"

"What I do best?" Mischief lights up his eyes. "Put on clothes you don't care about getting bloody."

I was so naive to think we'd never come to this point. It was so easy to get caught up in the changes of my life, but of course the real world had to come crashing in around me. The way

Berto described Valor comes flooding back. The cruel words and ghastly stories of the state of the bodies we managed to get back from the Cavanaghs fill my brain. *He fillets the skin right off the muscle, a thousand little cuts* . . . I force Berto's words from my mind.

Without argument, I pick up one of my suitcases and pull it over to a box to stack it. We change in silence, and when I put my hair up into a bun, I can't take the silence anymore. I can't take the noise in my head that I keep trying to block out.

The words come out in quick succession before I can over-think them. "Is it true what they say about you?"

"Depends on what they say," Valor answers, propped against the frame of the built-in closet doing something on his phone, but he puts it away.

With his head cocked, a glint passes through his eye. It's almost like they turn a different color for a moment.

"That you hurt others to get information?" I dance around the gruesome words and beg my stomach and its contents to stay in place.

"Is that really what you want to ask?" Valor steps forward, his eyes gleaming and changing again as he walks toward me.

I wonder if my eyes look weird in this light too?

He's well within reach. Warmth radiates off his body, practically begging me to touch him.

"You know I hurt people for information." Valor raises his hand slowly toward me. He pulls one of the short strands of my hair back out of my face and brings it back along my head, gently tucking it under the elastic band. "What you really want to know is if I enjoy it."

My mouth is dry, and I try to swallow. It's hard and I'm uneasy. But I nod a response for him.

"Yes," Valor says coolly. "I enjoy my work. I'm good at it. I don't expect you to like it. But I need you to see it for yourself. You need to be eyes wide open in this marriage. It's been too easy of a life this week. The D'Medicis were our largest and most vocal enemies, but that doesn't make them the only ones."

I draw shallow, steadying breaths. We're both stuck, examining each other, watching for something unknown to pass between us.

"Come on, I'll show you the entrance to my lair."

"Do you usually call it that, or is it for dramatic purposes?" I sass him.

That draws a slow smile across his face. "I like when you get sassy like that. Keep it up, and we'll get dirty in other ways."

My breath catches. I look away from him, and he leads the way out of the closet.

When we get downstairs, I head toward the kitchen. "How long will this take?"

"As long as it takes?" Valor says, following me.

I turn toward him. "Like I should put the dough in the fridge to slow the rise or we'll be done within the next two hours?"

Valor shrugs. "Leave it. We can take breaks and come put your bread in."

"This feels very much like a team-bonding exercise." I eye him before looking down at the dough. "And the bread probably needs ninety minutes to rise."

"So scientific," Valor notes, coming to stand behind me.

I stiffen. But there's nothing pressuring about it. Instead, Valor rests his head on my shoulder and looks down at the dough. With him so close, the rich scent of bourbon and chocolate floods my senses. And I relax. *How do I tell him I want more of this? How do I convince him to be this way with me more?*

"So, you can tell it'll be ninety minutes because?" Valor wraps his hands around mine on the sides of the bowl.

"How much it rose in the time it took you to bring the boxes in and carry them upstairs, then some estimations about the yeast and how much it will rise, continuing on the same scale," I explain with a small shrug, trying not to dislodge him.

Valor pulls his phone out and sets it on the counter. The screen saver of Kerrianne and Captain gives way to the phone screen, where it shows his recent call from an unsaved number. He goes to the clock app and sets a timer for eighty-eight minutes before pulling away from me. "Alright, let's go."

He tucks his phone back in his pocket, and I'm stuck following him. Dumbstruck by his care over my bread. He could have walked away and said nothing about it, but Valor took enough interest and concern for the work I'd done to set the timer.

I follow him back through the house, down the stairs like we're headed to the shooting range. But we veer off to the home gym, which I assume he uses during the day when I'm working since I haven't seen him in here. It looks normal, with only one way in or out. And then Valor puts his palm against the mirror, and a light blinks through the glass before the wall opens.

He pulls the wall back, like a door, revealing a small chamber. "Your palm print will open this. If the house is, for whatever reason, invaded, take Kerrianne and yourself and go out this way."

Valor flags me into the small dark chamber beyond the wall. A motion-activated light flickers on as I step in. He shows me how to pull the wall closed, and it locks behind us. Then Valor pushes another door open.

The butcher shop downtown looks dirty compared to the sparkling clean stainless-steel and white-walled room Valor leads me into. It's spotless and shiny. A computer table is set up on the left, with a tablet stand and monitor, followed by a wall with cabinets full of what I assume are torture implements and cleaning products. It smells clean but not sterile or bleached. A stainless-steel table is on the other side of the room, in front of a door, which I assume leads out. But perhaps the most intimidating part is the central piece.

A stainless-steel chair, with spikes and sharp corners, is

menacing. Chains and metal loops, clearly meant to restrain someone, make it all that much more foreboding.

"Afraid yet, princess?" Valor's voice drips with something dark.

He walks across the room, gesturing for me to follow, and pushes a swinging door on the other side of the room from where we came in. Beyond the door is an underground parking area.

"I'm not afraid," I tell him, looking at the vehicle stowed down here. "Though, I am wondering what your favorite way to kill someone is."

It catches him off guard, but Valor recovers flawlessly. "Depends on my mood. Now, as I was about to say . . . This tunnel leads two miles away from the property to a little shed owned by a friend of a friend of a friend of the family," he tells me. "Normally, the only people who see the tunnel are my most trusted confidants or my next victim. But the latter never get to see the way back out."

I follow Valor back into the stainless-steel room and ask, "Normally, because I'm not a trusted confidant?"

"No. You're not. But I trust you enough to get Kerrianne to safety and enough to keep your mouth shut about what you've seen."

Valor is back to being so cold with me that it almost hurts.

There's nothing more to say, but I wait with him. In five minutes, the low rumble of a vehicle driving down the interior driveway comes through the doors. Valor is still cold but now impatient. He walks back to the doors and leans, holding one open. I follow, slowly, and get there in time to see a van, which I'm certain delivered my boxes a little over an hour ago, deliver a whole new cargo.

After opening the back doors, Neil and another man drag someone from inside the cavernous interior. He kicks and shuf-

JAEGER ROSE

fles, trying to escape, but the bag over his head and his arms bound behind his back aren't doing him any favors.

"Quit your sniveling," Neil snarls at the man.

It's an almost animalistic sound, and it startles me more than seeing them drag the man into place. I hold one door open out of the way while they bring him in. And in response, I get a grunted 'thank you.'

"Table or chair?" the second man asks Valor.

"Chair," he answers. "My wife has bread rising, and I don't want the smells of intestines screwing up the joy of freshly baked bread."

I try not to let my face change and remain impassive, but at the thought of what Valor is saying, I feel my features contort. If anyone sees, they don't call it out.

They have the man strapped into the chair, and when I stand next to Valor, the second man offers his hand out to me. "I'm Gavin Cavanagh. Neil's youngest. Nice to meet you. I'm sorry I wasn't there for your wedding. Pleasant surprise to see you now."

"On such short notice, I don't blame anyone for not being able to attend." I shake his hand, indulging his attempt at small talk. It slowly creeps in, though, that we're doing so with a man strapped to the chair in the room.

"Are you two staying for the information or do you want the notes?" Valor asks, looking between Neil and Gavin.

"Staying. I don't want to make a second trip if you're not playing with your victim." Gavin nods toward the poor man.

"How fast this goes depends on our friend here." Valor steps toward the man and pulls the bag off his head. "Well, well, well, if it isn't my good friend, Marc."

When I see the man's face, recognition has me drawing a sharp inhale before rational thought leaves me entirely.

"Are you fucking shitting me? Marcell Lawrence Trakas!" I snap at him and lunge forward, rage brewing inside me.

Valor wraps his arms around my waist, holding me back.

"Oh, shit." Marc's eyes go wide. "Toni, I didn't know you'd be here. I'm so sorry. I didn't — It's a misunderstanding. These guys. I'll go. It's not like I came here on purpose. It's, I'm —"

Gavin rips off a piece of duct tape from a roll conveniently hanging on his belt and slaps it over Marc's mouth before muttering, "Jesus Christ, Valor's woman is as scary as he is."

Valor pulls me tightly against his chest. "Whoa, easy, princess. How do you know my friend, Marc?"

"This motherfuckin' asshole is the sleaziest son of a bitch I ever fucking met, and I promised the next time I saw him that I would gouge his eyes out of his head."

My blood boils with renewed malice at seeing him again, and I fight against Valor's hold around my waist.

"Patience," Valor says softly. His words are laced with a deep tone that settles in my bones and calms me down. "Steady, Antonella, Marc isn't leaving here alive. I have no problem sharing my toys. But I need a little information before he departs Earth."

Marc's eyes bulge, and he shakes his head, trying to talk around the tape.

He gets to suffer.

"Antonella, I'm letting you go, princess. I need you to not kill Marc right away, okay?" Valor isn't really asking. But his words pitch like a question.

Rather than answer, I stop fighting against Valor's arms. I try to draw slow breaths, and my fingers clench into fists. The crescents of my nails digging into the skin grounds me just a little bit. After a few more breaths, Valor must believe I won't charge Marc because he lets me go.

"That was fuckin' hot." Gavin looks me over, and I glare at him. He raises his hands in surrender. "In a completely platonic, 'you're my cousin's wife' type of way." Gavin — smartly — changes the subject. "Oh, and really, you can't trust a dude who spells Marc with a *C* instead of a *K*. It's like they're trying too hard."

"It was fuckin' hot in a 'she's my wife' type of way," Valor huffs.

He steps toward Marc and the chair he's been strapped to, wrists bound to the armrests.

It looks painful. I move my hands, thinking what it'd be like to be bent at that angle. *Ooft. No, thank you.*

Valor stoops to get eye level with Marc, and the patronizing droll of his voice cuts through the chilly basement air. "Marc, I'll untape your mouth. It seems like it's in your best interest to not aggravate my wife, and I know that'll be hard for you."

Marc whimpers like the sniveling sack of shit he is, but he nods, and Valor removes the tape.

"Now, Antonella, why don't you tell me how Marc ended up on your shit list?" Valor doesn't look back at me.

"Well, this disgusting pig used to take videos of girls in the locker room at Our Lady of Good Council Preparatory. Then he'd sell that footage to the boys of neighboring high schools. To be honest, I wouldn't be surprised if you saw some of it." I clench my fist tighter, fighting the urge to slam it into his face.

"Oh, Marc." Gavin tsks. "You're a special snowflake of a slimeball. See, what did I tell ya, Marc with a *C*? What a cunt."

Valor is calm, and I dislike it. He has a fucking daughter, yet he had no reaction. He doesn't even move.

Slowly, though, there's a shift in the air. It creeps in like frost inching over my body.

A noise comes from Valor. It's a growl, practically inhuman. His voice is much deeper than it was before. "And what happened to Marc after he was caught?"

"Well, when I caught him, I beat the shit out of him." It was the first time I ever hit someone. Slamming my knuckles into him hurt. I learned to do it better, but the pain was what stopped me from killing him. "And then Berto found out he was the one filming. Last I talked to Marc, he was in a hospital bed with two broken legs, all his ribs broken, and he was gasping for air when he promised me that he'd move states and wouldn't be seen again. Apparently . . . he's not a man of his word."

"Toni," Marc starts. My name comes out like a gasp and raspy, like when he said my name in the hospital bed.

Gavin puts the tape back over his mouth. "You never learn, do you?"

Valor stalks across the room to his cabinets. After pulling out some equipment, he brings the tools to the stainless-steel table, which he pulls toward Marc.

"Marc, I wasn't mad when we found out you were the one responsible for selling the fight locations to the D'Medicis. I was disappointed. Were the D'Medicis paying you? According to Neil here . . . They weren't. You were volunteering information."

Marc fervently shakes his head.

So much for Berto being on the same team. So much for Berto wanting the same things. I can't believe he'd even talk to Marc again.

Valor pulls the tape off Marc's mouth and puts it on his arm. He squats down and snaps his ankles into harsh buckles at the bottom of the chair. It must hurt because Marc winces.

"No, I never took their money. I thought they were coming to place bets. You know I want to make a buck on the easy marks. It's not like they'd know the fighters. Money is money. It all spends." Marc's nose is running, and it's disgusting.

"That's good. Noble of you trying to bring in business." Valor is calmer as he bends, so he's eye to eye with Marc. "Who else were you talking to?"

"Nobody!" Marc objects, but it's too loud, too quick, and obviously a lie.

Valor shakes his head and turns back to the table. He grabs some sort of long blade. It's mounted between two handles on either side. "Do you know what this is?"

Marc swallows and slowly shakes his head. "I swear. I didn't tell nobody nothin'. I didn't sell the footage. I stopped. I never did anything else again. Valor. I swear. Nobody else knew about the fights."

"See, Marc. I've got a special power. I can tell when people are lying, and you keep lying to me. This is a curved draw shave knife." Valor holds it up for him to see.

He shows Marc how sharp it is by pulling his thumb across the blade. The snick of metal is loud enough to be heard over Marc's harsh breathing.

My heart is beating heavily in my chest as I imagine how Valor plans to use the knife. It looks sharp enough for a decapitation, but Valor doesn't seem done with Marc. Seconds later, my guess is proven right.

Valor lowers the blade to Marc's lap and situates it on top of his thigh.

"Valor. I swear. I told the D'Medicis and no one else. I don't come to the cities except for your fights. Make some bets, get some money, then I leave again. I don't talk to no one else," Marc whines, his whole body shaking.

Valor's blade cuts through the fabric of Marc's pants. Marc screams out like he's in pain, but there isn't any blood. All Valor did was strip the fabric off his leg.

But a smell penetrates the air. It's an acrid pee smell I'm attuned to from teaching.

"I hate when they fuckin' piss themselves," Neil groans.

I pull my eyes away from Valor as he slices off Marc's pant leg to see Neil pat a very pale-looking Gavin on the arm.

"I'm going out to the van. You comin', Gavin?"

Gavin looks like he'll be sick, and there isn't even any blood. Apparently, he's squeamish at even the prospect of it.

He looks to me. "You wanna come too, A?"

I shake my head. "I'm good here. I want to see this fucker suffer."

Gavin and Neil leave as Valor cuts down the other side of Marc's pants. He throws the fabric aside and looks back to me.

Valor's eyes are dark, his face all stern lines and rage. "Did he sell videos of you?"

That question hits me like a punch in the gut. It makes me close my eyes, but that's not enough. I turn my head away from him, and it's still not enough. Rotating 180 degrees around is the only way I don't feel the full force of the shame. But for the first time I've thought about it in over a year, a new thought screams louder than the rest. *What if Valor doesn't want me because of this?*

There's a loud smack. The sound of skin on skin. It comes twice, thrice, and on the fourth, it finally stops.

Valor shouts, "You're a dead man!"

The words echo around the room. It eases but doesn't resolve the thought in my head about Valor wanting me.

Marc sobs, "I didn't know. I was a kid. I didn't know."

"You didn't know filming teenage girls changing was wrong?" Valor must hit him again.

"I didn't know she was yours," Marc wails.

"Who are you giving our fight information to? Who the fuck knows about the fights?" Valor presses.

I hear a snick of maybe shears of some sort as they open.

Marc's scream covers the sound of whatever Valor does.

"You've got nine more fingers. I'll let her kill you quickly if you fuckin' tell me all our secrets you've been sharing." Valor threatens him.

Or is it offering reprieve? I can't decide.

"D'Medicis." Marc whines through my old last name. "And some guys at the bar. I think they're Chinese? They're nobodies. But they asked where they could get brutal action, and I told them. Really, though, they only had one gun between them. Who could be dangerous if they have only one gun? That's it. They're nobodies."

Valor seethes, making a deep hissing noise like air between teeth in a clenched jaw. "Describe them."

"I don't know, man. Asian?" Marc whimpers. "One had a scar on his jaw."

"And let me guess. One had a really messed up nose. It had been broken a few times." Valor seemingly knows these men.

I finally work up the courage to turn back around. Marc's face is swollen on his left side. It's bright red and his eye is starting to swell. Valor's body is blocking one of his hands from my view, which I'm guessing is the one he removed a finger from.

"I guess." Marc looks at Valor and his hand. It's hanging at his side, and he's holding a scissors-like item, spring loaded with nasty, large blades coated in blood.

"You guess?" Valor doesn't let Marc off the hook.

"Yeah, it was bent, kinda to the left?" Marc questions what he knows.

"Yakuza. Fuckin' exporters. At least they already buy our weapons. Won't be hard to clean up," Valor mutters, turning back to the table.

Every rise and fall of his shoulders comes with great effort, the breath slowly leaving his lungs.

He looks up at me. "I'm seeing if Royal can find every video with you in it, and I'll personally kill anyone in possession of one."

"You can't just kill people for seeing a video over ten years ago." I shake my head.

Why is that the most romantic thing I've ever heard? What is wrong with me? I wet my lips and run a hand down my face.

Valor scoffs out a laugh but doesn't comment.

"Marc, how long have you been a lying sack of shit and been in Chicago?" I glare at him.

He's pale and looks like he's going to be sick. "A while," he whines.

"Like two or more years?" I snap at him, fist clenching.

"Maybe four? I don't know." Marc tilts his head and squints.

"Valor," I say quietly, drawing his attention away from glaring at Marc.

I don't know if I want to tell him this, but if the truce is real, then it's a show of trust, and there can't be any harm in it.

"I remember Berto saying at Christmas two years ago that the Yakuza were moving in on our territory. He suggested to Gregorio that we attempt a hostile takeover of their business, but Gregorio said it was too big, even for us. The network is so large that it's impossible."

Valor turns away from Marc and cocks his head to one side and then the other. He studies me closely.

"It was two years ago. I don't know what's happened since then, but if Marc's information is real, then maybe they're taking a bigger foothold here." I shrug, trying to offer help.

"Maybe. An enemy of my new friends makes for a very good team-bonding exercise." Valor's lips almost threaten a smile as he quotes me from upstairs.

I look at my smartwatch. We've been down here for forty-five minutes, but it's passed like ten.

"Don't worry. We have plenty of time."

I nod, looking over at Marc. "I'm not sure he does."

Valor turns back to Marc, choosing to pick up the two-handled blade again from the small table. This time, when Valor runs it down Marc's leg, he takes skin off with it.

His voice booms over Marc's screams. "When did you talk to the Yakuzas last?"

I force myself not to balk at the disgusting sight and the spray of blood. It's gruesome.

It's meat. It's like a beef roast. It's not human, it's beef.

Bile rises, but I draw deep breaths, distracting myself by watching Marc's reaction and not looking below his waist.

Marc's head wobbles back and forth before slumping forward. Valor smacks his face.

Coming to, Marc blinks, shaking his head.

Repeating himself, Valor steps away. "When did you talk to the Yakuzas last?"

Marc sobs, shivering, but I can't tell if it's the cries or his body going into shock. "I don't know how long it was. Like a few days after you all told us that all the fights were stopping."

"Three and a half months ago." Valor draws long, slow breaths. "At least you were smart enough to tell them after we moved everything."

"I told them I'd call the guy when we knew where the action would be." Marc's eyes are watering, snot bubbling, and gurgling comes from his throat. The sounds churn my stomach. "But I didn't."

I look away from his face and see the blood from his leg running down the chair to a puddle on the floor. I notice, for the first time, a drain a little ways away. *Practical.*

"Do you want to dirty your hands, princess?" Valor's voice is sweet, almost playful. "Or do you want me to do as you say?"

I've never been in this position. I made threats to Marc's eyes and his life, but I never knew if I'd be able to do this given the opportunity. Examining the table, I step toward it and grab the brass knuckles that are kinda shaped like a cat's head. Two pointing bits poke out from the top, and the space between them looks to be roughly about the size of a rib. I slide the knuckles on my fingers because I've hit someone before. I've punched more than a few people. This much I know I can do.

My heart rate picks up. I dreamed of killing him and getting some sort of revenge. Retribution for what I now know: there isn't enough therapy to ever make the violated feeling go away. I was one of many. But I'm the only one who will ever get a chance to make him pay for it.

Adrenaline sends tingles through my body as I flex my fingers around the metal, savoring the weight. I can't even contain the excited breaths sawing in and out of my chest.

Valor doesn't say anything, but his eyes are locked on me. Every one of my movements has been cataloged on some level since I stepped through the door. *Will he step in if I'm doing it wrong? Is there a right and wrong way to torture and kill someone?*

No. As I meet his gaze, something between us changes. It's less like judgment and a test to see if I'm fit for this and more like concern for my well-being. It feels like approval.

Before I overthink it, I step past Valor and look Marc in the eye. The one that Valor hit is swelling up so much that it's hardly open.

"Fuck you, Marc."

I thrust forward, twisting and correctly intensifying the force until my knuckles slam into his chest. Air escapes his lungs, and Marc sputters and gasps. I hit him again in a different spot. The knuckles are denting his shirt, leaving red marks on the white cotton where I puncture his skin.

Relief floods through my body. Vengeance feels so much better than I imagined. A weight slowly rises from the bottoms of my feet, pulling upward, and I want a little more violence. I need to let a little more of this rage go.

"You're done with him?" I confirm without looking at Valor. If I look at him, I might lose my nerve.

"Yeah. We have his phone and books. Royal can figure out anything he didn't tell us." Valor sounds almost bored.

"I told you everything," Marc gasps, his head falling forward. He wheezes before pleading. "Let me go. I'll leave. I won't come back this time."

"Let you go?" My rage sours the happy feeling of vengeance. I grab hold of his hair, yanking on the strands. I try to keep my voice calm, make him understand how ridiculous he sounds.

259

"You don't get a choice in this any more than I got a choice in you filming me. Filming us."

It's easier than I thought to ram the brass knuckles into his head. The sharp tines poke into both of his eyes. He screams and gargles. I hit him again and again. The crunch of bone turns soft as I start panting with the exertion.

"Antonella," Valor calls, forcing my focus off Marc. "That won't kill him. You're just burning energy, darling. Step back and let him bleed into his lungs and drown, or use this."

I look away from Marc and the pathetic lump of his body to Valor. He's holding out a pocketknife I don't remember seeing on the table, nor have I noticed it lying out with his wallet in the bathroom where he changes pants.

But when I look at that knife, I know I can't use it. Hitting him is one thing.

But that . . . that I can't do. I'm weak. Too weak to kill him. The self-deprecation sinks in. *Too weak because I'm a woman, because Gregorio is right, women have no place in this world, and because if I can't kill someone who hurt me, how could I have ever expected to stand next to Berto to kill for him?*

Tears well in my eyes, and the thundering of my heartbeat in my ears mixes with a deafening whine of tinnitus. I shake my head.

"You're brilliant, darling. Beautiful as you strike. It's okay to not be able to do this." Valor steps forward, and I move out of his way.

I close my eyes to avoid seeing what I can't hear over the noise in my head.

Marc's death doesn't absolve him of all the shit he's done, no more than it erases the memory of the videos from the boys' brains he sent them to. But there is peace in him being gone for good. That peace has me opening my eyes to see the proof in his limp body.

Valor steps between me and the corpse. His touch is gentle

as he unwraps my hand from the brass knuckles, and it settles me. The tinnitus and hammering of my heart relax, leaving me with a ghost of a headache.

He raises his free hand to wipe at blood or tears on my cheeks. "I'll be right back. Close your eyes and don't open them."

I trust him, letting my eyes fall closed without any objection. Valor's footsteps set a hurried pace across the floor. The door on the other side of the room flaps open and closed. Then two sets of footsteps return.

My body involuntarily jumps as a hand touches my shoulder.

Valor comforts me with kind words, but his hand falls away from my arm. "Easy. Turn toward the exit to the house."

I do as he says, and when I'm facing the opposite direction, I open my eyes to walk around the table and stand with the monitor toward the door. Valor is right on my tail the entire way. He opens and closes doors for me until we're finally back in the gym.

"It never gets less amusing. Gavin can't watch me torture someone but has no problem cleaning up my messes." Valor looks at me as he walks backward through the gym and into the hallway without touching me. It's casual, almost small talk.

He leads the way back upstairs to the kitchen. It's like a world away from the basement. The sun is still shining, and the house is warm and bright.

"Can you check your bread? We're early, but I think you'll want to shower," Valor says, walking to the counter where I left the dough to rise.

I nod and do as he asks. The dough is almost proofed the entire way. "If I hurry, I can shower and get down here before it's ready."

"No," Valor commands, and he's firm. "Tell me what to do and take your time cleaning up."

"Pull the cover back and poke the loaf. If the indent stays, it's ready. If not, re-cover it. If it stays, put it in the loaf pan I already buttered and put it in the oven. It bakes for thirty minutes." I try to keep the instructions clear and concise.

When I preheat the oven to the correct temperature, I see why he wanted to deal with the bread. My hand is covered in drying blood. But it's not only my hand. It's all the way up my arm.

Valor spins me back to face him, and it shakes me out of staring at my appendage. "You were magnificent. Go get cleaned up. I can take care of this."

The gentle touch of his lips on my forehead is unexpected and sends warmth through my body, and for a moment, I let myself want more.

CHAPTER THIRTY-FIVE

MY WIFE, MY DAUGHTER, MY FAMILY

I wash my hands and stare at the loaf of bread. When I poked it, the indent bounced back, and after looking it up on the internet, I know it needs more time.

But standing here, watching the bread rise, my brain runs on overtime, replaying the moment of Antonella's shame from what Marc did to her.

The way she clenched her eyes closed, then turned her head away. It wasn't until that quarter turn, when she faced away from me, that her shoulders rose and fell with what seemed like sobs. Ones I don't even think she was aware of.

She didn't wipe tears off her face. It was like she had been so lost in her head about it.

Our mate was wounded, and now we will make them pay. All of them. My wolf and I agree.

There's no way in hell I'll be able to leave that alone. I need to, at the very least, make sure it's not out on the internet. I may never be able to trace it if it was sent from user to user, but if it's out there for the world to see, it needs to come down at all costs.

My chest swells with pride as I recall the power she packed behind each punch.

Our mate is strong. My wolf pushes.

I haven't even corrected him that she isn't. Anyone would be proud to have a woman that strong. I'm married to her. She gets to be mine.

Gavin doesn't keep his fuckin' mouth shut when it comes to things like this. He'll tell people she helped me with a piece of shit in my chair. He won't disclose who it was or why he was there, but Gavin will absolutely tell them how she snapped and had to be restrained.

They'll respect her. It'll prove how right we are. How right she is for the pack. My wolf pictures us standing together before the pack and her acceptance into it. *All she needs is a wolf.*

A pit of dread sinks in my stomach. I showed her way too much wolf today, and I'm . . . it . . . Showing her has to happen sooner or later. I'll have to show her and then tell her that I have to give her a wolf.

I'm not squeamish. I just filleted someone's leg. But thinking of telling her makes me sick to my stomach. It makes me curl my toes in my shoes and grip the counter.

The timer beeps on my phone, and I'm quick to turn it off. Sometime, while I was lost in my head, the bread rose higher. I test it before following Antonella's instructions and double-checking the internet. After setting another timer, I look at the message on my phone from Royal.

It's a bunch of pictures of Kerrianne playing with robot controllers, shaking someone's hand, and another of her face in an astronaut cutout.

I smile before heading upstairs to the bedroom.

Antonella is quiet but not frozen. She goes through the motions of showering, maybe scrubbing her skin a little too hard, but not dwelling on it. And by the time I step under the water, she's ready to step out. I want to stop her and keep her with me, but I don't.

The little touches we share light fires in me, and I'm not sure how long I'll be able to quell them. I won't push her, especially knowing that she's been violated like that. Marc may not have touched her body without consent, but that doesn't mean I can.

She's in clean lounging clothes when I step out but is sitting on the vanity rather than having left the room.

Antonella whispers, "Thank you for not letting him live."

"No one hurts what's mine and gets to survive. My wife, my daughter, my family. You're all off limits."

Valor

CHAPTER THIRTY-SIX

A GROWING PUP

Winter break classes are underway, and Kerrianne is super excited. It's a good opportunity for her and Declan to start working together, fresh on a Monday morning. After this weekend and Antonella's intensity when she was pissed off, I have no doubts that, between her and Declan, little raptor is safe.

That doesn't change the damn near heart attack I have when I see her cell number come up on my phone early afternoon, right after the school's scheduled lunchtime.

"Hey." Antonella's voice is soft like she's keeping her conversation from being overheard.

"Everything okay?" I lean back in my desk chair and reach for the drawer with my gun.

"It's not bad." Antonella immediately tries to de-escalate my fear. "But Kerrianne isn't quite herself. I don't know. She's maybe coming down with the flu." Antonella continues, her voice low, and I hear her heels click on the floor. "Irritable, lethargic, easily frustrated. She's not herself. It's started to get worse since snack this morning. If she were anyone else's child, I'd have sent her to the nurse. But . . . I mean . . . what's the point

267

in having your daughter in my class if she can't get special treatment?"

My daughter. Antonella being very clear not to claim Kerrianne is so respectful that it gives my wolf a moment to calm down from his protective nature and shift to problem-solving.

Pup will grow. He's adamant that it's probably growing pains of the wolf variety.

I'm not ready for her to grow up, but if she's acting this way, it could be bad. She's a little old for an uncontrolled shift, but that's always a concern.

I pull my gun out of the drawer and close my laptop. "No nurse. Good call. I'll come get her. I'm nearby. I'll be there in like fifteen minutes. Is it possible to give her another snack?"

It's a bit of good luck that Kerrianne's having a growth spurt during the nonmandatory classes. But now it's accelerated the urgency to tell Antonella about who and what we are, or undoubtedly, Kerrianne will be the first one to show Antonella a wolf.

"Yeah, I'll hold her back when I send the rest to art," Antonella whispers. "Got to go."

"I'll be there soon." I'm not sure if she hears that last part, but it doesn't matter because the phone clicks off.

Jack is standing at the door to my office. "That the school?"

"Yeah? How'd —"

"You get a call and start it with 'Everything okay,' it's either your mother or your daughter, and I know for a fact Betty is with Ian and they're at home safe and sound," Jack explains.

"Yeah, Antonella called saying Kerrianne wasn't herself, so you can only assume what that means." I stand up and try to remember freezer contents.

I'll text Mom on the way home. Get more of Kerrianne's favorites brought over.

"Ahhh, crabby and about ready to take her schoolmates' heads off, then?" he asks knowingly.

I tuck my gun into its holster and shrug my coat over my shoulders to conceal it. "I call her little raptor for a reason." I laugh, knowing that my daughter is every bit as fierce as she is sweet.

"Isn't that the truth." Jack leads the way out of my office, and we take the elevator down to the garage where we keep the SUV. "Can't believe your kid is seven."

"Yeah. Can't believe I've survived this long." I sigh and lean against the elevator doors.

Good thing I sat Antonella down and divulged the family secret. My own sarcasm doesn't even amuse me. Especially not when my wolf scolds me for my choice too.

You should've told her. She's our mate, my wolf grumbles. *Then we could be a happy family. But no. You're too busy trying to look for a war like some fuckin' hero. Show her we're wolves, and this will be easier.*

I ignore him as per usual and climb into the passenger seat of the SUV. Tucked inside, I dial the number for Declan.

"Yeah, boss." He answers on the first ring.

"Change of plans with the raptor. Meet us at school for a pickup." I don't bother explaining myself. His first day and things are already abnormal.

"On it." Declan waits for more instruction or for me to hang up, so I close the line.

"What do you think of Declan?" I ask Jack as we settle into the drive through the city streets.

"Good guy." Jack nods, signaling before changing lanes.

He checks the rearview mirror a few extra times.

I check the side mirrors myself. "What are you seeing?"

Jack shakes his head, and we take a wrong turn away from Kerrianne's school. "Call Declan back. Tell him we need him."

With one hand, I dial Declan again, and with the other, I open the glove box to pull out another gun.

"Yeah, boss." He answers on the first ring.

"Change of plans. Again." I hate sounding like a flake, and I put it on speaker.

Jack knows what I'm asking for and starts talking about what he sees. "Follow our vehicle on the GPS. We've got a possible tick, and I don't like it. Gray late model hybrid of some nature. Not your usual assault vehicle."

"I'm comin' from the other side of the school. Give me a few. Keep them circling," Declan answers, accent thick.

I catch a glimpse of the car that Jack thinks is following us. He's right. It's not the usual style vehicle we'd see if they were looking for a shoot-out or a display of power. No, that's a vehicle designed to be invisible. To follow, to intercept and cause chaos, but then completely disappear.

Like the kind of vehicle someone would take our pup in. My wolf, on edge, agrees with me.

I chamber a round, and despite having Declan on the phone, I start texting, alerting those in the area of the potential threat. I hesitate when I get to Antonella's number.

Before I can dial, shots ring out. They pepper the back of the SUV before working their way up the left-hand side. The bulletproof sides hold strong with loud plinks of metal on metal. The windows crack and spiderweb, but the caliber of the round isn't enough to pierce it. When the vehicle pulls in front of us, they shoot, and the windshield also cracks up but holds in place.

The vehicle wobbles.

Jack curses. "They got the driver's side tire."

But as fast as the attack happened, they're gone.

"Think they're circling back?" Jack asks, slamming his fist against the wheel.

The vehicle comes to a stop in the middle of the road, rendered immobile.

Jack is dialing someone on his phone, and the screen shows it's my parents' emergency line.

"Jack?" My dad barks gruffly as he gets moving. "What's happened?"

"Valor and I were shot at. Vehicle is disabled. Declan is on the way to us, but it's suspicious. It's like they were waiting for us to leave the office." Jack growls, moving and bending to look through the fractured glass.

It's not the first time we've been sitting ducks in an SUV that's practically a tank.

"Where were you headed? Should I send a team?" my father asks, completely calm.

"No. No team. We need to move quickly. We're on our way to Kerrianne. She's irritable and Antonella said it looked like the flu," I say.

"A growth spurt," Dad groans.

"How convenient is that?" Neil asks on the line. "Antonella knew you were coming to get Kerrianne, and you're attacked en route? That's suspicious."

"What are you implying?" I snarl.

Neil doesn't back down. "That it's possible your new bride set you up."

Dad's phone is muted, and Declan pulls up on my side of the vehicle. I get out, gun drawn, checking back and forth as I walk around to the passenger seat of Declan's car.

Jack climbs through the SUV, also going out my door, before climbing into the back seat on Declan's side.

"School," I snap before Jack even has the door closed.

Declan guns it, flying through traffic.

"Ian is sending a cleanup crew and a tow for the SUV." Jack doesn't bring up what Neil said. He doesn't need to.

We'll kill whoever hurts her. My wolf paces inside.

We're anxious. My skin feels tight, and my fangs elongate as we drive to the school. I'm ready for conflict at a second's notice.

My focus is entirely on Kerrianne's safety and all the possibilities. There is one possibility I absolutely can't stand the thought of being true. *Could Antonella have set this up? What would she get out of me being dead?*

The rule has always been that, no matter what, Kerrianne goes with her bodyguard for consistency, but between the newness of Declan and being shot at, I can't wait for him to bring her out to me.

In a flurry of texts, I let Dr. Thatcher know I arrived at the building to 'check in' my presence and 'check out' Kerrianne. Finally, I text Antonella when standing outside of her classroom door.

My heart is thundering, and all I want is to lay eyes on them both.

I hear Antonella's heels click along the hard floors as she approaches the door. She asks softly, "Is it urgent?"

"It's me." I confirm for her. *Smart woman not trusting and opening the door.*

She unlocks the door and stands in the opening, looking behind me. She then opens it only far enough for me to walk through. Her scent of fear hits me like a shot to the chest. It floods all my senses, bringing my own back to the surface.

"What's wrong?" I examine her and step around her. *If this pup shifted uncontrolled . . .*

But Kerrianne is still in her human form, her head down, resting on her arms on her tiny desk. Her shoulders rise and fall with the steady rhythm of sleep.

"There's something strange with her eyes. I don't . . . They're not green." Antonella puts her hand over her mouth and pulls it away. "I didn't know if I should call an ambulance. I . . . She ate the same thing everyone else did today. I . . ."

"It's okay. It happens. We'll talk about it at home." I'm swapping one problem for the next.

Kerrianne is safe, but Antonella has seen a glimpse of my daughter's wolf.

Pup is safe. My wolf focuses on the important part. *Our mate is safe.*

I walk over to Kerrianne and crouch down by her desk. I run my hand up and down along her back. "Hey, little raptor. Let's go home."

Kerrianne growls. It's low and would draw a little one from me to scold her.

She lets out a soft whine before turning her head to face me. Her eyes are bright yellow with her wolf right at the surface.

I pet her hair and whisper, "Tuck the wolf away, Kerrianne."

It's agonizing to watch her try. But ultimately, she's not able to get the wolf to go back.

Pup is too tired. My wolf knows.

"Alright, I'll carry you. Eyes closed though, okay?" I murmur, and Kerrianne nods.

It's painstaking to watch her pull herself from her desk and into my arms. I scoop her up, carrying her like I've done so many times before.

With her in my arms, I walk back to Antonella. "Jack is staying here with you. I'm sending a couple cars to bring you home at the end of the day."

Antonella draws her brows together. "Is something wrong?"

I nod, not wanting to lie to her, but that kernel of doubt is in the back of my brain. The one Neil planted. "It'll be fine, but I'll feel better knowing you're safe."

She doesn't question me beyond that, but she does open the door and step out into the hallway first before flagging me out of the room. I effortlessly carry my little raptor back to the secured entrance and am flanked by Jack and Declan to get her in the car.

When she's buckled in, Jack heads back to the school's security office, and as Declan starts to pull away, I debate stopping and going back for Antonella and Jack to bring them home with us.

But I don't. I hold Kerrianne's hand and comfort her on the way home.

I've always allowed Kerrianne to shift anytime she's at home and we don't have company. So when we pull up in front of the door, under the covered parking awning, Kerrianne is barely out of the car before her wolf explodes from her little body, destroying the clothes she wore to school.

Which gets a chuckle from Declan. "At least she didn't shred the inside of the SUV."

I sigh and work the buttons of my shirt on my way to shift with Kerrianne. "Can you imagine if we destroyed two in one day?"

"Pft. Light day." Declan scoffs. "You want me to go back for Mrs. Cavanagh at the end of the school day as extra precaution?"

"Please." I nod, tossing my shirt on the bench by the front door, and kick off my shoes, watching as Kerrianne runs full tilt down the driveway.

Pup got faster. My wolf observes, and I stretch out, letting him take over my body.

Life is simpler with four feet and chasing Kerrianne through piles of leaves that the gardening staff has yet to pick up.

I chase her down, pushing her to run harder around the yard. Then I lead her back toward the house and repeat the process, running out again and again.

For almost two hours, we're out here as wolves enjoying the

elements before we collapse in the yard, both of us out of breath and panting.

She's falling asleep in wolf form when I shift back and pull on my clothes. I grab a dress from one of the gardening boxes we keep around the house and bring it over to her.

"Come on, Kerrianne. Let's get you cleaned up, fed, and put to bed." I hold the dress out toward her.

She groans and lets out the most dramatic sigh in puppy form before slowly shifting back. It turns into a yawn, and she pulls the dress over her head.

After a negotiation of dino nuggets and cauliflower or mac and cheese with hotdogs and broccoli, I get Kerrianne tucked in her bed upstairs right on time for the text to come in that Jack and Declan are on their way home, escorting Antonella.

Antonella

CHAPTER THIRTY-SEVEN

TRUTH IS STRANGER THAN FICTION

When the SUV pulls into the garage, Valor is waiting. He walks over to where I'm sitting in the back seat, Declan and Jack having taken the two seats in the front. I go to open my door, but he's faster and he offers his hand to help me out. I take it without objection, even if this is a strange development between us.

"Is Kerrianne okay?" I look toward the door to the house. "I can make soup?" There's a vacant spot in the garage and I indicate to it. "Is the other one out for service?"

Valor is quiet. Too quiet. It's like that stillness you're not sure you'll survive. The one that screams massive storm, batten down the hatches, and pray you'll see light on the other side.

He backs away, walking me toward the house, my hand in his. "Kerrianne will be okay. I put her to bed, but I bet she wouldn't say no to soup for lunch tomorrow."

I follow him diligently to the mudroom off the garage, where I take off my shoes.

The conversation doesn't pick up between us. Valor doesn't seem to want to elaborate. So, I embrace the silence. Maybe if I work around him, I can wait out the storm he's brewing.

I pull out a stockpot from a cabinet and grab ingredients out of the fridge. Valor's kitchen seems to be continually stocked, his house always clean and fresh. I know it can't possibly be what he does all day, so I assume he has staff, but I've never seen or sensed anyone. It hasn't mattered enough for me to ask.

I've got fresh ingredients chopped and ready to go. Celery, carrot, and onion browning in a pan all while I debone the chicken quarters that were in the fridge.

Finally, Valor speaks. "Someone shot at me today."

His words stop me dead.

My heart hammers in my chest, and I turn off the stove, looking at him. Hoping, praying, for some good news, I look to the stairs. His words implied Kerrianne was alive and fine.

"It was right after we talked and I told you I was coming to pick up Kerrianne." Valor's tone isn't accusatory like one would expect for the easy line of deductive reasoning.

But I don't immediately jump to defend myself. He can check who I've called and talked to with his access to my cell phone and the stupid smartwatch I wear per his request. I have literally zero time in the day between students, home, and bed to talk to anyone.

"I don't think it was you, but there was obvious suspicion that you'd been involved." He walks around the kitchen island that had been separating us and leans against the counter next to me.

His muscles flex beneath his shirt as he crosses his arms, and I go back to work. If he wants to play it cool, then we'll play it cool.

I finish deboning the chicken and toss the bones in water to boil with a bundle of fresh herbs and salt. After washing my hands, I turn back to him.

"Okay, you're doing the 'wait in silence' bit to see what I have to say, but the answer is I don't have anything to say. You don't think I did it. I don't know who would have said I did it.

And most importantly, I didn't do it." The accusation stings, sending violent pins and needles into my heart. I finish a slow exhale, then press the rest of the air out through my nose, trying to expel the hurt and rage before drawing a shallow breath. "To be clear, *it* is telling someone that you were coming to pick up your daughter at the school."

Valor cocks his head.

But now that the fury in my words has started coming out, I can't make them stop or hold them back. I raise a stern finger. "And furthermore, I love Kerrianne so much, and I don't think hurting you would be in her best interest. I don't think putting her in a position where she could be hurt is in her best interest. So, what motive could I possibly have at this point to get you shot at?"

He nods once and uncrosses his arms, resting his palms on the counter behind him. The muscles in his forearms flex with the movement, drawing my eyes — and the heat from my heart admittedly lower.

Could he stop being so fuckin' sexy? It would make it easier to be offended by this. I push the memories of us together out of my mind. *Offended. Not Horny. Offended. Not Horny.*

I cross back to the chicken on the counter and start cubing it.

"You love her?" Valor's voice is low and scratchy.

"Of course I do. What's not to love?" I don't bother looking at him because I don't care if he's offended by my feelings for his daughter.

And after torturing Marc in the basement, I think I could love you too. I keep that to myself. It's too soon for that.

Valor had called what he felt for me falling into lust. Maybe I'd believe that except aside from accidental touches and maybe all of three intentional ones . . . and the kiss to my forehead after killing Marc . . . he's made no move for anything more. I sleep in his bed, and maybe it's for appearances for whoever cleans the damn house, but that doesn't mean I can't or won't develop feelings.

"You're not her mother," Valor deadpans.

"I never said I was." *This man is so infuriating.*

Rather than let myself get angry with him, I slide the knife through the chicken with precision. Valor keeps his knives sharp. After seeing his murder basement, it makes sense that he wouldn't stand for dull kitchen knives.

"I said I love her. I don't try to mother her or step in where it's not my place. Today . . ." I think back to the haunting color of Kerrianne's eyes, something not being right there. "I knew I shouldn't send her to the office. I've never seen anything like how she looked today. Yet, you're not concerned. Not outwardly anyway, so I'm doing what I know how to do for someone who isn't well. Make soup. Gregorio would have a field day with me 'learning my place.'"

Valor steadies my knife hand, and it's then I realize I'm shaking. "This. This isn't your place."

I look at him, and his eyes are the same haunting yellow that Kerrianne's were. I tighten my grip around the handle. My heartbeat thunders in my ears, and my mouth runs dry.

"You were stunning downstairs." The words of praise from him stoke a fire within me. "It was a little under calculated, but we were both in a hurry. Marc deserved to die. You're far more than your ability to make food in the kitchen."

The fire within me, the thundering pulse in my ears, his eyes that are unnaturally yellow — it's all too much.

I step back, pulling the knife with me as I shake free of Valor's grip. "What the fuck is going on?"

Valor runs his hands back through his hair, clearly unconcerned with the knife between us. He walks from the kitchen to the other side of the bar and begins pacing. "Listen, no one has had to do this in at least the last twenty-five years. The best 'advice'" — he uses air quotes to punctuate his point — "is that I should trust you and that you'll understand. Which seems ridiculous. But worse comes to worse, you get locked up in the house and never get to leave again. It isn't exactly how I saw my marriage going. Especially when you just showed me how brutally perfect you can be."

"Okay." I shake my head, watching him pace, not entirely sure I'm following. The space between us lessens the thundering in my ears, but I can barely breathe with the anticipation of whatever it is that Valor is saying.

Locked up in the house forever? No, thank you. De-escalate the situation. I've gotta break it down. "I'm good with the illegal activity that comes with this life." I choose my words slowly, carefully. "I'm not afraid of the work our families do."

But this doesn't feel crime related. Crime doesn't make your eyes yellow and golden.

He turns to face me, stopping for a moment, and goes back to walking the living room repeatedly. "I wish it was as simple as criminal activities."

"Valor, you're scaring me." I warn him with the hope he makes this stop.

It's not a nightmare, but I yearn to wake up from this dream. The air feels thick with ominous tension.

"I know. I can smell your fear." He hangs his head and draws a long, slow breath. "Let's . . . go outside."

He can fuckin' what? I don't want to go. There's something comforting about being in the kitchen, probably the accessible weaponry. From the color of his eyes to the way he paces like a damn predator at the zoo during a field trip with small children, unsettling is an understatement. If he was going to kill me, it would be harder to clean up in the house.

Yeah, it's safer in the kitchen where there are more sharp implements to defend myself.

The sun is starting to set, and Valor holds open the door to the patio and yard. I don't want to go, but he isn't asking. It's clear from his raised eyebrow and stern glare.

I follow, keeping the knife clutched in my hand between us as I walk by him outside. *I'm not going down without a fight.*

He starts pulling his shirt off.

"What are you doing?" I glance back to the door leading into the house.

I'm not naive enough to think locking him out would help me long term, but it could give me time to get upstairs to the gun cache.

"I know, Antonella. I can smell your fear. But there's some arousal too. Afraid and horny . . ." He gives me a sultry smile. "Kinky, darling."

"You can smell my fear and arousal?" I quirk an eyebrow and readjust the knife in my hand.

He nods. "Antonella, my family are wolf shifters. We date back to the —"

"I'm *not* sorry. What?" The words come out before I can even stop them.

Okay, family of crazy people. Formulate escape plan. Berto will have a fucking field day laughing at me.

Valor undoes the button of his pants, and before my eyes, he changes. His body contorts and fur covers flesh, and then there's a large black wolf standing on top of his dress slacks.

"Jesus fucking Christ." I'm frozen in place, eyes locked on a massive wolf.

My phone is on the counter in the kitchen, which may as well be a mile away from me.

My mouth feels like it's stuffed with cotton, and I can't even make myself breathe. I don't know how big wolves are supposed to be, but this seems larger than I thought they were. Educated guess says they're not one of those convenient animals that follow the 'if you don't move, they can't see you' rule. No, that's black bears. Wolves have good eyesight. *All the better to eat you with.*

Really? I'm thinking about children's stories. Fuck!

Apparently, my self-preservation is shit today because I should do something more than stand here. *I should run. I should do something, right?*

"Okay. Good . . ." I don't know what to say. My words come out barely audible.

But it's Valor? Would he want to hurt me? Is he even in there?

I'm lightheaded and have to will my brain to tell my lungs to breathe when I find that I've locked my knees. The knife falls out of my hand, clattering to the ground at my feet as the world spins.

I wobble, and the wolf moves, almost charging toward me. I gasp and stumble, trying to put one of the large deck chairs between us.

Oh, there's the self-preservation button. For fuck's sake, Antonella . . . right on time to fall and get eaten.

But Valor — the wolf known as Valor? — moves way faster than I expected. He's there in an instant, steadying me on my feet. My fingers latch into the fur as I instinctively hang on to stand. The topcoat is coarse and not quite soft, but my fingers sink into the undercoat, and it's cozy like down feathers.

I pull back the second that I'm steady.

My husband is a wolf, and clearly, the wolf is not planning to kill me or let me accidentally get hurt.

He stalks as I walk back around the chair and plop down in it. I cup my head in my hands, resting my fingers on my temples and looking at the brick pavers. *Wolf. He's a fucking wolf. Wolf.* The computer of my brain still not quite catching up, I bounce between disbelief and shock.

Massive black paws come before me, and then I see a wet-looking black nose, and Valor lies down in front of me, looking up. Golden eyes stare at me. Like they were in the kitchen.

Like . . . Kerrianne at school. They're both wolves. He said his family. Royal? Ian? Elizabeth?

I keep my eyes locked on him. They're not expressive like a dog's eyes are. It's a flat look, like when Valor is unimpressed with something.

And then nervous laughter kicks in. I sit back, looking at him, and I can't stop the giggles. "This is my fucking life. I'm forced into a marriage because apparently, I'm the only compassionate person in a massive feud. I protect someone else's daughter on principle and come to find out I'm married to a dog."

Valor snorts.

"Wolf." I correct. "Married to a fucking wolf." I drag a long, steadying breath and shake my head. "Thus the 'will keep me locked up' bit. Because I can't tell anyone, and if you don't trust me to keep my mouth shut well . . . that, yeah."

Valor gives a massive sigh, resting his head on his paws.

"Your secret is safe with me. I was willing to kill Berto for Kerrianne, and we both know you can't trust the government. What would reporting you do? No one would believe me anyway." I press my hands together like in prayer, tapping them against my mouth, self-silencing.

What will this mean for me? How will this change me?

I swallow hard. "And now I'm expecting you to talk back because clearly I've lost the plot."

Valor stands and I freeze. Every muscle tenses as he takes two tiny steps forward and brings his big muzzle toward me. The big muzzle full of big teeth that would probably hurt. Valor runs his nose up between my breasts and then nuzzles his cold nose against my neck.

I squeak in surprise and immediately regret it. I'll get myself killed at this rate.

Then his big, long tongue licks up my neck and flicks my ear as he moves, giving me a big lick up my cheek. I scrunch every-thing together.

"Ew, Valor." I push at the fluff.

The fur on his neck is softer than on his back where I'd used him to hold myself up.

He stops licking me but doesn't back away. He lies back down, and he's so large he has no issue lying on the ground and using my lap as a pillow.

I put my arms on the armrests and take him in. This bouncing back and forth between fear and understanding is giving my heart all the cardio it needs for the week. For a lifetime.

"I'm going to pet you because you're kinda soft, so if you don't want me to, then quit acting like a big dog." I warn him and try to hype myself up to do it.

Picking up a hand, I place it on his massive head. The dark fur is so soft, and when I pet the ridge of his forehead, he closes his eyes.

Valor relaxes, and I keep running my fingers through the short hair on the top of his head and out toward his ears. The cupped triangles are almost as big as my hand, and I wonder if this will be some sort of dream. I'll wake up in Valor's bed with him wrapped around me and laugh it off as having too much wine at dinner and watching a science fiction show before bed. Or maybe I've caught what Kerrianne has?

One of Valor's big ears twitches, and he stands suddenly. He lifts his nose in the air and draws deep breaths, pulling them into his lungs and then exhaling. It's hurried.

He steps back and nudges my leg with his nose. When I don't move, he does it again.

"You want me to stand up?" I ask while pushing to my feet.

Valor flicks his nose to the house, and I don't bother ques-tioning it. The movement very clearly says go inside. I follow his 'instructions' and walk back to the glass door, holding it open for him to come in behind me.

I smell it instantly. Burnt food and hot metal. I leave the door to do what it will and dart into the kitchen. The celery, carrots, and onion are burnt to a crisp in the pan. It smokes and threatens to start on fire.

Valor comes inside. Human and dressed.

I try to deglaze the pan with warm water to clean it up.

But as I do, it doesn't seem to be helping anything.

My head is still reeling as Valor approaches. I note the knife he carries in his hand, and he tosses it into the sink unceremoniously.

"You took that surprisingly well." Valor rests his forearm on the countertop and looks up at me. "And I love to be petted."

Valor

CHAPTER THIRTY-EIGHT

IT TAKES REAL SKILL TO BURN THE SAME SOUP TWICE

"And literally everyone else in your family?" She throws her hands in the air. "Royal? Ian? Elizabeth? Kerrianne?"

"Yes, we are, but that doesn't matter, Antonella."

"What does matter?" she asks while walking the burnt pan to the sink to soak.

She nervously wanders to the fridge and then the cupboards before settling on a water glass and filling it up at the refrigerator.

The scent of burnt food clings to the air, and I want to take the whole pan out to the trash can. It's not worth trying to salvage, but I can't leave Antonella while she's in shock like this.

"Did you mean what you said about keeping our secret?" When I ask that, she stiffens.

"Well, good to know you could understand me." She sighs and sets the glass down.

We lock eyes, and hers are brimming with tears.

Cautiously, I step closer to her. She doesn't smell like fear. She doesn't look away or try to flee. Nothing speaks to the waterworks threatening to unleash.

"Talk to me?" I place my hand over hers on the counter,

caging her in and yearning for more. Seeing her while in wolf form awakened something so deep and needy.

I fuckin' told you she's our mate. Did you listen? No. Now here we are. You finally see it. My wolf berates me.

And I shove him down deep inside because he can rub it in later, but I can't comfort her later. It has to be now.

"Please."

"I'm scared," she tells me, her voice not wavering.

"No, you're not." I contradict her. "You're in shock and handling it well. But there's no fear. Outside, sure, little afraid. Not right now."

I turn her to face me in time to see a tear escape, and I raise my hand quickly, wiping it away. She doesn't recoil so I pull her into my arms. "I'm sorry I scared you."

"I promise, your secret is safe with me," she whispers, resting her head against my chest. "You don't have to do anything to me. I promise, it's safe with me."

I squeeze her tight because those words come with a fear scent. I kiss the top of her head, and she molds against my body. My mate is afraid of me. That hurts deep in my soul. She shouldn't be afraid of me.

"You're safe with me."

Antonella lets me hold her for a minute. Then, in an instant, she pushes out of my arms and narrows her gaze at me. "Kerrianne isn't sick, is she?"

I scrub my hand down my face, trying to keep up with her. "No. She's having a growth spurt, and her wolf is developing more. Luckily, it's happening over winter break."

"And you were letting me make soup and look silly when she wouldn't be ill tomorrow?" Her stern words make me laugh.

"Kerrianne loves chicken noodle soup. She wouldn't think you're silly at all, not after I told her you thought she was sick." I try to downplay my clear negligence on the subject.

Antonella mutters while going to the cupboard where we keep the frying pans, "This man will be the death of me."

"I heard that." I try to draw on some of the ease we'd found over the last week and a half. It hasn't been perfect, but there's been a peaceful vibe between us.

"All the better to hear you with, my dear," she says in a mockingly deep, gruff voice and shrugs her shoulders before retrieving more vegetables.

I grab clean knives and cutting boards and ready myself to help. She lets me, not trying to tell me to stay out of her way but going about our normal every night deal of making food together.

She's so fucking good for me. The wolf was right. Now to make her fall in love with me too.

My smooth chopping strokes stutter for a moment before I recover.

Love.

Shit. I really do love her.

"Alright. Give me 'my husband is a wolf shifter 101' because I'm still not sure if I'm awake, and at least this'll make an interesting dream," Antonella demands as she stirs the new sauté items.

I work to cube the dark meat into Kerrianne's bite-size pieces. "Well, we don't get sick. So anytime Kerrianne isn't her normal, cheerful self . . . it's probably a wolf issue. Hearing, smell, eyesight are all above average. We heal fast. Need red meat regularly. We have pack functions once a month, and you'll need to be there."

And I'll have to turn you into a wolf sometime in the next year. I can't make those words come out of my mouth.

Just tell her now. Let's not make this another round of surprises. My wolf laments with disapproval.

"Okay. So, full moon? Silver bullets? Wolfsbane?" She starts running down the 'typical' wolf things.

"We go running on the full moon because there's brighter light in the sky, makes for better running conditions. Silver is a metal on the periodic table. Bullets are bullets, and a good shot to the skull, heart, or lungs can kill. Wolfsbane is poisonous to everybody, not only wolves." I shrug, finishing the chicken, and head to the sink, where I put the knives in the dishwasher and wash my hands.

"Magic cleaning house and magic grocery pantry and fridge?" Antonella's question comes from left field.

I lean against the counter next to her as she finishes cutting more vegetables to stew. "That's not a wolf thing?"

"Well, how am I supposed to know? I never have to dust or grocery shop for things. They seem to be done by themselves. I've never seen anyone else clean or shop." Antonella gestures around the kitchen.

"Housekeepers and personal shoppers, Zoe and Winnie. They're part of the pack and come over to clean twice a week. They do laundry and take out the dry cleaning too." I can't believe I didn't mention these things sooner. But they're such a normal thing to me that I didn't think of it. "They're in your phone. If you text one of them something you want or need, it'll turn up the next time they're here. If it's urgent, say so. You can also send them pictures of things that can't be washed or need certain treatment. They're ridiculously thorough."

"You sound like Gregorio talking about Leticia and Sarena." She straightens with the realization of what she said. "Sorry."

"Don't be." I nod, hearing her criticism. "If it matters, or helps me not sound like a douchey sleazeball with too much money to spend . . . I'm their only job, and I pay their college tuition as well as a salary that they can more than live on." I grimace. "Yeah, okay, now that I say that out loud, it's not exactly helping the 'way too much money to spend' thing."

"No, it doesn't but yes. It does matter." Antonella purses her lips and looks at me. "Does Kerrianne like egg noodles from the bag or should I make some fresh for her?"

"Bagged egg noodles are fine." I try to reassure her, but there's a stern cock to her head, and she glares at me.

Mate is angry. You stepped in it. My wolf warns, backing up.

"Of course they're fine, but would she like something else?" Antonella snaps and then draws a slow breath, softening a bit. "Oh God, I sound like my mother."

I snort, trying to hold back the laugh and failing. "Would it make you feel better to make her pasta?"

Antonella sighs, and her shoulders slump. "I feel terrible for saying it, but I'm exhausted and really don't want to make fresh pasta."

"Nearly passing out will do that to you." I leave the radius I'd been hovering around her in to fetch the packaged egg noodles.

When I come back, she's still cooking. Chicken in the pan with her vegetables, Antonella doesn't stop moving.

Weirdest case of shock that I know. None of her behavior is expected. I thought yelling, screaming, crying . . . fighting back and the obviously wrong choice of trying to run. Not . . . making my child soup.

"To be clear, you're not currently planning on killing me in my sleep, right?" I set the bag on the counter, knowing they won't go in until much later in the process.

Antonella slowly shakes her head. "No, I won't kill you in your sleep. Where's the fun in that?"

"That's fair enough."

I look around. She's every bit as controlled and relaxed as any other night. The bones are on and boiling, the burnt pan is soaking, and she's searing the chicken. There isn't anything for me to do but watch her.

"This has to boil for a bit for those nutrients. If it's okay with you, I'd like to sit and process." Antonella covers the pan of seared chicken and turns off the heat.

"Yeah, I'll be in my office?" I offer, despite the strong urge to stay by her side. But I'm willing to trust her.

Antonella moves to the sink and washes her hands, addressing me while drying them off. "You don't have to go hide away. I'm not mad at you. I can't figure some things out, and my brain is moving a hundred miles an hour toward a waterfall, and I'm pretty sure there are sharp rocks at the bottom."

"Wine, cheese, and conversation? Or I can order us wings from our first date?" The way I'd move heaven and hell for her right now if she asked.

"Wine, cheese, and conversation would be good." Antonella backs up toward the 'drink fridge' I keep in the kitchen.

I walk past her to the cupboard and grab crackers.

Ten minutes later, we've got an adult snack tray, sippy cups, and an awkward second date in my living room.

"How the fuck did we not know you're wolves? Our families have been fighting forever. Fuck, I've lived here for practically two weeks, and I *just* noticed something weird last night." She draws a big sip of her wine.

I pull my phone out and then use the app to turn on the fireplace. It's not cold in here, but it gives that ambiance that says 'safe' and 'warm' that maybe she needs right about now.

"We've been hiding who and what we are for centuries. It gets harder every year with modern surveillance, but that's why packs buy big pieces of land, hell, entire towns. It gives us space to exist." I pick up one of the slices of cheese and salami, forgoing the cracker.

"So when I said we didn't use protection and you wouldn't say you were sterile . . ." Her eyes are distant, and I'm watching all the things come into alignment.

"We can't get pregnant unless you become a wolf." It clarifies a question she's asked before. One that must be important to her

Antonella sips more of her wine.

She didn't ask to be one of us. My wolf cocks his head. *Does she not want our pups?*

Whoa. Who said I wanted more pups? I argue with him. *Have you not seen the holy terror of the pup we have?*

My wolf doesn't see it that way. He pictures the great afternoon, running with her and all the learning she's doing. The asshole isn't wrong. She's a pretty perfect kid overall, but it doesn't change my feeling that one is enough. *Unless . . . No, the wolf is right. She didn't ask. If Antonella wanted kids, she'd have asked.*

I don't push, and we end up in a comfortable silence, absent-mindedly eating cheese and crackers. When her wine is gone, she pours another glass, and it's halfway to her lips when she springs up off the couch.

"Soup!" she shouts, running, glass in hand, to the kitchen. "God, it would take real skill to burn the same soup twice."

I follow, knowing by smell that nothing is burning, but it's not worth reminding her. "In your defense, the first time was my fault?"

Antonella rolls her eyes with a headshake. "I should know better than to walk away, leaving a burner on. Burn the house down is exactly what this family needs."

"For sure, we don't have an arsonist. Explosive tech, but he's not great at the slow-burn type thing." When she looks at me to check if I'm serious, I shrug and smile.

"Slow burn." Antonella nods. "Yeah, something like that."

Antonella

CHAPTER THIRTY-NINE

ENOUGH IS ENOUGH.

I'm starting to think Valor will give me high blood pressure and is trying to worry me to death. Something stressful happens, we get a day or two off, and then another incident occurs. Saturday, we torture Marc, then in true biblical fashion, we have Sunday as a day of rest. Monday, we have Kerrianne sick at school, a drive-by, and my husband is a wolf. Then Tuesday and Wednesday were fine . . . I'm literally waiting for the other shoe to drop all the way up until I get home, and when nothing bad happens, I don't know what to do with myself.

One thing is for damn fuckin' sure. I need *relief*. The lack of privacy is getting to me. Valor and I get up at about the same time in the morning, and we go to bed at the same time at night. A woman has needs, and I'm close to my boiling point.

"Okay." I psych myself up in the mirror. "We've literally tortured someone together. There really isn't anything more intimate than that. It's sex. He showed you he's a massive wolf sometimes. You've had sex with him once already. You're sleeping in his bed. It's not like you're asking him to take you on a murder spree. Fucking ask him, you wuss."

My reflection doesn't seem to have any more faith in me than the voice in my head does.

Valor clears his throat from the bathroom door.

Like the fraidy-cat I am, I jump, holding my hand to my chest while looking at him. *How the fuck did he sneak in like that?* My cheeks heat with embarrassment.

"Sorry." Valor hangs his head.

"How much of that did you hear?" I murmur, trying to become invisible like the kids in my class by closing my eyes and barely breathing.

"We have already had sex. And if you really do want to kill someone with me, I have a few hits that I could use a hand with." I open one eye to see him rub at a spot on the back of his hand, looking at me like he could probably devour me. "I came up to tell you that we've been invited to my parents' house for dinner tomorrow night and ask if you wanted to attend or if it would be me and Kerrianne. Clearly, uhm . . . we have more to talk about than dinner with my parents."

"Yes." I nod and realize there wasn't actually a question with that.

"Yes, we need to talk, or yes you want to go to dinner with my parents tomorrow night?" Valor clarifies.

"Yes, for dinner tomorrow." I turn away from him and back to the sink, where I run the tap with only cold water.

"Antonella." Valor doesn't leave the doorframe.

But even with his panty-melting tone, there is exactly a zero percent chance I'll turn to face him, so I acknowledge him simply. "Yes?"

God damn it, how many times can a woman say yes without it being suspiciously weird?

Valor moves, and the bathroom is enormous, so there's no mistaking it as an accidental touch when he presses his hand against my hip. I try to sidestep, but his hands have closed me in, and in the mirror, it's clear he's not trying to move me. We lock eyes in the reflection. His front is pressed against my back, and with long arms, he reaches forward and turns off the tap.

The press of his body against mine isn't crushing by any means, but it doesn't help at all with my feelings of lust.

"Antonella." He says my name again, but this time he doesn't wait for me. "I've been a neglectful husband. Please forgive me."

My mouth goes dry. I'm burning up. His heat against me, my embarrassment, and those words, stick a fork in me. I'm done. *Fuck me. Literally and metaphorically.*

Valor leans forward and noses my head to the side to kiss down my neck. He drags his tongue along my skin with each movement, and then he whispers. "Every time you get extra sassy with me, I think about how much I want to see you on your knees in front of me. I want you to show me what else that mouth does."

A shiver racks my body, and I try to move away from him, but there's nowhere to go. My pussy clenches, and the ache I felt from our 'wedding night' feels like it was forever ago.

He circles his left hand from my hip around to the front of my body. "I keep wondering if you're a good girl or a brat because I know you're looking for praise. Is that fiery nature of yours because you're looking for me to set limits and enforce them, or do you want me to prove myself as someone strong enough to handle you before you'll submit to me?"

My mind is blank, but then it whirs to life, trying to process. I understand in part, but what is he truly asking? What difference does this make? And why, even though I'm not sure I understand, am I getting aroused?

"I think I can hear your brain operating on overdrive." Valor lets out a chuckle as he runs his hand down and across my stomach. He expertly pulls up the hem of my shirt before playing with the waistband of my yoga pants I had changed into after school. "Do you want this?"

Yes? No? Yes? No? My brain cycles through the options. *If we do this, what will it do? How will it change us? I want to know what he's talking about. I want to understand why he makes me feel this way so easily.*

I search his eyes in the mirror, and he keeps his gaze on mine. I nod, afraid to speak and ruin the moment.

Without wasting any time, Valor runs his hand between my skin and the fabric of my yoga pants. Forgoing underwear for the ridiculous purpose of not having panty lines haunts me.

"Oh, fuck." He bites his bottom lip. "No panties. Had I known, I might not have waited so patiently. The only thing sexier than a woman in matching lingerie is one who usually wears underwear but opts out."

At an almost tortuous pace, he slides his fingers between my folds, and the pressure of his index finger on my clit sends sparks through my body.

But it's not enough. I adjust by rising on my toes before rolling my ass out toward his hips. The movement has his fingers, which are curled upward, grinding against my clit.

"So needy, taking what I'm not ready to give." Valor clicks his tongue. "I know you want my praise. You light up every time I give you the littlest bit of attention. But how would you like a punishment? Would you take that like a good girl?"

My eyes had felt heavy, but I force them wide open, examining Valor's face in the mirror. He's serious. His stoic neutrality gives nothing away to the interiority of his brain.

He slides his hand out of my pants. "Kerrianne is on her tablet for the next twenty minutes. I'll give you a little punishment for being so needy and denying us both. And then, I'll fuck your mouth while I make you come all over my fingers."

I . . . What? Fuck.

I grip the edge of the counter to steady myself because his words almost make my knees buckle. I'm warm all over, and when I catch a glance at my reflection, my pink cheeks are giving me away.

Valor bites at the side of my neck, and then his hands are back on my waist. He pushes me over the counter, away from the sink.

My body is pliant under his touch, moving easily.

Once my chest is pressed against the surface, he tells me to stay put in that commanding voice he uses so sternly. It's so fucking hot, and I listen.

Except then he grabs my waistband and starts to tug.

"Valor." I object, trying to push myself up.

"No." He grabs my wrists, pinning them behind my back with one hand while he works my pants down with the other.

Once around the curve of my ass and past the lip of the countertop, they fall to the floor, puddling around my feet.

"I was going to give you thirteen for every day I've been denied this beautiful body because you didn't communicate that you wanted more. Two for trying to fuck my fingers without permission. So now you'll get a nice round fifteen for disobeying me." He almost reverently rubs his hand across my ass as he speaks.

I'm lost to the attention of his hands until his words register in my brain.

"You're spanking me?" I ask to clarify.

I've never been spanked a day in my life. My parents never laid a hand on me. And well, Gregorio is too much of a coward to hit me.

"Yes, princess." I can hear the smugness in his voice but can't lock eyes with him in the mirror anymore. "I'm going to spank you. I'll be gentle . . . this time."

The first comes without warning with a sting to my ass, and I yelp in shock.

"Count them. I want you to count and thank me." He prompts me.

I'm quiet. The disbelief in what's happening takes over.

"Don't test me, Antonella. You're already up to fifteen.

Should we make it twenty? Too many and I won't have time to make you come until we go to bed tonight."

I can feel my arousal even without the fabric of my pants against my core. *What the hell is wrong with me?* But, dammit, I need an orgasm. Defeat and embarrassment send a cool chill down my spine as they settle like rocks in my stomach.

I whisper, "One. Thank you."

The next smack comes as I finish saying 'thank you.' I wince. It's a bit harder on the same cheek.

"Two. Thank you."

Valor switches sides, then gives me two smacks, waiting each time for me to tell him thank you between.

We're at eight and my ass is on fire. My eyes are scrunched closed, and I'm barely breathing enough to get the words out.

"You could have been almost done," Valor says, squeezing my ass cheeks. "But you had to disobey me."

The pain from the next one is worse. He hits me harder, and the skin is already tender.

"Nine, thank you."

By eleven, tears are welling in my eyes. He's started switching them one at a time on each side.

"Twelve," I sob, forcing it out. "Thank you."

But it's not shame. It's guilt. It's sickening guilt that I disappointed him. I didn't realize how much I had been working to be perfect for him. It wasn't self-preservation but something deep inside, wanting to prove that I could be everything, but instead I've proven nothing.

"Three more," Valor says softly as he pets the soreness away. He's sweet and encouraging about it. "You can do it, be strong for me."

I sob between thirteen, thank, and you, followed by a quicker gasping fourteen, and finally, mercifully, fifteen.

Tears stream down my face, and I can't figure out if it's from the guilt or the pain.

Valor helps me up from where I'm bent over the counter and turns me to face him. Brushing my hair out of my face, he smiles.

No, now I know for sure. Because the way he looks at me has me crying harder. My knees are weak and my shoulders shake.

As he wipes a tear away, he praises me. "You are such a good girl for me."

He kisses me softly, tongue probing. I feel more in control of my body as the emotions ebb.

His approval doesn't melt away all my disappointment with myself, but it eases it.

"Come to bed." He takes my hand. His touch is gentle and leading as he walks me out of my yoga pants.

When we're in the bedroom, he lets go of my hand. "Head off the end of the bed."

I'm nervous but don't dare disobey, despite how my ass stings when I sit on the bed. Carefully avoiding any unnecessary pain, I lower myself to my back, letting my head hang over the side.

I get a perfect view of Valor, upside down, while he frees his cock. He's hard, and the tip is a beautiful bright pink.

Leaving his slacks on the floor, Valor walks over to me. The head of his cock is almost brushing against my lips.

I want to lick it so badly.

"Good girl, waiting for me. Open." Valor instructs me, and I do, pushing my tongue out, hoping for a taste.

This I've done before. I know I like it. Never from this position, but I'm positive it'll be just as good.

Valor leans forward and sinks his dick into my mouth. And I couldn't hold back my moan if I wanted to. He slides his hand down my stomach and in between my legs. His fingers find my clit, and he strokes it perfectly.

I breathe around his length in my mouth, pressing my

tongue along his shaft to encourage him. Valor doesn't move his dick, but he sinks his fingers inside me. He probes until he finds that spot that makes my body jolt with arousal.

"You're so fucking wet, princess. You're horny for me and that makes me so pleased."

In time with his fingers working my core and my clit, Valor fucks my throat. I struggle to breathe, and gag with each thrust, but I feel how wet I am. The sounds coming from me are pornographic — half choked and gagging between desperate moans.

"That's it." Valor's praise fans the flame of my desire further. "Fuck, Antonella, you take my dick so well."

He works faster, and breathing isn't an option. I shatter, and unable to breathe, the intensity causes me to see stars behind my eyelids. Wetness coats my core, and distantly, I worry about the feeling, but I struggle as I fight the urge to move.

But then Valor cusses and thrusts into my throat. "God, you're perfect. You just fuckin' squirted for me, darling."

A moment later, he shoots his load down my throat. The hot jets choke me as I swallow them, sputtering against his cock. I take everything, and when he finally pulls out of my mouth, I'm panting.

Valor doesn't let me relax for long. He bends forward once more, and I lick along his still-hard shaft as he grabs hold of my legs below my knees. He spins me on the bed, and I squeak in surprise.

"Shhh." Valor scolds me. "We're running out of time. We wouldn't want to be walked in on."

He drops to his knees before me and pushes my legs apart.

When his tongue sinks between my folds, I almost scream, but I clamp a hand over my mouth. The stimulation is so much, too much, and I try to close my legs, to move them, but Valor is relentless. As he licks and sucks, it's a dedication to my body like none other.

He brings me to another orgasm in seconds. I writhe under his touch, and Valor groans.

At last, he breaks the connection between us and climbs onto the bed next to me.

My legs tremble without him supporting them, so I let them drop to the side as I try to control my breathing.

He relaxes alongside me. "What did I do to deserve a woman like you?"

"Can't answer that. I, however, ended a century-old feud by calling for the truce and brought chaos on both our houses." I sigh, my body cooling off, and I shiver. I feel more like myself and calm again.

"Well, when you say it like that, it makes it seem like this'll be a great tragedy." Valor pulls me closer to him.

I revel in his warmth and embrace it. "But we're not star-crossed lovers, only lusters."

Valor stiffens ever so slightly but then relaxes, resting his forehead against my head. "Mmm. I can't wait to get you naked tonight."

He was going to say something else, but I could never prove it.

As the orgasm fades, the reality of what he did to me sinks in. "You fucking hit me."

"Spanked, there's a difference," he murmurs sleepily against my head.

I roll out of his arms, and he grabs me, pulling me back and holding me closer this time.

Our eyes meet, and his are soft, almost sleepy. "Did you enjoy yourself? Not the two orgasms."

"Valor." I start but then bite my tongue.

It wasn't what I expected. It fuckin' hurt, and I don't understand where the emotions came from.

"Say what you're thinking." Valor's words, a soft command, ease the heat.

"I never thought I'd be okay with something like that. I don't understand why I am. It fucking hurt. But I wasn't crying from physical pain." I feel so weak saying those words, and the image of him in front of me gets blurry.

But Valor runs a thumb across my cheek and dries a tear. "Overwhelm, emotional release, and pain can all bring tears. I'll admit to maybe pushing you too hard. But I'm an asshole through and through. Stop me if I say something that's wrong, okay?"

He waits, and after a second, I nod.

"You don't cry. You don't let people see you upset. Angry? Sure. But never when you're honestly wounded or hurt. You're in control at all times, always trying to prove that you're worthy of attention and respect." He pauses, giving me an opening to interject, and as much as it grates me that he clearly knows this part about me, I say nothing. "You carry your pain deep in your soul, never to see the light of day."

His words rouse feelings from within me, like water slowly bubbling up through a fountain turned on for the first time after a long winter. My breathing is ragged, and I'm at a loss. It's not like me to fall apart.

Valor knows what to do though. He pulls me against his chest and holds me while delivering words into my crown, his breath warm against my hair. "If you never want me to do that to you again, I'll understand. It can be a wrong method in the search to find the right thing, but part of you needs that release. I want to be the person who gives it to you."

I nod, accepting, because the shock that pushed me away from him before pulls me deeper into him now. "Promise me one thing?"

"Try me?" Valor doesn't make the promise before he hears it.

"You can't be cold toward me and expect me then to be this soft toward you." I can't make my voice loud to drive home the point, but he doesn't need me to.

"I'll make every effort. Tell me if you're not feeling me as you feel me now." He gives me a soft squeeze.

Valor pulls back a little, bringing his hand from around me to pull my chin up to meet his gaze. The seductive smirk on his face tells me all I need to know.

"I don't understand why sometimes you freeze me out or leave me in the dark about things. Is it all stuff because you're . . ." I let that trail off, and Valor pulls his eyes away from me as he cocks his head.

"Kerrianne is done feeding the tortoise." He sighs but brings his attention back to me. "Don't worry, princess. I'll be sure to be mindful not to bring out the ball gag until you're ready."

Whatever face I make has Valor kissing me deeply. He pulls away, giving my thigh a love tap before getting out of bed. "Come on, we're underdressed for dinner."

"I thought dinner with your parents was tomorrow?" I sit up, wide eyed, feeling the sting of the way he so thoroughly spanked my ass.

"Mmhmm." Valor won't look at me.

"Valor," I groan, trying to wrangle all the emotions of the past half hour. "Who's coming to dinner tonight?"

"Well, it was meant to be a surprise but . . ." Valor's sheepish smile does nothing to ease my tense shoulders. "Leticia will be here in twenty minutes."

"You better not be lying to me." I glare at him. "And she better be coming in through the front door."

"Where else would she be c —" Valor snorts. "Of course she's coming in the front door. I have some morals and respect for the truce. She's hardly my first choice of your cousins to kill."

Valor

CHAPTER FORTY

THE IN-LAW IS NOT AN OUTLAW

"I can't believe you live here," Leticia whispers to Antonella, looking around the house. "I'm pretty sure there are gargoyles on the roof."

"No gargoyles," Antonella whispers back. "But there is a tortoise."

"On the roof?" Leticia unzips her boots and leaves them on the rug, her coat already hung on the rack by the door.

"Solarium," Antonella says before looking over her shoulder to me as she leads Leticia, arm in arm, to the kitchen. "Okay, will you tell me how you planned this?"

"That was all me." Leticia giggles. She draws a big, deep breath. "You see, it wasn't enough texting you every day, so I called up the Clark Enterprise office and pretended to be a vendor, started reading a bunch of technical jargon off the internet, and asked for answers or the person who would be in charge of this sort of top-secret project. The receptionist, after like, thirty minutes, transferred me to Royal, who was surprisingly nice and informal, and with a little flirting, I got him to put Valor on the line."

"Ha." I laugh before I can stop myself.

"What of that wasn't true?" Leticia looks me up and down. "Because your receptionist, Margret, is very nice and, I say, deserves a raise if she regularly puts up with that bullshit."

"No, it's just that Royal was positive you weren't flirting with him," I explain while taking out a bottle of wine, offering the label out to Antonella.

She shakes her head and opens the fridge before pulling out three beers.

"You're going to make it so hard to go home if you spoil me like this." Leticia eyes the beer before making grabby-hand motions, like Kerrianne does when she really wants something.

"Beer goes better with the pork I'm making," Antonella explains, and I use the church key to open the bottles, handing Leticia hers first.

"Thank you." She beams and looks around the house. "This is nice. A lot brighter than I was expecting, not that I would know because you're like the single-word answer queen. I'm not lying when Valor told me he had no problem with me coming to dinner tonight. I thought he was full of shit, and you'd be gone or something. Maybe chained up in the basement."

"I should have made it clearer that you were supposed to talk with your cousin." I take the heat for Antonella.

The truth is, she probably didn't think it was a good idea to text Leticia. But without previous message history to see how much they spoke before . . . It hadn't raised any sort of alarm that she wasn't texting regularly.

They look at me like I'm growing a third head. "Should I maybe give you two some space?"

"No." They answer at the same time, tones sharp and accusatory.

"Well, Leticia, you're welcome here anytime, and, Antonella, anytime you'd like to see Leticia, you two can meet up in public if you'd prefer. I don't trust Gregorio or Berto and don't want you at their home without me, but I have no problem with you two speaking and getting together." I shrug and take a sip of my beer, trying to catch my breath.

"It's so weird." Leticia's words are singsongy, delivered through clenched teeth and with a melody. "He's almost normal. Toni, are you sure he's a Cavanagh? Did you look at his driver's license? Did you marry the wrong rich guy?"

Antonella rolls her eyes and answers at regular volume. "Oh, I'm pretty sure he's the right rich guy. The Irish do things differently."

"Clearly," Leticia murmurs.

"Daaaad!" Kerrianne calls from upstairs.

"Yes, Kerrianne?" I echo back.

"Can I wear pants?" she shouts down the stairs.

"I told her one time that she had to wear a dress when company came over, and now we go through this every time she meets someone new," I explain before answering back at a louder volume. "Yeah, pup. Pants are fine."

"Pup?" Leticia squints at me.

And it's then I know I fucked up. The hair on the back of my neck rises.

"Term of endearment. Kerrianne is kinda unique. You'll like her." Antonella is quick to explain it away.

"Nope." Leticia shakes her head. "Bullshit meter is off the charts. He stiffened, and you're about as subtle as a freight train. You're not actually offering an explanation. I wanna know."

How is she so perceptive? My wolf homes in on her. Leticia is most certainly human.

My wolf momentarily flashes in my eyes, despite my best efforts. He's tight against the surface, and Leticia gasps.

Antonella looks at me, and I know it'll come out eventually. But fuck, Dad will be pissed at me for blowing this in less than thirty minutes of having another D'Medici in the house.

"Leticia." Antonella draws her attention. "Not tonight. But we will tell you later. When have I ever lied to you?"

"I don't like this." Leticia narrows her gaze on me. "I saw your eyes do something. If you're getting her messed up or on some shit, I'll be really pissed. I may have absolutely no skills to take you down myself, but do not think I cannot come up with something."

"I swear to you. The only trouble Antonella will find herself in is whatever she chooses to walk into. She will always have a choice for an out." I step closer to Leticia and offer out my hand. "I'll tell you in two weeks when you come back for dinner again, you have my word."

Leticia scrutinizes me a bit further before switching her beer to her left hand and shaking on it. "Deal."

We separate, and awkward silence descends for all of sixty seconds before we're saved by my little raptor.

Kerrianne comes tearing into the kitchen, sliding on her socks across the floors. "I thought you said she was Antonella's cousin."

"I am." Leticia pulls her long blonde hair over her shoulder and stands like Antonella.

The resemblance is there but nowhere near as strong with Leticia's blonde hair to Antonella's dark brown.

Leticia looks at Kerrianne, eyebrow raised, and taps her pointer finger against her lips. "I like your outfit."

"Thanks! Tortoises are my favorite." Kerrianne beams. She's wearing a T-shirt with little tortoises mixed into the paisley print.

"I heard there's a tortoise here. Is he yours?" Leticia isn't as natural with Kerrianne as Antonella is, but their conversation turns to 'let me show you my tortoise,' and Leticia waves over her shoulder at us as she leaves to visit Captain.

"I'm so sorry." Antonella apologizes as she walks over to the oven and grabs oven mitts. "She doesn't know how to let things go."

"It's okay. You two are close, and I'm serious about you having a life. Eventually, she would need to learn the family secret. But I should have been clearer that you should talk with your cousin and truly talk. Obviously, with discretion but . . ." I take the oven mitts from Antonella and use them to pull her cooking vessel out of the oven. "You don't need to hide away from her. You're allowed, encouraged, to have a life."

Antonella's cooking smells divine. It's had me salivating all afternoon. But in the last hour, it's really started to develop a robust aroma.

"Well, it's nice that you've said that because Leticia and I had planned, earlier this year, before well . . . this happened . . . to reinstate a family tradition my mom and I had. I wasn't sure you'd . . ." Antonella stops talking as she pokes the roast with a fork. She shakes her head. "Ten more minutes."

I re-cover the roast and put it in the oven, then try to bring her back to what she was saying. "I wasn't sure you'd?"

"I wasn't sure you'd agree to it." She admits with a sigh. "In my defense, it's not like —"

"You don't need a defense." I take off the oven mitts and grab her by the waist, pulling her close to me. My cock pulses thinking of how I had her today and how I want more. *Focus, Valor.* "As long as it's safe, and you're not actively trying to undo the truce . . . there's nothing I can think of that you couldn't do with the right level of security."

"Take Kerrianne shopping and then to lunch with us?" Antonella winces. "I thought it'd be nice to include her because then she could get you and your parents something without all of you knowing by default. But completely understand if it's a no."

"It's not a no, but why does this sound like lunch is deep in D'Medici territory?" I narrow my eyes.

"Oh, that's because it's deep in D'Medici territory at La Fatal Piedra." Antonella wraps her arms up over my shoulders. "But the days we wanted to go, Berto, Gregorio, and Eduardo will all be in Italy for their yearly pre-Christmas trip. I would be the highest-ranking D'Medici in the entire city, and I don't even have that last name anymore."

"Okay, but you're taking a full team of security, plus Jack and Declan." *And I'll probably be hiding in an SUV down the street.* It seems strange to want to be so deep in the heart of the Gold Coast, but she said family tradition. It must be a part of it.

"That's fine. I'm not asking you to pu —"

"Put Kerrianne in danger. I know." I rase an eyebrow. "I like my wife and have every intention of keeping her too."

"First you're falling in lust with me, and now you even like me." Antonella fakes a gasp, shaking her head before letting out a sigh and pulling away from me.

I grab at her, wanting to pull her back, but she picks up her beer and knows exactly what she's doing when she pushes her tongue out to taste the rim.

My cock gets ideas, and I can't pull my eyes off her. Antonella is playing with fire.

Let's sink our teeth into her and give her a wolf. We can keep her forever. Wouldn't even need to —

"Ope. Looks like I was wrong, and dinner isn't ready yet," Leticia says loudly as they're coming back down the hall. "Though your dad might eat Antonella if it isn't done soon."

Kerrianne giggles, "We don't eat people."

With the interruption, the moment passes between us, so I move us on from the awkward 'pup' and 'we don't eat people' tells of the non-humans in the room.

Reaching for the cupboard, I wave her over. "Kerrianne, do you want to set the table?"

"Okay." She holds her hands out dramatically for a stack of plates.

I pull them out of the cupboard and then find Leticia standing behind her with her hands similarly outstretched. I eye her but grab the right amount of silverware and offer it to her.

"What?" She looks like I offended her. "In the last year, I've cooked all but five of the family meals. The least I can do is set the table."

CHAPTER FORTY-ONE

THE NEW RELATIONSHIP

Seeing Leticia off into the back of one of my uncle's SUVs was hard, but with multiple promises from Valor and more than one set of plans on the books . . . . I know I'll see her again, and I'm trusting of it.

I find Valor carrying the last of the dishes to the kitchen, and I head over to the sink. I know we have staff, Zoe and Winnie, but there are things I can do to make their jobs easier.

"I want you naked in my bed in two minutes," Valor whispers in my ear as he stands behind me. He reaches in front of me and slides his hands into the top of my yoga pants. "No excuses, Antonella."

"Or what?" I sass, turning in his arms.

He keeps still as I move, his hands warm against the top of my ass when I'm facing him.

His eyes grow heated, the fire sparked within them, and he wets his bottom lip with his tongue. "Or neither of us get to sleep until we find some of the limits locked within you. I want to see more of that masochist from before."

My heart thunders in my chest, and Valor pushes one hand down between my ass cheeks. He brings his other hand to the nape of my neck and tugs on my hair. I wince, tears welling in my eyes with the sting.

"I'd like to eat you, fuck you, and put you to bed pleased with my treatment of you. But if you need an attitude adjustment, I've no problem giving it to you." He's almost whispering, and the butterflies in my stomach aren't contained. They take over my whole abdomen, and I even get tingles in my feet.

"Do you want to be a brat, or do you want to be my good girl?"

His question sparks a pulse in my pussy.

"I'll be good." I nod against the tug of his fingers in my hair.

"Show me, princess." Valor lets me go, and I try not to collapse from the swoon that overtakes me.

But I'm halfway upstairs when there's a knock at the front door.

"Valor?" I question.

"Two minutes," he repeats, but he doesn't sound as sure.

I go up to the top of the stairs and tuck myself out of sight.

Valor

CHAPTER FORTY-TWO

THE VISITOR IN THE NIGHT

My suspicions are heightened, and I grab the gun from the lockbox under the entry table's decorative lip as I approach the front door.

But through the weather stripping, I get the scent of a trusted member of the pack and lower the weapon to my side.

"Good evening, Father." I open the door for the clergyman, not wide enough to let him in but polite enough to talk.

"No one could get ahold of you, so they sent me. We're reading someone their last rights." He speaks mostly in code.

News of the shooting, and we don't want to talk over the phone.

Stepping back, I invite him into the house. Antonella's breathing gives away that she's still at the top of the stairs, but the good priest is human and won't notice.

"Your new wife is awake?" Father Michael asks, looking up to the staircase.

I shrug. "I had tied her to the bed, and we were about to copulate when you knocked."

His eyes go wide.

Serves him right for asking about our mate, my wolf huffs as I lead him to the heart of the home.

"We have a problem. And I do have to say it sounds like quite the conundrum." He stands at the counter, practically stick straight.

"Can I offer you a cup of coffee?" It's polite, but I hope this conversation won't last that long.

"For the road, perhaps." He nods with a thought. "They pulled the bullets out of your SUV, and I don't have any good news."

"Well. They're bullets, embedded in my SUV. I wasn't antici-pating good news." I turn on the coffee pot and begin measuring out the grounds.

Father pauses, and it gets me to turn to look at him rather than the coffee pot.

He tosses his head in the direction of the stairs. "They're ones we recently sold."

"To who?" I ask, not wanting it to be true and needing him to say it.

"They're the ones Gregorio wanted as part of the negotia-tions," Father whispers.

"You can't be serious that they violated the truce already." *It doesn't make sense.*

"Well, the evidence is circumstantial. It could be that they sold them. They recently seemed to solidify their relationship with the Russians. A daughter of the brother married to the next Pakhan," Father Michael huffs.

I go back to making his coffee. That information was discussed at dinner when Leticia updated Antonella on every-thing back at home. Their cousin, Sarena, was married off to the man Gregorio intended for Antonella.

Kill him for proposing to Antonella, my wolf suggests.

We have no claim to hurt him. She wasn't ours yet. I remind him of the same conclusion I forced myself to come to at dinner. The realization I could have been married to an eighteen-year-old for the truce chills me. I don't mind the single-year difference between me and Antonella, but ten years? She'd be right between me and Kerrianne in age.

"You know this information?" Father Michael startles me, standing next to me. I'd frozen thinking that through, and he takes over making coffee. "You're clearly too tired to make coffee."

With a sidestep out of his way, I lean my hip against the counter so I'm facing him, arms crossed, not caring that it's a defensive maneuver. "Antonella's cousin, Sarena, was married off to him. It was organized before the existence of the truce. If it was the Russians, and it was a deal struck before the truce, I don't know what that would mean. Are we sure that would be a breach?"

"Using our own bullets against us?" Father Michael implies heavily that he thinks it should be considered.

"What bothers me, though, is that it's not a Russian-style attack." I tilt my head back and forth. "Though . . . our friend Marc did say that the Yakuza were interested in our business."

Father Michael is already shaking his head before I finish my thought. "No, Gregorio pissed off the leader of this area. Badly. I think there was a game of poker or something that went bad. It wouldn't be the Yakuza."

"We have plenty of enemies Gregorio could have sold that ammunition to. If selling it to someone who uses it against us isn't a violation of the truce, then this isn't as big of a deal as we're making it. I don't like it any more than you do, but there are rules in place, even if they weren't negotiated well."

I dislike it. I dislike it very much, but I wasn't part of the negotiations, and every time I think of that . . . I feel myself getting more wound up.

"Your father is reaching out to the arbiters since this time of night is the best time to contact them."

Father Michael's coffee is pooling in the pot. I cross the kitchen and grab one of the composting travel cups that Winnie insists are better for the environment, since I can't seem to keep track of reusable ones, and bring it to him.

He pours a cup and asks, "Sugar?"

"Brown or white?" I ask, headed to the pantry.

"White. You young people and your coffee, making it too fancy." Father Michael scoffs. When I come back with the container and a spoon for him, he mixes his drink before looking at me with a distinctive set to his mouth and pitying eyes. "Neil is adamant that it was your new bride who gave them the information about your whereabouts."

"If Antonella informed them of my whereabouts and the D'Medicis are trying to strike the pack where it hurts, wouldn't they have waited until I had Kerrianne in the vehicle? Take out an entire path to succession? It would move to Royal then rather than him caring for the pack until she's of age. It's the easiest path to take." I question the logic of it. I know I should be rebutting against Dad and Neil directly, but the man of God is here, and it's the best I can do.

Father Michael bobbles his head, considering it before attempting to draw a sip of too-hot coffee. He stops himself before burning his mouth. "That's a very good point."

"What bothers me about the day the truce was called is one thing I don't have eyes on." I add the suspicion I haven't spoken before. "We're believing that Berto D'Medici managed to take down a fully trained, highly armed wolf?"

"Well." Father Michael pauses and furrows his brow. "Was there proof he acted alone? Perhaps if there were several of them or he got the drop on Sean somehow."

"It may be nothing, but it's been bothering me. I watched the footage from Kerrianne's school. Antonella isn't half assed in her defense of Kerrianne. It didn't seem scripted in the slightest." I defend her outright, but the longer it sits in my brain . . . the more uncertainty brews.

Could she have called the truce and regretted it?

"Kerrianne has nearly fourteen years before she can rule. That's plenty of opportunities to take her out of the running. Maybe the D'Medicis have a greater plan we don't know about, and even if Antonella acted on her own and called the truce, we all know women can be softer for children. She called the truce against her family's wishes and, as a result, is paying atonement by feeding them information on your movements." Father Michael voices what feels so unlikely to me.

I pinch the bridge of my nose. It is possible. I don't like it, but it is possible.

This evening has turned from fun and lighthearted to a chaotic nightmare of what-ifs that come with an infinite number of conclusions.

"It may be that only God knows. Stay sharp until we can learn more." Father Michael heads toward the door.

I follow him, showing him out before locking up behind him.

Mind reeling, I head upstairs. Antonella isn't at the top of the staircase. But I find her pulling back the covers on the bed.

Antonella

CHAPTER FORTY-THREE

NO ONE LIKES CONFRONTATION

"Outside of Leticia I haven't talked to a single D'Medici since we got married." Bed stripped, there's nothing for me to do with my hands but stand here and stare at him, ready to defend myself. "You can check my text messages. I'm sure you could tell if there was a new device connecting to something or other in your house."

Valor doesn't move, hardly even blinking.

I grab my phone off the nightstand and throw it onto his side of the bed, shrugging. "I don't know what Neil is telling everyone or why he'd be saying something like that, but we've been married almost two weeks. I hadn't even been comfortable enough to do more than text Leticia, let alone ask to see her."

"I know." Valor's statement does nothing to help with my own defense.

With a small sigh, I climb into bed and lie down, looking at the ceiling before closing my eyes. "Valor, what do you really want?"

The bed dips next to me, and I roll my head and open my eyes to see that he's sitting beside me, offering my phone back. I take it from him and unceremoniously toss it onto the nightstand. Fuck it. I don't need it. Let the damn thing die.

Valor rolls his eyes, stands up, and walks around the bed. I track his movements and watch as he picks my phone up and plugs it in. He sets it down with much more patience than I did and then looks down at me. The flat irritation is gone and there's a fire back in his eyes. Not the fun fire though. *Anger.*

"How would you explain the bullets? The timing?" Valor furrows his brow.

He bends toward me and wraps his hand around my throat.

What the fuck? Instinct has me wanting to struggle, but I force myself still, conserving energy. I blink up at him, waiting for him to start choking me, but his hand rests there, and in the span of at least thirty seconds, he starts running his thumb up and down the column of my neck.

"Valor, I'm not working with the D'Medicis. I don't have a death wish. Period." I swallow and can feel the weight of his hand against my throat. "I don't know what's going on."

Valor lets me go. "I'm not sure I understand what's going on either."

His admission is decidedly not settling. But whatever I've said is answer enough. He walks back around the bed, stripping his clothes off. He's in his boxers by the time he gets to his side.

"Are *you* planning on killing *me* in *my* sleep?" I don't know if I should have to ask this or not. I'm not even sure if he'll tell the truth. But I can't quite contain the question he asked me earlier.

Valor smiles as he climbs onto the mattress next to me and curls up facing me. "No. I don't plan on killing you in your sleep. We're both dedicated to one cause."

"Kerrianne." I state the obvious.

Valor pushes up and rolls me onto my back, then he kisses me deeply. He wraps his fingers into my hair, and I push back against him to match his intensity, remembering how he made me come earlier, and the flame of desire crackles to life within me.

I want more of Valor's touch, but just as I'm so sure he'll give it to me, he retreats. "Let's get some sleep. I've a feeling dinner with my parents tomorrow will be eventful."

Immediately, my heart rate picks up, and my brain plays through every possible scenario for that dinner. *No, what could possibly go wrong? . . .* That's a laugh. I can't even convince my brain to let it go. *What the fuck do I wear?* I'm cold and shivering but can't force myself to move and pull up the blankets.

"Antonella." Valor is between me and the ceiling again. I feel the weight of his body next to me, his hand cradling my face. "Hey. Don't panic. Let the fear go. I didn't mean that in any sense that they'll be difficult toward you. They're eccentric. It wasn't meant to scare you."

The cold dissipates, and I warm under his touch. From his hand on my jaw to our chests pressed together, I start to relax.

"That's it." He rests his forehead against mine. "I'm trying to not be a dick. I dislike not knowing what's going on with the business. For the first time, nothing is as it seems. There's been so much change, but I know it isn't you. I'll do better."

I nod with my forehead pressed against his, moving us both but not finding words.

"You're trembling," Valor mutters and reaches for the blankets. He pulls them up over us and then rolls me toward him until I'm curled in against his chest. "When I brought Holly home to meet my parents, they were in the kitchen cooking dinner. And for the first time ever, they had decided to get and butcher their own pig. It took them hours longer than they had anticipated. Anyway, dinner was supposed to be at seven, and we arrived at six thirty to my mom screaming and my dad chasing her around the kitchen, living room, and even outside with pig testicles, shouting, 'They're just like oysters!' on repeat."

How is this supposed to make me feel better? "Oh, okay?"

"Holly and I had to pick up carryout pizza and help them finish butchering the hog. It's a good thing she came from a pack in the South and was familiar with hog butchering because my parents were severely underqualified for that activity. Dad kept saying 'It's nothing like butchering a deer and making canned venison,' and honestly, I thought she would leave me because of them." He laughs, and the shuddering of his chest makes me feel the fondness of the story, easing my nerves a little bit. "Besides you're already their favorite person."

"Oh?" I push back so I can look him in the eye.

"You saved Kerrianne. They already love you." He reassures me, running his fingers through my hair.

"But that doesn't save me from suspicion of something that I could never have done." I can't even get those words out beyond a whisper.

"It's not coming from Dad. It's coming from Neil." Valor wrinkles his nose. "My uncle is always looking for an enemy where there isn't one. I need to remember that and not be pulled into his theories. I'm more worried about what my parents will embarrass me with rather than their acceptance of you."

"Well, if it's any consolation, you don't have to meet my parents?" I can't help it. The words come out, and I wince, laughing uncomfortably. "And, well, you're already familiar with Gregorio. Leticia is pretty much the only one you had to impress, and other than practically outing wolves all by yourself at dinner . . . I think it went well."

"Don't remind me." Valor buzzes his lips on a long exhale. But he circles back to what I glossed over. "I think I'd have liked to have met your parents. Your dad might have had tips to raise a self-reliant daughter." Valor surprises me with that. He pulls me closer again from where I'd pushed away. "I don't know what's going on. But I trust that you have Kerrianne's best interests at heart."

Valor

CHAPTER FORTY-FOUR

THE ODD JOB

My phone vibrates more than once in my pocket. I pull it out to see the reminder flashing and an indicator of some text messages from Antonella.

CALENDAR REMINDER:

> Dinner @ 6:30 with Parents at Estate. Bring Rolls and Butter.

ANTONELLA:

> You're 100% sure that store-bought rolls are fine? I could have made some quickly.

> Kerrianne swears you always bring these ones so I'm going with it. Be safe.

Attached is a photo of three bags of rolls from the local grocery store and the butter my mother likes on our kitchen counter.

VALOR:

> That's perfect. Excited to be home. Buyer is late.

I hit send the same second there's an explosion. It startles me, and I snap into focus. Even with the echo of the warehouse, I know it came from out front.

Neil is quick to shout and wave his arm, beckoning us to follow him. "This way, we'll go out the back before they can get there."

No. Danger. Go out the front, they'll have moved away from the explosion themselves. It'll be an ambush. My wolf and I agree that Neil is headed the wrong way.

"No!" I shout, letting the alpha command rip through me. "It'll be a trap out the back. They won't expect us to walk into an explosion."

"That's ridiculous! We can't take the ammunition and C-4 past the flames. They'll explode." Neil has a point regarding the explosives, but precious seconds are ticking by.

My gut disagrees with his orders. The men are clearly conflicted, looking between me and Neil.

"Leave it. It's five grand, not worth worrying about." I turn and leave them to their devices.

It's not up to me if they come or go, but I'm trusting my wolf.

Pulling my gun, I head toward the front where we came in. I don't know what they blew up. It sounded like one explosion, not multiple, so chances are there's a vehicle in good enough shape to limp out of here until I can get somewhere on foot. I test the doorknob for heat.

It's cold.

Footsteps come from behind me, and I look over my shoulder to see three men have followed me with their guns drawn. Two of them were recently shipped in from Ireland, and one is younger in the business, leaving Neil and two others to go out the back.

I count down on my fingers.

Three.

Two.

One.

Guns raised, we sweep, heading out of the building.

Danger. My wolf draws my attention to a single enemy standing by a vehicle.

He raises his gun, but one of the fresh-from-Irelands shoots the gun out of his hand rather than to kill.

"Fresh body for the basement." I huff a laugh as we jog past what was one of our throwaway SUVs, burning from the explosion.

Our heads are on a swivel, watching for threats.

One Irishman grabs the injured man's gun and then drags him, kicking, swinging, and groaning in pain, to our other SUV that looks drivable.

The young gun and the one with the prisoner watch our backs as the other Irishman and I sweep the vehicle for explosives. The tires aren't even sliced, and we don't find any detonation or tracking devices of any nature. *What sort of amateur hour is this?*

Gunfire is coming from the back of the warehouse, but they knew the risk. We're not a no-man-left-behind agency. Neil will have to handle his fuckin' self.

I get in the driver's seat, and the rest of the men climb into the SUV with the captive before I throw it in gear. Out in less than two minutes.

Home to our mate and pup. My wolf is on edge, forcing me to watch for tails and other potential threats.

"Quit your bitchin' and moanin', would ya?" the Irishman in the back snaps at our wounded capture.

I catch a glimpse in the mirror of what's happening.

The Irishman looks over the wound on the man's hand. "A flesh wound. You're grazed at best. Valor will do far worse to you."

The man groans, and I take a corner harder than I need to

JAEGER ROSE

while trying to listen closely, but the Irishman doesn't use the opportunity to question him. That's okay. It's my job anyway. He'll have to wait until after dinner with my parents.

Once we're finally far enough away and I'm sure no tail is coming, I slow, trying to avoid looking suspicious or breaking traffic laws. Nothing worse than being pulled over with a hostage in the back. My phone vibrates in my pocket, and I pull it out. Not being the SUV my phone is connected to, I answer it and hold it to my ear.

"The hell happened out there?" my father snaps. "I got a call from Neil that you were ambushed. A shoot-out, four dead? Two of them ours?"

"One of the SUVs exploded. Neil went out the back. I took a team out the front. We left the goods. I don't know what happened to the others who went out the back with Neil. I wasn't staying around to figure out what the fuck was going on. We took a hostage. Headed to my place now." I answer as concisely as possible.

Dad's silent for a moment, and I figure out that his hand is over the speaker. "No, I know Valor will want mashed potatoes and gravy."

Then Royal comes on the line. "Send me a picture of him and any tattoos. I'll see what I can figure out, and for the love of God, please don't forget the buns. They're acting like Antonella is the pope."

"Got that Valor?" Dad is back.

"Yeah, I'll get it sent over." I immediately regret not taking the time to learn my teammates' names, but we worked well as a unit.

Bad of us not to know. We should know our pack. My wolf agrees, and I'm already feeling guilty enough as is.

I hand my phone to the back seat. "Photos of him. Anything he's got, face, tattoos, et cetera. To my brother, please."

"Yes, Alpha," he answers.

I don't waste the seconds it would take to correct him that I'm not alpha yet.

My wolf, however, doesn't hesitate to puff up with pride that he's accepted me in that position.

"Want me to arrange transport for us off your property?" the new kid asks from way in the back of the SUV. "I don't know if you want Kerrianne to see all of us."

"You haven't heard of Valor's lair?" the second Irishman asks loudly over his shoulder.

"No?" The kid sounds embarrassed.

"Valor's the best interrogator the Mafia has known. If Valor can't make them talk, then they don't know anything," the Irishman in the front answers. "He's got a whole outfit hidden away in a secret bunker. His daughter and the mate will never know we're there. It's legendary. Talks are all across Ireland of how Valor works."

"That's . . . interesting," the kid in the back answers, clearly trying to pick words that aren't offensive.

"Sent," the Irishman in the back says, passing my phone forward.

I realize I haven't heard any moaning and groaning and look over my shoulder. "He die or pass out?"

"Had a little help passing out," the Irishman admits. "Can't stand wussy nonsense like that."

But my brain has moved on to other things.

Like the fact that the two men who went with Neil are dead. It was their job to get him out alive, so it's not beyond reason that they died carrying out their duty. Plus, we don't know how many they were up against. We may not be a no-man-left-behind outfit, but I'm going to need more answers to respond to the call of violence.

But even more disarming than that train of thought is the sinking feeling in my gut. *How did they know we were there?*

We were meeting usual buyers, people we've worked with

for years. It's why we had such a small, nonconforming shipment. I'd never cut a deal so small. For just anyone.

My phone rings again, and I don't check the screen before answering. "Valor."

"Valor. What the fuck? We get to the warehouse, and there's a burned-out SUV. Two of your guys and three other dead bodies all around. Did the cost of these shipments increase in price now that you're working with the D'Medicis?" It's the buyer, and he increases my suspicions with every question. "I don't really think the cost to clean this up is worth what little product we ordered."

I drum my fingers on the dash. *Do I believe it wasn't him?*

"Clean it up. On the next shipment, I'll have two of the custom M-9s you've been bugging me about for a while." I try to negotiate.

Royal won't be happy. It takes forever to make the customized pieces in his printers. But body disposal isn't cheap, especially when they're shot to pieces.

"You know that only covers one man." He negotiates right back.

This is the part of business I like.

"Well, we want our dead back to bury. That's a delivery charge at best. So that only leaves two and an SUV to clean up." I sigh like it's such a big deal to compromise. "What do you want if the M-9s aren't enough?"

"You get me two of those fully armored SUVs that you got off the Callahans and my kid into that fancy private school that Kerrianne goes to? The one in River North?" He groans. "The wife is all sorts of pissed about a current administrator at our school and the bodyguard situation."

Good. My wolf sighs with some good news. *Not everyone knows our pup moved to someplace safer.*

"Two SUVs fully loaded, and I'll get you in touch with the administrator at River North who was willing to talk about nontraditional tuition options. You're on your own to buy your way in, but I'll act as a reference." I won't budge on. I'm not spending money on a school I don't use.

"Fair enough." He agrees. "Text me with a new meet, and I'll get your men back to you by dawn."

One thing's for certain: There was no way Antonella could have known about this meeting, and it got sabotaged anyway. This couldn't have been something she had a hand in.

CHAPTER FORTY-FIVE

THE FULL TURKEY DINNER

Valor comes home in a different vehicle than he left in, and I only noticed because I was anxiously pacing the first floor of the house and saw him, from a window, get out of the vehicle some ways down the driveway.

"I'm fine," he whispers, coming inside, and I pick up a distinctive burnt metal smell. "Delivery went poorly. I'll go shower and dress, then we can go. I don't want Kerrianne to see and smell me. I have work to do tonight."

There's someone in the basement. I read between the lines.

"I'd hug you or kiss you hello, but you look too pretty to grime up." Valor walks past me, making a show of keeping his hands to himself, holding them upward and away from me.

"Well, for the neglect, you'll owe me double later." I try to flirt.

Valor nods, and a dangerous glint in his eyes is quickly replaced with the yellow of his wolf. "That's one, princess. How many more can you earn yourself tonight?"

My mouth drops open in shock, and I turn away from him.

I barely hear his footsteps as he prowls away from me and up the stairs. Kerrianne never even looks up from the bonus workbook of word searches and pattern drawings I brought out for her to work on to pass the time.

Ten minutes later, Valor is coming down the stairs, and I immediately feel underdressed. Slacks and a dark green shirt seem much more formal than the flowy dress I pulled out of my closet and paired with black stockings.

"You look fine. Don't." Valor loops his fingers in mine as he approaches.

"Do you read minds?" I whisper, leaning in toward him.

That gets a full belly laugh, and he shakes his head. "No, your face said it all for you. If you lose focus from that perfect Mafia wife facade, it's like your face doesn't know what to do, so it broadcasts every single one of your thoughts."

"Oh." I try to school my emotions, keeping my face neutral, but my cheeks flush anyway.

He lets it go without another word, and with a little pressure, he pulls me with him toward the kitchen. "Ready to go, little raptor?"

"Let's goooo!" Kerrianne charges past us to the garage.

We make the twenty-five-minute drive to his parents' place, and the gatehouse opens for us without even checking the inside of the vehicle. We drive up to the house before I have a chance to process my surroundings. I'm not even sure what to expect, but as we pass through a row of fir trees, the home comes into view.

It's a traditional style home complete with vinyl siding and a Welcome to the Den painted wood sign on the stoop leaning up against the house.

Valor carries the rolls, and I fuss with the skirt of my dress on the way up the walk.

Kerrianne doesn't knock. She flings the door open and darts across the threshold, disappearing into the house while screeching, "Grandma!"

"Kerrianne, inside voice, please," Valor says in a normal

speaking voice, to which Kerrianne repeats the word at a whisper-yell volume.

"In the kitchen," Elizabeth calls from the back of the house.

I take in the very traditional furniture — a recliner and a soft-looking sofa — the warm rug on hardwood floors, and a gas-burning fireplace with holiday decor adorning the mantel. The home is warm and welcoming. It's almost too suburban and more classic, turn of the century than what I anticipated.

"Oh, there you are!" Ian Cavanagh says, rounding a corner from down the hallway. "You brought her in the front door like she's some sort of esteemed guest." I'm taken aback, stiffening, but then he smiles and opens his arms wide. "Rather than the family that she is."

Before I comprehend what's happening, Ian pulls me into a hug. Valor walks past us deeper into the house with a sideways glance at me. *Smug asshole.*

"Come on, come on, come on. Betty will be so happy to see you. She's been hounding me to force Valor to bring you over for dinner." Ian releases me from the hug but doesn't let go entirely. Instead, he leads me into the house with his arm wrapped around my shoulders. "I've been stopping her from popping by with breakfast daily."

"Oh, my shoes." I try to stop him, knowing my little kitten heels could scuff the hardwood.

"Leave them on. Floors are meant to get dirty. Homes are meant to be lived in." He continues bringing me into the house. When we hit a larger great room and the kitchen, he takes my coat. "What can I get you to drink?"

"Water would be great," I answer, and Betty turns to look at me.

She then decks Valor on the shoulder. "I thought you said she . . ."

"She does know." Valor winces, faking pain, holding his hand over where he was hit. The hit that was a love tap at best.

337

"She sure doesn't look like she knows," Betty growls.

It sounds more like some of the sounds Valor has made than I was expecting.

"I did not know water wasn't an acceptable choice of drink. I'm fine with whatever." I look to Ian for help.

It takes him a second to stop his silent snickering before he goes to Betty's side. He wraps his arm around her lower back. "Just because Valor told her doesn't mean they jumped right to making grandbabies. They've only known each other two weeks."

Betty huffs.

Valor pours me a glass of water and ice from the refrigerator door and brings it to me. "I uhm, uh, should have warned you that my mother is really excited about the prospect of another grandchild. I had hoped in seven years Royal would have stepped up but . . ."

Heat flames my face and down my neck. Children hadn't crossed my mind beyond the basic 'I can't get pregnant because we're physiologically different.'

I position him between me and his mother, and with my voice as low as I can possibly make it, I whisper, "You said I'd have to become a wolf, and it's not like we talked about what exactly that entails."

"You didn't even tell her that," Betty groans. Clearly this wolf-hearing thing is way better than I anticipated. "That's it. Ian, we're marrying Royal off. It's the only way."

"Betty. Don't rule Valor out so quickly. It's not like we've locked them alone in their house this entire time. They both have lives and things to do and a daughter to take care of." Ian comforts her.

"Speaking of, is Royal's lair where my daughter ran off to, or did we let her run feral?" Valor sighs, interlacing his fingers with mine.

"Yes, he's in the middle of business, but I'm sure with Kerrianne finding him, he'll switch to something more appropriate." Ian nods, and while it's not absolutely clear what Royal is working on, I would wager a guess that it has something to do with Valor smelling like an explosion when he came home.

"Takeoff!" Kerrianne giggles from somewhere in the house, and footsteps running up stairs interrupt us.

Royal comes skittering to a stop, sliding stocking footed across the floor with Kerrianne clinging to his back like a little koala. "Everything you need to know is sent to your printer. Should be enough to get us what we need. Beyond that, hello! Welcome. Mom decided we need to have Thanksgiving . . . again."

"I love Thanksgiving!" Kerrianne's eyes are wide and beaming. "Two is the perfect number of Thanksgivings. No, maybe three."

Royal shakes Kerrianne free before coming over to me. He wraps me in a hug, too, and a throat is cleared.

"Jeez. You married her, it's not my fault you haven't claimed her. I'm just excited to see her." Royal lets me go, and I look to Valor. His eyes are narrowed, his lip curling, and his shoulders are tight up around his ears. "Especially since I also got you the other information concerning her that you asked for and I have good news to report."

"Valor." I put my hand on his chest. He covers it with his own, and there's more of that warmth from last night between us. "If you kill your brother before dinner, then we won't get to eat the food when it's fresh and hot, and that would be a massive disappointment to me."

My words draw his eyes from Royal. His features soften and he mouths, "Two." I roll my eyes, and he turns my head back to me before mouthing, "Three."

Shifting away from him, I hope no one was paying attention to us. Royal is picking out chairs for him and Kerrianne at the dining room table, and Ian is helping Betty pull the pan from the oven with a whole turkey roasted to a perfect brown color.

Thank goodness for small mercies.

"Now, no one get any crazy ideas. I had help." Betty beams at the turkey.

"Probably for the best," Royal murmurs a little loudly behind us.

I draw a sip of my water, not wanting to say anything, but I'll for sure offer to bring more food in the future and no more store-bought buns.

After much insistence, Betty lets me help her do the bare minimum of carrying food over to the informal dining room table to eat. Even being 'informal,' it seats eight, so the six of us have plenty of room.

Food is placed out on the table, prayers are said, and we're ready to eat as Ian asks, "So, what's this other thing that Royal worked on for you?"

"It's nothing important." Valor dismisses his father's inquiry.

"Nothing important or not fit for the company?" Ian presses for more while he continues cutting through the piece of turkey on his plate.

"The latter." Valor raises an eyebrow.

I try to disappear into my chair at his side because if it has something to do with me, which Royal implied it did, I don't want to make myself more ostracized than I am. *It would be nice to know, though, what it is they're saying about me. Maybe get a chance to defend myself against whatever it is they think.*

"So, Antonella. You'll maybe wait until summer to become wolf, then?" Betty is trying to be helpful, I think, changing subjects from 'work.'

But without even knowing the answer, I'm quick to throw a piece of turkey into my mouth to buy myself some time.

"Mom, she doesn't even know how it works. I was letting the first half of the information sink in." Valor defends me.

I don't know why, but him being protective of me feels so unexpected. Good, but unexpected.

The ominous way everyone talks around becoming a shifter brings an uneasiness, my chest tightening with it. Having very recently found out about wolves, and only half of the information at that, it's not instilling confidence that becoming a wolf, whatever that entails, is something I want.

"She's a teacher, Valor." Ian starts in where Betty left off. "Unless she's taking time off work, there are only so many times a year you can do it. Unless you two have decided she's not continuing to work?"

Dread sinks through me, drying out my mouth, and I choke on my bite of food. Quickly raising my glass, I swallow down some water.

"That won't happen," Betty huffs and waves the idea off the table with a flick of her wrist. "She's too good at her job, and her students need her. Isn't that right, Kerrianne?"

"Antonella is the best! She's got me doing more fractions than any other student, and I get extra fun sheets." Kerrianne nods. "I think Antonella should always be my teacher, like third grade, fourth grade, fifth grade."

I close my eyes for a moment as overwhelm hits on every level. I force those things down, stuffing them deep inside.

Valor brings his hand to rest on my thigh. He squeezes gently and then moves his thumb in soothing movements back and forth. "Antonella will continue to work. It takes a lot for a teacher to impress Kerrianne, and if that's something Antonella wants to bring to other children in other families, then I don't see an issue with it so long as we can ensure her safety."

It's too much. I have no choice but to wipe a tear, the moisture overflowing from my eyes.

"Oh goodness. We've upset her." Ian's dismay hangs in his words. "Quick, change the subject. Did you see the latest rugby match?"

Royal and Valor start talking with Ian about sports, and it gives me a minute to pull myself together, thankful for the redirect as I enjoy the beyond-divine stuffing Betty made. It's made from scratch, not from a box. The bread is thick and moist and not so salty that the gravy over the top is overwhelming. I focus on enjoying the meal and the pleasantness of a real family.

Betty helps me clear the table before she takes Kerrianne to the living room. I move to go with them, leaving the men to talk as Gregorio and Eduardo would, but Valor calls me back. He pats the seat beside him on the opposite side. It brings me squarer with Ian and Royal.

"Before you go on your hunt for justice. I'd really like you to think the consequences through." Ian crosses his arms and leans back in the chair. "There's a reason we don't venture outside of business ourselves."

"Hunt? Business?" I ask, looking between the two of them. *Why does that sound like it's not for animals?*

"Oh, yeah. Uh, Dad . . . we weren't telling Antonella about that," Royal whispers, leaning over to talk to Ian but not quite enough.

Ian puts his hand over his mouth as if to silence himself, but Valor is already shaking his head. He looks at me directly, readying to reveal the information apparently not originally intended for me. "I had Royal do some digging into Marc's previous exploits. Because I wanted to be sure it was taken care of. That there wasn't . . ."

"There wasn't anyone out there actively jerking off to his new wife's teenage image and being all pervy." Royal gets up from the table and heads to the kitchen. "I did find the footage and was able to scrub it off the ancient net, without watching it, to be clear. I did some digging through the —" Royal cuts himself off while mixing a drink. When he's stirring the ingredients together, he starts again. "Doesn't matter. I found the people it was shared with. If they have a local copy, it would be the only way that it could ever see the light of day again."

I look at the three of them, wishing I had something to do to distract myself from my discomfort of them all knowing what happened to me. *At least Royal didn't watch it.*

Valor brings his arm around my shoulders and gives me a reassuring squeeze as he watches his father, and in the more masculine version of Kerrianne's sass, he defends himself. "I'm not implying that we go and kill them all."

"No, he's suggesting some good old-fashioned breaking and entering and arson," Royal speaks loudly from where he's at in the kitchen.

"It's unfortunate you don't have an arsonist." The men around me go still, and I catch a side-eyed glance from Ian. "What? I can't learn things? I accidentally burn soup and make a joke about burning the house down, and Valor explained maybe I should take up arson as a skill set."

"I mean, it would be unexpected. She'd be suspected much more forwardly if it was poison." Ian nods and then runs his hand back through his salt-and-pepper hair, much like Valor does. "And no, there is nothing wrong with you learning our business. Betty has missed Kerrianne and is soaking up all the grandma time, or she'd be out here too."

It's foreign being wanted at the table.

Royal comes back to sit with a drink in his hand.

"I've thought of the possibilities of what a failed hunt would mean." Valor brings his hand to my thigh like he did earlier and runs gentle circles with his thumb again.

Is he soothing me or himself? It doesn't matter either way.

"It would feel less suspicious if there were a bunch of burgs with multiple methods rather than burning families' homes to the ground." Valor shrugs and looks over at me, and mischief lights up his features with a half smile and a glint in his eyes.

He would. He'd burn them all to the ground if he thought he could get away with it. I shouldn't be turned on by that.

"Good." Ian nods in approval.

It's impossible not to note how relaxed and carefree he seems with talks of business. The lack of formality is less stressful than anticipated, but not a lack of formality in that it doesn't matter, only that it doesn't need to be life or death.

"And the drive-by?" Valor looks at his father with the same indignation I've afforded Gregorio before. "I don't like that we're implicating Antonella in that attack."

Okay, we'll talk about this with me at the table. I keep my head down and pretend to be fascinated by the pattern in the table runner. *What happens if there's a disagreement?* God, I've never even considered this. Flashes of a body torn apart by what we thought were a thousand stabbings could have been a wolf attack. *Is that what could happen to me?*

"Antonella." Ian draws my attention back to him. "Whatever you're worried about, I wouldn't. Neil is so certain it's you and Berto working together, but I cannot rectify why he is so sure given the lack of evidence."

Royal gets out of his chair and heads over to the fridge. He opens the door, and I hear the rattle of aluminum foil before he sets a container on the counter.

"Dude, are you growing again?" Valor watches over my head as I hear food storage containers opening.

"Well, for all the times you called me your little brother, I decided to grow." Royal microwaves his food but comes to stand at the table and talk to us while it ticks by. "For what it's worth, I checked. There is no way Antonella has another phone or is using her phone, watch, email at work, personal email, or anything to communicate with Berto. So, unless she's outfoxing Jack and Declan to see him in person and making her devices somehow follow her regular paths of movement without her . . . it's unlikely."

"Still in the room." I look up at Ian before looking up at Royal. "As much as I like that you're implying I'm that tech savvy, I am sadly not."

"Well, if you hadn't already decided to specialize in starting fires, I could use a hand, but fire and computers aren't friends." Royal pats my shoulder and goes back to the kitchen, stopping the microwave early.

Royal vouching for me is unexpected. It eases my fear that they're really considering me as some sort of spy. It's one thing to have Valor more certain of me being loyal to them. But the approval from his family lets me slouch slightly into my chair.

"I wouldn't put it past the client, however, to do this in order to get a better deal on something." Ian drums his fingers on the table. "What did he want for the cleanup?"

"A couple of tanked-out SUVs, two of Royal's custom M-9s, and my contact to get his kid into Kerrianne's old school in River North." Valor scrubs his hand down his face. "If he's having money problems or security problems it makes sense. We all know the lengths I'd go to get Kerrianne the best things in life."

"Would explain the smaller purchases." Ian considers it and furrows his eyebrows. "Who else do they do business with?"

"No idea, they're newer players on the scene, coming up here from the Bible Belt for their guns because they don't want to seem weak in the new area. They took international shipments before Doyle kicked them to us." Valor draws a sip of his drink.

But the soothing circles of his thumb have turned into broader passes of his hand, pushing my skirt between my legs and slowly stroking my inner thigh through the fabric.

"Who is it?" I try to be helpful and distract myself from the heat and needy throbs in my pelvis.

"They call themselves the Brass Skull Company," Ian answers. "Ridiculous name but —"

"Well, this is awkward." I scrunch up my features. "Berto and Gregorio were backing them in a pot-growing operation last year. Berto was pissed when they lost a whole crop because he had a buyer in Canada lined up. But they smoothed it over with a massive amount of absinthe and moonshine."

"Well, that'd do it," Royal huffs. "Know what strain they were growing?"

"I have no idea other than it was high-quality pot. That's not something I knew about. He was interested in using the D'Medici network because everyone knows Italians have run illegal substances since long before Prohibition. If there are no illegal liquor or drug sales . . ." I laugh. "Well, the joke used to be that it's because the D'Medicis lost to the Cavanaghs in the truce."

The irony of it makes me laugh and gets a similar reaction from Royal.

A weight lifts again at the table. They don't seem concerned with my involvement and are accepting the information.

"I bet his kid goes to school with my cousins currently, and he's afraid . . . after, uhm, well, that Berto might try something with his kid," I say.

"Logical." Valor nods, sitting back in the chair. "Brass Skull Company starts buying from us because they're afraid of Gregorio and Eduardo after the deal fell through. It's a bigger jump to believe the idea that they'd ambush us only to then ask us to pay them to clean it up. Except if they're cash short and having security worries."

"Let's try to confirm this theory with your next victim." Ian pushes his chair from the table, clearly ending the conversation, and he gives me a smile, "Antonella, it was great to spend time with you. I'm so grateful for you, but this old man goes to bed early. Since Valor will be up late, we'll keep Kerrianne. The little raptor awakens early."

"It was good to meet you too." My smile is genuine. The belonging here in this conversation eased my fears more than I expected.

Valor

CHAPTER FORTY-SIX

NOT THE RIGHT FUN

Kerrianne fell asleep listening to Mom reading. So, after a quick kiss to her forehead and a hug goodbye for my mom, we head back home to deal with the 'project' in the basement.

I follow Antonella up the stairs to our bedroom to change. She reaches behind her, arm bending at an awkward angle for the zipper.

"I'll help you." I step forward, reaching for her.

She huffs but continues to reach for it. "I've been doing this long before you came into my life."

"Four."

I salivate at the thought. I had two plans depending on how many 'infractions' she earned herself. At four, there's still a high possibility that I'll edge her or force her into four orgasms. But more than six, and I'm taking my hand to her ass again.

I get hard no matter which option I think of.

Antonella quits fighting me, and I hold the fabric away from her skin as I slide the zipper down its track.

Stroking her leg at the table, I could feel a seam in her stockings, and maybe it's wishful thinking, given that lingerie under wedding dresses is usually more common than daily wear, but that seam could mean . . .

She slips her dress off her shoulders, and it drops to her waist before she lowers it the rest of the way.

Garter belt, garters, and thigh-high stockings.

"Fuck." She lets her hair down, and it tumbles across her shoulders and down her back. She's the picture of a pinup cock-tease. "Let me see you."

Antonella turns slowly, her brows scrunched together. "Valor, it's hardly the first time you've seen me in my undergarments."

"Five. I assumed you only wore them because it was our wedding. It's a regular thing, isn't it?" I'm salivating.

I step closer to her, dancing my fingers along the band around her waist.

"What are you counting?" She crosses her arms in front of her chest and leans back.

"Six." I smirk at her. "Every time you're a brat, I add one more to what I'll do to you."

"Mmmm." Antonella cocks her head forward and looks at me in what I assume is the disciplinary look she gives her students. "And what is it you're planning to do to me?"

"Seven." I move my hand up over her arm, across her chest, and up to her neck. "Wouldn't you like to know?"

Antonella opens her mouth like she's about to tell me 'Yes, I would like to know,' but she keeps it to herself.

I run my thumb up and down her throat.

We could put our mark there. My wolf and I both want the world to know how deeply we'll have claimed her, mind, body, and soul. I got to mark Holly where it was regularly visible, but I don't want to make Antonella's career difficult.

"But something tells me you're open to whatever I have in store for you," I whisper against her lips.

"Can we torture the guy in the basement before you make a

sexual deviant out of me?" she murmurs before pushing against the grip I have on her neck to press our lips together, but not kissing, as she reaches for the buttons of my shirt.

"You don't have to help, darling."

I'm hot under the collar and don't want to go to work tonight. But leaving my captive downstairs in the torture room until tomorrow morning isn't good for getting information. After a certain level of delirium, my victims can't give reliable and coherent information.

Releasing her neck, I bring my hand away from her and let her finish unbuttoning my shirt and my cuffs before sliding it off my shoulders. The warmth of her hands leaves trails of comfort along my skin.

When she brings her hand to my belt buckle, I stop her with my hand on top of hers. "Ask," I say, letting a low growl from my wolf through.

"May I, please?" Antonella's voice is barely above a whisper.

The scent of her arousal in the room is unbelievable and has me barely restraining myself. But I have plans for her.

With a single nod, I grant her permission.

The release of pressure from the constraining fabric against my cock draws a sigh, and I lean forward, resting my forehead against the top of her head. "Do you know how badly I've wanted you all night?"

"I bet you'll tell me." Antonella finds that spark again.

She knows I have something in mind that she may or may not like, yet she's pushing the envelope anyway.

"Eight." I don't object as she slides her fingers into the band of my boxers and drags them down my legs, dropping to her knees in front of me. I'm throbbing, and pre-cum beads on the head of my cock. "Lap that up for me, darling?"

Antonella doesn't even blink. Locking eyes with me, she sticks out her tongue and slowly drags it across the tip. Her tongue is warm, and the move sensual, as she cleans me.

I hook my finger under her chin, and when I apply pressure, she knowingly rises from kneeling. She stands on her tiptoes and reaches up to kiss me. Placing a hand on Antonella's shoulder, I nudge her back down and bow my head to kiss her with that deep intensity she loves so much. *That I love so much.*

I taste myself on her. The saltiness mixing with her sweetness.

Antonella doesn't stop there. She wraps her hand around my cock and gives it a squeeze before working it between us.

Grabbing her wrist, I stop her. "Not now. We've got to get some answers. Change into something you won't mind me ruining later. I like how you look in this far too much."

Antonella lets out a massive sigh. "What's a girl gotta do to get laid in this house?"

"Nine." I chuckle, following her to the closet.

It's not like she's alone in her desire. It's torturing me too. Especially watching her strip. Her beautiful tits are free from the bra, the warm color of her nipples against her skin demanding to be sucked on. It's mouthwateringly beautiful.

The garter belt comes next as she unsnaps the clips from her stockings and slides it down over her hips, taking her panties with it until they drop to the ground. She may not be trying to be seductive, but Antonella's naturally graceful movements are undeniably sexy. She turns slightly away from me to roll one of her stockings down her leg, her ass presented to me, her pussy on full display, and it stays that way as she rolls down the other.

"Ten." I manage a whisper over the knot in my throat when she turns back to me.

"That's hardly —" Antonella stops herself with a quick intake of air.

"Nice try, eleven." I force myself to pull my watchful eyes from her.

"So, you're making me wait to figure out what and how

you're fucking me until after we torture whoever ended up in the basement?"

I sigh. My previous resolve to spank her fades because the throbbing of my cock demands more attention. "The mixed number of how many edges and orgasms you'll get. Don't worry, there'll be more orgasms than edges."

Her eyes are wide. "Oh, fuck."

"That's the plan." I kiss her forehead. "I've got to get downstairs. You don't have to come. Get some rest. Sometime in the next twenty-four hours, you're getting tortured for talking back and torturing me all night."

The obedience in her nod swells my heart, and I wrap my fingers into her hair and wrench her head back to kiss her again. This time it ends with a gentle bite to her bottom lip.

We could bite her there just like that. We could change her. It doesn't have to be love bites. My wolf encourages me.

Too little time. We want her to succeed. I remind him. Winter break will be done before I know it.

"I'm coming with." Antonella clears her throat, wobbling for a moment as she shakes her head. "As soon as I remember how to breathe when you're in the same space."

CHAPTER FORTY-SEVEN

SHARP AND POINTY

"Hello." Valor sounds so cruel with such an ordinary word.

Walking in behind him, I see what happens when Valor isn't here to receive his 'special shipments' himself.

A captive, a nondescript, twentysomething male, is sitting in that cruel-looking chair. He blinks against the harsh light and squints, quickly becoming more alert from what must have been a disappointing nap. "Let me go! I didn't do anything. I was to stay with the truck and shoot anyone who comes out."

"And that doesn't seem a little bit problematic to you?" Valor flicks on a tablet, showing camera feeds of the house, and then retrieves paper from a printer and starts flipping through the pages.

"A job is a job, man. Guy paid us good money too. I got kids to feed." He defends himself. "You get it."

I take it he's trying to talk to me.

"No. I don't." I shake my head. "Sexist to assume that."

"And you don't either. I can hear it in your voice." Valor tsks condescendingly.

This Valor more aligns with the one Berto says to be afraid of. He hands me a page without looking at it.

Fred Smith. Lives with a roommate. Not communicating with his parents. One sister, lives in Washington. I skim the document . . . Valor is right. No kids. *Can he tell if someone is lying based on tone of voice?*

"The kids, not the money, that is." Valor clarifies. He keeps reading a document but engages the twentysomething in almost casual conversation. "I understand the love of money, Frank. But you took the hit job from an unknown number to kill how many people? For what, a measly ten grand?"

"Fourteen, ten up front, four when the job's complete, and that was just my cut," Fred argues.

"My hit men don't get out of bed to even hear about the mark for a penny less than twenty-five thousand. That's strictly consultation fees. That's such an insult that even if I wanted to let you out of this basement alive, which I don't, I couldn't." Valor sets the papers on the table and then braces his hands against it, looking at the captive. "This can go easily, you can tell me everything I want to know, you don't get hurt at all, and then at the end, when you've given me all the information, I'll kill you nice and painless."

"Fuck you!" Fred snaps.

"Awfully bold for someone strapped to a chair in arguably the creepiest basement in the suburbs," I muse, stepping over to Valor and leaning against him.

Fred watches me like a hawk.

Valor stiffens as he notices. It has his arm snaking around me, holding me close to him.

I turn my head into his chest and murmur, "He may respond better to someone less assuming?"

Valor nods but moves my head away from his chest, kissing my lips, then my cheek, and whispering, "He might, but . . . I've another idea. Have you ever had an audience?"

A chill runs down my spine, ending at my pussy, which throbs with need. I'm already worked up from upstairs. Hearing

356

him count every time I smarted off built my anticipation. Then to learn it'll be the number of edges and orgasms he'll bring me through was sexier than it had any right to be.

I clarify as quietly as I can. "Here, with him?"

I miss Valor's warmth as he steps away to face Fred. He gets up close and personal with him. "Listen, Fred. I like the hard way. My wife likes it when I start making you less and less comfortable until you're in so much pain you're begging to die. The smell of blood and the sound of bones breaking is an ideal night for me. You, fighting back . . . it's almost like foreplay. If you'd like to keep that attitude, go right ahead. Make our night."

Valor is threatening a man, and I'm fucking lightheaded at the thought of how Valor will fuck me. I never considered having an audience. I didn't like knowing that Marc and his shitty friends would be watching those videos he took of us in the locker room.

But Valor isn't letting this man leave here alive. Valor and Royal hatched an evil genius plan to literally hunt down those tapes and make sure no one else can watch them again. *How am I supposed to not fall in love with a man like Valor?*

"Antonella," Valor purrs. "Could you get something sharp and pointy to play with?"

I walk over to Valor's tool cabinet and look at the shelves. Many implements are both sharp and pointy, but a shorter, curved knife draws my eye.

I bring it back to Valor and place it in his open hand.

"Cobbler's knife. Good choice." Valor praises me but looks at Fred with dismay. "I'll start with an easy question. If you answer honestly . . . Antonella will take off a piece of clothing. If you don't . . ." His words hang in the air with the threat as he tips the knife. "Who contacted you for the job?"

Fred swallows hard and tries to fight in his chair. It doesn't go well for him. Valor doesn't repeat himself. He grabs hold of

Fred's hand and slices up, from the webbing of his thumb to the wrist.

The scream echoes around the room, and Valor waits for the noise to die before he tries a new question. "Is it someone you're afraid of?"

"Listen, man. I just took a fuckin' job," Fred groans, his head rolling back and forth.

Valor doesn't take mercy on him, slicing another line up from between his middle and second index finger.

Fred yowls, "The guy who hired us paid cash but did an in-person pickup with the lead of the crew."

"See, Fred, was that so hard?" Valor scoffs.

He looks over his shoulder at me. His eyes are warm and focused. They turn that slightly yellow-gold color. The one that matches his wolf.

I grab hold of the waistband of my yoga pants I'm willing to sacrifice for this sort of work. They slide down my thighs, and I step out of them. My shirt is long, covering my underwear and ass completely.

Fred is hardly in a state to admire, but he does raise his head and look at me.

Valor sets the knife down on his workstation and comes to me.

"Seems like I owe you five edges and six orgasms," Valor says loudly enough for Fred to hear.

He fists his fingers into my hair and moves me, forcing me forward, then around to the table, where I'm well within view of Fred as Valor shoves me down against it.

I close my eyes, the feeling of being manhandled raising my heart rate. The white underwear I'm wearing surely has a wet spot from the arousal I've been trying to crush all night.

Valor pulls my panties down, exposing my ass. "See how wet she is for me, Fred? My wife is hot from watching you get tortured. If you tell me everything you know quickly . . . you won't suffer. I'll let you watch before I kill you. You can get to watch her come all over my cock."

Effortlessly, Valor pushes his fingers into my pussy. The feeling builds between my legs, and I try to hold off my growing desire, but Valor scolds me. "I can feel you clenching on my fingers. You're close. If you come without permission . . . I'll triple the eleven you've earned and take it out on your ass with my hand and belt."

"Oh, fuck," I whisper.

"You two are sick fucks," Fred murmurs.

Valor laughs, full and deep from his belly. "Don't think I can't see your hard-on. You think we're sick fucks, but you're the one being tortured and you still want to fuck her." Valor brings his hooded gaze to the hand at my pussy as he strokes my inner walls. "Which . . . I can't say I blame you."

Valor withdraws his hand from me, and I look over my shoulder at him. With heated eye contact and a smirk, he swipes his tongue out, licking away my arousal. "Mmmmm."

When Valor steps away, I push myself up from the table and exhale a shuddering breath. My shirt falls, and I pull my underwear back in place.

The loss of Valor's touch is a blessing because it stops the growing orgasm. Maybe. The release from his hand on my ass was unique. I felt free. Would the belt be the same?

He heads over to his tool cupboard. "Who was your crew leader?"

"How the fuck should I know?" Fred snaps back.

"You don't know who your crew leader is?" Valor looks at me, and we share the same 'what the actual fuck' look between us.

"All I know is that he calls himself Viper, and he sets these kinda jobs up from time to time." Fred panics, talking more as Valor goes back to looking through his tool cupboard. "I know he said he met with a guy. Viper said the guy —"

Valor turns, coming back with another tool I had considered. It's more of a punch of some nature.

"He said the guy looked like a typical businessman, suit all done up, graying hair, older guy. Apparently had big money, which is why he could pay a crew so much." Fred's words come out in rapid fire.

"Did Viper mention this guy's name?" Valor growls. He pushes the implement against Fred's hand.

I look away as Valor works. Only hearing Fred's yowling.

"I don't know. All he said was old white guy."

"Where is Viper?"

"Dead. I heard on the radio before you grabbed me. Someone said, 'They shot Viper.' I'm betting the guys are wondering how we're gonna get paid. Please."

"I believe you," Valor tells him. "But if you don't know his name, then you're not useful to me. We'll find Viper and his things without you."

"No," Fred whines.

With my back to them, I can only make out Fred's barely understandable begging and whatever Valor is doing to torture him further.

"There, now you'll get to bleed out nice and slow while I take great care of my wife."

Valor's footsteps draw closer to me.

He sets the implement far away from me before drawing my face to look at him instead of the table and his 'tool.' "It's okay to not enjoy the same bloodlust the way I do. You're perfect nonetheless."

Perfect. I can't even stop my stupid heart from fluttering.

Fred groans. Whatever Valor did to him didn't kill him.

"Moderately slow bleeding out," Valor explains. "I wanted to give him a little time to watch as I fucked you over my workbench. I've dreamed of this moment for so long. Never thought I'd have a woman so willing to walk down here with me."

"Is it funny that I lose confidence when it actually comes to the killing?" I force myself to glance over at Fred, but Valor guides my chin back to him before I get to look that far.

"No, princess. I'll make a killer out of you yet. But not today." His words are spoken with the same admiration one would promise undying love or affection.

It awakens something deep in my soul, and I rise up to my toes and kiss him. Valor lets it happen. He's sweet and tender as he kisses me back.

I've fallen in love with him, and while I'm sure that thought will never be reciprocated, nor will it be voiced to the world, it doesn't change how I feel. Valor Cavanagh is exactly the kind of man I was made for, and I'll live or die by his side.

Valor

CHAPTER FORTY-EIGHT

EYES ON ME

When I raise my hand to her throat, Antonella is breathing heavily, and her heart rate is through the roof. The rich brown of her irises turns nearly black with the lust shining through in her gaze.

"He has about fifteen minutes left to live," I tell her, trying to find at which point she loses interest.

But the muscles in her neck flex against my hand as she swallows. She parts her lips with her tongue, like she's about to say something before stopping herself.

"So, do you want to come for him? Give this sick, dying asshole one last look at how glorious a woman looks when she comes, or do you want something just for you?" I offer her, wondering how she'll make that decision.

Silent for a minute, Antonella chews it over. I can almost see the flashes of thought pass in her eyes as the gears in her brain work through her choices.

"Exactly how sassy do I need to be to get that taste of your belt you promised?"

"Fuck." I look over to Fred.

He's bleeding out, and it's slow enough that I could give her what she asks for and fuck her until she comes. But the last time I gave her pain, the emotions flowed freely with it. She was already a little soft at dinner.

No one sees our mate vulnerable. My wolf agrees. *Skip to ending his life. There will be plenty of opportunities to have fun with problem people.* My wolf urges me to kill faster. A welcome but unusual development since he also enjoys the bloodshed.

"I'll have to fuck you in front of a victim another time, princess," I tell her at the same time Fred releases a gurgle as blood escapes into his lungs. Antonella almost moves her head within the grasp of my hand. "Don't look, darling. Eyes on me."

She does as I say, following the light pressure I keep on her neck as I walk backward, leading her out of the hidden passage into the main portion of the house.

My hand feels cold when I pull it away from Antonella's warm skin.

I leave her, hoping she won't follow as I head back into the room with Fred. I don't let him suffer alone in the dark. Instead, I end his life quickly by slitting his throat the rest of the way, and he slumps forward in the chair.

After a quick text to Gavin asking for a cleanup, I toss the flash papers into the burn bin. The match flares hot in my fingers, and when I toss it in the can, the records go up in a ball of flames in less than two seconds.

There are too many suspects who could be behind this latest hit job. But one thing is for sure — Eduardo and Gregorio D'Medici don't have graying hair. They have black hair. I speculate it's dyed, but it does rule them and Berto out as primary suspects behind whatever is going on.

Antonella is where I left her, waiting for me when I come out of my lair, and she lets me interlace our fingers as I lead her in silence out of the basement and into the main living area.

It's so tempting to bend her over the couch, the counter, and hell, even right on the stairs, and get a look at her sexy, barely clad ass. But I behave. And it isn't until we're finally in our bedroom that I take back the controlling tone that gets a rise out of her.

"Strip."

Antonella cocks her head. "Make me."

Oh, the mate is so fierce. My wolf is almost condescending with that, but we like the challenge.

I step forward and quickly grab the bottom hem of her shirt. Tearing it, the fabric rips easily, and she leans back as if to get away from me. It's halfhearted at best. The scent of her arousal overrides every sense of logic in my brain.

"Take your bra off before I rip it off," I snarl at her, letting the wolf inside rise to the surface.

Seductively, Antonella unclasps the garment, slides it over her shoulders, and drops it to the floor. With her gorgeous tits on display for me, I reach for her underwear. It's a practical piece. Not delicate lace or the like that, apparently, she has stocked in her wardrobe. I have no qualms about tearing it to shreds, ripping it from her body, as I drag her closer to me.

She gasps, but it's from surprise because not a hint of fear comes off her body nor does the desire fall from her eyes.

"Do you really think you can handle my belt?" It's the only chance she's going to get to tell me no.

My uncertainty is ever growing. *What if she can't handle me?*

Then we'll give her a wolf, and then she will. But you've so little faith in our mate. My wolf encourages me. *Look at how she's looking at us.*

"I want to." Her answer isn't a yes or a no. Antonella leans toward me. "Let me try?"

"If it's too much, say stop, and this time I'll stop. In the future, I might not be so nice." I lean into her and press my lips against hers.

She kisses me back, and it's chaste at first, but in another heartbeat, it gets more intense. I wait, kissing her until she reaches toward me.

I capture her wrist and spin her around, bringing her hand behind her back.

"Fuck," she gasps on a ragged breath.

But I don't stop moving because she didn't say stop.

I push her deeper into the bedroom and then face down against the bed. One-handed, I undo my belt and pull it from my pants. There are so many ways I could do this, but when I see Antonella's delicate fingers fisting the sheets, I move past all the options to set this up and, with my teeth, fold the belt in half. I grasp the ends together and choke up until I've got just the right amount of leather in my hand, the loop ready to smack against her soft curves.

She's shaking, but there's no mistaking the scent of her arousal.

To give her a small taste, I run the leather over the globe of her ass. Antonella clenches instinctively.

"Relax, darling. Tensing only makes it hurt more." I lie to her.

It's the body's way of lessening an impact, but after her emotional response just over twenty-four hours ago, I don't know if she's truly ready for more. Selfishly, I want to push her to her limits. I want it to hurt so she tells me to stop. Her asking for pain is out of character, but now I want more.

I pull my arm back, and after a single swat of the belt against her skin, I wait.

A gasp, a writhe, and a calming breath. Antonella breathes steadily again.

I raise the belt again, and then she fights. She wrenches her wrist, and I release my hold on her. "Stop."

"Good, darling." I praise her, dropping the belt to the floor and helping her roll to her side. "What happened?"

She shakes her head and pulls her hands up over her face. "I can't . . ."

"Can't what?" Bitter dread sinks through me as I kneel next to her on the bed.

Antonella pulls her hands off her face, and her words are stronger than anticipated. "That was too much, but if you don't fuck me, I'm going to riot and get a toy to finis —"

I shift her onto her back, and she tries to scramble away, but I'm faster, unbuttoning my pants and opening my fly before grabbing hold of her ankle and drawing her back to me. With one hand, I restrain her, holding her leg back, and with the other, I push my pants down and kick them off.

Antonella fights, and it's fierce until I wrangle her underneath me. Her legs are splayed out on either side of my own, and my hand is on her throat.

"I'm the wolf and you're my prey. I'll always take care of you. I love a good toy as much as the next man, but until we at least get a full month of marriage under our belt, the only way I want you coming is on my fingers, on my tongue, or speared on my cock."

"And after that?" She taunts me but reaches for my neck, pulling me toward her.

"Then I'll get more creative with how to make you scream my name." I thrust into her.

She's so wet, she's *been* wet, primed and ready for me.

My balls throb as I fuck into her. She moves her hand from behind my neck and wraps it around my throat. *Fighting for control, hmm?*

I shift to my back, pulling her on top of me, and fuck her from beneath, taking her cunt.

"Fuck." Antonella's eyes roll back as she moves her head from side to side.

The motion pushes her throat into my hand, and I give it a soft squeeze.

Instinctively, she rocks her hips forward and back, taking me all on her own and pressing into my hand every time she moves forward.

I'm mesmerized watching her. Tits bouncing as she grinds against me. It isn't until the edges of my vision go dark that I realize her hand is still on my neck. But fuck, I'm so close, and the noises she's making grow louder with every movement. I'm loving every second.

Lust and love. They're both four letter words for how I feel.

I thrust up into her, and the movement drives Antonella over the edge. She screams, arching up and out of my hand. She grinds and rocks her hips, meeting my thrusts. I'm on the brink, and when she looks down at me, sweat glistening on her skin, sleepy but happily well fucked, I lose control and come deep inside her.

Give her a wolf. Bite her. My wolf begs. *Make her ours, keep her like this forever.*

He forgets that I already have her forever. The mind-blowing sex is only a fraction of it.

Breathing heavily, I pull Antonella down next to me. My cock slips out of her and leaves me cold and disappointed. I could use her cunt as a sleeve and stay inside her warmth longer, but when she curls up against my chest, I forget all about it.

"Thank you," Antonella murmurs. "That was so good."

"Anytime, darling." I kiss the crown of her head and reach to wrap her up in a burrito of the blankets around us.

When we're nice and snuggly, I finally let myself drift off to sleep.

It's love. She's my mate and I need to tell her that soon. All of it.

CHAPTER FORTY-NINE

LE TRADIZIONI DI FAMIGLIA

"Wait, where's my new niece?" Leticia asks, looking at the table where I sit alone in the front section of La Fatal Piedra.

"She's coming. I may have lied to get out of the house a little early so I could pick up a few gifts she wouldn't see. Declan is bringing her in a little bit. Besides, it gives us a little time to catch up," I answer and usher her to sit down.

"It's weird sitting up front and not being squirreled away to the back room with the family. I like it." She slings her purse over the back of the chair, where I set my purchases and purse, before looking out through the big glass windows to the street. Her attention span changes quickly. "Oh my God. That means we can finally talk about how hot Valor is."

"Yes, he is very hot." I roll my eyes as Leticia fans herself with her hand.

"Leticia. I haven't seen you in forever!" Our waiter greets her. "I thought you were avoiding good food. Get you the usual?"

"Rude, but yes, my lover, please bring the usual." Leticia giggles as the man walks away.

"Isn't he like our fifth cousin?" I squint at her. I'm terrible at keeping track of the extended family, and it's only gotten harder the longer I lived away from home.

She shakes her head. "Not by blood. His mom married my mom's cousin. She had him before they met."

"Well, okay then." I draw a sip of my water.

The server sets a large glass of wine in front of Leticia, and after a quick check-in that we're good, we're alone again.

"It's still so weird you're twenty-three."

"Yes, well, that's what happens when you move so far away for so long. Your little cousin becomes not so little." She hums while taking a sip. "Okay, Valor. Is he like amazing in bed?"

"Could you have said that any louder?" I glare at her, flicking my eyes to the rest of the restaurant.

"So, does he make you come?" she whispers, leaning forward.

I press my fingers into my temple, trying like hell to hide the fact that I'm blushing but knowing that's never going to happen. "Yes, okay. God, why are we talking about this?"

"Because you're getting laid, and if a man so much as looks at me, Berto gets so overprotective it hurts." Leticia groans.

With a sigh, I drop my hand from my head and sit back in my chair. "You get two questions, and that is the most I'm discussing with you today."

"What is he like in bed?" Leticia chooses her question carefully, not boxing herself into a yes or no answer.

An animal. The first answer that comes to mind is so obvious and kind of fitting, but I can't reveal his secrets. "Strong, skilled, and reciprocates well. He always tells me that he's falling into lust with me."

"Eeee!" Leticia makes a quiet shrill noise. "That's so swoon worthy. Level ten swoon. I love that for you. I know you've avoided dudes before, but like . . . that sounds like he's worth the extra —"

"Oh-kayyy cutting you off." I interrupt her. "Second question?"

"Is it all big dick energy or is he backing that cool swagger up?" Leticia quirks an eyebrow, her cheeks turning pink.

"You're seriously asking about size?" I groan, wishing my cup of water was wine, but Kerrianne is coming and she's my responsibility. I absolutely won't risk it.

Leticia nods and presses her hands together in front of her chest. "Oh, come on. I gotta know."

"It's not just energy," I deadpan.

She fans herself again, wiggling in her seat. "I'm so happy for you!"

"Thanks, me too. As far as my theory on being married to some underling . . . I'm okay with being wrong if it means spending time with Kerrianne and Valor."

Through the window, I see Declan walking Kerrianne down the sidewalk toward us.

She sees me and waves excitedly.

When I wave back, Leticia looks over her shoulder. "Gah, she's so stinkin' cute! You going to make one of those?"

"Oh, don't you start too." I glare at her but stand as Declan and Kerrianne come through the door. "I'm enjoying my life as is. Not thinking too much about it. Not putting any labels on it."

I walk toward Declan and Kerrianne.

"Valor wants me to stay in the building. Not to be an intrusion, I figured I'd stay at the bar, watch the doors?" Declan offers, nodding toward the large mahogany bar at the side of the room.

"Not an issue. Put it on my tab." I reassure him before turning to Kerrianne and offering her my hand. "Are you ready for lunch?"

Kerrianne nods, taking my hand, and looks past me. "Is that Leticia?"

I stop walking, her question sounding off. "It is. Is everything okay?"

"I really like her. She's super cool. I didn't know if she wouldn't spend time with us anymore 'cause Dad doesn't like her brother." Kerrianne leads the way back toward our table.

"Sometimes who we're related to doesn't define us. I think your dad sees that Leticia is a good person, and that's what matters. But he approved us seeing her today. Would it make you feel better if we called him?" I offer to her.

"He said she'd be here, so I know it's safe. And Declan is right there." Kerrianne looks back to double-check that she can still see him. "Plus, I trust you. Dad said you're not my new mom, but he said you'll protect me just the same. And I know that's true because you're already lookin' out for my back."

"Absolutely." I agree. My heart flutters with the recognition.

I never want to replace the memory of her mother, but the fact that she knows she's safe with me is more than I can ever ask for.

Kerrianne sits in the unoccupied fourth chair at the table and looks at the kids' menu set in her place. She seems intimidated by the arguably way fancier than they need to be paper menus with full-on maps of Italy. "This place is fancy."

"It is a little fancy. My mom used to say fancy restaurants are the world's way of saying 'celebrate even if it's for something small,'" I say before leaning over to look at her menu with her. "The lasagna comes in a little dish made in your size." I demonstrate its size with my fingers. "The edges are crispier, and they can make it with whichever type of ingredients you like. So, choices like lamb or beef or chicken, and it can have tomato sauce or more of a white sauce called béchamel."

"My favorite is the meatball pizza, or if you're feeling very adventurous, the porchetta sandwich," Leticia chimes in and then hides her mouth from me with her hand. "If they let me, I order off the kids' menu anytime I'm here."

372

Kerrianne giggles at that. "What is a porchetta? It sounds funny."

"Porchetta is pork and how they cook it to make it soft and tender," I answer before Leticia can say how young the pig is when they cook and kill it.

God knows I don't need to traumatize her like Uncle Eduardo did to me at her age.

"Okay." Kerrianne nods, and our server comes by.

Kerrianne efficiently orders her beverage, and we're given another few minutes to decide.

"Are we celebrating?" Kerrianne wrinkles her nose, her brow furrowing so much like Valor's does. "You said your mom said celebrating, even if it's small."

I nod and explain. "When I was your age, my mom would take me out to a fancy restaurant. Most of the time, it was here, and we would eat lunch and then go shopping for everyone's Christmas gifts. I could pick out a little something for everyone I loved so much. Then my dad would meet me for dinner and dessert, and then we'd go buy my mom something for Christmas."

"Like we are today." Kerrianne nods, clearly picking up what I'm saying.

"Exactly." I smile.

She squints at me. "Is Dad meeting me for dinner?"

I shake my head. "No, Leticia and I decided since my mom and dad aren't alive anymore that she would come with me, and now we have you. So, the tradition has changed. We're going to make it a 'just the girls' thing."

"I'm really glad I get to come." Kerrianne beams.

My heart stings, and I fight back tears, my emotions getting the better of me. Leticia finds my hand under the table and squeezes it. I hadn't realized how much that seemingly small memory meant to me. I didn't expect to miss them this much. I didn't expect this to hit so hard. Maybe it wouldn't have if it was just Leticia and me, but Kerrianne's presence sharpens the ache of my grief, yet I wouldn't want it any other way.

"We can pretend Declan is a girl. I'm sure he won't mind," Leticia chirps, and I flick my eyes to see him laughing at the bar.

Antonella

CHAPTER FIFTY

THE UNEXPECTED

Snow is falling from the sky, and I look up, admiring it as it comes down among the buildings.

Kerrianne is all too excited to pick out gifts for Valor, Ian, and Betty. She's stumped when it comes to Royal. The store we stop at doesn't have anything Royal would seem to have a use for.

"Oh!" Kerrianne squeezes my hand. "Can we go to the hockey team's store? He said that if he ever met number seven, he'd smash him. Could we see if they have a bobblehead?"

"Absolutely." I elbow Leticia, who is not handling that nugget of information well.

She steps back behind us to get herself under control.

When we get down the street to the SUV, Declan isn't the only one waiting for us. I'd recognize that profile anywhere. Valor's angular features are softened only by how he's smiling and chatting with Declan, standing across the sidewalk from him, leaning against the building.

"Well, this is a surprise." I eye him, but nothing screams 'I've got bad news,' so I force myself to lower my guard.

"It is." Valor smiles at me. "Are you all done shopping?"

"We were going to the hockey team's store to get something for Royal to smash." Leticia pipes up.

Valor nods like it's a perfectly normal statement. "I don't want to interrupt too soon. I'll go with Jack and meet you there."

He seems like he's firmly decided so I don't argue with him, especially not when he wraps an arm around me and pulls me in for a kiss.

"I'll see you in a bit," I whisper against his lips.

The soft smile on his face is unexpected. He was nervous this morning about sending us off without tagging along, and I expected to find a vehicle tailing us, with him in it, all day. But that never happened.

At the hockey team's store, they had three different sized statues and bobbleheads of number seven. Kerrianne picked the medium-sized one because it had the most bobble to the head. I don't know how Royal will explain to her that he won't smash it into pieces. But it's also not my problem. Oh, to be a fly on the wall . . . Maybe I can make that happen.

Valor is outside with Declan again, and he's quick to stoop down before his daughter to meet her at eye level. "Do you mind if I take Antonella out for a little while? I'll send you home with Declan, and we'll be back before bedtime?"

"Okay, but no looking at your present." She narrows her eyes at him, giving him the signature Cavanagh glare.

"I promise." Valor kisses her on the forehead and gives her a tight hug. To Leticia, he adds, "I've a car waiting to take you back to the Gold Coast. Trusted men, I promise."

She laughs. "I think you're afraid that Antonella will kill you in your sleep if you don't get me home safely."

"Why does it always seem to be in our sleep that one of us is getting murdered?" Valor murmurs and offers his hand out to Leticia.

"Oh no, I'm a hugger." She wraps her arms around him and squeezes before releasing him. "I'll catch you all later."

In less than thirty seconds, I'm left holding hands with Valor along the Riverwalk.

"I know you normally did dinner with your dad, but I thought maybe as part of the new tradition we could go together instead." The tears I stuffed down earlier come out this time, and he's quick to wipe them away. "If I don't meet the minimum age requirement, Dad said he'd come down and take you to dinner instead."

I lean into his touch. The comfort and familiarity shouldn't be so easy. He shouldn't make me feel so safe.

After a few seconds, I realize I haven't answered. "Of course I'll go to dinner with you. That would be a good tradition."

"I'm glad you said yes. We have a stop to make first." He grabs my hand and squeezes. "I'm so glad you were thrust into our lives."

"Me too," I say with a small smile.

Valor drives through the city, his right hand interwoven with mine on the center console. Every once in a while, he brings our joined hands up to his lips and kisses my knuckles.

We pull into a parking garage, and Valor motions for me to stay put. Being a complete gentleman, he opens my door for me.

Hand in hand, he leads us down the sidewalk to the front of a jewelry store. The business is closed, but he knocks anyway.

I'm surprised when someone opens the door and welcomes us in with their arm extended toward the shop's interior. We walk farther inside, and I admire the sparkly stones glistening in the case as the shopkeeper locks the door behind us.

"I was wondering when you'd bring in your new bride." A woman comes from the back, her gray hair glistening in the light. "She's lovely. I can see why you picked her."

"Mmm, she's a spoil of war. The rarest prize in all the land." The adoration in his eyes as he looks at me is a shock to my system.

I raise my eyebrows but keep my mouth shut. *Damn. That was smooth.*

"I don't love the ring we started with. I was hoping you could help." Valor leads me closer to the counter farthest at the back.

The sparkly nature of gems catches my little raven brain, wanting to see them glint and gleam in the light. I'm so fascinated with the case that I don't notice Valor bringing my hand up to the counter until a feminine touch grazes my fingers.

"You never were a fan of the more traditional shapes. I'm surprised this is what you proposed with."

I shift my gaze to her. A silent scolding passes between them.

"It's a long story but . . . my father." Valor defends himself.

The woman shakes her head. "Well, you know I always take care of you."

"Antonella, this is Galina. Galina, I present you my wife, Antonella." Valor introduces us.

Being invited into the conversation, I smile. "You have so many beautiful pieces."

"Thank you. I know what Valor likes, but you wear it every day. What do you like?" she asks.

"I've never been a jewelry girl. My mom had my ears pierced when I was a baby. Beyond a few simple necklaces, I'm new to this." Flitting my gaze between the two of them, I can tell it's not the answer they were hoping to hear.

But Galina doesn't waste time. "It means you get to see more gems. Valor, I'm guessing budget is not important."

He shakes his head. "Next alpha of the pack, there's a certain expectation."

My eyes go wide with the notion that she knows, but I'm unsure if she's a shifter or not.

Valor fills in the gaps. "Galina is from a pack in Eastern Europe. She comes here to manage her many jewelry stores every few months."

Galina pulls out a piece of black felt and then lays a velvet cloth over it. From within the case, she selects a few pieces, setting them out on the counter. "Now, these are just to determine shape. I've got what you're really after in the back. Valor is like a little magpie. He always wants the most sparkly. Which normally is a round radiant. But a regular radiant or emerald will look best on your hand. You've got long, graceful fingers." She gestures to my hand. "Take off the abomination, dear."

I look at the ring before sliding it off. *It seemed fine to me.*

The woman moves quickly, taking the 'abomination' and setting it aside. She then slips a new ring on my finger. It's too big in the band but the diamond is a lot more sparkly. And I do like how it looks.

"Ah, look. She likes it." Galina takes it back off and puts on another. This one's much more subtle. It's as if she's reading my mind. "But she prefers the emerald cut."

"And we'll need —"

"Valor if you're about to tell me that you need the full three-piece set, I'll come right around this counter and deck ya." Galina looks up at him, her chin tucked down and eyes narrowed.

It's thirty minutes of trying on rings and sets, Galina pulling cut diamonds out of trays from the back, before she and Valor seem content with my reactions, which I wasn't aware were giving so much away.

"Alright, I'll get this on order." Galina is beaming when she herself, not her assistant, lets us out the door again.

The sun was setting when we entered the store, and with the short days of winter, we're only illuminated by the streetlamps.

I look at my ring in the glint of artificial light before looking up at Valor. "You didn't have to replace this one. It's beautiful."

"It's not and it's been bugging me." Valor laughs while wrapping an arm around me.

He leads me down the block past the parking garage to a fine dining restaurant.

The maître d' immediately leads us to a table toward the back, away from the bustling door leading to the kitchen.

"Do I even want to know how much this costs? I know what Gregorio spends on gifts for Francesca, but I have a feeling what you bought is more." I wince.

"Why are you uncomfortable with me spending money on you?" Valor counters.

"Why did this turn into an interrogation?" I push back.

He smiles at me. "About the same time you seemed to get weird about money. Though I've recently come to understand how much you have."

"Okay, could I buy this ring?" I keep my voice quiet as our waiter brings over wine and an appetizer. In confusion, I look at Valor and the plate.

"I know it's gross when men order for women, but this is the special tasting course, and it's allegedly an amazing experience. I've wanted to try it for a while, and it's a 'meal for two' type of thing." He runs a hand across the back of his neck. "Forgive me?"

I nod. "Forgiven, but answer the question."

"If you liquidated your assets and it wasn't already paid for, you could buy your ring," Valor answers. "Why are you uncomfortable with me spending money on you?"

My spine stiffens, and I try to relax, but there's no way to say this without sounding ungrateful. I try anyway. "Until recently, things had been extremely tense between us, and in some cases,

I wasn't sure you believed me or trusted me with everything that's going on."

"I like you. I trust you." Valor nods with each statement. He draws a deep breath in through his nose but doesn't say more.

"I like you and trust you too," I tell him, but my heart is screaming *I love you, and I want you to love me too.*

Valor

CHAPTER FIFTY-ONE

THE MESSAGE

I read it again.
I read it another time.
It doesn't make sense.

NEIL:

> We're headed to your house. Be there in an hour.

> Antonella betrayed us. Bringing proof.

> Kerrianne isn't safe with her. None of us are.

DAD:

> It doesn't look good, Valor. I'm sorry.

> They broke the truce. Secure your bride. We can't let anything else happen.

My heart shatters in my chest. I trusted this woman. I let her into my daughter's life. I could have kept her locked up in a tower away from the world, but instead, I let her into my home, into my bed, and if what Neil says is true, she's betrayed us, and Kerrianne is in danger.

I don't want to believe it. I don't know what to believe. I rack my brain for signs of her deception that I may have missed. Maybe the deception started at the beginning. Her sexual inexperience, her softness, her willingness to explore new experiences with me — it was all an act. The smartest of ruses to play right into her hand.

My wolf is silent but with me, our hearts being ripped from our chest at the prospect.

I ball my hand into a fist around my phone and bow my head, taking a deep breath to contain the rage at being made a fool of. Fire burns through my gut, and I can't control my heart as it pounds in my head.

With one last look at her, taking a tray of cookies out of the oven before turning it off, I let this be her last moment of peace. I let it be perhaps the last good memory I have of her. Moments are fleeting and something you can't ever hold. We've had so many good moments.

Striding forward, I steel myself for what's to come.

Maybe it's a mistake. Maybe she didn't know what she was doing. I need to know now, before they get here. Whatever it takes to know the truth.

Transforming from Valor the husband to Valor the interrogator, I stalk into the kitchen and grab hold of her ponytail. I drag her to the wall outside of the kitchen and press her face-first against it, pushing my body against hers, caging her in.

"Valor!" she shouts, pushing against the wall, trying to get out from under my weight.

But it's no use; the size difference between us puts her at a disadvantage.

"You need to tell me what you did right this second. I might be able to save you, but I need to know what the fuck you did," I snarl into her ear.

"I don't know what you're talking about. Move," she orders, still trying to push me away. "Get off!"

"Don't lie to me. What did you do?" I repeat, wishing I had more information to prompt a response.

Maybe she's just done so much dirty shit she doesn't know what I caught her in. That sickens my stomach. *How could I have been so wrong about her?*

Antonella kicks out, trying to strike me, but I have her pinned, so she can't land anything more than a ridiculous tap against my body.

She quits struggling and draws slow breaths. "Valor, I don't know what you think I did, but I assure you, I didn't do it."

"My father and Neil are on their way over here right now. They say they have evidence that you betrayed us. You put Kerrianne in danger. So fucking tell me right now, and maybe I can make this easier on you. Maybe I can make this look like it's something it's not. A life locked away in an apartment with a view is better than death." I warn her, talking fast, hoping she hears me and what I need from her.

"I don't know what the fuck they could possibly be bringing, but I didn't do it. Whatever they think I did, I didn't." She's drawing ragged breaths. Her forehead is pressed against the wall so I can't see her expression.

With a snarl, I step back enough to forcibly roll her to face me. "Just. Tell. Me."

Her eyes lock on mine, the autumn-leave tones glossy with moisture. "I don't know what you think I did, but I didn't do it."

I want to believe her. From her soft lips, furrowed brow, and the sincerity in her eyes, I don't sense deception, but maybe she's that good. That's been the plan all along. Make me think she's giving everything away, but really she's got it locked inside her. Was this some elaborate long con?

It rolls my gut. I don't have time to waste.

With force to show her I'm serious, I grab her by the back of the neck and shoulder, turning to put her in front of me.

Antonella walks on her own two feet as I steer her through the house.

Until we take the stairs down to the basement.

"Valor." Her voice wavers with a near sob. She digs her feet into the floor, stopping her movement. "Don't do this."

"You're not giving me any choice." I hate that my voice isn't strong, that it's filled with gravel. She's made me weak.

My wolf howls in mourning. *No, our mate wouldn't do this. She wouldn't.*

I ignore him, my heart breaking enough without him dying inside me as well.

Antonella fights me the entire way, reaching back to try to dislodge my grip. Her feet dragging and scrabbling against the floor, searching for purchase that doesn't come. It's clear she did have training, albeit not enough to fight me off.

I throw her up against the wall alongside the door to my torture chamber.

Antonella keeps fighting, her voice edged to a sharp point. "Valor. I don't know what is going on. Let me go. Talk to me."

That sound, that pleading, normally excites me, but this time it leaves my mouth dry and ashy. My stomach turns again. But I have orders. I tried to get her to tell me. So now we'll see what my uncle brings with him.

I could chain her to the wall, or hang her from the ceiling by her wrists and let her dangle, or strap her to the table. But I can't make myself leave her in such an exposed position. I force her into the metal chair.

Antonella doesn't go without a fight. She claws at me when I move around her to put her into the chair. Her long hair makes for an easy handle to maneuver her. Her knees buckle at the edge of the chair as I drag her backward. Her ass hits it hard, and Antonella lets out a gasp trying to reinflate her lungs.

Using her hair, I drag her up to the position I need her in.

Her ass comes off the chair, and she's forced to stand, leaning backward with her shoulders pressing against the spiked back.

The collar on the chair works like handcuffs, opening to wrap around the unlucky person's neck and then clicking back, tightening and latching into place, then it's attached to the chair with a chain.

I lock the steel collar around her neck but don't adjust the chain, keeping her bent uncomfortably.

The last man I had in this chair was a foot taller and had a hundred-plus pounds on Antonella. Maybe if I make her uncomfortable, she'll realize how serious I am. Maybe she isn't telling me because she thinks I'm messing around, that I won't hurt her.

If she does think that, she's wrong. I'll do anything to protect Kerrianne, even if it means hurting her. Even if it means hurting myself.

My wolf whines, fighting against me. *Our mate wouldn't betray us. She loves us.*

She continues to fight, digging her fingers at the collar's edge, but it's far too tight. There isn't any room to grab hold. The thick metal makes it hard to grasp.

I walk around and stand before her, bracing myself on the arms. I'm well within striking distance, but with wild eyes and a red face, she's too busy trying to save herself, so she doesn't take the opportunity to attack me.

"Tell me what you did," I order her, but my voice decides pleading is better, and it's soft, vulnerable, and I hate her for making me this way. "I can save you if you tell me."

"I didn't do anything, Valor. Why would I lie to you?" She gasps for air, the collar far too tight.

"Self-preservation?" I offer, pulling one of her hands away from where she's grabbing at her neck.

I extend her arm to lock it into the armrest and do the same with the other. Her gasps for air grow more desperate.

Antonella's face begins to turn red, her eyes soft and plead- ing, her lip trembling, and this is all it takes to reduce a strong woman to silent begging. Begging that gets her nowhere.

I wait until her eyelids get droopy before I release the chain holding her at such an abnormal angle.

Her ass finally comes to rest in the chair, and she takes deep breaths. I let her catch her breath before I start again.

"What is it that you did? What is it that you told someone? What could it possibly be?" I don't recognize my voice anymore.

It's not me. I wouldn't talk this way to anyone in my chair like this. I wouldn't let them see me break.

"Valor. I don't know what you're talking about. If I knew I'd tell you, but I haven't done anything." Antonella is panting, her breaths fast and heavy through an open mouth. "Talk to me."

"They're bringing evidence. I need you to tell me what it is." I can't look at her anymore. I can't see her panicking in my chair. The one I've used hundreds of times before.

Busying myself, I go to the cabinet, open it up, and look at the tools available for this job. Everything here is meant to maximize pain. They're all things that hurt like hell, but none of the pain they can inflict compares to what's going on in my heart.

"What have you talked about with your uncle?" I growl at her, hoping it jogs her memory.

"I haven't spoken to Gregorio since the wedding. He told me that he hoped you'd kill me because I was a disgrace."

Again, sincerity in her voice.

She isn't lying. My wolf fights me and what I'm doing, but he's the one who convinced me to love her. It's clear he's wrong about many things, including her being our mate. No mate would betray the other. A human can't be suitable for a wolf.

"You're a fantastic liar." I take two implements out of the cupboard. "So, if you want to play that it wasn't your uncle, what about Leticia? You two text all the time, what is it you've been telling her about our life?"

"Get my phone." Antonella pleads. "You can read any message on it. But I've told her nothing. We talk about recipes, the children in my class, the overbearing, protective parents, and the television show we're watching."

"And what is encoded in those messages?" I ask, wheels turning.

If it were an encoded message, then it would be Royal with the information, not Neil.

The clock is ticking.

I approach her with a razor-sharp knife I pulled from the cupboard.

"Nothing is encoded in those messages." She keeps her eyes on me and writhes against her restraints, pulling her feet up into the chair like she'll mule kick me.

I set the knife on the table and close the distance to the chair. Grabbing her legs so she can't kick me, I lock them into place. Her calves locked together keep her knees closed. "I can't lie for you. I can't make a plea for your life. Not unless you tell me what you did."

"You wouldn't have to lie for me if you'd listen to me. Yesterday, you told me you trusted me."

Antonella knows which buttons to push. She's spent weeks learning them, and that thought sets my stomach on a spin cycle again.

"And it was misplaced." I push myself away from her, disgusted.

But the more I ask, the more and more it feels like she's telling the truth.

My chest tightens, and I feel hopeless, like maybe I'm doing the wrong thing.

I dig the heels of my palms into my eye sockets.

Have we been wrong before? No. But, Christ, there's a first time for everything.

Maybe I'm making a mistake. Minutes pass like seconds, narrowing the window to get the information and formulate a lie before they get here. *I need to make a judgment call. Whose side am I on? Who is right and who is wrong?*

My orders are to secure her and hold her, so my job is done until they arrive.

We're stuck staring at each other. The overhead lights, the obnoxious fluorescent lighting, washes her out and makes her look less like the strong woman I married. The woman my daughter loves. The woman I love. *I love her.*

We love her. She's our mate. Protect her. My wolf urges me.

"Antonella, this isn't me trying to trick you. I can't save you if I don't know how." I approach her with the knife.

"Stop." She shakes her head. "Don't do this."

Stop. That one word from last night.

My wolf howls at the loss of that tender moment.

"You're not giving me a choice." I barely get those words out above a whisper. They're practically drowned out by my wolf howling in my head.

"No," she whines as I slide up the skirt along her legs, the tip of my knife slicing into her skin at the same depth as a papercut.

I'm not trying to inflict damage. But I need her scared enough to tell me. I need her afraid enough to say something I can do to help her.

She doesn't say anything. My actions don't bring any words or confessions, and as I run the blade up the other leg, I study her features. She closes her eyes. Tears escape the corners and run down her face. Hands clenched in fists, she pulls against the restraints, probably the instinct to wipe those tears away.

This isn't the way I like to watch the tears stream down her cheeks. I only want to see her tears when my hand is on her ass or my cock is in her mouth. I don't want to see her in pain, not like this.

My actions can't be helped as I remove the knife from her flesh and point it away from her to wipe the tears off her face with my thumb. She flinches away from me like I slapped her.

"What did you do?" I whisper, hoping maybe she'll answer me this time. That maybe she'll tell me everything, and I'll find a way to spin it. To fix this. To keep her, even though I shouldn't. "What did you tell someone, even if it seemed benign? What did you say that they could have used? Did Berto reach out to you?"

"No. Fuck. Why would I talk to Berto?" Her chest heaves as she fights back sobs. "Whatever they tell you I've done will be false."

I set the knife on her lap as a peace offering. *I can't do this. Not to her.*

I plead with her. "I love you. Let me save you."

"If you really loved me, you wouldn't have dragged me down here." Her body is racked with a shudder. It guts me to watch. "Whatever you do, just tell Kerrianne I didn't want to go and that I loved her. Don't let her think I didn't. I wouldn't betray you. I wouldn't betray her. Not when there's so much for me to lose." Antonella draws a deep breath. "Do what you've got to do, Valor, but I'm not hiding anything from you."

There isn't any deception. There hasn't been any deception. I've made a mistake. For what? A few words in a text message?

I'm reaching for the latch to release her when the door from the underground garage slams open and my father and uncle walk in.

"Oh, you started without us. Did the bitch start talking already?" My uncle laughs, and it's dark and murderous.

He doesn't talk of our mate this way, my wolf snarls, snapping.

He walks over to the table and drops a stack of papers on it. It's a small stack, but even a single line of text or a single photo can be damning evidence. We've killed for less. I need to get to the bottom of this. *Now.*

Antonella

CHAPTER FIFTY-TWO

THE EVIDENCE

I've feared for my life before in shoot-outs and drive-bys. I've had a chill run down my spine as I've felt stalked while walking home at night. But nothing compares to the spiked back of the chair cutting into my flesh. It's pierced my blouse in several places, and I can feel blood running from my shoulders down my back.

Valor's accusations, the pleading, the way he said 'I love you' as he put the knife he just cut me with in my lap. He could have cut me deeper. I've seen him do so much worse.

The cuts burn but not as intensely as Valor's eyes as he waits for something — anything — but he doesn't even seem to know what it is. That's what doesn't make sense.

He steps back away from the chair. The warmth of his fingers as they brush against mine. Furrowed brows and hard-set lips. Valor looks over my head at his uncle and father as they approach. Their footsteps, loafers, step lightly across the solid floor.

Neil Cavanagh purposefully doesn't look at me as he drops a stack of papers on the table. He's smug, disgustingly smirking at

Valor like he's figured out some dirty little secret. Like the cat who caught the canary.

Whatever Neil *thinks* he has will be a lie. You don't bite the hand that feeds you. You don't pick on the biggest kid on the playground unless you can win the fight. And you don't double-cross when you've already crossed enemy lines once.

But I don't know that guilt or innocence matters in this room.

I admired Valor's secret lair before. The way it was a fortress of solitude from the outside world. Now the feeling of being trapped, knowing that this is where I'll die, I understand the pain of those who have been here before me.

Yet up in the light of day, when the sun rises tomorrow, life will go on.

Hopefully they won't tell Kerrianne I left her. I didn't want to go. I'm not guilty of whatever they think I did, but hopefully they'll give her closure.

I draw a fortifying breath as the second-in-command of the Irish Mob holds up a picture, and he begins like he's starting a perverted story time. "Here we have little Miss D'Medici sitting at a restaurant. Or should I say 'ristorante'?"

As he continues with the show, he flicks to the next picture and it's zoomed out farther, so the gold letters on the red trim of the restaurant are visible, and you can still tell it's me.

"She's at La Fatal Piedra, which, as we all know, is the preferred spot for Don D'Medici to do business." Before I can interject, Neil goes back to the first one and points to my hand. "Look at her wedding ring glistening in the light. So, we know this was recent."

This is clearly an attempt — a poor one at that — to frame me going to an Italian restaurant as evidence of the outing being somehow related to my family. But why? Given the clothes I'm wearing in the photo, I immediately know what day it is.

I open my mouth to object but close it again, thinking better of the situation.

What the hell is Neil up to, or does he just have bad information?

"Get to the point," Valor growls, not disclosing to Neil that it was just yesterday that I was there. Not even disclosing that Valor had also been in D'Medici territory yesterday.

"Shhh, Valor. Let an old man tell you how your wife betrayed us. How she's the one who already broke the truce like she forgot it's her life on the line." He scoffs and points. "Look at how she points to something on the paper, showing it to . . . oh, who is that? It's her cousin, isn't it?"

This time he asks me, and I answer because this proves nothing. "My third cousin, Humberto. He's studying here for the semester from Italy and works as a waiter in that restaurant. I'm asking a question about the —"

"Ah, ah, ah." Neil cuts me off. "But look and see, there are four place settings at this table, and, oh, who is that?" He holds up another picture. This one is of Gregorio, Eduardo, and Berto entering the building.

But the photos can't possibly be from the same day or the same time. I know they weren't there. It's why I picked La Fatal Piedra. Because it would be safe, not crowded, and the heads of the family are in Italy.

Valor turns to face me, his eyes narrowed.

Immediately I start talking. "That's not the same day, and if it is, then it's not the same time. The D'Medicis are in Italy. Leticia stayed behind to get the house ready for Christmas, it's why we could do lunch and shopping yesterday."

"Likely story, Miss D'Medici." He clicks his tongue.

I want to correct him. I want to take ownership of being a Cavanagh, but it feels too heavy.

Neil puts the photos down and grabs the knife out of my lap. I force myself to stay still as the blade bites into my skin.

"Tell us what you told Gregorio and Eduardo," Neil snarls

but then draws back. "Tell us what you told them, and maybe Valor will kill you quickly."

I plead to Valor and then to Ian. "You can check the cameras at the restaurant. I'll convince Nonna Farinelli to share them with you. I have nothing to hide. Leticia has nothing to hide. I think she likes her father even less than I do."

Neil pulls the blade along my skin under my jaw with more pressure than Valor used earlier, but I don't know how deep he cuts. It hurts like hell though. I struggle, trying to raise my hands to push him away, defend myself, or stop the bleeding. Anything.

"Get her phone," Ian commands.

He's the least cold of the three but as equally calculating.

Valor is darkness. For a moment, it had disappeared when he told me he loved me.

I had hope that he'd hear me or be on my side. That whatever was happening between us would be strong enough. *He told me he loved me. I guess I wasn't clear when I prayed for his love.*

Valor moves, not quickly, but he does go, leaving the heavy, soundproofed door open behind him, Kerrianne asleep upstairs in her bed. *Please, God, be merciful and don't let her wake.*

"We should just kill her and get this out of the way. Your son is clearly soft for her." Neil postures.

He pulls the knife down the side of my throat, and it's not as deep as the cut under my chin, but it stings, bringing tears to my eyes.

No. No. No. He's a bully like Gregorio. We don't let them win.

"Not until we see the whole picture. If she's guilty, then Valor gets to kill her himself." Ian's use of the word 'if' sends a flutter of hope through me.

Maybe I won't die after all. But blood runs down my neck and soaks my blouse, and it scares me. I force myself to focus on steadying my breathing.

Valor comes back with my phone in his hand and his eyes on

the screen. He's unlocked it and is flipping through it. He puts it on the table and pulls out his phone.

Ian and Valor start comparing information from just yesterday.

"She went to some shops first and then went to La Fatal Piedra." Ian defends me.

Valor starts, "There's Kerrianne at home and then La Fatal Piedra."

Immediately I jump in. "I would never take Kerrianne to meet with Gregorio. First, because he hates children, and second, the family is old school. Women are not to be part of business, and he barely tolerates me. A female child? They would never."

"And yet, you were the one who called the truce." Neil chides. "To protect, Kerrianne."

"Anyone of age could call the truce. That's been the rule since it was implemented. Anyone can call the truce so long as they're willing to put their life on the line for it to be upheld. I did. I was willing to put my life on the line to protect —"

"Enough!" Neil moves forward, thrusting the knife into my stomach.

A scream flies from my lips with the impact, and I try not to pass out. The pain rips through my body, causing the world to flutter in and out of focus. I try to lock my eyes on something to tether me to this world. All my brain can do is focus on Valor.

He pulls Neil away from me, but not before Neil turns the blade. I scream until my lungs give out, until the darkness threatens to take me under, and I wish that maybe it would. They're going to kill me anyway. Maybe it's easier if I die now.

"She could have met with her uncles before Kerrianne got there. Look! She's clearly conspiring with the waiter. Her uncles sat at a different table. Passing messages is plausible." Neil argues with something that Valor says.

"They weren't there," I murmur, fighting for my life and

consciousness. *I should hold pressure on the wound.* I can't move my arms. "I knew Gregorio and his consigliere wouldn't be. Talked to Leticia. Italy . . . for a purchase. Ev-every y-year before Christmas." I focus, trying to get my words to form. "Berto. He went this year too. Some . . . thing . . . about earning it."

"When?" Valor is in front of me.

I didn't see him move. His greenish-brownish-glowing eyes are piercing me. His thumb sliding up and down along the side of the blade.

"They left?" I can't focus. My brain is foggy. "Wednesday? Tuesday? Leticia texted me. Francesca redecorating my room."

I swallow, my mouth dry but my palms sweaty.

Valor steps back from me, and I whimper.

A moment of clarity strikes me harder than the pain in my gut does. Logic. "Declan. He sat at the bar. If Gregorio D'Medici was there . . . ask him."

Ian pulls out his phone and dials Kerrianne's bodyguard. My head throbs in the seconds between rings.

It goes to voicemail. A simple message of his phone number is read out by an automated woman's voice.

Valor pulls out his phone as the silence ticks by for a fraction of a second.

Neil distracts him, pushing on. "If it wasn't for whatever she told them, my Gavin would be alive."

"What?" I gasp. The sharp inhale sends a stab of pain through my stomach, but I study, try to study, the men. The shock sends my heart beating faster. "Gavin is dead?"

Valor turns to look between his uncle and father, shaking his head in disbelief. Ian nods in confirmation.

"Don't look surprised, Miss. D'Medici," Neil sneers.

I know my grip on reality is slipping, but he doesn't look like a man grieving. There is no sadness with the hatred. It's not well contained mourning or shock. *Psychopath story time. Party of one.*

I just know it. I've seen enough loss in life to know that it's not right.

"You killed him."

The words come out before I mean to say them, before the implication of saying them crosses my mind.

"You're accusing me of killing my own son," he deadpans.

"Did you?" Ian asks.

Neil spins and looks at his brother. "Don't be ridiculous. Why would I kill my son?"

"Royal?" I ask.

I keep trying to find the man I loved through logic and questioning. He wouldn't hurt me like this. I draw a breath, but it's hard to get air in, the wound in my stomach not letting my chest expand. Everything hurts, but lack of oxygen makes me lightheaded, and I forget the pain. "Order of succession . . . follows eldest. Kill Ian . . . family head to Valor. Kill Royal . . . Neil's son second in . . . consigliere."

Valor nods, understanding what I'm saying. "Kill Gavin, frame the D'Medicis to break the truce. I would put myself on the line for my daughter. You and I would be out of the way without Royal to —"

Ian starts dialing his phone.

"That's preposterous," Neil growls. It's feral.

Scary. But I can't be scared. You can't be scared when you're not alive.

"Sacrifice." Spots dot the edge of my vision, but I force myself to stay awake through it. "Gavin is youngest. I bet . . . you have an heir."

Royal doesn't answer his phone.

Valor slams Neil up against the wall. Metal rattles and clanks, but if I try to turn my head, the pain in my neck gets worse.

At least Kerrianne is safe. The truce holds.

I'm fading in and out of consciousness.

The world bustles around me, and I try to speak. "Make it look like an accident."

I don't know what the world hears, but I feel nothingness.

Valor

CHAPTER FIFTY-THREE

THE TRAITOR, THE WOLF, THE REMORSE

Neil is securely chained to a wall. Dad is tracking Royal and scrambling all the guards we know we can trust. I lock down my home into an impenetrable fortress. Kerrianne is visible on the monitor, but it doesn't stop my fears.

Antonella is covered in blood. It coats the chair and the floor beneath. The mess from the knife piercing her side. It shouldn't have hit anything major. But 'shouldn't' and 'didn't' are two different things. Not to mention the cuts to her jaw and throat. She's lost a lot of blood.

I dart to her chair and press my fingers to the wound on her stomach, trying to feel for bleeding. I strain to hear what my ears are telling me. Her heartbeat is far too slow. Her breathing is practically nonexistent. I let go of the wound in her stomach, and my hands are slick with her blood.

"Antonella." I start releasing the binds on one side of the chair.

Dad is at my side, unstrapping her other arm, her leg, her neck. "We don't have time, Valor. She won't survive this. You need to give her a wolf."

The noise that comes next, I'll never forget. It's almost like a death rattle, but she's fighting.

My wolf is nowhere to be found.

Dad's right. She's not going to survive.

I look for the monster inside me. But he retreated deep in my mind as the evidence was presented against her. And he didn't resurface as we learned more. As she poked holes into what Neil was saying.

I'm afraid, lost, and looking for him.

Dad pulls Antonella from the chair, and blood stains her blouse on the back from the spikes cutting into her shoulders. He sets her on the stainless-steel table I had her over not that long ago.

"Valor!" my dad shouts, and his alpha command presses through the air. "Shift."

It awakens my wolf, and he whines. I force it, pushing myself to shift.

This isn't how it should be. This isn't how any of this should be.

I find my four feet and approach her. She smells like death, the literal life force seeping from her.

The wolf knows what needs doing. Lifting his paws onto the table, he opens his mouth and digs our teeth into her flesh, tearing through the fabric of her shirt and straight to the bone.

Some ask if wolves are venomous. The truth is no one knows what magic is at work here. But a bite, bone deep, to a human on the edge of death, is all it should take.

I let her go carefully. Lowering myself to the floor, I press my nose against her head and gently lap her neck, cleaning the bite.

You can't die, Antonella. Princess, until death do we part shouldn't be so soon. It shouldn't be like this. I whine, thinking about all the things I said and did incorrectly.

"There's nothing you can do for her right now, Valor. Let the magic of it work. We need to find Royal." Dad tries to pull me away from her, but it's like standing and seeing her body in the morgue.

The stainless-steel table and sterile room. I can't tear myself away from this spot. I'll have to burn this house to the ground because I'll never be able to forgive myself.

"Valor!" Dad commands again, but he turns soft. "Let her rest. Your mother is on the way. We need to find Royal."

I groan, forcing myself away from her. Her heart is still beating, and her chest rises and falls. *She isn't dead. If she's dying, she'd be dead.*

Shifting back is agonizingly painful. Torn between wanting to stay and needing to go, picking a form between wolf and man is a battle of will. Until finally I'm naked and standing on two feet.

I can't keep my eyes off her, keeping her in my peripheral vision.

My wolf is hyperfixated on her, demanding I make glances between pulling up memories of us together.

Every time my phone hits Royal's voicemail, I call again.

Jack comes hobbling in through the underground garage, practically carrying Declan with him. He leaves him to slump against the wall before running out the back doors again. My father follows Jack back out to help.

I go back to searching for Royal, using my credentials to patch into my parents' security camera feeds. There's just too much footage for me to sort through on my own, even with six tiny screens at a time on my tablet.

"What did you do to Royal?!" I snarl, forcing myself to look at Neil.

He's been quiet for a while. Unlike most people in my basement, he's standing, not trying for any sort of relief, and then this fuckin' asshole shrugs.

I'm torn between torturing it out of him and just killing him. But killing him would leave me trying to figure out the pieces from the cyber trail, and that's usually something Royal does. He's better at it. I sit atop a throne of a tech empire, but it's always been his domain.

I keep watching the screen.

Declan writhes on the ground before sputtering, "Fuckin' hell. Get the goddamn bullet out."

"Just a minute. Quit your belly achin'. No one wants to hear it." Jack scolds him as they drop a very bloody and broken Samuel, Neil's eldest son, and prop him up against a wall next to his father. He's in and out of consciousness. Jack nudges his thigh with his shoe. "Tell the alpha what you told me."

Samuel rocks his head back and forth on the wall. "Dad'll kill me."

"Don't say anything," Neil growls, and his teeth click with a snap.

"Dad'll kill me but they're —" He turns his head to the side and vomits bile and blood onto the floor. "They don't want anyone to find him. Not until it's too late. Took him out to the nature preserve."

"Tell me which one," my dad snarls.

The command is evident, and it'll have to be followed, but Dad wraps his fingers around Samuel's throat for good measure.

I search through more footage of my parents' driveway, finally finding what I'm looking for. A vehicle pulls up and Royal comes out of the house. He suspected something because he has a gun tucked in the back of his pants.

I fast-forward through the struggle. I don't need to watch him lose, knowing that what's done is done. I can kick his ass in training if we get him back. Finally, the van moves, and the idiots Neil used were incompetent. The license plate is still on and clearly visible.

"Got the plate," I mutter and quickly start using the automated link Royal hooked into the city's traffic cameras.

My phone rings, and Royal's name flashes across the screen. Hesitantly, I answer. "Valor."

"Fuckin' hell. It's not Antonella. Don't hurt her. I couldn't get the damn thing to call out or answer. They shattered the damn screen. It's not Antonella." Royal is gasping for air.

"You're okay?" She's well past the point of hurt, but there's no point in telling him now.

"Neil and fuckin' Samuel are trying some shit. They're —" His phone cuts out a little bit. "God fuckin' damn it. What good is a fuckin' indestructible case if it breaks and destroys the phone? Can you hear me?"

"Yes, I can hear you. Can you get here?" I don't bother telling him everything we already know. Information only slows us down at this phase.

"Yeah. I'm on my way as soon as I fuckin' find the goddamn keys. Fuck it, faster if I hot-wire it. I'm on my way. Don't hurt Antonella."

It's too late. I hurt her and then let her die. I try not to look at her. To not confirm she's dead.

My wolf forces my attention back to her, where I'm sure to see her lifeless. But she's still hanging on. Antonella's chest rises and falls. It's shallow, but she's still there.

Mate is strong. She'll fight. She'll heal. He assures me. *She'll be wolf.*

Maybe I'd believe that if blood wasn't pooled all around her on my table like the rest on the floor by the chair.

CHAPTER FIFTY-FOUR

THE VIOLENT LITTLE THING

No sooner had I fallen asleep than I wake again.

Gasping for air, I scream, pain radiating through every part of my body.

Valor's voice is loud, coming in stereo from around me. "Let her take you. Don't fight. Relax. Breathe. Please breathe."

My body bends and breaks.

Each breath I take is more and more excruciating. Stabbing pains shoot through my abdomen and along my spine. It's agonizing. I want nothing to do with this pain.

I want nothing to do with him.

Grinding my teeth, I try to scream, but I can't get air.

Nothing moves.

Everything refuses to move except for the shivering that's overtaken my body from the cold in the dark.

He didn't listen, didn't defend me, and now I'm dying. *Fuck. Valor.*

But then my lungs expand. The world feels different. Brighter. Like the sun against my face. When I try to blink, I open my eyes to find the sun high above in the sky, and the ground beneath me is snowy and bright.

Pine trees are dusted in snow, and a thick blanket is on the ground beneath me. The gray sky isn't even as ugly as it normally feels.

I'm no longer cold.

It's glaringly obvious something is wrong. Something has changed. Everything is wrong, so very wrong.

The world doesn't make sense. My body moves, but it isn't my own. I have four limbs at different angles like a dog. A wolf.

What in the fever dream is this? No. Not a fever dream. I'm dead, gone to hell, and it's frozen over. What unlikely event led to this? At least hell is pretty.

"Come on, princess." I hear Valor's voice again.

Ahhh, yes, all eternity listening to that nickname. The way he made me feel. It's only fair to be tormented by him in death. I groan, fighting down the anger and the betrayal coming in waves. *Eventually, I'll learn how to ignore him. He's less obnoxious than most second graders anyway.*

"Try to stand. If you keep fighting her, it'll keep hurting." Valor approaches me from somewhere off in my side vision and kneels beside me. We're practically nose to nose.

At least I know he's not just an audio hallucination in death.

Pain and heartbreak pierce me. Every memory and the way he looked at me refreshes the physical pain that's still so fresh in my mind and body.

My begging and pleading as I told him I didn't know. His anger as he didn't believe me. The physical pain superseded by the emotional as Neil plunged that knife into my stomach.

I try to speak, but the hallucination I'm caught in feels too realistic. I'm silent. Unable. *Wolves don't talk.*

At least this time no one can hear me beg for mercy.

"Quit fighting your wolf."

Just a hallucination. A shitty as fuck hallucination who is bound and determined to make even death miserable.

Valor hesitantly reaches out and runs his hand over my head.

He huffs, inching closer, then he sighs out a massive exhale. "You need to stand. Come on. It'll feel better once you move. Don't overthink it. Don't fight her. Just stand."

'Just stand,' he says. 'It'll feel better,' he says. I close my eyes and think upward, following the fever dream that's apparently not actually hell.

My mind flashes back to that conversation. *'To be gifted a wolf, you need to practically die.'* And now I'm here. I almost died in his basement, only to end up here. Wherever the fuck here is.

Trust me, a new voice says.

I open my eyes, turning to look around, but no one's there. It's just me and Valor out in what appears to be the middle of nowhere.

Valor cocks his head.

Relax and trust. I won't ever let him hurt you again. We'll tear him limb from limb. Her voice is strong. She feels ravenous, and I believe her.

I let go and just feel. My body moves, and it's so freeing to take steps, walking away from him. It takes a minute, and soon I hear her voice again. *Lead the way.*

To think and to move is as easy as it seems. Two steps, then three, darting left and right. It's a full sprint, running to destination unknown, leaving Valor in our past.

Until his large black wolf comes running up alongside me. I push to move farther and faster, but he's constantly there, chasing. I turn hard, going back the way we came, but he spins alongside.

Just go the fuck away, I think.

Valor cuts in front of me, coming to a stop, forcing me to come to a full halt.

I try to walk past him, but he snarls at me, and the wolf in my mind snaps. She lunges forward, and our teeth sink into him, reaching for skin, but we come back with a mouthful of fur rather than blood.

It's not enough for her. It's not enough for me. We charge, surging forward once more, and when we connect this time, it pushes him to the ground, throwing him off kilter. Valor doesn't fight back.

He lets the wolf within me, the wolf I'm within, get ahold of him at the neck by his shoulder. The taste of blood hits my tongue, filling my mouth. My jaw clamps down, pushing farther. But even then, Valor doesn't fight back.

Attack after attack, Valor accepts the beating we give him. The pain we inflict on him until all that's left of my energy is panting and wobbly feet.

I collapse to the ground, and when the darkness comes, with it comes peace.

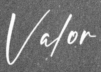

Valor

CHAPTER FIFTY-FIVE

THE AFTERMATH

I deserved it. Every bite and scratch. Hell, I probably deserve that ten times over. But she's weak, still coming into herself. The newly minted wolf only has so much strength.

It's been days of fighting. But this is the first time Antonella has seemed alert.

When her wolf retracts, she collapses, unconscious. My gorgeous mate's long hair puddles in the snow around her.

For a flash, I remember the blood, but I force myself back to the present, to her.

It's easy enough to scoop her up into my arms and walk across the yard to my family's hunting lodge. I set her on the bed by the wood stove to warm up and then close the door behind us.

Antonella stirs when I pull a blanket over her. When she curls up into a ball, refusing to look at me, my guilt intensifies.

I pull on my sweats and sit next to her feet. "Can we talk?"

"I'm thinking annulment. I get my money, you keep yours, and we pretend we never met. I'll find a new teaching job, and you can fuck all the way off." Her words are sharp with a cutting edge.

"No." I shake my head and scrub my hand down my face, covering my mouth. *She's never going to forgive me. Not like I'll forgive myself either.* "No annulment. Yes, you can keep your money, you can have my money too. There is no pretending we never met. And Rothschild-McClintock Magnet School will never fire you."

She closes her eyes and sits up, her body wobbling for just a second as she stabilizes. "Did you find Royal?"

"Yeah, he saved himself. As he says 'It was fuckin' amateur hour. They were asking for me to kill them' but it's only because Neil underestimated Royal. According to Samuel, it took five of Neil's guys plus Berto and his two friends to take down Sean, but Neil only sent three to take care of Royal." I look over at her, hoping to find some of the joy we shared together from before. Anything.

You hurt our mate. My wolf reminds me. *Of course she won't want us right away.*

I keep rambling with the intent of opening the conversation. "Royal may be the tech genius, but he can handle himself."

The silence that settles between us is awkward. *I said the wrong thing.*

Even when we were newlyweds, our silences were never awkward. Maybe if they had been, it would make this easier now.

"What happens next, Valor? What fuckin' happens next?" She looks straight ahead, blankly watching the flames dance in the little window of the woodstove.

"We talk. I apologize. In time, you forgive me. We go home to Kerrianne and our life together." I offer what my ideal solution looks like.

"Oh no. I'm not pretending this never happened. I'm not pretending you didn't drag me to the basement like one of your victims." Her voice holds that sharp cutting edge, but she wraps the blanket tighter around herself. "That I didn't just get turned into a wolf *because* you almost let me die. You told me the process, Valor. It's not hard to figure out what happened." Her eyes go more distant, her voice softening. "You wouldn't listen to me. Not once did you even pause to consider that I might be telling the truth."

I don't argue. She's right.

Neil almost killed her because I put her there. In my basement, I strapped down the woman I love and threatened her to give me secrets that she knew nothing about. I demanded so much, offered nothing, and didn't wait to know more.

It probably wasn't smart to approach her with this when she's so freshly conscious. My wolf points out. *Feed our mate and get her sated before we try again.*

I stand and walk over to the kitchenette. Jars of canned venison are in the cupboard, and Mom made sure to send me with enough fresh vegetables to feed an army.

Without a word, I start making her food. Canned venison and cauliflower over egg noodles with gravy. I laugh to myself as I put the egg noodles on to boil. *If I could make her fresh pasta, I would.*

It would be terrible. We don't make pasta. My wolf scoffs at the idea.

Antonella turns to look at me briefly but then returns to face the fire.

I'm done with cooking dinner when my phone rings. I answer, recognizing the ringtone set just for her. "Hey, little raptor."

"Dad. Grandma said that you said you were worried about Antonella. And then she said you would call, and you haven't called. I tried to call her, but her phone doesn't ring. Grandma said she was hurt. When are you coming home?" Kerrianne hiccups and gasps her entire way through those words.

The sound of her pain hurts like arrows to the chest, one after another. Both of my girls are hurting, and it's all my fault.

Antonella rips the phone out of my hand. "Hey, Kerrianne. I'm okay."

Her hearing got better. She got faster. My wolf is smug as he watches Antonella take my phone and walk away. The blanket wrapped around her hides her body from me.

"No. Oh, it's okay, Kerrianne. No. No." Antonella growls but self-silences the sound like she's done it her entire life. "Kerrianne, flat tire."

Focusing, I hear a little 'shhh' on the other end of the phone.

"I am okay. I'm with your dad. We're at a cabin, and there's snow. Is there snow there?" Antonella handles my daughter with expert care, a welcome mothering touch. "No, I don't know when I'm coming back to the house. It could be a little bit. A lot of things have changed. I don't have answers, but we'll put it in the parking lot and wait for the knowledge bus." Antonella's voice cracks, and it shatters my heart. "Yeah. Go play with Royal. I'll make sure your dad texts with updates."

They disconnect the call, and Antonella breaks down. She sets the phone on the bed next to her and sobs, wrapping herself tighter into the blanket. Her whole body shakes, and I fight between going to her and giving her space to grieve.

I've already bound us together for the rest of eternity; it's bad enough that I've put her in this position. *Would my presence comfort her?*

I let her cry it out and am sent back to the weeks I spent standing outside Kerrianne's door as we tried the 'cry it out method' to get her sleeping in her own bed. I'm just as helpless then as I am now.

Ten minutes pass before Antonella draws a deep breath and pushes herself up off the bed.

"Kerrianne okay?" I try to ease into communication by talking about the one person we both care about.

"She wants to know when we're coming home. If I'll be ready to go back to school after Christmas." Antonella blows out an exhale, pulling the blanket tight around her as she approaches. "I figured it wasn't my place to make those decisions anymore. I don't even know my own body anymore. Is the offer about getting locked up in an apartment with a view still on the table? If you're not up to Gold Coast, I would gladly settle for River North, city facing, even."

"No. The apartment isn't still on the table." My knees feel weak, and there's a ringing in my ears at the suggestion. "But if you want some time, Kerrianne and I can move into my parents' property for a little while. Give you some time to calibrate."

"Calibrate." She huffs. "Is that what we're calling this?"

The question leads me to believe I'm making a little progress with her. "It's an adjustment period. You'll feel a little different for a while, and then it'll become normal to you."

Antonella doesn't comment, but she does swing her gaze around the small space before looking back at me. "I don't suppose you brought me clothes?"

"Several dozen outfits. New wolves tend to shred." I nod toward the bags of clothes on the dresser and then, with my spoon, direct her to one of two doors in the cabin. "There's a bathroom through that door."

CHAPTER FIFTY-SIX

THE TRUST

Valor, or whoever packed my bag, had at least some idea of the things I liked or disliked. The soft fabric of yoga pants, T-shirts, and bralettes were a welcome sight over something rigid and formal.

It's soothing to have something comfortable to put on when your insides feel disheveled enough to be a jigsaw puzzle. I'm unsettled, and my brain feels fuzzy.

I cried, and I'm not even certain I know the whole reason behind my tears, but everything feels so heavy. I couldn't hold it in. Valor doesn't deserve to see me weak, but I couldn't stop it if I tried.

I don't know how to act or how to behave. A little voice inside me says *Fuck him, fuck this, fuck it all*. A louder voice says *He's ours and he sees that now.*

The shower in the small bathroom is in a clawfoot tub. I debate trying to clean up, at least the parts of me that can be scrubbed anyway. Instead, I dress and run my fingers through my hair until it lies moderately flat. Then I wrap it up into a small bun using the hair tie I found in the bag.

Valor is where I left him when I leave the bathroom.

The louder voice that I keep hearing, my wolf I guess, sighs. *Our mate provided for us. He's made us food again. He loves us.*

He must be receiving a similar message from his wolf because Valor looks at me with one of those caring glances that he gives Kerrianne. He sets a bowl, dished up with food that smells delightful, on the counter with a fork tucked in it and cautiously slides it toward me.

I approach, eyeing the offering. It's egg noodles with a protein, something that doesn't smell like beef, and gravy poured over the top. Hesitantly, I raise the fork and take a bite. It's delicious and not in the way all food tastes when you're starving.

Valor whines and then clears his throat.

He wants us to like his offering. My wolf apparently translates.

I look up to see his eyes trained on me. They're beautiful. The flicker of gold makes them a little more animalistic but beautiful all the same.

Because I'm petty and immature, I lie. "My wolf said to tell your wolf to fuck off."

It sounds dishonest even to me, but Valor nods and then laughs, "I bet she does."

I take my bowl and head toward the bed, feeling too awkward standing at the kitchen counter.

A few steps behind me, Valor follows. He drags over a small stool and sits on it, facing me where I sit on the bed, feet curled underneath me.

After a few seconds, he tries to break the silence. "Do you want to see a picture of your wolf?"

I still the fork midway to my mouth. "How long have I been out?"

"Well, out is a . . . not quite the right word." He stumbles over that. "It was four days ago I turned you. It's been four days since you were in human shape."

I lower my bowl from chest height to my lap, scrutinizing him. "What have I been doing for four days?"

"Well, the first one you slept. Your body was healing, and the next two, your wolf was busy trying to exact revenge on your behalf." He gets up and pulls his phone from his pocket before unlocking it and setting it on the bed next to me. "But when she was too tired to try and maul me to death, she let me grab some pictures."

I hesitate at first and then pick up his phone. There's a stunning gray wolf with warm eyes and sometimes a bloody snout. I flip through a few, forward and backward, looking again and again. Using two fingers, I zoom in and out on the photos, flicking between the nearly two or three dozen he took.

That's us. My wolf encourages me to recognize the wolf as me. But I don't remember anything about these photos being taken. I have no attachment beyond what the voice in my head is telling me is real.

It is real though. My heart beats a little harder at that sentiment. It is real. I'm a wolf. Valor made me a wolf like him.

The last photo in the reel is of Valor and me. He's in the foreground, taking a selfie with me over his shoulder in the woods behind him. He's smiling, and the sun is shining bright. *We could be happy like this.*

"You're such a dad," I mutter before thinking it through a bit more. "What have I been eating for two days?" I narrow my eyes. *Please don't tell me you've been letting me eat weird shit.* "This wolf's snout is almost always bloody."

"Uhm." Valor runs his hand across the back of his neck before giving me a cheeky smile. "That's mostly my blood. Good news, you're a great hunter. Bad news, you still suck at killing things."

"Only you would think that's bad news." I turn off his phone screen in favor of my bowl of food, and I force my jaw to unclench in order to eat.

"I've been feeding you frozen cuts of meat and helped you take down some smaller game. You tried to take us after a whitetail and almost got kicked in the head, so, not great yet." He tries to muffle a laugh.

I roll my eyes and, with a shake of my head, finish my food quickly. When I go to take it to the kitchen, Valor follows me. I dislike him at my back, so I turn to face him. "I don't need your help."

"At the risk of sounding conceited, yes, you do." He places his bowl on the counter and then steps back, giving me space. "We need to have a conversation."

The relief of him stepping away is met with anxiety over the same action. More back and forth in my brain of being mad at him, being afraid of him, and being lost without him. It's a never-ending conflict, and I wish I could pick a spot and stay anchored to it.

"I deserve for you to be mad at me and to hate me." He steps back farther, walking backward to the stool he ate his dinner on. When the backs of his knees hit it, he sits down. "Nothing you ever did gave me reason to believe that you're not exactly the woman you claimed to be from day one."

I leave the kitchen and absentmindedly walk toward the door, where I lean against the wall alongside it, listening to him talk.

See, he loves us. My wolf urges.

I slide down the wall until my butt hits the floor.

"I've learned so much about trust since I met you." He hangs his head, looking at his hands. Valor scrubs them together softly like he's remembering something. "The most important lesson I learned too late."

"Which was?" I quirk an eyebrow and cross my arms in front of my chest. But admitting he was wrong and willing to have a conversation already is so much more than I anticipated from him.

"Trust in a relationship isn't determined by how long two people have known each other but rather the depth of the souls intertwined. I trusted Neil because he's been there my entire life. I took the near-thirty years I've known him and didn't examine beyond that. Because if I had, then I'd have seen that the strongest relationship I ever had was telling me the whole truth." Valor closes his eyes and then forces them open to meet mine, but a weight drags his shoulders down. He looks worn and tired. "What you saw in seconds took me too long to recognize."

"And?" I push for more, not worried if I'm making him uncomfortable.

"And I'm so fuckin' sorry. We talked, I don't know how many times, about trust and how I could trust you with Kerrianne. Yet when it came time for me to back that trust, I didn't. I said the words but didn't believe them when it mattered."

I can *feel* the sadness in his eyes.

It warms the hollowness inside my heart.

Our mate is sorry. He is remorseful. We've punished him, and he knows he's wrong. My wolf urges me to recognize the truth, but I'm still wrestling with the way everything unfolded.

The anger is still there, but the sadness at his betrayal subsides with his conviction. It's the first time anyone has ever apologized for their actions against me with real contrition.

I believe Valor is sorry. That he is remorseful. And that whatever my wolf has been doing to him, whatever anxiety he's had over my well-being, and whatever wrath he's received from Kerrianne has pained him enough to know how badly he screwed up.

It doesn't fix the relationship. It doesn't ease all my anger and my pain.

But when Valor leaves his perch on the stool, crosses the room, and sits beside me, I don't move away from him. Our eyes lock while I wait for some sort of divine providence to tell me what to do.

None comes, and Valor places his hand on mine, giving it a little squeeze. I don't pull away or fight the touch.

Our mate. My wolf pushes, wanting every part of us to be touching him. The change, the pull, and acceptance of what he is saying has me leaning against him.

"I trust you with Kerrianne," he reiterates.

I draw in a sharp breath. My chest constricts, and my face heats. "I don't trust *you* with *me*. I don't *trust* you at all."

"And I am going to earn it every day. It's why you can't live in the apartment in the city. I'm going to spend every day trying to earn back your trust. Wolves have complicated belief systems, and one of those beliefs is that two wolves can make a great pairing, claim each other as mates, and work on that bond. The belief is that if you both work hard and well . . . not fuck up everything like I did this week, you can form an intense and long-lasting mating bond. It can become the bond that fate intended you to find." He squeezes my leg, his large palm spanning across my thigh.

He means it. My wolf encourages me.

"Then on the other end of that is fated mates. It's someone you meet one day, and instantly, you know. Your wolves just click together. It's two halves of a whole being reunited. It's rarer and more unexpected, but it's celebrated as the best relationship you can have. Because the two are so perfect for each other in their unity they don't struggle and get bogged down by the little things. No one claims it's without challenges entirely, but it's not as hard."

He's our fated mate, my wolf whines.

I hang my head and swing it back and forth. I can't stand it. I dislike being pulled in a direction like this. Not after everything that's happened.

"Holly and I weren't fated mates. I loved her so much, and I wanted her to be. We both knew we weren't. That didn't matter to us though. We had a wedding, bonded ourselves to each other, and got pregnant right away. We were willing to give up the possibility of perfection for the hard work we had ahead of us."

I lift my head to watch Valor speak and find his eyes filled with unshed tears.

"The voice inside my head says you're my fated mate," I whisper

"So does mine." He snorts and squeezes me one more time. "You probably shouldn't call her the voice inside your head though. Even other wolves will look at you funny for that."

"Well, do they have names? Or is this just a 'my wolf' situation for the rest of my life?" I grumble. "I sound ridiculous."

"Not once have I ever been asked that question." He cocks his head, considering it. "I don't think there's any harm in naming her if you'd like. Again, that may get some funny looks." A smile tugs at his lips, and he nudges me playfully. "It's kinda cool, though, you get to claim all their good ideas as your own and can blame the dumb ones on them too, because how is anyone gonna know which consciousness came up with something one way or another?"

I can't help it. I snort before laughing. But I quickly compose myself. "I don't forgive you. You make me laugh, but that isn't forgiveness."

"I'm not asking for you to forgive me, not right now." He nods, as though resigned. "I know I don't deserve it. I'm so fuckin' sorry. Don't think I'm not beating myself up for this."

"I don't care, Valor. It's done." My words are a lie, and now I know what he meant when he said he could hear it. It's like little trickles of deception cling to the words, and they sound false, like when someone says something you *know* isn't true.

"You do care, and while you're right, I can't take it back, that doesn't mean it feels done to you."

Valor isn't patronizing, but he's good at voicing what I can't. My body relaxes a little bit.

"But I think we're getting there."

"How am I ever supposed to trust you?" I loathe how pathetic I sound. The question is absurd, and in this moment, it feels like the answer is I can't.

"I don't deserve your trust. But you know that." Valor leans against me a bit more.

He is sorry. My wolf reminds me.

"I had doubts and acted anyway. He told me Kerrianne wasn't safe with you, and if Dad hadn't texted that the truce had been broken, I would have maybe thought more clearly, but he had Dad fooled too."

"What?" I snap and glare at him. *Could this get any worse?* "The truce was broken?"

I push myself up off the floor, and my body twitches. Shivers rack my spine, and I feel so tense I can hardly move . . . except I'm already pacing the floor.

"It wasn't. I promise, it wasn't." Valor shakes his head, and the calmness oozing off him draws me to stop as he stands still, patient, waiting. "I have questions about how things happened, but I spoke with Berto personally, and Dad talked with Gregorio. As far as we can tell, they're unaware of anything that's happened since the truce. Though, Berto admitted to having help taking down Sean and gave me a play by play of how it went. I'm sure there were some embellishments, but the fact that Sean didn't survive made more sense when he explained it."

There is no way in hell I'm apologizing for Berto. I didn't do anything wrong. I'm not accepting responsibility for any man's shitty actions.

Not Berto's. Not Valor's.

"It isn't right that I believed Neil over our experiences and my heart. It wasn't fair, nor did it boast trust in our relationship." Valor's remorse continues to chip away at the guard around my heart, carving out a little piece of the bitterness. "I meant what I said though. Had you inadvertently or unintentionally done something that compromised our safety, I would have lied for you and found a way to make it look like it *could* have been something else."

"I think you're trying to talk me into forgiving you." I look at him. His green-brown eyes look back at me, and I melt a little. His brown hair hangs into his face, and I want to brush it out of the way. "But know that you were angry at me for calling the truce, and that's exactly what you were doing. You were offering to put your life on the line for me."

He nods. "I would have, and I'd do it again."

"I'm still so mad at you," I fume. "I cannot reiterate enough how hurt I am. I was willing to die for her, and that hasn't ever changed. It will never change. It's who I am, but you didn't even pause." Hot tears are welling up in my eyes, and I hold them back.

"And you have every right to get angry, to yell, to want to hurt me back. I'll take it. All of it." He raises his hand but stops himself before he can wipe the tear off my cheek that escaped.

Suddenly, a question springs into my head and rattles around my brain until it tumbles out. "What happened to Neil?"

"Nothing," Valor answers flatly.

"Nothing!"

I clench my fists, turning away from him, because my tears only boil over instead of freezing, my rage bringing the precipitation with them. *How could he be sorry yet nothing happened to Neil?*

My wolf is snarling too. At least I know my anger in this isn't one sided. She may want me to forgive Valor, but we're not letting this go.

Valor's hands are on my shoulders, and he spins me around, gripping my chin and dragging my face back to him.

I narrow my eyes. "I almost die, and he's what—"

"Nothing happened to Neil because he's still in my basement waiting for you. Well, us. I have more questions I need answered," Valor explains.

Those words calm my rage, and I force even breaths before raising an eyebrow. "Me?"

"He committed treason, but the most egregious offense was against you." Valor tries to explain what must be a complicated system of laws, and he pauses to reframe. "Kidnapping Royal, hurting Declan and Jack, killing Sean and Gavin were all offenses against wolves. But you were human when he hurt you. That comes above anything else."

"When you let him hurt me." I don't pull that punch. I correct him with the ferocity of my wolf backing me.

"And you can torture me for the rest of our lives for that." He assures me before continuing. "Neil, however, is yours to do with as you will. I recommend making him suffer and killing him, but you're within your right to do whatever you please."

"Whatever I please?" I straighten and tilt my head. "And if that's taking a little bit of him apart and dismantling him until he dies?"

"Then I recommend you pick parts at random to inflict the most pain," he advises, sounding a little bit more than 'slightly' unhinged. "There are many ways to make it hurt for as long as you'd like."

"You haven't questioned him or anything?" I ask, testing the ability to hear falsehoods.

"I refused to leave you longer than I had to. I wanted to make sure you transitioned cleanly. You were my priority." Valor's gaze holds the intensity of his dedication I've seen before, but now it's directed at me.

I'm a priority. His words don't come with that itching feeling of a lie. *Huh.*

It's because we are his and he is ours. My wolf weighs in. *We can be angry, but it doesn't make him less ours. Let him show us he can do better.*

I blow out a breath and sit back on the bed, but Valor stays where he is.

"Neil is getting his bare minimum needs met. Food, water, a bucket to shit in. We'll question him together when you're ready to go home."

We'll go home soon. My wolf reassures me like she knows where home is. *Starving him to death is an option though.*

"And no one will be angry, there will be no retribution, if I kill him?" I need to clarify because this sounds too good to be true.

"If you don't kill him, I will." Valor shifts on his feet and slides his hands into his pockets. "Neil has to die. Fast or slow, it doesn't matter so long as it gets done."

Death and murder shouldn't soothe me, given everything that's happened, but my shoulders drop. I'm not cold, but I pull the blanket around me, needing comfort.

Valor moves over to the woodstove and stokes the fire. He turns around to face me again and clears his throat. "I know this cabin isn't very large, so if you wanted some alone time, I could maybe shift and go for a run or something?"

Space doesn't feel like what I want, especially since my wolf seems to settle with his proximity, but the longer I'm around him, the harder it is to be mad at him. He deserves for me to be mad at him.

I shake my head, and Valor doesn't waste a second to sit next to me on the bed. He runs his hand across my shoulders, and I lean into his warmth.

"I don't remember much since the basement," I murmur.

"That's normal." Valor isn't fazed by my abrupt change in conversation. "The first few days, the wolf is driving. There isn't anything science based I can point to, but we believe it's because she's making space for herself in your brain and body."

427

"Will it ever feel normal?" I know the answer, but I want to hear him confirm it.

Valor nods. "It'll become second nature."

Being that having a wolf is quite literally having a second nature draws laughter from me, and I snort mid-laugh at his choice of words.

"Okay, yeah, I deserve that." Valor leans against me before pushing back as if to jest.

The easiness between us brings me more comfort than the blanket did.

He hesitates to speak. "I've missed you. I've missed your laugh, your smile, this feeling between us."

God, if I don't feel that too. Closing my eyes, I can only nod in agreement. I didn't want to forgive him like this, but my heart is pulling me toward him.

Valor is our mate. My wolf gives me answers. *He can't ever hurt us like that again. It would kill him to do it.*

Her reassurance means everything. The honesty of it, and the fact that his words and actions seem to back it up.

Maybe it's foolish to put myself into his hands again, but at least now I have a wolf and I can fight back.

I shift on the bed to face him and cup his jaw, running my thumb over the stubble covering his cheek. Valor just stares at me, as if he's afraid of moving and spooking me. His Adam's apple bobs with a swallow, and I move my gaze to his lips. Slowly, I lean over to him, and Valor mirrors the movement. He lets me kiss him first, but the intensity deepens quickly.

I run my fingers into his hair and hold him to me as we kiss. Valor does the same, pressing his tongue into my mouth. I accept, letting him closer to me.

By the time we stop kissing, we're both panting, and when I look into his eyes, I don't want to kill him. I don't want to fight back. I'm still angry, and it simmers within me, but I don't want the anger to consume me. I've never wanted to be a hateful person. Even if Valor deserves it, I know I won't be mad at him forever. I know I won't be wary of him forever.

Neil deserves my anger more than Valor does.

His features turn devious with a playful smirk and darkened eyes. "Gonna kill me in my sleep tonight?"

"Well, if my wolf hasn't killed you yet, and it's not for lack of ability, then I guess you might get to live through the night." I huff. "Never go to bed angry, or in our case, never go to bed with murder on the mind."

"If you're up to it, and we're both alive in the morning . . ." Valor speaks softly. He draws slow, steadying breaths. "We could go home in the morning."

Home. It's a foreign concept. Valor's house felt homey. It felt like a place I could be comfortable. I don't know that it'll be like that anymore. But I nod anyway. There is no hiding out in a cabin, there is no apartment in River North, and that just leaves facing the new reality head-on.

Valor

CHAPTER FIFTY-SEVEN

HOMECOMING

I'm secondhand nervous as I steer the SUV up the driveway to the front of the house. My wolf is feeding off the constant energy from Antonella. Her wolf must be pacing inside her. I've seen the telltale signs of wolves on the edge of snapping before, and she's strung like a tight rubber band.

She's not ready to come home, but she's not getting any better being out at the cabin either. Mom and Dad said there is no rule book to this sort of thing. Grief for what she lost, her humanity, isn't linear.

Antonella examines the house, and I stop before pulling close enough that any of it would go out of view.

"I'll burn the whole thing to the ground and rebuild, on this lot, on another lot, anywhere, if it makes you feel more comfortable."

Antonella doesn't say anything. She just stares down the mansion like she can intimidate it.

I offer her an out. "Say the word. There are tons of different places we can go. I'll go inside, grab Kerrianne, and we can go to my parents', or any of the places we own in the city."

She inhales, steady and slow, as if thinking each breath through. "Don't. Not just yet."

I ruined her home. I ruined the place she should feel safe. I wait a few more seconds and ease off the brake, letting the SUV crawl its way forward. The garage door opening slowly gives her every extra second to stop and change her mind, but I park the car and turn it off, and Antonella opens her own door.

She walks to the door to the house and lets herself in before I'm even out of the SUV. I hurry but try not to make it feel like I'm chasing her.

She's stock still, staring at the stairs leading to the basement. The stairs I carried her down against her will. I'm sick looking at them. I can only imagine what it feels like for her.

"Princess, you don't have to —" I cut myself off, letting her work through it.

Kerrianne lurks around the corner, and Leticia whispers for her to come back to where they were waiting for us.

A few more seconds, and Antonella moves past the stairs, her eyes looking over the kitchen. The cookies she had been baking are long gone, and order has been restored.

In a snap, she changes herself. Not fixes but changes. I sense her fear and frustration, but she's pretending to be fine for those in our home. She puts on a perfect facade, a shield against scrutiny, and reminds me just how strong she can be despite the emotions running rampant inside her.

Arms wide open, she stoops down and pulls Kerrianne into her arms for a tight dancing hug.

Leticia takes a turn, wrapping her arms around Antonella. When they part, Leticia is wiping tears out of her eyes but pretending they're not there.

Royal is last. He makes his way over with a slow healing limp in his step — from the shit those fuckers did that he still hasn't told me about. When he gets to her, he wraps his arms around her, and they whisper to each other. I'm too far away to hear, but if she wants me to know, she'll tell me.

Leticia gets her wits about her the fastest. She moves to the kitchen and starts a pot of hot cocoa, urging Antonella to sit down and put her feet up by the fire because they'll get cold.

With Leticia's back to us, Antonella mouths, "Does she know?"

I nod and look between Leticia and Antonella, the differences between them only growing.

"I don't think I have to worry about my feet getting cold anymore," Antonella says as she takes a seat, but it's halfhearted teasing.

Kerrianne climbs into Antonella's lap and snuggles up. Resting her head against Kerrianne, Antonella wraps her arms around her.

Look at our girls. My wolf wags his tail, and I'm propelled forward to the living room, needing to be by them.

Royal steps into my path. The glare, tight jaw, and body movement say everything. His loyalty is to her, not me. I don't push it, and I divert my path to the far end of the sofa away from her.

I outrank my brother as pack second in the wake of Neil's treason and imminent death, but I don't want to fight a challenge against him. Not when I agree with his judgment.

"Grandma says we might not go back to school after Christmas. Is that because you're part of the secret now?" Kerrianne questions.

"It is," Antonella answers without missing a beat. "You know how your wolf gets tired and cranky sometimes?" Kerrianne nods, which prompts Antonella to continue. "Mine is like that a lot too. So, I might not be a good enough secret keeper for a little while. I may need to take some time to make sure I'm good and ready to be a secret keeper."

"Grandma says Leticia knows the secret and is keeping it but doesn't have a wolf. I didn't know that was supposed to happen." Kerrianne looks up at Antonella, who looks to me and Royal.

"There are special times when secret keepers don't have wolves, like Father Michael doesn't have one, but he knows." I try to offer an answer. "If you're ever not sure if someone knows our secret, it's best not to tell them. Not even to test and see if they know it."

Kerrianne squirms uncomfortably. "Are we going to give Leticia a wolf like we gave Antonella?"

"Not unless we absolutely have to." Royal answers for me. His tone is sharp before he takes it back to a joking rumble. "It's kind of nice having a human around."

"Hardy, har, har. Asshole." Leticia comes in carrying a tray of mugs of cocoa. "For the best cousin." Leticia holds one out to Antonella. "For the asshole I like." She holds one out to Royal. "For my favorite little bestie." She gives one to Kerrianne and leaves mine on the tray on the table before sitting down with her own.

"Be nice, Leticia." Antonella warns her.

"He has arms," Leticia answers before bringing the cup up to her mouth. "I could have poured it down his shirt . . . or worse."

One hand holding a mug, the other keeping Kerrianne close, Antonella can only sigh and look to the ceiling to voice her dismay.

I stand and take the cup, looking at it. "Should I be concerned this is . . . different?"

"Should you be?" Leticia cocks her head. "Do you require something different?"

Royal holds his mug out to me, and I take it instinctively as he swaps it for the one I grabbed. "Speak now . . ."

Leticia rolls her eyes. "The only thing different here are the two of you."

"Manners, all of you," Antonella says over the lip of her cup before she takes a drink.

Kerrianne giggles. "Different isn't a bad word."

"Oh, in this case, it most definitely is. They're using it as an insult." Antonella groans. "And it's not one we'd repeat at school because?"

"Insults are bad and meant to hurt people. Even if we think they're funny, it could hurt," Kerrianne recites.

Royal looks over at me and whispers behind his cup, "The fuck are they teaching the kids at the school?"

With a shrug, I shake my head as I sit on the sofa again. "I don't know, but maybe I should take some classes."

"You can't come to class," Kerrianne huffs, the attitude strong. "You'd never fit at my desk. Your legs are too long."

"Excellent logic." Leticia nods and takes another sip. Her phone rings, and she groans answering it. "Berto, for the last time. Mind your own business and not mine."

Antonella must hear whatever Berto said because she taps Kerrianne's leg, and Kerrianne scrambles out of the way, coming over to sit with me.

When Antonella holds her hand out, Leticia hesitantly gives her the phone.

Antonella's voice is glacial as she rumbles, "Berto. You did not just say that."

Leticia has gone ghost white. She leans forward and sets her mug on the table.

"That's the second most ridiculous thing you've ever said." Antonella is on the verge of growling, and Royal gets up, going over to her and steadying her with a hand on either arm, demonstrating breathing.

"I'm not letting that happen." Antonella is firm but then hangs up the phone. She raises her gaze to her younger cousin, repeating herself. "Leticia. I'm not letting that happen."

"Don't be silly. Look how well it worked out for you, aside from like, say maybe, the last week, arranged marriage can work quite well. It's time anyway. I shouldn't be putting it off." But her words and smile don't match the dread in her eyes. The lack of fire and fear of the unknown.

"I'll figure you a way out of this." Antonella shakes her head.

"You've got enough on your plate. I know the man Berto is talking about. I'll keep his house in order and dinner warm and on the table. Nothing I don't do now."

It's noble the way Leticia has resolved herself to this, even though she's more shaken up about this than she's letting on.

But she doesn't let us dwell on it. "Sorry for the interruption. Now, where were we? Talking about putting a Christmas tree up in here? With such high ceilings, surely we could get one at least a respectable height. Maybe ten feet?"

"Better go twelve with these ceilings." Royal looks up, playing into her change of topic.

I hug Kerrianne tighter before downing the rest of my cocoa and nudging her off me so I can take my cup to the kitchen. Kerrianne runs over to Royal, and they talk loudly about ornaments and how she likes colored lights on a tree because they're just that much more 'Christmas.'

As I stand, Antonella does too and swipes Leticia's discarded cup from the table.

Rinsing the mugs at the sink, I try to reassure Antonella. "We'll find a way. They can't make her do this. Not on our watch."

My comfort only goes so far with her. "Berto says the papers are done," she whispers. "It means that as soon as they're back in the US, they'll file the documents. She's already married. The next year will be planning a wedding that's just for show."

I wrap an arm around Antonella's shoulders and press my mouth against her temple. "The Cavanaghs aren't exactly ones to let something like a little paperwork stop us."

CHAPTER FIFTY-EIGHT

FACING FEAR AND FOE

I've walked past the top of the basement stairs a few times today. Each time it gets easier. Valor, however, hovers like I'm going to shatter. Though a tiny piece, a fragment of brokenness, wants to, I refuse to let stairs, and a room, define who I am.

"I have a second location if you want me to take him somewhere else for you to get your revenge," he offers. Hell, he offered to build me a whole new house just so I don't have to stare down these steps. "I mean it. We'll move tomorrow and go to a hotel tonight if you want us to."

But this is Kerrianne's home. It doesn't feel right upturning her sanctuary because I have an issue to work through.

I draw in a deep inhale and release it slowly. "It's just a flight of stairs. It's just a room."

The first step is the hardest, but once I get myself moving, muscle memory takes over.

Valor comes down the stairs behind me, and it quickens my heart rate. I bite back the panic. Repeating the logic again and again that this is just stairs, it's just a basement, and I'm not the one who is about to die.

We're just as strong as he is. My wolf assures me. *He couldn't kill us, not anymore.*

I don't know how much of that is true, but she certainly believes it.

Neil is chained to the wall, dozing, head slumped on his shoulder, when we walk in. He doesn't look comfortable, but he does look deep asleep. There's nothing to throw, so instead, as soon as the door closes and I know Kerrianne can't hear, I scream at the top of my lungs.

Neil jolts awake and looks around, his chest heaving, and he gasps. "I see she survived."

"She survived," I echo his mockery. "No thanks to you."

"And I think you'll probably be her first kill," Valor muses.

I can hear his finger tapping against the screens of the tablets. He's setting the security system and whatever he uses to make sure Kerrianne is safe while we're down here. Well, in addition to Declan and Jack being stationed in the living room and upstairs hallway.

I hate that Valor is right about killing him. Not because I'm shying away from death, but that this is what it took for me to get angry enough to do it. There are questions I need answered though. Pieces to the puzzle that have been bugging me all afternoon.

"How the fuck did you mess up a drive-by?" I start with the least recent event I haven't been able to figure out. "His car was literally still headed toward the school. If you're looking to take out the heir and his successor, then why wouldn't you wait until his car was headed in the other direction with his child in tow?"

I glare at him, guessing I'm out of striking range based on the length of chain holding him to the wall.

"Idiots didn't know where the school was." Neil doesn't even bother lying and saying it wasn't him.

"Who did you hire?" I clench my fist.

Valor comes up behind me and places one hand on my shoulder and the other on my stomach, holding me back to him.

"Members of my pack." Neil's claiming word 'my' makes Valor growl.

"Don't worry. We've already started flushing out your little militia. You'd be surprised how many of them already transferred to different packs or simply disappeared. For someone who used to own quite a bit of stock in a tech company, you knew nothing about hiding your evidence." Valor is cold, the unwavering version of himself. "It was smart to short the inventory of those custom shells coming in. I never even considered that you would be smart enough to cut a deal for extra ammunition but stupid enough to use something so customized in a drive-by shooting."

"It was convenient. That I could blame it on your new bride's family." Neil taunts, again not distinguishing me as a member of the pack and family, even though it was his actions that made me part of 'the family secret.'

Valor steps around me and goes to Neil. Wasting energy, Neil tries to fight and attack Valor, but much younger and stronger, Valor moves his restraints and muscles him over into the very chair I suffered in.

Neil struggles, trying to stay out of it.

Was that what I looked like, fighting back? Is that how pathetic and weak I was? I blink and turn away, not wanting to watch this part.

No. My wolf pushes inside me, and I follow her lead, forcing my gaze back to Neil.

Wolf healing, as Valor explained, is why I have just a barely there silver scar from the wound that almost killed me. If it weren't for the vividness of the memories, I'd say it was nothing more than a dream.

Valor has him completely secured within another minute or so.

"Go to the toy box, darling. Pick out some toys. But remember, we've got to get some more answers first." Valor indicates to his cupboard of implements.

The way he said 'toy box' and 'darling' sends ridiculous little butterflies to my stomach. They bring to mind his promises from before the world got fucked up. That he's open to using toys. Days and weeks seem to be blending — Christmas is already later this week. But the night I threatened to get myself off feels so long ago yet also like it was yesterday.

Valor comes up behind me, looking over my shoulder into the toolbox. "Maximum pain and short, or draw it out long and slow?"

I shrug, not even sure what you'd call many of these things.

I pick out a knife, and Valor wraps his hand around mine. He adjusts my grip on it like he did the gun. "You use this with upward force. It sheers off the surface. Going up produces the best impact."

Well, if there's a right and a wrong way to torture someone, Valor Cavanagh would know. I try not to laugh at the morbid humor of that.

Valor follows me as I take the knife back to Neil. This time when we approach, his face pales.

"It's all fun and games until you're the one in the chair, isn't it, Neil?" I grit my teeth, trying not to haul off and jab the knife into his head.

But as I get closer with the knife, I freeze. "Why don't you tell us about the warehouse bombing?"

"Wh-what do you want to know?" Neil is hoarse. He tries to swallow. "You mean the Brass Skull Company shipment? And the idiots I hired to attack us?"

"I didn't expect him to cooperate so easily," Valor grumbles like he's disappointed his own flesh and blood is folding to torture so easily.

440

Then again, if it were Gregorio and Eduardo . . . I'd maybe feel the same.

I use the knife as Valor showed me. Flesh moves so easily with it.

"It was too fuckin' easy," Neil sputters, his face turning red. "This stupid up-and-coming crew your dad told me to disband. They'd take any job for a fraction of our prices. So stupid they'd even attack us."

"Let me guess, you're the one inviting the Yakuza in too. You probably, what? Promised them something for giving information to Eduardo and Gregorio?" I muse, thinking back to what Marc said.

"Enemy of my enemy is my friend." Neil coughs and swings his unfocused gaze in Valor's direction. "You'd been so intent on revenge for Holly for how long?" Neil draws a short breath. "It was too easy to dangle the carrot over the D'Medicis. It's shit you didn't die when I killed Holly. But everyone said she wasn't your fated mate. I tried anyway. Your loyalty to her . . . bred too much hatred. That hate must've kept you alive."

Neil's head wobbles like he's going to pass out. I slap him, the knife still in my hand slicing a gouge across his face.

He yowls as he comes back to with slightly better focus.

Valor stalks forward, but he doesn't touch Neil. "All of this for what? To take over the pack? What is it that my father did that made you want the pack?"

He levels eyes with Neil.

Curiously, I step around him for a better view and find they both have golden-yellow eyes. Eyes that I now share with them. My lip curls in a snarl as I look between them.

It's all Neil's fault. Valor did save me. He fucked up, sure. But we're both victims of Neil.

Neil shakes his head, coming around, and the blood running down his face drips onto his days-old shirt. "You're the problem. Not him. You and your ideas for the future. You can't just leave good enough alone." Neil gurgles and splutters but gets himself together to lash out his vengeful words.

Valor steps back and looks to me. "I don't think I have any more questions. Let it out, darling."

I didn't need Valor's permission, but knowing we have all the answers lifts a weight off me. But something else rises in its place.

We'll kill him for hurting us. My wolf is there. Jaws snapping, snarling, and ready for blood. She's strength amid the nerves and adrenaline running through my body.

"It'd have all worked out except your bride is weak. Had she just been strong enough to turn the other way when we sent Gregorio's loyal soldier to fetch Kerrianne."

Neil's insult earns him another slap and then another. This time, knowing what the knife can do, I angle it so more deep red gouges join the first one as I whip my hand across his face. But it doesn't feel like enough. Not enough torture. Not enough pain. Not enough eye for an eye.

My strikes don't seem to hurt him as much as the pain in my soul hurts me.

"Had she just been docile enough, as well trained as Gregorio said she was, then this wouldn't have happened. You'd be dead and none of the family or pack would be the wiser. It's too easy to kill off such a small family line." Neil spits blood, and it lands in his lap.

My lip curls in disgust as drool dribbles down his lip and chin. *Pathetic.*

Neil wheezes in a breath. "You know, Gregorio was right about females, not worth the trouble."

Bile rises in my throat, and a roar bellows from deep inside me as I drive the knife into his stomach. Pulling it out, I slam it into his shoulder.

I give in to the rage, wanting my pound of flesh but also

wanting him to shut the fuck up. His voice is grating on my nerves.

Neil screams out again, and I try to find an ounce of humanity to take mercy on him.

But nothing, since the last time I was down here, has given me any desire to show mercy.

I sink my blade into his body two more times, the knife going all the way through and nicking the fucking chair, before he loses consciousness and is sufficiently bleeding out.

I watch and wait, not wanting to miss his death, and within his final exhale, I find freedom.

CHAPTER FIFTY-NINE

THE PROMISE

Valor led me by the hand while walking backward up the stairs out of the basement, then up to our bedroom, keeping his eyes on me like if he lets me leave his sight, I'll disappear.

And maybe I would.

We won't leave him. My wolf, the voice inside my head, argues. But it's not like she needs to convince me because her 'argument' only affirms what feels right in my gut.

I won't leave Valor, not because I can't, but because I want to stay. Despite his flaws, nothing about Valor is wicked or evil. For me to heal and trust him, I need to be here and present the opportunity.

No annulment, no divorce, no murdering him in his sleep.

Him picking me over Neil helped.

He closes the bedroom door, then leads me into the bathroom and closes that door behind us too. "Declan and Jack don't need to hear how much I missed you."

Valor's words send a shiver down my spine, and I don't bother trying to suppress it. With my hand still in his, Valor spins me, facing me toward the mirror, our arms wrapped around my waist like the first day we met. Except instead of staking a claim, he's holding on to me for dear life, worried about where I'll go and what I'll do if he releases his hold on me.

But this image is a far cry from our wedding day, and I don't miss the opportunity to admire us together like this. My brown hair, braided over my shoulder, barely avoiding the blood splatter on Valor's T-shirt that I borrowed. The red tinge to our skin from that same blood of my first kill.

The look of adoration is in the softness of Valor's eyes and the small smile pulling at his lips. Warmth blooms in my chest. Despite the havoc that's upturned my life on the surface level, nothing has changed.

That is, until our eyes do.

Valor's first, going from the green-brown to the bright, vibrant golden-yellow of his wolf. Then, as heat rises in my body, mine do the same. Maybe more orange than yellow, but unnervingly animalistic.

So pretty. My wolf decides, pulling my focus to the picture of the whole. *He looks fit to be our mate.*

"Let me take care of you." Valor leans down, not taking his eyes off me in the mirror as he kisses my neck.

My stomach flips, and my pussy throbs at the idea. The memories of how good Valor has made me feel flood forward, dissipating my resistance.

"Hands on the mirror, darling." Valor's voice is gravelly, a growl, the noise I can now make.

I lean forward over the vanity, resting my forearms on the mirror rather than my hands. It shuffles my ass backward, pressing against his crotch. Which must have been Valor's plan.

Valor slides my pants down my legs. And when they're on the floor, he gingerly lifts each foot, placing a small kiss on the back of my ankle before setting it back down.

He runs his hands up the outside of my legs, fingertip-light touches, teasing me along the way.

The sharp flick of a knife blade opening cuts through the otherwise silence. A sound I've heard before.

"Valor," I say in warning, but I'm not sure against what.

I try to look in the reflection to see what he's doing, but the vanity blocks my view. Pulling one hand off the mirror, I try to twist, only to freeze as Valor slides his fingers into my panties.

Unexpectedly, my anxiety of the unknown rises.

"Valor," I snarl.

It comes out just as sharp and angry as I intended. *Maybe a wolf has its bonuses.*

As if commanded, Valor stops. He withdraws his fingers and steps back. Knife pinched between his thumb and palm, he keeps his hands open, showing me in the mirror that he's no longer touching me.

So much for trusting him. I spin around to face him. *No. I'm going to trust him again. I'm going to give him the opportunity to give me reasons to trust him.*

Valor slowly lowers his hand and offers the knife out to me.

I don't take it, but I nod, and Valor understands. He starts at the collar of the blood-splattered shirt. The fabric is more drenched than I thought because blood squelches out as the knife cuts a path through the material, and cool liquid runs down my torso and to my thighs.

After slicing through the bottom seam of the shirt, Valor sets the knife on the vanity next to me and brings his hands to my waist. He runs them up under my breasts, reaching behind me and unhooking my bra.

With the closeness, I lean forward and kiss him. He's soft and pliable, letting me set the pace. All the while, he keeps undressing me tenderly, pressing the T-shirt sleeves and straps of my bra down my arms before tossing them away.

Valor hooks his fingers into the waistband of my panties.

I place my hands over his and scold him through uneven breaths. "Where's the fun in that?"

His mouth falls open, and after a beat, he picks up his knife. Using his finger as a barrier, he protects me as he slices down the center. I clench the muscles of my core, willing myself to stay as still as possible and staving off the violent shudders threatening to course through my body.

Arousal and fear, feeling so much the same yet so different, wreck my nerves. They heighten every piece of this experience.

The fabric of my panties sounds tortured as it's cut away, and he drops to his knees before me, waiting. Choosing to trust him after being on the receiving end of his rage is hard, but I do, with a small turn and a deep breath. Facing the mirror again, I give Valor the opportunity to redeem himself.

The mirror is cool against my fingers, and I hesitate.

Trust our mate. My wolf encourages me.

When I've settled, Valor continues, his finger protecting me from the knife along my underside and up to my ass.

I can't help the breath that leaves me in almost a moan as he drags his finger along the knife's path between my legs.

"Much better." Valor hums in approval once the waistband is cut again and the fabric naturally falls down my legs.

He makes a show of putting the knife away and setting it on the granite vanity far away from us. Then, through the mirror, I get to watch him strip.

I curl my fingers as my need only increases.

His shirt, less bloody than mine, mars his skin with a smattering of red, and I look down in the mirror to take in the sight of it on my abdomen. Blood acts as evidence in the war of taking myself back.

When I raise my eyes back to Valor, he's waiting. He tucks his thumbs into his jeans, already unbuttoned and unzipped, and removes them with his boxers down his legs.

I'm only woman. No one can blame me for the lust at seeing Valor hard for me.

Because I know how good he makes me feel, my hesitation is

forgotten in an instant. Especially when he drops behind me, down to his knees, and out of sight below the vanity. I lean more weight against my pelvis and raise up onto my toes, allowing him better access to me.

Valor slides his tongue along my slit, all the way up to my asshole, and I clench, shocked by the sensation.

He groans. "You taste amazing. I've wanted this for so long."

"Well, we often want what we can't have," I grumble, trying to be playful, and it earns me a well-honed smack to my ass.

I practically lose myself in the bite of that sting. My body relaxes under the pain and what it does to me.

But Valor doesn't strike again. He goes back to eating me out, sucking my clit, his nose teasing my entrance.

He murmurs against my pussy, "That's it, princess. You're so wet for me."

I draw a slow breath, trying to enjoy the pleasure he's offering. It's not hard to do because Valor knows what he's doing. He works my clit in a figure-eight movement with his tongue, the soft underside so tender, and my legs tremble. I let out a low moan, ready to come.

"Easy." He shuffles from his knees to standing and comes into view in the mirror.

I glare at him for stopping me from coming. *This is why he put the knife so far away from me.*

"Do you have any idea how wet you are right now?"

His crooked smile is the only warning I get before he slides his fingers inside me, then runs them over my clit, my heat and slickness allowing him to glide with ease.

"I've a pretty good idea." I grit my teeth.

Drawing ragged breaths, I focus on not letting a moan escape. He drives me closer to the edge of an orgasm one more time as his fingers find my G-spot and work me over.

Valor squeezes my clit once before stopping again. "Turn to face me."

The command sends a throb through my pussy, but I don't turn around. Instead, I wiggle my ass at him. *I just wanna come already.*

"Trying to get me to punish you?" Valor raises an eyebrow. "I thought for sure you'd be more interested in punishing me after everything."

"Shut up and fuck me before I change my mind." I raise an eyebrow right back.

Pressing his chest against my back, his cock hard between us, he moves slowly and trails his hand up my stomach, through the mostly dry blood on his way up to my throat. Valor gently wraps his fingers around my neck with no pressure, testing me, himself, and the tension between us.

The tension between us holds as I lift my chin and ever so slightly push into his fingers. He tightens his grip. The heaviness of arousal and how simply right this feels, this *is*, makes my body respond.

I relax, and it's met with Valor's other hand smacking my ass. Hard.

I gasp, "Fuck. That hurts."

Valor huffs and palms my ass, fingers digging into the stinging flesh, before slipping his cock between my legs. He rocks his hips, sliding through my core, coating himself in my arousal but not penetrating me.

"Are you here to play or here to fuck?" I antagonize him.

It feels so different from how we'd been before, but I crave what he's holding back. It felt right when he spanked me, when he used my body, there was a balance, but we feel off kilter now.

Somehow, Valor gets it. He understands and squeezes my neck tighter for just a fraction of a second before he adjusts my hips to give him access to my pussy. He slides his cock in slowly, and the familiar stretch has my head tilting to the side as I groan. Seated all the way inside me, Valor brings his hand back to my neck and gives it a slightly harder squeeze. He bends forward, and the change in angle stretches me further.

"I'm here to do what I need to get my wife back." He nips at my ear before whispering, "And if that means fucking her like the brat she is, until she's coming on my cock and begging for more, then so be it."

And he does.

Valor withdraws and then thrusts into me over and over again. With his hand around my throat, he pulls me hard against his chest. The pressure against my neck — a threat and a promise and a turn-on all at once.

I have one earth-shattering orgasm, my body tense and wound tight, as I scream out, but Valor doesn't stop fucking me, not until the last shiver of that orgasm subsides. Still sheathed inside me, Valor bends, placing a soft trail of kisses up my shoulder to under my ear.

Letting my neck go, he slides his fingers into my hair as he withdraws.

I crave to have him back within me. He hasn't come yet, and I want him to. No, I need him to. Valor bends me over the vanity, my ass jutting out and his cock slotting between my cheeks.

"Valor," I growl.

It sounds raw, echoing how I feel. But it accomplishes what I need it to. He slips his cock into my pussy, and I breathe a sigh of relief at how he fills me.

The first smack to my ass rivals the shock of the first time it happened, but it's more welcome than it's ever been before. I relax into the way he handles me.

Short, quick thrusts partnered with a hard and heavy smack make my eyes roll back in my head.

Then he switches to long thrusts and peppers my ass with swift smacks.

I don't count, I don't even bother trying to remember how

many times his hand brings a sting of pain. The pleasure I'm getting is too much.

My pussy throbs, the deep angle rubbing against my sensitive spot on each withdraw and thrust.

"Valor, I'm close," I moan, praying he doesn't stop.

He untangles his fingers from my hair. His hips stop pounding into me, and on one last push, he withdraws.

This fuckin' asshole. I press up hard with my hands until I'm more or less standing.

Valor smiles smugly as he runs his tongue over his teeth. "What's wrong, darling? Too good?"

I grind my ass against him, needing more, needing him to come. This time, my antagonization doesn't work. I shove off the vanity and spin to face him.

Like he's done nothing wrong, Valor leans forward and kisses me, in that possessive way he does so well, placing his hand up alongside my neck. He runs his finger along my throat, and I forget how to breathe at the feel of it.

In a smooth movement, he raises me up onto the vanity. Instinctually, I spread my legs, putting him between them, but then the fear of him withdrawing again has me wrapping them tight around him. The head of his cock presses against my clit. All it would take is a small adjustment, and he'd be back inside me.

Our lips part, and he murmurs against them, "So needy."

"I'll handle it myself if you don't finish the job." I bite his bottom lip.

He pulls back, releasing his lip from between my teeth, and then adjusts us. Until we're just right, and he slides back inside me. I wrap my arms around his neck, holding him to me as he finds a new rhythm, taking me harder, faster, and deeper than before.

I squeeze my legs around him, the desire to be one with him settling in like none other.

Bite, the voice in my head whispers.

I roll my head to the side as Valor kisses my neck.

Bite, the voice says louder this time.

With my nose at Valor's ear, I nip at the lobe.

Bite! the voice screams, and I have no real reason not to obey.

I grab hold of the base of his neck near his shoulder with my teeth, and it alleviates some of the intense desire.

Again, I bite but a little harder.

Valor groans, his hips pistoning in and out. "Fuck. Antonella, darling, that's it."

He cups the back of my head, pressing my face closer to him, and I bite harder.

Claim him, the voice, my wolf, demands. But I don't know what she wants from me.

Two more thrusts and I'm screaming, my body tight and rigid in his hands.

A strong urge overcomes me, my mouth feeling oddly full. I bite down with all my strength until the coppery taste of blood coats my tongue.

Satisfied with my orgasm, Valor chases his release until he's coming, his fingers bruising into the skin of my hips. His snarl echoes off the solid surfaces of the bathroom.

The pain of Valor's teeth cutting through the flesh of my shoulder sends fireworks across my vision. But it passes as quickly as it comes, the pleasure, aftershocks of an orgasm, overtaking the unpleasantness.

The weird feelings leave my body, but the taste of blood remains in my mouth.

At least five minutes pass before we're able to move. The exhilaration subsides, and we're left drawing slow inhales, looking into each other's eyes.

Until my eyes fall to his shoulder.

The wound doesn't make sense. *What the fuck is this about? What is this?* "How did this happen?"

Valor cuts me off with a kiss. "It's a mating mark. It's a primal instinct to claim each other as mates."

He helps me down off the vanity and spins me so I face the mirror. When he brushes my braid off my shoulder, I see the mark.

"It'll turn into a silvery scar, showing we own each other — forever." He kisses it and then up my neck, "Till death do we part."

"Mmhmm." I lean forward, looking at it.

The bite is four puncture marks, not half circles like I'd expect.

"Fangs," he says, and it's almost as if he's in stereo inside my head.

I look up in the mirror and squint at him. *Why does his voice sound different? What the fuck did this asshole do to me?*

"One of the perks of being a mated wolf. It's the bond. And . . . It's not nice to call names." He smirks, but his lips don't move as I hear the words.

"You can talk in my brain. You can hear me, in my brain." This new reality of not being normal — again — settles over me all at once. My body gets stiff, and I want to run or do something. I cover my face with my hands.

This is so not good. How did life get to be this way? It's rhetorical, of course. The road here was quite clear.

Valor pulls my hands away and wraps his arms around me, holding me to him. "I can hear some of your thoughts in your brain. Just like you can only hear some of mine. It's kind of like if you think about me or to me, it passes through. Sometimes, the big thoughts just kinda happen automatically. So, I'd fully expect to hear something like 'This fuckin' idiot' no less than four times a day when I'm working."

I snort, thinking of how relatable that is, but then the deviousness of how I can make this more fun sets in. It doesn't have to be scary. "I can only imagine how many times you're going to hear all the teacherisms at school."

"God help me." Valor holds me tightly again.

My heartbeat slows, and my shoulders come down from around my ears. When he's sufficiently satisfied with the hug, he takes me by both hands and leads me to the shower.

Enveloped in the glass-walled shower, Valor cleans me. Lightly massaging, he works my muscles under the soothing hot water as he scrubs.

I hear Valor in my mind, small requests and adorations like, 'That's it' and 'Good.'

The blood of the day washes down the drain.

My mind wanders to Christmas cookies, and Valor kisses me, redirecting my focus back to him. He must hear more of my random thoughts than I anticipated. But he doesn't bring it up. Instead, he uses intimate touches and praise while wrapping me up in a towel.

Almost an hour later, in the quiet hours of the morning, despite how tired I am, sleep doesn't come.

Wrapped up in the familiar chocolate and bourbon scents of Valor, I'm physically at rest, my body letting go of the last bit of tension as I embrace the feeling of safety. But closing my eyes and trying to rest does nothing.

Valor's breathing hasn't evened out to peaceful sleeping sounds.

So we're both awake, lying here, looking up at the ceiling.

I roll my head to look at him, and the darkness no longer seems that dark with how easy it is to make out his features. But a question has been eating at me. No, it's been clawing at the back of my brain, trying to get out. The smallest thing has been bothering me until it no longer feels small.

"Did you mean it?"

"Probably, but what are you talking about?" Valor yawns and rolls to face me.

Immediately, the warmth radiating off him reaches me.

"Did you mean it when you said you loved me?" I swallow hard.

Am I ready for the truth? Do I want him to love me? Will it destroy me if he doesn't?

Unhelpfully, my wolf is nowhere to tell me her thoughts. She was so opinionated until I bit him, and now she's gone. Maybe that's a good thing.

I roll to face him, bringing my hands up like I'd normally sleep, close to pressing on his chest.

"I love you, Antonella. I will never hurt you again." Valor places his hand on top of mine.

He squeezes my fingers, rubbing his thumb across my knuckles.

That last little resistance wrapped around my heart, which held onto the fear, anger, and resentment of what he'd done, evaporates. In its place, a new warmth fills me.

"You better not." I wrap my hands into his, squeezing. I shuffle closer until our thighs meet, and I feel all of his body pressed against mine. "Because I love you too."

Valor

CHAPTER SIXTY

CHRISTMAS

If it weren't for Kerrianne, I wouldn't even suggest any Christmas activities. But when we woke up the next morning after ending Neil, Antonella went to work. She found a tree lot with twelve-foot trees. She personally called Royal and demanded he come over to help Kerrianne put the lights on and program them to dance around in special ways. But then, in a tender way, she let Kerrianne help with the assortment of Christmas cookies she baked.

I knew part of it was to distract herself from the change, from the truth, and from me.

My heart hurts for all of us. For Kerrianne, who doesn't need to know the darkness we know, for Antonella for the betrayal of her trust and our relationship, and for my own sick grief that didn't let me see the obvious right in front of me.

Two women in my life called for the truce for my daughter. While I wish Holly's death wasn't in vain, I at least feel a little lighter with the unexpected closure.

And as I finish packing up the rest of Antonella's present, I know it's the right choice. Paper is usually reserved for the first year of marriage, but Antonella and I have lived a year in the last thirty days. It's not the most luxurious paper in the world, but I'm hoping it's the thought that counts.

"Daaaaad," Kerrianne calls, "it's present time."

"I'm coming." I tape the last corner down and carry Antonella's gift, along with the rest of my stack, out of my office.

After Kerrianne helped Antonella wrap my gifts and I carted the little raptor off to bed, Antonella wrapped the majority of the gifts in the formal dining room last night while I 'didn't look,' but I watched her intently in her element of paper and scissors and tape.

"The youngest goes first," Kerrianne declares, holding a finger up in the air and pointing at herself.

We decided that the three of us would do gifts on Christmas morning at home before lunch and gifts at my parents'.

"Not this time, Kerrianne." I hold up the stack of odd-shaped gifts in my arm. "I want Antonella to open these first."

"Uhm. Where did those come from?" Antonella eyes me suspiciously.

"What, I don't know how to shop?" I scoff and bring the packages to where she's curled up on the couch. I set them on the coffee table in front of her.

"Is that what I think it is?" Kerrianne stage-whispers.

The conversation we had while I was tucking her in kept her up way later than it was supposed to one night this week, but it let Antonella and me have sleepy early morning sex that we both desperately needed.

When I nod, Kerrianne puts her hands over her mouth, exaggeratedly stopping herself from spoiling the surprise.

"Okay . . ." Antonella is hesitant as she picks up probably the worst wrapped present in the entire house.

I should have just stuck a bow on it.

I'm not even breathing as she rips open the paper and looks at the legal documents. I know what it says and the attorney fee I paid to rush the paperwork. I debated forging her signature, but I wanted her to have the choice. Even if I'm pretty sure she'll sign.

"I need a pen." Antonella has tears in her eyes. She looks up to me and repeats it. "You can't take this back. I need a pen."

Kerrianne darts off to the kitchen, and coming back, she says, "Does this mean I can call you Mom now?"

Antonella signs the paperwork, and I don't miss that she signs Cavanagh. "You can if you want, but you don't have to."

The paperwork barely makes it to the coffee table before Kerrianne attacks Antonella. They're hugging, and Antonella is holding her close. When Antonella opens her eyes, she locks them on me, and I know the feeling. The feeling of getting to hold your daughter for the first time. It maybe came seven years apart for both of us, but it doesn't change the way it feels.

"I promise." Embarrassingly, my voice cracks, and I wipe a tear off my cheek. "I promise the next one isn't as urgent."

At a loss for words, I hand her the cylindrical one.

"Is it a telescope?" Kerrianne asks, taking in the long tube.

"Hmmm." Antonella raises it up like she's going to look through it. "Only one way to find out. Wanna help with that end?"

Antonella pretty much lets Kerrianne pull the outside layer off, and it reveals the architect's case. Then she works the buckles open to reveal the predictable blue paper.

"These were the alternate plans for the first floor and basement," I explain. "The footprint of the house stays the same, but we can move things around, make it new, and —"

"Wipe away all the spaces that I hurt you in." I push through the bond.

"Well, as long as it has a bigger kitchen." Antonella closes the case. *"I'd like that very much. A fresh start with my new family."*

"Is it my turn now?" Kerrianne snuggles in next to Antonella, arms open for a present.

"Yeah, little raptor, I think we can get you a present now."

OTHER TITLES

By Sarah Jaeger - The Ardelean Bloodline:

Smoke

Haze

Blaze

Scorch

Smog

Stay up to date on all things Sarah Jaeger and Jaeger Rose.

Follow me on social media:

ABOUT THE AUTHOR

Sarah Jaeger is a human being from the Upper Midwest, even though she is certain she was born to be a shifter. A dreamer since birth, the idea for the Ardelean Bloodlines popped into Sarah's teenage brain and refused to leave. Finally, that idea is came to fruition in the form of a fully-fledged paranormal romance series.

Subsequently her dark romance pen name, Jaeger Rose, has begun a new journey for Sarah.

When she's not writing, Sarah likes to recharge with solid TV show binges, playing cards and games with her family, and caring for her fur babies. Stay in touch with Sarah at:

www.authorsarahjaeger.com

Made in the USA
Monee, IL
04 May 2025

16810672R10262